RECKONING

PETE ALDIN

For Liz and for Dave.

You are the village that helped raise this Child.

RECKONING

PETE ALDIN

FOREWORD

I highly recommend you read the ebook *Rescue Mission* before reading this novel. It's not a dealbreaker if you don't, but several of these characters have their origins in that short novelette. You can read it on your phone or tablet in an hour. It's available for $0.99 at several online ebook stores.

If you're a read-to-music type, please get my Doomsday's Child Spotify playlist going in the background: https://tinyurl.com/2yw6t7y2.

In this book, most spelling is American, since the story is told from Elliot's point of view. Other spelling is Australian for local accuracy and authenticity (e.g., metre, the Centre, etc). Elliot uses a mixture of imperial and metric measurements because of various influences on him: growing up in the USA (imperial); a career in the military (metric); almost four years of living in Australia (metric).

In Australia, the car's "boot" is its trunk. *Tassie* is an abbreviation for the large southern island *Tasmania*, but it's pronounced *Tazzie*, and I've spelled it that way to avoid confusion.

Some Tazzie locales are true and accurate while others are invented, or embellished.

All flora and fauna references are true. Except, of course, for deaders ... as far as we know...

"He'd make a lovely corpse."

Charles Dickens

PROLOGUE

North East Tasmania
March 27
Year 5, Post-Collapse

CRAIG WAS A DOER.

And doers did stuff.

But if Craig hadn't been so desperate to get laid, he wouldn't be doing this.

No way. Uh uh. A resource run like this was dangerous—the most dangerous thing you could do when it sent you way out here, out from behind the moat, all alone, out at the full limit of the territory deemed "safe".

Five days and five nights he'd been at it. And he was more than ready to head home. It wasn't really the dwindling food supplies or the fact he'd been sleeping rough and cold each night. The risk of injury was high. The potential for death was real. That's why everyone else had stayed behind the moat and left him to it. Out here, Craig was vulnerable and tired and cold and, yeah, bored. He hiked his pack into a better position, bending tree branches aside as he took the straightest route back to the car, muttering to himself to keep his mind occupied.

"These bloody useless, pointless, dangerous resource runs," he grumbled.

Scouring dilapidated homes and caravans, hoping to find a packet of ibuprofen. Scavenging through roadside trash and rusting traffic jams with their adult skeletons or half-rotted children that would be right there smiling their death grins at you when you opened a closet or the boot of a car...

"Bloody dead children."

But bloody dead children were better at least than *half-living* children snapping at you and reaching for you, he supposed. Thank God *that* hadn't happened this time out.

"Bloody freezing."

The words came out in a cloud of breath to prove it.

"Bloody dangerous."

Here he was, wandering around central Tazzie, armed only with a broom-handle spear and the crappy .22 that Caufield had given him. A .22 rifle and just three rounds, since bullets were in short supply now. Two years ago, three bullets would have been next to worthless if he was anywhere near the undead. These days, so long as Craig was careful, the broom handle would be enough. Well, as long as he didn't come up against a biker, or that pot-head faction out west. The Westies grew and smoked their drugs—Dazza and Rita had both seen it on previous runs—but they were anything but chill. Craig knew from experience the bastards would shoot at you the moment they saw you.

They still have bullets? he wondered. *Been a while.*

He jumped and checked over his shoulder when a stick snapped twenty or thirty metres back. He stopped and strained his senses. Nothing to see, but there were sounds. A series of scratches—a rat, maybe, or a feral cat. Hopefully not dogs.

Dogs. Undead gimps. Bikers. Westies.

God, he hated resource runs. And honestly, if it wasn't for the hope of attracting Rita's interest, he wouldn't be out here.

Craig pushed through more trees, moving faster than he wanted to, while telling himself things like "There aren't any more bikers" and "Relax, old mate, relax" and "Find something nice for Rita". When part of a wattle branch slipped from his grip and flipped back to slap him in the mouth, he swore loudly and asked himself for the hundredth time if *anything* was worth this crap.

"Doing is everything." Caufield was fond of saying this and Craig repeated it aloud now as he snapped off the offending branch to punish the tree for assaulting him. "The human race needs doers to survive. Doers do and doers reap the rewards." Then to cheer himself up—and put things in perspective—he added, "And I know what reward I want."

Rita. Rita with that long red hair. Rita with those wide blue eyes.

With his vigor renewed, Craig pushed ahead, hearing the burble of Grey's Creek ahead, picturing the Nissan he'd parked across it. Sunlight touched his right shoulder, peeking through the tree cover and failing dismally as a great source of warmth. His mouth stung where the branch had scratched his lip. Still, the run was almost over and if a cut lip was the worst that came of it ...

"Bright side, Craig," he whispered. "There's been no crazies, no Westies, no dogs, no biters, no kids' bodies."

And not much in terms of finds, he added sourly.

Apart from a box of Mars Bars, a packet of ibuprofen and six boxes of Kleenex, all found in the back of a rust-pocked car, he'd unearthed nothing good that other scavengers had missed. At least tissues were valuable: people hated wiping their arses with grass and mushed-up printer paper. Rita would smile when he gave her a box. Oh, how she'd smile.

And picturing her, he smiled along with her.

Then scowled and swore when his boot skidded off an exposed tree root. Grumbling, he focused on the task at hand, trying to keep his feet away from snags and slimy wallaby droppings. The creek was soon in front of him. He felt proud that he'd found his way back without using a map, trusting his instincts. There, on the other side, was his Nissan.

And there was his Doberman. Lying under the car to shelter from the early morning dew, she heard him coming, her ears pricking. But she didn't make a sound. She was a damn good dog, the only person from his former life still with him and she was well-disciplined: a single command of "guard" had been enough to get her to plant her butt at the back of the SUV when he'd left her.

A mist lay across the muddy brown water of the creek

and he knew it was going to be bloody cold wading through it. But he was distrustful of the bridge downstream. In the year after the infection and the breakdown of society, he'd sneaked around on his own except for the dog. And he'd quickly learned that bridges were often watched by bad people. He knew of three people who'd been injured by booby traps in those early days then set upon by the scavengers who'd laid them. In he waded, gasping when the water rose above his boots. He slogged out until the stream was knee-deep, wishing it was clear so he could see where he was stepping. With his rifle over his back, he held the backpack to his chest, using it to balance, treading with care on the uneven bottom. A sudden drop in gradient brought the water to testicle-level and tears to his eyes. He gasped, breath catching until he got his lungs working by sheer willpower.

"Holy Christ!"

Maybe the bridge would have been better. Even getting his head shot off would be better than this, surely.

Push on, he told himself. *Old Caufield wouldn't complain. He wouldn't wimp out. Nor would Rita.*

Yeah, but Rita doesn't have testicles.

Out in the middle, the current tugged at him when the water rose to his chest. He had to hold the pack above his head, hoping the creek bed wouldn't dip further and plunge the rifle into the water. His shirt rode up as the creek tickled at his hip and belly.

There came a sudden stabbing pain in his side. Craig yelped, startling the dog. He stumbled sideways, staggering with the current until he found his balance and righted himself. The side of his stomach above the hip stung like hell. Heart racing, he looked back, but saw nothing in the water. What if it had been a gimp?

"That's stupid," he whispered aloud. "It was a stick. Just a stick, that's all." There were always submerged branches and similar crap in creeks. Shit it hurt, though. Maybe it was metal. Maybe bits of the bridge had floated down here. Maybe he'd get tetanus. "Dammit."

He made it to the other side without further incident, knees sliding on the slick grass and weeds. The dog came to the bank with her stumpy tail wagging and ears down. He shoved her away, dropped the pack and lifted his shirt. Five distinct punctures, an arc with two punctures on one side and three on the opposite. A pattern. A bite pattern. Maybe. Or maybe he was seeing a pattern that wasn't there, imagining things. Scaring himself. He lifted the shirt higher, probed the skin around the wound with a finger, wincing. If they'd been teeth, they were awful big for a freshwater fish. The skin was torn, drooling blood. No, no pattern, just something jagged and ragged that had caught him in the side as he'd brushed past. A branch could do this. His mouth was dry, but that was just fear. Surely. He looked out to the middle of the creek. Was that churning water there? Was there something under it, something trying to rise? Nothing did, though the water swirled and swelled. Just a branch. Or a garbage bag full of tin cans. A piece of that bridge. Or maybe a fish got him. Sure, fish were growing damn big these days.

"It wasn't a gimp," he insisted. "It wasn't." They were all gone, rotted away. But he gathered sticks and lit a fire and put a billy on it. The backpack with its dry treasures got tossed into the car while he waited for the water to boil. When it had, he washed the wounds as best he could, then poured the last of his homemade hooch into the punctures, stifling a sob. He sat by the fire a few more minutes and joked to himself that his sobbing was more about the loss of the booze than the pain. He didn't laugh at his own joke. The dog looked on with concern until he told her they were going. She bounded to the car.

Five minutes later, he was twenty minutes from home, carefully navigating roads littered with detritus and brazen wildlife. And he was sweating.

Ten minutes, and he had to pull over to throw up the chocolate bar he'd eaten for breakfast.

Twenty-five minutes and he pulled into sight of Bournstowe. He had a fever and the dog had retreated to the back seat to keep away from him.

His SUV crossed the earthen bridge through the moat. The sentries pulled back the gate and waved him through with nothing more than a curious glance into the back seat, looking for goods. The dog whimpered and he ignored her. He pulled his car down the quiet side street behind the main shopping drag, intent on getting home, getting to bed. He was sick, that's all, a spring cold caught while sleeping rough. He'd be better after a little shut-eye, some peace and quiet.

Quiet.

The street was quiet.

Apart from those on sentry duty, everyone else would be at breakfast.

Rita would be there. In the communal kitchen.

At breakfast.

Suddenly, Craig was hungry. And lonely. He wanted other people. He wanted Rita.

His tires screeched as he took a corner late, changing direction away from home and toward the eating hall. Let them check his car after breakfast and award him some kudos. He could gift Rita her tissues then.

Pulling up outside the Chinese restaurant which now hosted the communal kitchen, he shouldered the car door open and had to catch himself against it to stop from spilling out onto the asphalt.

Noise rolled out through the restaurant windows. The place was teeming.

Craig got out of the car. The dog flew out through the door behind him, shot past him like a bat out of hell and bolted away along the street. Craig couldn't find the strength to care. It wasn't the dog he wanted anyway. He got himself to the restaurant's front door without anyone inside noticing his drunken stagger, and he leaned against the bricks by the entrance. His clothing was soaked with sweat, but it no longer bothered him. His mouth became slick with saliva. Apart from a little trouble balancing, he felt good now. He felt strong. The aroma of cooked food—the aroma of people—reminded him that he was hungry. Very very hungry.

As a matter of fact, Craig was ravenous.

He opened the front door and went inside where the food was.

PART ONE

HAUNTING

But the subjects of the kingdom will be thrown outside, into the darkness, where there will be weeping and gnashing of teeth.

The Gospel of Matthew 8:12

1

"WELL, ALL RIGHT," Angie puffed, rolling onto her back. Twigs snagged in her jacket; her movement rattled the hedge above the hollow that she and Elliot lay in. "That was a nice way to greet the day."

Elliot drew a lungful of crisp pre-dawn air and made a quiet noise of agreement.

Moments passed while they caught their breath, rearranged clothing, felt around in the dark for their small packs and weapons.

When Angie spoke again, her voice was a murmur and still unsteady. "You happy?"

Did she mean happy with the *entire* night's activities, Elliot wondered, or with those of the past fifteen minutes?

Either way...

He reached around to flick a stone from under his shoulder and said, "Very."

With the sun tucked behind the horizon, she was a soft smudge beside him. But he could imagine her adrenaline-laced grin—he heard it in her voice. He patted her thigh gently before flipping onto his belly. A second later, he heard and felt her do the same, rattling the bushes again. He raised his head until twigs pressed into his scalp through his wool cap. The terrain outside their hollow was moonscape-grey. A cracked bitumen road before them. A grassy verge and wire fence the other side of that. In the paddocks past the wire, cattle and sheep. A lone horse. Fifty paces to their right, an open gate and gravel driveway, bird-netted fruit trees along one side, poplars the other. Two hundred metres along the driveway, a farmhouse and outbuildings designated on their map as a *Militia Homestead*.

Angie's hip and thigh had come to rest against his. "Got anything?" she whispered.

He scanned the area a second time, ears straining. Nothing but breeze. He whispered back, "Nope."

"Me either." She sighed through her nose. "Seriously don't believe that no one's seen or heard us tonight."

"They're all ass-clowns," he replied. His breathing had slowed but his heart still pounded from the hard sprint they'd made along the driveway's grassy fringe—and the other shenanigans that had followed in the hollow here. First time *that* had ever happened on mission. *Definitely* a first. And a sign of how much they could get away with inside of Jericho. "Complacent. And dumb as house bricks."

Two hours earlier, working in wan moonlight, they'd found this hollow under the roadside hedgerow and marked it for falling back to. Then they'd approached the militia compound down that driveway. It had zero security besides its high fences. They'd cut a large gap in the wire, then located the quad bike that Driscoll had said would be inside. While Angie stood guard, Elliot had rigged a small gasoline-and-detergent bomb to go off when someone turned the key, big enough to seriously burn or even kill the driver—and maybe anyone standing right alongside. They'd then drilled holes in the compound's rainwater tanks. Inspired by an old Mujahedeen tactic, they'd left a "night letter" attached to the gate, warning the militia living here to pack up and leave Jericho or suffer the same fate that the SERPs would. And the whole time they'd been inside that compound, no people had come out of the homestead to check on the yard, no dogs had been there to bark at them. The occupants were as arrogantly sure of their minor fortifications as their SERP masters were of Jericho's larger ones. In the hours preceding this mischief, he and Angie had performed a dozen similar acts of sabotage around the area, all without detection.

Dragging his wool cap tighter on his head, he said, "I could lie here whistling *The Star-Spangled Banner* and they wouldn't wake up."

"You don't know the words?"

"Hey, I know the words. I'm just a better whistler than singer."

"No argument there."

The breeze momentarily changed direction, gusting

toward them, carrying scents of damp earth and manure. He dropped his head as it scooped up road grit and tossed it at him.

Angie's hip and thigh rolled away from his. "Time to get the hell out of Jericho, sir?"

"Don't call me 'sir'. I work for a living." Old army joke. And already an old joke between *them*.

"I think we should exit via that stormwater drain."

"We'll climb the orange shipping container."

His team had designated a dozen reasonably secure ingress/egress points around Jericho's makeshift walls, some of them over, some under, some through. The SERPs had seriously misplaced their trust in their barriers' ability to keep out danger. Especially when they'd never had sufficient manpower or CCTV to monitor all of it.

And they have even less now.

"Drain's way closer," she said.

"Container has that ladder their watchmen left against it."

"And the container doesn't smell as bad. Is that the main reason?"

"It's a selling point."

"Easier to spot us, though. *If* they actually have a sentry nearby."

"There's something on the way to it that I wanna look at."

"And you didn't tell me till now? Thought we were over this *making big decisions without discussion* shit."

It's my fireteam, he thought. But he was smart enough not to say it. "It's not that big a decision."

"Is if it means climbing their walls in broad daylight."

"It won't be *broad* daylight."

"Sunrise soon, so there'll be *some* daylight," she grumped. "What exactly are we taking a peek at?"

"Driscoll told us a lot of things under interrogation."

Oh yeah, he thought. *A lot of things.* Locations of infrastructure. The twelve CCTV camera hotspots. Troop strengths. Troop weaknesses. He'd called the SERPs' civilian conscripts *militiamen*. Men. And so far, every one of them Elliot's team had seen carrying weapons *had* been male.

"You weren't there for everything he said," he continued. "And I can't remember all of it all the time. I just remembered this one thing. There's a compound in the forest past this farm—"

"How far?"

"A klick-and-a-half."

"Halfway to the orange container."

"Yup. Compound's in an old Boy Scout camp. Driscoll said the site was originally set up for tents, but there's a dining hut that people sleep in now. Militia responsible for patrolling the eastern perimeter. And seeing as how we want to weaken perimeter defenses..."

In the dark, she felt for his wrist and tapped his watch. "Leaving it very late, Elliot."

"Just a recon. See what we see. The more of Driscoll's info we confirm, the more we rely on the rest of it."

"Been true so far."

"So far." He paused. "You don't wanna check it out?"

"I'll do what you want to do."

"If it comes to a firefight, we're not too far from the boundary."

Another sigh through her nose. "Let's get on with it."

Pushing his MCX short-barreled rifle ahead of him, Elliot dragged himself from the hide.

He held Angie's biker-adapted Glock as she followed suit. With its double-drum "C-Mag" holding a hundred rounds, the pistol was as almost as heavy as his rifle.

They turned left along the road—north. One hundred metres later, they jumped the fence into a field with decent cover: an old pine tree, a small and empty hay shed, a rusting tractor, a wattle tree. They headed due east. The next cow paddock went back a long way and also held good cover: the trunks of white gums made ghostly presences in the gloom around them.

Clouds clotted in the sky above. Elliot could feel the small clouds of his own breath against his cheeks as he walked through them. This night had been colder than an old man's fingers, but at least the sporadic cloud cover had kept the temperature above the frost zone—unlike many a Tasmanian morning. By the time they reached the next hip-high fence, the creeping predawn light had begun revealing their small puffs of breath—another fifteen minutes and it'd be a telltale for anyone who might be hunting them.

She's probably right. We shouldn't linger.

But three weeks of scouting had shown that the petty tyrants running this region were not only complacent, but lazy too. SERPs and militia rarely ventured from paths and roadways; they preferred to drive rather than walk, so he'd hear them long before any came in sight, even if the vehicle was a golf buggy or electric scooter; and they rarely released "workers" from their prison-billets before ten on any given morning.

He crossed the fence first, watching the field behind them as she followed. Magpies warbled from the trees now, anticipating the day. A solitary kookaburra laughed from the bushland east. Parrots complained.

Slinging the rifle, he flipped the cover on his newly acquired Swiss Army watch. Not yet 0600.

"Still time for one last piece of assholery," he said.

THIRTY DAYS AGO, ELLIOT'S FLEDGLING FIRETEAM HAD DONE battle with the SERPs in Settlers Downs territory, preventing the abduction of most of their community.

Thirty days ago, he thought as he and Angie trudged through knee-high sedge and bracken at the edge of a native forest.

Feels like yesterday.

Feels like forever.

The past three weeks of scouting had led to this first night of hard-boiled guerilla action, Elliot's smaller group beginning to undermine and harass Jericho's larger and better-armed forces. At 2100 hours, Elliot had scaled the electricity pylon two hundred metres outside Jericho's northern gate where Jericho militia had established a plank-and-wire sniper's nest twenty metres up. Using his SERP-issue sidearm with its newly fashioned suppressor, he'd killed both men. Then he'd smashed their walkies, taken the magazines from their hunting rifles, jacked out the loaded rounds and dropped the weaponry to his team below. While Angie and Spider had hidden the weapons to be retrieved later, Elliot had cut off both sentries' heads. He'd washed his hands and boots using the dead men's water supply, then perched those heads on the rim of the nest and stuck unlit cigarettes in their mouths. A dark prank. Inspired by things the Gurkhas had done to the Viet Cong in the 1970s. Intended to inspire fear, to make the enemy wonder who was next, *where* was next. Maybe, just maybe, it might turn militia against SERPs— or cause them to evacuate Jericho...

From the sniper's nest, the team had split three ways, scaling Jericho's walls in different places.

Rit and Sturgis had several objectives to complete, chief among them using bolt cutters on livestock fences before eliminating the lone militiaman they'd earlier observed manning a poorly-hidden hide near one of the north-eastern walls. Stupid to have one man out on his own, Sturgis had said; a mistake he was happy to exploit. Most militiamen seemed to prefer the woodsman look: thick beard, flannel shirt, hunting jacket. The plan was to bury that hunting jacket and the man inside it under twelve inches of soil somewhere near his hide.

Because he'd always preferred solo endeavors—back when he'd been a Vike—Spider had been allowed to circle around and enter Jericho from the west. He'd spent part of the last three weeks catching spiders and snakes. His primary mission tonight had been to infiltrate small homesteads and leave his creepy-crawlies inside boots, cars, toolboxes, food bins, and, if possible, inside a kitchen cupboard.

Trailing Angie through the bush now, Elliot considered just how far this fledgling fireteam of his had come in a short space of time. They were far more polished than they had been thirty days ago when forced into improvised battle to prevent the kidnapping of their entire community.

Thirty days ago, Elliot thought again. He stepped carefully onto a log, testing the surface before committing his weight. *One whole month*.

The score from that day of ambushes and skirmishes had been four dead SERPs plus one captured; twelve dead Downsers, most of whom had been sick people the SERPs murdered out of convenience. Elliot would never shake the memory of what he and Sturgis found in that Infirmary. And he'd never forgive any of Kyle's people for that atrocity. Uniformed or militia—all were complicit.

Few Downsers had been back inside their former sheep farm since. It was better that way. Less traumatizing. Safer. Most had made the trip to Barnabas Island after Sturgis secured them sanctuary—albeit sanctuary with a firm time limit on it.

Six others were scouting locations in the mountains between St Marys and Upper Esk where the Downsers might need to make a new home.

If this doesn't work.

And what if it does? If it all worked the way he hoped it would—if the SERPs were dealt with, the Jericho slave-workers released and happy—would there be a return to peace? Could there be?

And what would that mean for Elliot and Angie?

He snuck a look at her now as she slipped through bracken ferns, appraising her.

Any other woman seeing her man cut the heads from two human beings would be appalled enough to reject him utterly. Elliot had spent the last month waiting for Angie to reject him, like all the others had across the years. Tonight had been her big chance—but when he'd climbed down from the tower and she'd returned from burying the sentries' weapons, her only reaction was to plant a kiss on his forehead as he stooped to retie his laces.

This was the woman who had, three years back, held one of their captors down while Elliot stabbed them to death. This was the woman who, alone, had chased down a SERP truck filled with captive Downsers, forcing it off the road and shooting the driver dead before bringing her people back.

Luck was a fickle bastard all right, but it had gotten him this far—and it had brought him Angie.

The light was good enough now that she caught him looking and gave him a wink.

Shit.

Angie was good for him. Angie was *right* for him. She'd asked him earlier if he was happy.

Elliot had to admit that—if it hadn't been for the imminent threats from well-armed modern day slavers, serious influenzas, feral dog packs, and the drybones still out there in the forests and barren farmlands—life could not be better.

THE SCOUT CAMP WAS A NETWORK OF SMALL CLEARINGS carved into bushland so dense Elliot and Angie had to approach it via the small dirt track linking the clearings.

The first clearing held nothing but two ancient four-person tents. Come loose from some of their pegs, they looked like a pair of giant lungs, rippling and flapping in the breeze. Elliot gave them a quick once-over while Angie covered. *Nada.* And no one. They moved on, keeping to opposite sides of the track, stepping on patches of weeds to keep from crunching twigs or leaves or gravel.

The second clearing was much larger, with old climbing equipment, a small dam and a storage hut that probably held kids' canoes for the dam. No noise. No movement.

The third clearing sported two structures twenty-five metres apart: a cinderblock amenity building and a wooden hut with an iron roof. These were surrounded by a newer-looking fence of barbed- and razor-wire, head high with a gate made from the same stuff. The hut seemed big enough to house a kitchen and dining hall for maybe fifty people. The gate was shut and fastened to the fence with four large padlocks. Neither Elliot nor Angie had bothered carrying heavy bolt cutters with them, but both had wire cutters in the side pockets of their hunting pants.

Faint clattering sounds emanated from within the compound, the creak and scrape of footsteps on old floorboards. A little smoke curled from the stovepipe chimney, a—

Freeze! he signaled Angie. She dropped into a crouch faster than he did.

A woman had come out the front door, baby in one arm, steaming mug in the other hand. She eased herself onto the short set of steps, placed the mug beside her, hiked up her pullover to offer the baby a breast. Then she reclaimed her coffee. Mother and child drank.

From across the way, Angie gave him a *what now?* look.

Elliot cursed. Was the woman a militia cook, one of the workers? Was she...?

You idiot.

It had never occurred to him that militia—SERPs even!—might have families. Evil people who enslaved others to do their hard work for them didn't have families, right?

You stupid idiot.

The idea was confirmed seconds later when a heavily bearded militiaman appeared behind the woman and stooped to play with her hair. She leaned into the petting. Snatches of their murmured conversation carried to Elliot; it sounded mundane, pleasant, middle class. Normal.

He exhaled his frustration, then signaled Angie to withdraw first. His rifle stayed up, covering her. Before it was his turn to edge back along the dirt track, the man had walked across and disappeared inside the amenities block. Not once had he glanced outside his small compound. The woman's head bent low over her baby as she talked to it. Another woman called from inside, something about breakfast. The mother called back, "Just eggs, thanks!"

Eggs, Elliot thought and commenced his retreat, hunched over and facing the buildings. He smelled bacon cooking, but he was sure it was a phantom, imagination.

Eggs. From chickens no doubt raised by slave-workers.

Jesus. How much messier can this get?

Being this close to the Jericho boundary and to escape, he'd intended to terminate whoever slept in that building, leaving a handful of militia bodies for the SERPs to deal with, fomenting further discord among militiamen.

But women, children?

Wives?

Well, if they *were* wives, then they knew full well what their husbands were involved in. They were complicit. Possibly some had held weapons on slave-workers themselves at some point. And if—*when*—Elliot's team freed the workers, retribution would surely come against those wives. But it wouldn't be Elliot discharging it.

He backed up far enough that the fence and the buildings behind it were no longer in sight, then jogged after Angie.

Once upon a time, all these people had been neighbors, Australians, Tasmanians.

Once upon a time. Just a few short years ago.

Christ, what an unholy mess.

ELLIOT LAY ATOP THE ORANGE SHIPPING CONTAINER THAT formed this part of the wall, covering Angie as she scrambled up behind him, went down the other side and sprinted across the firebreak outside the walls.

His turn. Once down, he raced across the open ground to join her inside the tree line. A hundred feet to his left, six Tasmanian devils crowded around their breakfast, something larger than any of them, a roo carcass maybe.

Angie huddled in a hollow between two thick eucalypts, facing the way they'd come, her field glasses pressed to her face, her focus on the group of coughing, grunting marsupials around the carcass. Why was she kneeling there watching wildlife? Why wasn't she already moving deeper into bushland? She was the one that had pushed him to get away faster.

Elliot took a knee in the damp mulch beside her, scanning the walls they'd just crossed. The tree to their right provided shadow from the rising sun. He asked her, "Filming a documentary?"

"Fuck off," she said. "Check this out."

He took her glasses.

The black-and-white, beagle-sized scavengers were clustered around a body all right. A human one, lying exact-center of the firebreak between Jericho's walls and the bushland beyond. The man hadn't been there two days ago when Rit last scouted this location. He was clothed in a light tan polyester jacket, still zipped up, dirty jeans and hiking boots. Not a Jericho slave-worker then; and not in militia costume. His arms were splayed to the sides and the six feasting animals had pulled off a glove before tearing away three digits from his left hand. The squat and stocky devils had gone for the exposed skin first. Which hadn't left much of his face. His scalp seemed untouched and his hair was jet black, no grey to be seen there; Elliot's free hand scratched under his wool cap at his own greying buzz cut. Three devils were yanking chunks of meat off the neck and left hand, while a fourth worked its way up under a jacket sleeve. The final two tugged at the same pants leg, stopping every few seconds to cough and mewl aggressively at each other.

"One of you move to the other leg," he muttered. *Plenty to go around*. He panned the glasses up and down the body again. "See the death wound?"

Beside him, Angie *hmm*-ed. "Dark patch on the jacket."

"Chest shot." He handed back her glasses. "Wonder if a sentry thought he was one of us? Would they think we're out here? I mean, any moment now, maybe already, a lot of them are gonna *know* we're in the neighborhood, but—"

"He wasn't a scav-rat," she said thoughtfully. She had the glasses up again. "Maybe there's people in Hobart or further south."

"Whatever his story, he's dead now. And we need to keep going."

Time to regroup, compare notes.

"Did pretty well to live this long. Deserves a little appreciation for that."

"He avoided the pusbags, the Druids and the scav-rats. Then he came to these walls and thought he'd finally found safe haven. All that good work for nothing."

She put her glasses away inside her jacket and punched him on the arm. "I love it when you empathize."

"You know I'm all heart." He shuffled around to face east. They'd left mountain bikes a half-klick that way. They could be at the safe house in well under two hours. There he could debrief, eat, sleep, shower and shave—and in that order.

"He doesn't deserve even a 'poor bastard'?" She delivered the phrase in a gruff imitation of Elliot's accent and voice. Unflattering, but fairly accurate.

"What I'll do is learn the lesson he taught us. They've had sentries up on that wall recently. And I don't want to wait for them to return."

"Good point," she said, then stood, starting off. "So, I'll *take* point."

Movement drew his attention one last time to the crowd of devils. Each one had their heads up and toward the tree line, their noses in the air. Two bolted, suddenly scrambling over the body and heading north. The others shuffled about, agitated, emitting snarls and barks of anger. Or alarm. A shape appeared through the line of knee-high weeds along the trees near them. Elliot didn't need the glasses to identify the thing as it crawled—or dragged itself—toward a fresh meal. Drybones. Two more devils took to their heels, headed after the first. The remaining pair gave ground grudgingly, retreating to the dead man's hips, then lunging forward a little to issue threats at the encroacher before retreating further back. The newcomer was only six metres away from them when the final devils decided their buddies had made the correct decision and fled.

Elliot's lip curled. Tiny hairs lifted across his forearms, the back of his neck. He got up and followed after Angie. *Poor bastard, all right*, he thought, mind on the dead man. *If you'd come just two weeks later, you might have been safe here.*

Still, a quick and clean death may have been preferable to any time spent in the hands of those psychopathic cops. Elliot—and Jimmy, and Woodsy—had spent less than twenty-four hours there. Woodsy had lost joints from fingers before Kyle or Da Silva took him Christ knew where. Jimmy had been forced into trial-by-combat, only to be bitten by Da Silva's "jury" of deaders.

Fifty feet in front of him, Angie reached her hand toward him in a *halt* signal. She ducked. He crouched too, hearing what she'd heard, a big body moving in the bush, a hundred feet ahead and left. A moment later there followed a low, rhythmic thumping. Angie's shoulders relaxed at the same time as his did; she'd recognized it too.

Kangaroo.

A couple of seconds later, the roo bounded into view and passed by thirty metres away, veering as it noticed Elliot.

And then the two humans were up and moving again, Elliot maintaining that fifty-foot gap between them. He slow-breathed his heartrate back down, watching the bush around them, behind them, watching Angie's ponytail bobbing as her gaze also swept the forest, both of them taking care where their feet landed.

Was she as fatigued as he felt, he wondered, now that the night mission's adrenaline was burning away?

Angie's ponytail swung around as her head snapped left, thinking she heard something. A moment later, she unfroze and moved on.

And Elliot thought, *Nope, still sharp as a tack.*

Yes, sir, he'd gotten lucky when it came to her.

He was thinking of conversations they'd had, wine they'd drunk, and he was admiring the movement of her hunting pants when a twig snapped beneath his boot.

She shot him a *really?* look.

He scowled at himself, thinking, *And maybe, soldier, you should get your mind out of the clouds and onto the ground in front of you.*

2

THEY RETRIEVED two bicycles a short ways outside of Jericho. The ride from there was uneventful and soon they were pulling up in back of a weed-garnished petrol station.

The station's signs were so faded, they'd probably needed painting even before the Collapse. Halfway up the low hill behind it lay the safe house they'd used for the past week. The couple weeks before that had been spent cold camping in the bush or using hay sheds, farmhouses and even a small community college in the town of Lemont. Forty klicks east of here, Lemont had been devoid of the living, littered with skeletons of the long-dead, and peppered with the occasional drybone. Rit and Spider had used blades to dispatch more than a few of those undead.

In sync with each other, he and Angie hopped the safe house's low brick fence. They started up the tiered patches of lawn and garden beds toward the house, stepping expertly over the noise makers, the fishing-line-and-fishhooks traps, the shotgun-shell traps and spike traps.

"What's the password?" Spider called from the petrol station roof.

Elliot's head snapped around to scowl at the young man's shit-eating grin. There was no password. And the joke wasn't funny. He slashed his hand across his throat in a *shut the hell up* gesture. Angie simply flipped Spider the bird without breaking stride.

Sturgis met them at the safe house door, closing it behind them. He went to the living room window, picked up the sniper rifle he'd leaned by it, and recommenced cleaning it. He'd borrowed the SRS from his former navy buddies when negotiating sanctuary on Barnabas Island. Meg—the elected boss of the island, who'd once been Sturgis's C.O.—had grudgingly contributed the rifle, but only one 10-round magazine to go with it. Although he had used it plenty on the Navy patrol boat's long journey from the Timor Sea to southeastern Australia, Sturgis had yet to fire it on his current mission, conserving that ammo.

Ammunition, Elliot complained as he lay his MCX down and flopped into an armchair. *We're doing okay in terms of weapons, but it's the lack of ammunition that continues to undermine us.*

Despite conservative Tasmania's relative scarcity of firearms back before the world broke, there *had* been weapons. Tazzie contained not a single military base, but people had hunted for sport, and there'd been cops, and robbers, and three drug-dealing biker clubs. Within its first year, Settlers Downs had become reasonably well supplied with firearms: newcomers had brought a handful of hunting rifles; Elliot, Claire and Jimmy had taken handguns, automatic rifles, and shotguns from a Death Druid biker compound. The skirmishes with the SERPs a month ago had lost them some firearms, then gained them more.

But there weren't a lot of bullets for any of these firearms. Not at Settlers Downs, anyway.

To leave decent protection with the other Downsers, each member of Elliot's fireteam had brought along one sidearm plus an assault weapon, or—in Sturgis's case—sniper weapon. The men carried police-issue semiautomatic handguns, two full magazines each, and newly fashioned suppressors, or *silencers* as Spider kept calling the damned things. They had three MCX rifles between them, two full magazines each, sixty rounds per man. No suppressors for those. In addition to her Glock and drum-magazines, Angie carried her sawn-off double-barrel in a pouch she'd sewn onto the back of her tactical jacket.

When, back at The Downs, Elliot had counted up his team's total ammunition, it totaled less than three hundred and fifty rounds. Lewis had commented that it sounded like a lot. It wasn't. Throw in the single flash-bang on Elliot's belt and they weren't exactly a well-armed posse. And, if Driscoll was to be trusted, they still had eleven remaining SERPs and thirty militia to face.

We need to take more scalps over the next couple weeks before we start rescuing "workers".

"Everything went as planned," Sturgis said before Elliot could ask, his eyes on his rifle as he cleaned it. "No trouble at all. For us, anyway. The enemy got plenty." He tapped the 16-channel walkie-talkie on the coffee table by him. "Lewis and Heng checked in from St Marys half an hour ago. No contacts up there, but they've secured that old medical center where we first met Nance. As a temporary base. Easily defensible even with the six of them."

"Potential home for us?" Angie asked. She'd collapsed onto the rug in front of a radiator Sturgis or Rit had fired up. The old house had very modern solar panels and an excellent battery. Elliot unzipped his jacket as the warm air started thawing him out.

"A possible base, yeah," Sturgis said with a shrug. "They reckon there's a small housing estate nearby we could wall off."

"Another Jericho," she said. "That's working real well for *them*."

"If we go there, we'll do it better," Elliot said. These days, a settlement needed walls. And a home in the mountains might be better than by the coast. If Heng's scouting party made contact with friendlies in the area and got them on-side, it would be even better. "Where's Rit?"

"Out cold in the back room. He's got next shift on the roof."

"You should go sleep too."

Sturgis shook his head. He was a man who rarely joked, and he didn't smile as he said, "With that bloke's snoring? Not a chance. I'll wait till he's up."

"Spider went okay with his snakes and spiders?"

On the floor, Angie shivered and let out a cartoon character, "Brrrrr."

"So he tells us." Sturgis lay the SR98 aside and swept dirty cotton makeup pads and cue tips into a waste paper basket. "Reckons there's a dozen militiamen who'll be getting some serious 'jump scares' right about now."

Elliot made a face. "I wanted bites, not jump scares."

Sturgis shrugged, collecting his rods, brushes and oil canisters, placing them in the kitbag he'd made for the gun. "I said the same thing. So *he* said, 'I reckon ten of 'em will get bit'. I said, 'You *reckon*?'. He said, 'I did my best. I don't give money back guarantees, y'know'."

"Dickhead," Angie said softly, meaning Spider. To Elliot's knowledge, she had nothing against Sturgis.

"He's not the brightest crayon in the box," Elliot replied, "but he does okay. In the end it's all useful, whether the enemy get real sick from snake- or spider-bite or just mentally sick from the worry about what other surprises we've left around their home."

"Just tell me he used them all up," Angie said to Sturgis. "Like every single one of them."

"So he tells us," Sturgis repeated.

"I'm not gonna go in one of the bedrooms and find another box of funnel webs?"

"Didn't see any."

"No tiger snakes?"

Sturgis made a calming motion. "He didn't have anything when he returned."

"Good."

Unlacing his boots, Elliot asked Sturgis, "You took out that sentry okay?"

"Currently occupying a shallow grave." He zipped up

his cleaning kit, picked up the rifle's magazine. "His walkie and his shotgun are in the kitchen."

"And the name on his name tag?" Elliot couldn't understand why every militiaman he'd seen had half-assed home-made nametags sewn onto their jackets. Was it fan-boy imitation of the SERPs' better quality name plates? Was it meant to legitimize their roles?

"Richardson." He slipped the magazine in and lay the rifle back down again.

"Elliot," Angie said from the floor, her lips quirked in a dark smile. "Your idea for using his name is pure evil genius."

"None of what we're doing is evil," he said, too weary and impatient to let her joke stand. "And none of it's genius. Just necessary."

She made a conciliatory gesture. "Okay. Fair enough." Then she pointed to the kitchen door and asked Sturgis, "What kind of shotgun?"

He leaned against the wall and stretched. "Remington over-under."

"Dibs."

"All yours."

"Don't try and carry *two* shotguns," Elliot said. "Too heavy." He had his boots off now so he leaned into the chair back and rubbed his eyes, opened them, studied his hands. His palms and fingers were dirt-stained. They weren't shaking. That was good.

"Duh," Angie replied. "I was going to leave it here for later anyway." She turned back to Sturgis. "How many shells did he have?"

"Twenty," Sturgis said.

"Bonus! I'll take those then. Unless Herr Kapitan has any objections?"

Elliot shook his head grumpily, resisting flipping her the bird the way she liked doing to others.

"We also took out another lone sentry. At Pankhurst."

This was the part Elliot was most interested in. Along with the original facility out in the boonies—the one he, Woodsy and Jimmy had tried to infiltrate—Pankhurst seemed to be the hub for SERP activity. Which made sense given it was the sole town center within the walled-in farming region. The original hamlet of Jericho itself was nothing but a grouping of farm houses and a general store. According to Driscoll, Pankhurst was where most people lived or at least slept, slaves and slave-masters. There was a small regional hospital there, an old school, houses, a small shopping precinct. There was also the stage, bleachers and holding pens for Da Silva's "Night Court" and its undead jury.

"SERP or militia?" he asked.

"Militia, unfortunately. Didn't see a single SERP."

"Neither did we," Angie yawned.

"Good work, all the same," Elliot said. "That's one less for later. What did you find out there?"

For the first time in a long time, Sturgis actually smiled. "On the kitchen table is my schematic for getting into the Night Court's zombie holding pens. They lock them in a pumping station off the storm water system."

That must've been real fun, Elliot thought, them snooping around down there in the dark. He said, "*Real* good work. And you weren't detected at all?"

"Nope. Rit's good at this. I'm getting better."

"Too hard on yourself, Carrot," Angie said, using the navy nickname the man had long ago received in honor of his red hair. "You're a legend at sneaking around."

"I'm so-so." He reached down to pat the SR98. "I'll be much better with this."

"And you'll get to use it," Elliot said.

"Can't wait."

Angie had finally warmed enough to unzip her own jacket. "How long before last night's nasty pranks start messing with their heads, do you reckon?"

"Hopefully it's already happening," said Elliot. "Few more nights of this and we should see some infighting erupt. Some desertions. I'm thinking we let Sturgis use his baby there in a couple of days."

"Really?" Sturgis straightened. "I'd definitely be up for that."

That was understating it, Elliot thought. Sturgis and Rit had lost family in the SERP raid on Settlers Downs. Sturgis his sister-in-law, Rit his brother-in-law. And of course, there'd been the dead children Sturgis had helped to bury. The man was as hot for justice as Elliot was.

"Angie had an idea about setting a wooden area of their walls on fire," Sturgis added. "That could draw them in and I could hit a couple, then let it burn."

"Mmm. Maybe. I think after last night, they'll become a little leery of obvious ploys like that."

Angie sniffed. "Gee, sorry to be *obvious*."

Christ, she could be ornery when tired.

"I think the next priority is using the drones to observe the Facility for a day," he continued.

"Watch their comings and goings?" Sturgis said.

"Yup. There's that observation point on the hill outside their southwest gate. You and Rit could park the ute the other side of it, fly them from off the top."

Sturgis pursed his lips a second. "Range should be right. It'll chew through batteries, though."

"We have six of them. Maybe take Spider as well, to help you carry them and recharge?"

"If we have to."

He'd said it seriously, but Angie sniggered. Whereas Sturgis was always polite to Spider's face, Angie's feelings for the former Vike had never been hidden.

"It'd be a good use of time, confirm what Driscoll told us about the place."

Sturgis gave him a thumbs up, then groaned wearily as he pushed off the wall. "Solar battery has plenty of juice. I boiled the kettle when I saw you arrive."

"Coffee," Angie pleaded.

"Rit opened the last jar. Says it's not great."

"Does it have mildew in it?" she asked.

"No."

"Does it have caffeine in it?"

"Of course."

"Then I'll drink it. Okay with you, Kapitan?" she added with a tart smile at Elliot.

"You know it isn't," he growled back. "I'll stick with that stuff Lewis made up." The concoction of herbs was drinkable, it was fresh and there was no way it was poisoned. "You both should too."

"I drink tea," Sturgis said, making for the kitchen.

"Lewis's brew." Angie made a puking noise. "Wattle-seed and dandelion root. You know dandelions are *weeds*, yeah?"

"Well now, darlin'," said Elliot, "the day someone drinks instant coffee and gets Sick, you may just change your mind."

She scoffed. "How many times do we have to go over this? I ate shitloads of packaged food before and after the outbreak and I never got Sick."

"No, you got lucky. I *saw* a guy turned by food."

"You saw a guy turn."

"You weren't there."

"Sturgis, can you tell Elliot he's being an idiot?" she called out.

Sturgis, wisely in Elliot's opinion, did not respond.

"You know, you once called me the asshole," Elliot muttered.

In the kitchen, cups and spoons clattered and clanked. A full minute passed before Angie said, "See why I need the coffee so bad?"

"I'm beginning to."

"If you don't call me *darlin'*, I won't call you *idiot*."

"Darlin' is affectionate."

"It's patriarchal."

"Oh, Jesus, really?"

Sturgis returned with two mugs. Avoiding eye contact, he handed them over. Angie's went on the floor beside her and she turned over to blow steam from it before sipping. "God, that's bad." She sipped again.

"Good stuff's long gone now," Sturgis replied.

Beyond the windows, the sun had broken through the clouds. From this elevation, Spider was easy to see sitting in his deck chair on the petrol station roof, binoculars to his face. He seemed to be watching the next hill over, a swelling of the earth, grass-carpeted, denuded of trees.

Much nearer, a couple of sparrows had alighted on the garden beds to hop about seeking food. The gardens, though wild, were ablaze with spring colors.

Elliot's stomach rumbled and he cleared his throat loudly to cover it. No one reacted. When he could be bothered moving, he'd get up and refuel from the dried apple and rabbit they'd brought from The Downs. He lifted the mug and tried Lewis's brew, grateful Angie didn't see him grimace: it wasn't coffee, and it wasn't great. But it was warm and Lewis had claimed it was good for him, so he sipped more before putting it aside to cool.

A loud snore rolled out from the back rooms and Angie snorted, choking on coffee.

Elliot grunted a laugh also, relaxing. "They probably heard that inside Jericho."

Angie caught his eye. She winked. He couldn't tell whether it was born from a desire to conciliate after their minor argument, or rooted in residual lust left over from their earlier dalliance—or just her being Angie. But it warmed him a lot more than Lewis's herbal coffee, more than the electric radiator nearby. He winked back. She closed her eyes. He closed his, putting his head back.

The room fell silent, as the three of them became lost in their own thoughts. Elliot's turned again to how lucky he was to be alive and warm in this room after surviving four years of hell.

Yeah. Lucky. Again. Billions of others get totally screwed over while good ol' Elliot skates on through unscathed.

Triggered by the thought, the honor roll of dead started playing yet again through his mind. Kim and Dylan. Little Abby. Jimmy. Birdy. A dozen vets he'd served with in the Middle East, including—

Eames.

McGovern.

Radler.

In his mind's ear, he heard the ghost of Radler whispering, *Don't sweat it, Sparkles. Gotta make the most of all these second chances.*

"I'm trying," he whispered, then flushed when he realized he'd said it out loud and the others were frowning at him. "Talking to ghosts," he explained.

Another snore came from the bedrooms and the three of them chuckled.

Sturgis pushed off the wall by the window again. "Well, we've been back for five hours. Time he woke up. Who's next for sleep?"

"Me," smiled Angie. "Coffee didn't work."

3

October 27th
13:00

THE HILL ELLIOT sat on was really more of a butte, a kind of geological pimple in the landscape, a pimple poking seventy metres into the air from the midst of the treeless meadows beyond Jericho's southwest gate.

Elliot and Sturgis had taken cover in the family of eucalypts sprouting from the side of the butte facing Jericho. Birds swooped above the open ground between them and the gate five hundred metres away. A pack of feral dogs loped through the long grass below them, oblivious to their presence. Sturgis had his black sniper rifle propped through the bole of a tree. His ass was settled on a milk crate beside it; he clutched a drone controller on his lap, his thumbs on the twin joysticks, his eyes glued to the small video screen. Elliot held an identical handset, but he sat cross-legged in the dirt, his back to another tree.

The looting of a small town's *Outdoors R Us* store last week had provided them with plenty of these drones—they had the best and quietest in play right now. They'd tested these units yesterday and Elliot was satisfied that their quality—especially combined with the noise from the local flock of black cockatoos—would make it hard for any hostiles to notice them. Elliot squinted but couldn't make out Sturgis's unit with his naked eye. That was to be expected: the tiny object was white against a clear sky. Plus it would be well over a kilometre away by now, over Jericho "airspace".

"See anyone else?" he asked.

"Just those sentries. Nobody else visible."

The two heavily-bearded militiamen had been behind the gates when he and Sturgis had relieved Spider and Rit up here, three hours back. Elliot had snuck a glance at Sturgis's screen when he'd first flown high over them. Elliot had snorted: they were calling them "sentries"—but the men weren't moving around much. And they weren't manning the posts secured to the walls by the gates, preferring to stay twenty metres back from there, behind a curved screen of car tires, wooden pallets and sheet iron. They had a white ute parked there too—when Elliot was watching them, one man appeared to be napping in the vehicle's tray, while his buddy kept a rifle trained on the gate from the protection of his trash-screen.

Elliot snorted again now. "'Sentries', my ass."

"I can see the corner of that ute from here," Sturgis said from behind him. "Reckon I could scare them out of cover with the first shot and take them down with the next ones."

Elliot made a face Sturgis couldn't see. The navy man had been itching to lay aside drone duties and take a shot at the two militiamen for an hour now. Problem was, any shooting now would likely send them hunkering down behind the barrier, not send them running from it. He stroked the backpack beside him. "Let's rely on what we have in here to flush them out. It'll give you better odds."

"I can make the shot. I've hit dogs and roos over this distance."

"The rifle and its user aren't the problem," Elliot reassured him. "That's why you're here. We'll just wait till our surveillance is complete."

"This drone's battery doesn't have long," Sturgis grumbled. "Bloody Spider's drained it."

"He was only doing what we asked him to."

"He should've taken it back to the car and recharged it."

There was already one depleted drone on the slope behind them, leaning against another gum tree. Later, he or Sturgis would have to lug it to the SUV that Rit and Spider were guarding at the back and bottom of the butte. "Spider already had three to haul back there on his own. And we're almost done, man. All you need to do is take a closer look at where Rit thought there might be a security cam Driscoll didn't mention."

Sturgis grunted. "Just don't want this thing dropping out of the sky into enemy hands. Don't want to give 'em ideas."

"No, we do not." If the SERPs caught on to using drones too, it would even the playing field. With his toe, he nudged the unit he'd brought along. "If the battery's too low to get back here, just ditch it somewhere they won't notice it."

"Copy that. Can't believe how quiet this model is."

"Well, we paid top dollar for 'em."

Sturgis didn't laugh. Angie would have.

Elliot wished she was here for this. Had he done the right thing, leaving her alone today? What if something happened to her? What if—

She's fine, moron. She can handle herself.

Another grunt from Sturgis. His lips twisted as he adjusted the sticks on his controller. "Coming up on the creek you followed when you came here with Jimmy and Woodsy."

Don't remind me of that, Elliot thought.

Sturgis continued, "Wind's pretty light today. Great flying conditions." A quick look up at Elliot before his focus returned to the camera feed. "Even better sniping ones."

"Not long now, Great White Hunter."

A third grunt. This time, it might have been a laugh.

"Okay," Sturgis said twelve minutes later, "there's definitely nothing there. No camera. No anything. I have less than five percent battery. Ditching the drone in a tree —" He paused, his tongue slipping out to lick dry lips. "—now. Done." Shoving the controller in his pack, he met Elliot's eyes with fire in his own. "Time for some action."

Elliot unzipped his pack. "Roll those shoulders, crack those knuckles and get ready for the boom."

As Sturgis stretched, Elliot affixed the tennis ball bomb to the drone's payload mechanism. For the last month, he'd considered all the kinds of explosives, using Tovex gel the guys had retrieved from the mining site, Tannerite, even the crap they'd taken from a high school chemistry lab. There was plenty more available out there at mining sites, hardware stores, chemical stores. If they were going to break into the Facility, they'd need explosives to do it, since the door codes would have been changed since Driscoll's capture.

But when it came to the crunch, he just hadn't been able to do it for this mission. Partly, it was the danger of a bunch of hamfisted amateurs like him dicking with things they'd had no training in; partly the idea of dropping high explosive IEDs on Jericho buildings and moving vehicles made him feel too much like the people he'd once fought against. There was the memory of Al-Kasrah, for starters—

He shook that thought off before it could trigger the flashback, focused shaking hands on finishing what he was doing. The tennis ball was attached now. With its innards of a few hundred matchheads, striker strips from matchboxes and the little taped-up sandwich bag of kerosene, the object was worthy of a teenage prank. Its purpose now was far darker and more practical.

Elliot shuffled his ass up hill, getting out of the drone's way, then grabbed the controller again. The quadcopter lifted from the grass. Its humming was low, almost polite, unlike the giant-bee noise made by cheaper drones. With Sturgis taking position behind the tree, rifle stock tight against his shoulder, Elliot sent the drone high into the air and then whizzing away toward the gate. This would in no way be fun, but it was necessary. When he'd told Spider he couldn't come watch, the young man had pouted like a kid denied his Christmas wish.

"Psychopaths think killing people is entertainment," he'd told him. "You a psychopath?"

Spider's head had dropped at that and he'd mumbled a negative.

As the drone accelerated, Elliot hoped the mix of crap inside the ball would work—it was twenty-five years since he'd last made one—hoped he could hit the target from a hundred feet up.

A flock of small birds suddenly darted into his drone's path. Elliot slowed and dropped altitude to avoid them, restarted his breathing once he was sure there'd be no collision, then ramped up the acceleration, rising into a kneeling position as the little object passed high above the gate. Seconds later, he was braking it above the sentry post, zooming in for a moment. The napper was awake, both men standing at the back of the tray sharing a smoke.

"You ass-clowns couldn't make this more of a challenge?" Now all he had to do was pray against wind gusts. He zoomed out a little, then said, "Safety off, Sturgis."

He flicked the switch assigned to cargo release, watched the ball fall away from its carrier.

Stay on target. Stay on target. Stay—

On the video screen, the ute's tray disappeared from sight behind an orange flash and bloom of brown-grey smoke.

Baby!

"Nice!" Sturgis gasped, presumably watching through his scope.

A second later, the crack of the explosion reached them from down in the valley. With one hand, Elliot got the drone heading back toward him, lifting his field glasses with the other. Above Jericho's protective screen of scrap-and-crap, a burgeoning smoke cloud reached for the sky. He dropped the glasses, concentrating on getting the drone back ASAP, his attention split between the controller, the smoke cloud and Sturgis beside and behind him. He'd forgotten about the pack of wild dogs, but there they were again, fleeing for their lives up the grey ribbon of country roadway.

"Anything?" he asked Sturgis.

A wordless growl told him *no*.

The drone separated itself from the sky around it, a pale missile inbound. Elliot slowed it, guiding it in to land hard five metres to his left. He got to his knees.

"*Anything?*" he repeated, raising his glasses again.

Sturgis's next growl had words in it. "Lemme focus."

Through the binoculars, Elliot saw one of the sentries stagger out of cover to Elliot's right, weapon forgotten, hands over his ears.

Excellent.

A moment later, the other appeared beyond his former screen, running, tripping, stumbling as he tried to flee. Though his movements were erratic, his trajectory wasn't, providing easy anticipation to the watching sniper.

"Bingo," Sturgis said softly. Five seconds later, the SR98 barked.

The militiaman dropped, rolled, writhed. But he didn't get up again.

Elliot's glasses swung to the other man; surely Sturgis's sights were doing the same.

If he'd heard the shot or seen his comrade fall—which Elliot doubted—the militiaman wasn't showing it. He had a handgun out now, an automatic. He fired blindly toward the wall, the gate, a patch of bushes twenty metres left. Perhaps he thought someone had tossed a grenade from the last place. Elliot couldn't hear whatever the man was saying or yelling, not from this far away, but his jaw was sure working hard.

The SR98 barked again.

The militiaman stayed standing, emptying the last of his magazine into the bushes. Sturgis swore, worked the bolt. The militiaman was turning in circles now, a hand still over one ear, searching, scanning. His gaze must have stuck upon his fallen colleague for he froze, facing that way. Sturgis fired again. The target's head snapped forward. He dropped, blood spray suspended in the air above him.

Elliot got to his feet, strapped his MCX across his back. Lifting his pack and shoving the drone controller inside, he said, "Let's boogie."

BACK OF THE HILL, THE TWO MEN JOGGED AS HARD AS THEY could while carrying an awkward array of drones, packs, weapons and controllers, following a dirt track to the waiting car.

As they neared it, Spider emerged from the bushes to join them.

"Heard the bang," he said.

"Bangs," Sturgis corrected him.

"What was your score?"

"Me: two. Them: none."

"Nice."

Equipment loaded, Elliot drove.

A kilometre along the track, they connected with the road, half expecting a SERP vehicle to appear on intercept. Nothing waited for them.

Elliot turned left and away from Jericho. A half klick further on, they took a bend and their tires clunked crossing a double set of chains. Elliot pulled up hard. Sturgis exited and sprinted back behind the car. Rit appeared from the roadside to assist him, hauling on the chains until a plank-and-spike rig slid across the asphalt from the opposite verge. The rig resembled the one they'd used against the SERP BearCat a month ago.

Once the two men were safely in their seats, Elliot took off again. They'd discussed waiting to see who might hit that trap, hoping to riddle the crippled car with bullets Bonnie-and-Clyde style. But the enemy might send nobody. Or they might contact other gates and send vehicles ahead to intercept them, leaving them cut off if they lingered. Elliot planted his foot.

"The score?" Rit asked.

"Two confirmed kills," Elliot said.

"I *hit* the first guy," Sturgis said. "He might live."

"Doubtful," Elliot replied.

"Who cares about the technicality," Rit said, reaching forward to pat Sturgis's shoulder. "You got two. That's good."

Downshifting to take a corner, Elliot said, "My math says they're down to eleven cops, twenty-seven militia."

"If Driscoll was telling the truth," Rit said quietly. "Was it an extra camera in that tree?"

Sturgis shook his head. "Nothing there."

"Driscoll was telling the truth," Elliot said. Jesus, what he and Sturgis had done to that guy before finally disposing of him. Elliot was proud of none of it. But this was war; it was necessary. "He was most definitely telling the truth."

THE WEATHER STATION WAS A CORRUGATED IRON HUT dumped out in the middle of national forest. The chain link fence around it had a narrow gate; while the men had been gone, Angie had cut two more gaps in the wire in case she needed a fast escape. Elliot parked the car facing back the way they'd come. The four men climbed out, stretching and wrinkling their noses at the drybones piled against the fence near the original gate.

Presumably these deaders had chased someone inside years back, then fallen dormant. Or, Elliot mused, they'd backed their victim against the fence, piling on top of them in a feeding frenzy. Whatever the case, they'd been here stacked through several cycles of seasons. Where their body fluids had once leaked onto each other, these had now dried and glued them together. All had lost the capacity for movement beyond the weakest of limb and jaw twitches. Only one still seemed capable of seeing.

"Gives me the creeps," said Rit.

Spider moved to the edge of the pile. "Oh, they're not hurtin' anyone. Are ya, little fellas?" He poked one with the toe of his boot.

"Don't bloody *touch* them!" Sturgis snapped.

"Chill, dude," Spider laughed. "I won't catch cooties this way."

"You will if I throw you head first in the middle of them."

"Now, now, children," Rit said. He gave Sturgis a light clip over the back of the head, making Sturgis's lip peel back like an angry dog. "Squabbling's what we want Jericho people to do, not us."

Angie had come to stand on the other side of the fence without anyone but Elliot noticing her.

Spider, Rit and Sturgis caught sight of her at the same time, freezing guiltily. Rit pointed to Spider. "He started it."

"Fuckwits." She shifted her attention to Elliot as he passed through the gate. "Successful?"

"Lots of new intel, two militia down," he said.

They shared a kiss before Elliot moved through the tight little compound and into the weather station hut. One of their regular cold-camps, they'd cleared out its original crap ten days ago, leaving room for a tiny table and a camp chair, and three swags. Procedure was for two people to stay on watch out in the car at all times, one resting, the other alert, while the others enjoyed downtime in here. Elliot lowered himself into the chair and rubbed at his face, smelling dirt on his hands.

Outside he heard Angie ask, "You made kills?"

Sturgis grunted an affirmative.

Angie said, "Nice."

Conversation continued out there a little longer while Elliot drank from a water jug on the table.

"Rit, you'll take watch?" Angie asked.

"No probs."

"I'll stay with him," Spider said. "Need to take a dump first, but."

"Thanks for sharing. Make sure you write us a full report."

Angie and Sturgis entered. Elliot made to vacate the chair, but Angie pushed him back into it. She leaned on the wall by him, hand on his shoulder.

Sturgis stood his rifle in the corner before kicking off his boots and stretching out on a swag. "Oh, that's good."

"Well, fellas," Angie said, "you've had your fun for the day. Is it my turn yet?"

Sturgis made a noncommittal sound. "Good a time as any. They'll all be stirred up now, so someone should be listening to their radios."

On the table near Elliot lay the walkie-talkie liberated from the militia sentry Rit and Sturgis had buried in the forest two nights back. Elliot handed it to her. "Know your lines?"

"I've been practising all afternoon." She selected the

channel they'd agreed upon, then cleared her throat. "One Academy Award performance coming right up." She depressed the call button.

"Scheduled transmission to Miller. Scheduled transmission to Miller. Richardson made it here safe and he's insisting you bring the rest of his gear when you join us. Says you'll know what that means. And he says you're doing the right thing, it's way better over here. You should also bring as much meds and ammo as you can."

She let go of the button and waited. Elliot could hear her counting to thirty under her breath. Elliot pictured Miller listening, the flat-faced thug who'd brought Kyle the cauterizer used on Woodsy. Angie's idea to cast suspicion upon a specific person had been golden.

Her count had reached sixteen when the radio squawked and a voice said, "Who the hell is this?"

Elliot's heart thumped hard under his ribs. The voice was male. Steel-cold. Dripping with menace. And the last time he'd heard it, its owner had been ordering Elliot to be taken to the Pankhurst hospital ice room.

Da Silva.

This could not be better.

Angie's eyes were wide with delight. Though she couldn't know who she had reached, she appeared ecstatic someone was listening. She composed herself before pushing the button again. In the same tone, she repeated her message in different words, pretending not to have heard Da Silva at all. She counted again—this time there was no response. At thirty, she repeated the transmission a third and final time then turned the walkie off.

"Well," she said and gave Elliot's shoulder a squeeze. "That should stir up some shit."

He reached up to stroke her hand. "And the Academy Award goes to..."

Stretching and groaning, Sturgis said, "They start fighting amongst themselves, and killing each other, there's less of them to shoot back at us."

Picturing Da Silva shouting accusations at Miller, and Miller getting angry and shoving Da Silva or throwing a punch, Elliot replied, "We can only hope."

Tomorrow if it rained as the weather station barometer suggested, they'd sneak into Jericho for some more guerilla activities.

But this was enough for today. This was plenty.

Today, he thought, had been a very productive day.

4

THE TEAM'S long hike came to an end outside Jericho's western gate. Crouched within the tree line, wiping drizzling rain from their eyes, they glared across eighty metres of cleared ground at the message the SERPs had left them.

A worker hung from the framework above and outside the gate.

A woman.

Her hands had been secured behind her back, rope knotted around her neck. Her malnourished body had been stripped of clothing, leaving her naked to the elements, exposed to the crows perching on her shoulders.

Our enemy are worse than deaders, Elliot thought, his chest hitching, his half-empty stomach clenching, memory fragments surfacing to superimpose themselves across the scene at the gate. *Because these bastards know exactly what they're doing.*

Overlaid across the swinging worker's body he saw other bodies, the bodies of innocents in dusty streets and dry fields, bodies mashed by mortar fire, burned and blistered by phosphorus, beheaded by jihadists, perforated by Alliance ground fire—

Angie gripped his forearm hard, bringing him back. "It's not our fault, Elliot."

He deep-breathed himself back toward control, hissing, "Goddamned right it isn't."

"Right," she said. She gave a low whistle in Rit's direction. His eyes on the bodies, it took him a moment to notice. She told him, "Say it."

"Say what?"

"Not our fault."

"Not our fault," he repeated, teeth grit.

She pointed to Spider. "Say it."

"Not our fault," the young man mumbled. He was staring at his hands now and his eyes were wet with more than rain.

Angie pointed to Sturgis.

"Not. Our. Fault." His hands were stretched in front of him and clenched together, as if he were strangling the perpetrators. In a steady voice, he added, "Shit like this happens in war."

"Worse before better," Elliot agreed.

A pause, then Sturgis added, "But I didn't think I could get any angrier."

"Copy that." Elliot looked both always along the line. "We cancel the current action. All of it." Stares greeted this announcement. They couldn't continue their pissant insurgency, not this way, not if it started costing this.

Elliot wasn't wearing a ballistic vest, having given his to Rit, so it was easy to jam a knuckle in his chest and rub at where the stomach acid was rising and burning.

As much as he respected his new team, as keen and clever as they were, they weren't Rangers, SEALs, or SAS.

He suddenly had the beginnings of a better idea.

"Nipping at their heels this way, we're risking lives for very little short-term gain. We haven't hit a single former cop yet and the militia are small fish. If we want to end this, we need to end the SERPs."

"Cut off the head," Sturgis said.

"Exactly. I might have an idea for drawing them out and ending this quicker."

Rit turned a palm upward to catch the lightly falling rain. "The barometer says this'll set in at least for today. That help?"

Elliot shook his head. "Won't make any difference. And my idea will take us two or more days to set up. We get one shot." His gaze returned to the hanging woman—then passed on quickly. "I wanna do it properly."

"I still think I should go get Mafia and the others," Spider said.

"We talked about this," Rit replied.

They had. And Elliot along with the others had dismissed the idea out of hand. But things were changing —*had* changed. A few extra sets of hands and eyes—and weapons—might make a massive difference. A smaller team of Vikes could keep out of the main fireteam's way, monitoring the ground around the Facility, making ready for a targeted follow-up assault.

The only thing sticking in Elliot's craw about using Vikes was the guy who called himself Mafia. That sonofabitch had been worse than unreliable last time they'd worked together; and he still hadn't brought Elliot's BearCat back.

"Okay," he told Spider. "You leave in the morning and meet us at the safe house tomorrow night."

The others stared at him in open surprise, Spider looking the most shocked.

"Good," said the young man, regaining his composure. "Awesome. They won't let you down, promise. They hate these pricks as much as we do."

Elliot stopped him talking further with a raised hand. "Three conditions. One, you listen carefully to the new plan we're gonna develop and you memorize your part in it perfectly."

"Right."

"Whoever you bring back needs to understand exactly what they're getting into."

"Totes, boss."

"Second, you get two or three reliable individuals. And I *mean* reliable. Neither one of them is Mafia, you hear me? We need people who'll follow instructions to the letter."

"Reckon I can do that. I'll get the ones who's been takin' care of me spiders and shit."

"Three, I want my goddamned BearCat back."

Spider's face screwed up. "Mm. Last time I asked—"

"You didn't ask hard enough. The trade-off is they'll

get extra weaponry and medication once the dust settles here."

"Okay. Yeah, they might go for that."

"Hope you know what you're doing," grumbled Angie.

"Might be good to have the extra help," said Sturgis. "I guess."

Rit grunted reluctant agreement.

Angie sighed.

"Alright, fall back," Elliot said and one by one, the others melted into the bushland behind him.

These days, dates had largely lost their importance. But checking his watch, he noticed the date for the first time in a long time.

In three days' time, it would be October 31.

Perfect. Absolutely perfect.

"Trick or treat, bitches," he told the murderers beyond the wall.

5

October 30th
15:18

ELLIOT'S COMMAND post was a newly-erected tent set halfway up the tall hill behind the gas station—the *petrol* station, he corrected himself—and pegged across a hiking trail. He moved around the inside of it in a crouch, checking he was happy with the positions of the seven small monitor screens he'd set up, testing their reception. It was the fourth time he'd run these same tests—or was it the fifth? Paranoid, maybe, but everything depended on having secure connections with the hidden cameras down in the safe house.

The network of cameras and monitors was an eclectic one, all of the units pilfered from local homes and stores: four truck reversing cams that hooked into the split-screen on a 7 inch cabin display unit; a couple of expensive baby monitors; two dummy air humidifiers with hidden spycams transmitting to separate 5 inch screens.

Four of the five monitor screens ran off internal batteries; he'd hooked the 7 inch monitor to a car battery.

On hearing a whistle from the hiking trail where it turned to run across the face of the hill, he powered everything down and came outside. Angie trotted into view, carrying her sawn-off shottie and a long-handled shovel.

"Mission complete?" he asked when she was close enough that he didn't need to yell.

"Task complete," she replied, a little breathlessly. She pecked his cheek and dumped the shovel between the tent's guy ropes, out of the way. "Laid a pit trap right across the trail where it curves down toward the road in case they come up this way."

"Excellent. I wouldn't put it past them to have some local maps. Though I seriously don't think they'll send anyone up and around here."

She gave him a dubious look. "That why you put a camera down at the trail mouth?"

"Doesn't hurt to be sure."

"Exactly. So you don't tell someone who just dug you a pit trap that they wasted their energy."

"Nothing's wasted—and you're the best." He tilted his head as he offered a cutesy grin.

She cuffed his arm, trying not to smile back, then nodded at the tent. "Sure you'll pick up the camera feeds from here?"

"Tested them four times."

Or was it five?

The command post sat one-hundred-fifty metres from the safe house and behind it. That placed him well within the three-hundred-metre range the camera units all boasted on their packaging. It had been a relief to discover the manufacturers weren't guilty of false advertising.

Angie hummed a second. "So many things can go wrong, babe. That's all."

"Things already went wrong." He hooked an arm over her shoulder, drew her in. "That's why we're here. *This* time, they'll go right."

She leaned her brow against his chest. "God, I hope so."

"The equipment's good. The plan's good. The enemy has no idea what we're doing. They'll come in fast and straight, keeping in a tight stack, doing what they've trained to do. They're predictable. And predictable is a flaw. For them, a fatal one."

She reached for his arm with the wristwatch, turned it and checked his time. "Three-twenty-three. Few things to do before I make a certain phone call—"

"Radio call."

"—and really get the show on the road."

"Only thing I want to do right now is this." He lifted her chin, put his lips to hers. When they broke off, he said, "Make it through this alive. You hear me?"

She touched his cheek. "The plan's good, remember?"

All plans are good, he thought, suppressing a sigh. *Until they ain't.*

THEY TOOK THE HIKING TRAIL BACK DOWN THE HILL WITH

Elliot memorizing every dip and knoll, every tree root and half-dried mud slick: he'd be doing this again in near-dark tomorrow. Emerging from bushland, they paused a moment at a hip-high wire fence to peer south and over a couple of buildings into the dale below and beyond them. The fallow farmland and native forest there had been carved into a patchwork of uneven rectangles by the narrow rural highway, by farm driveways, by ranger access roads, and other hiking trails.

"Think it'll ever be back the way it was?" Angie asked. "You know, in a hundred years or so?"

"Do you want it to be?"

"If I'm honest? I probably do. I'm still like most people pre-outbreak. I want perfectly sealed roads, internet, supermarkets, electricity. But I don't want the pollution and social problems those things caused."

"See how green it is?" he said. "Hear how peaceful it is? If you can live without internet and major manufacturing, you could still have food and roads and electricity and decent housing and clothing, and without the pollution and the social problems. The human race in this country has a chance to try and create something new like that."

She chewed her lip, thinking. Then: "So. Same question, but turned around. Do you think *that* will ever happen?"

"If *I'm* honest? I think good people like you will try to make it so. And bad people will always get in your way."

"Well, that cheers me up."

That's why they used to call me Sparkles, he thought, then said, "You asked."

"Yeah, stupid me. Then what are we fighting for?"

"We're fighting," he said as he hopped the fence, "to make the bad people pay."

They were now in the overgrown grass behind the safe house. Neither thought of anything more to say as they came around the west side of the house, past the back door and clothesline, continuing downhill. They crossed the gardens and lawn at the front without any need to tread carefully this time, since Rit had cleared away the traps, repurposing some materials, hiding others. Elliot didn't want SERPs tripping them when they came up from the highway: he wanted them contained within the house before any action started.

When they reached the back of the station, Rit beamed down at them from the roof. "Beautiful day to prep for an ambush."

"Toolbox meeting in two minutes," Angie told him.

He gave a thumbs up and vanished momentarily before the ladder he'd pulled up after himself came over the side.

Elliot and Angie went around front of the petrol station. Earlier that day, Spider had returned with two more Vikes in his car. Those newcomers now lazed on the weed-ridden concrete between the fuel pumps and the glass doors. The young guy named Bourbon broke up twigs and tossed the pieces into a plastic bucket a couple of metres away while the fortyish woman named Wolfsister told him a story about her job in the "old days". She had a Jericho militia hunting rifle balanced across her thighs. Pausing her story, she gestured a casual hello to the new arrivals.

Angie said, "Take Rit's position while the rest of us have a team meeting?"

"No worries." Wolfsister got to her feet easily. "Tell you the rest later," she told Bourbon. The plastic bucket plunked as another of the young guy's twigs found it.

Once they were back in the safe house garden and out of earshot, Angie asked, "Think we can trust 'em?"

"For what we need them for?" Elliot shrugged his eyebrows. "Better than nothing. At worst, they'll keep any remaining militia off of us. And they'll be a long way from the main action, out of our way."

"I just wish they'd actually be vigilant," Angie replied as they kept walking. "Like, right *now*. Not just sit there discussing career highlights."

Elliot grunted agreement as they continued around to the safe house front entrance.

It had been a warmer day than the ones before it, hinting at the summer to come. Sturgis had stretched out on some cushions on the small porch, stripped to shorts and t-shirt, soaking in sunlight. He startled when the wooden boards creaked beneath Elliot's feet and sat up, wiping drool from one cheek.

"Nodded off," he mumbled.

"All good," Angie replied. "Rit was watching. You deserve a rest."

Elliot smiled a little at that, given what she'd just been complaining about. If it had been Spider napping on that porch, she'd have driven a boot up his ass. He wondered what the former Vike had to do to earn the trust and affection Angie bestowed on Rit and Sturgis.

He said, "Time for a final briefing. Living room."

Sturgis groaned as he rose, lifting the walkie-talkie he'd had balanced on his lap. He pointed it at bushland to the east of the house. "Spider's checking the rabbit traps for dinner. I'll call him back."

Rit was wandering the house when they entered, sniffing the air.

"You chroming?" Angie asked him. "Or coming down with something?"

He entered the living room. "Can't smell a thing. You really put petrol in here?"

"Out of sight and secure in containers that don't leak vapors," Elliot told him. "Perfectly safe. For now."

"Yeah, right, but I'm sleeping outside tonight," Rit replied.

"Sleeping bags in the bushes, mate," Angie told him and slapped his shoulder.

He made a face at that and fell silent, leaning against a wall.

When Spider and Sturgis returned, Elliot regarded the group soberly. No doubt, they expected a pep talk from him. As if he'd ever been good at that.

Too hard on yourself, murmured Radler's ghost. *'Member all that shit you used to give us about remaining circumspect? That was some good pep-talkin', right there.*

They'd assembled in a ragged circle around the room's perimeter. All had dark circles under their eyes. What Rit had just said echoed in Elliot's head. They all needed sleep and soon: Elliot was certain the SERPs would arrive at dawn—or shortly before it.

The plan they'd developed called for a coffee table dead center of the room—for some reason Angie shoved it to the side now. Was she going to get them to do some stretching? With fatigue chemicals seeping into his muscles, Elliot thought he could do with that.

She cleared her throat. "I expect you're wondering why I called this meeting. Well..." She moved to a book-shelf. "Look what I found in a cupboard." Her hand stroked the lid of a record player.

When had she set that up?

And why?

"Old school!" Spider crowed. "Does it work? I could do some DJ-ing. You know, scratching. We could party tonight."

Angie slipped an old LP from a shelf full of them; the album cover was a faded deep blue, its edges worn and white in patches. She told Spider, "If you scratched *this*, I'd kill you."

She turned it to face them. The album's title read:

UNFORGETTABLE — Nat King Cole

To Elliot's mind, Angie—blonde, white, late twenties, and tough as leather—did not look right holding that record.

She beamed at them and said, "My grandparents had this when I was little. I used to listen to it all the time."

Spider muttered as he read the cover aloud. Louder, he said, "Never heard of it."

Rit offered her a shrug.

Sturgis scratched his head. "I remember the guy's *name*."

"Before all of our time," Elliot said. "But, yeah, the man put out some damn fine tunes."

"Damn fine," Angie agreed and lifted the record player lid to push a button. The speakers came alive with a deep electric hum. "One of my favorite songs of all time is on this." Carefully, she slipped the record from its sleeve and put it on the turntable. She lined up the needle with the start of a track and lowered it carefully. The speakers snapped, crackled and popped. And then came the opening strains of horn and strings.

"*Pretend*," he said, naming the track. "Great song."

Into the center of the room, she stepped and beckoned with one hand. "Elliot, dance with me."

He glanced uncomfortably around the other men. "You're kidding."

"I'm not."

"Now?"

"Yes."

"I can't dance."

"Can you shuffle awkwardly? Coz that'll do."

He rubbed at the back of his neck. "Haven't shuffled awkwardly since I was..." He had to think. "Nineteen."

Jesus. A lifetime ago. Longer than Lewis's lifetime ago.

"Elliot."

"Yah?"

"Get over here."

Joining her, he avoided another glance at his fellows, taking her hand, reaching the free arm around her back as hers went to his and she lay a cheek against his shoulder.

"Commence awkward shuffling," she murmured.

So he did. His first tread clipped her instep, prompting a chuckle from both of them. And then, after a couple of bars of music, they fell into the same groove. Angie led.

This ain't so bad, he had to admit.

By the end of the first verse, she'd turned him around until his back was no longer to the others. Elliot had expected Rit and Spider to be razzing him, and Sturgis to be staring at the floor in embarrassment. All three returned his gaze with frank and serious expressions. Rit nodded encouragement. Elliot flashed them a tight smile.

Then Sturgis was stepping forward. "May I cut in?"

Wordlessly, Elliot and Angie separated. Angie held out her arms as Elliot went to stand beside Rit. She and Sturgis joined in more formal pose, a chaste pose. Maintaining several inches of space between them, they saw out the short song. Sturgis was a way better dancer than Elliot was—perhaps navy officer duties had given him practice.

When the track ended, when the needle scratched across the gap to the final song on the A-side, Angie kissed Sturgis's cheek. He gave her a nod, wiped an eye and went to stand by the window.

Angie returned the needle to start of *Pretend*, then turned toward Rit. "Your turn, bud."

"Me!"

Palm upturned, her fingers flicked in a Bruce Lee *come-get-some* gesture.

Blushing fiercely, he shuffled through a full verse and chorus with her before breaking off. She pecked him on the cheek and shoved him gently away, then pointed to Spider.

"Your turn, dickhead."

Grinning, he came over. Their dance was awkward but Spider never stopped grinning the whole time. If he noticed she hadn't kissed his cheek, he didn't show it. When the song was over, Angie lifted the needle from the record and turned off the player. And remained there, staring down at the black vinyl disk. Spider performed a little shimmy as he returned to where he'd first stood.

Sturgis grunted, leaving the window to rummage in his pack. He brought out a slim shaving kit case, causing Rit and Spider to exchange a perplexed look. He unzipped it, pulled out a mini-bar-sized bottle of booze.

"Scotch." He handed it to Rit. Angie turned as Sturgis pulled out a second tiny bottle. "Vodka." He tossed it to her. The third bottle was rum; Spider got that. Next came bourbon which Sturgis tossed to Elliot. The final bottle was again a scotch which he kept for himself, ditching the empty kit case. "Found these a few months back. Kept 'em for a special occasion. Lady, gentlemen, please crack them open."

There came a chorus of clicks as lids were twisted from bottles.

Sturgis stared down the neck of his. "Not much here. Maybe each of us could make a toast before we drink together?"

"I'll start," Rit said. "May none of us die tomorrow."

"Hear hear," said Spider. Then: "Better a stout heart than a sharp sword."

The others blinked at him, as astonished as Elliot at

the sound of profound verse coming out of that mouth. Then all eyes turned to Angie.

She said, "Here's to clear heads, steady hands, and stupid enemies."

Elliot caught every eye and added, "To the bravest team I ever served with."

All of them—even Angie—blushed.

In Elliot's mind, Radler's ghost murmured, *Yeah, they ain't too shabby at all, Sparkles.*

Closing out the circle, Sturgis thought a moment, then said, "To absent friends."

Five tiny bottles were raised toward the center of the room. Five tiny bottles were drained.

Then Elliot said, "Let's get ready for the morning."

6

October 31st
Halloween Morning
04:56

EXACTLY ONE HOUR TILL SUNRISE, Elliot thought and tugged the sleeve of his dark sweater back over the wristwatch. The same hand rose to flick a super-keen mosquito away from his ear. He'd come out of the tent for fresh air and the freedom to pace around. To keep his nerves under control. To give the body and brain something to do.

The sky above was almost completely clear of clouds. A three-quarter moon had risen to the north-north-east a half hour earlier; it peeked now around the face of the hill, low over the trees. The strong northerly breeze tasted of summer and promised another warm day. It had made the hours he and the team spent hiding outdoors less uncomfortable than they might have been. In fact, he thought, the conditions were near-perfect, as if a higher power was backing them.

Finally.

From within the tent came some soft radio crackle. Then Spider's voice, professional-sounding, unusually clear of dumbassery. "Contact."

Right on time, Elliot thought as he ducked through the flaps. Da Silva's SERPs were well-drilled people, people of professional habits, *predictable* habits.

A pause, radio static, then Spider again: "Three SUVs, electric motors, real quiet. One came in fifty metres ahead of the others. They're slow and careful. Wait..."

Another pause. Elliot braced to hear gunfire in the distance.

Spider came on again, ending his concerns. "Okay, all three passed us. Can't see no other vehicles 'cept theirs, or hear any. SUVs have pulled up. Hundred metres up the road. Unloading ... I count ...eight. Eight SERPs. Full cop gear. Looks like they have glasses on, so might be night vision lenses."

"Won't help 'em," Elliot muttered to himself.

"They're moving. Headed your way. Good luck." The static-ridden transmission cut out.

Elliot didn't send him an acknowledgement because he didn't want radio noise giving away Spider's position. He alerted Rit, Angie and Sturgis on another channel with a simple eight clicks. Moments later, one after the other, they replied with two clicks each, indicating they'd heard. And that was that, as far as comms went for the next short while.

In Hobart—when the outbreak originally happened —the private security team Elliot had been with had all owned earpiece microphone sets. But he'd left his—and theirs—in the hotel when he'd fled that city. He hadn't imagined ever needing such things again. His *current* team had found nothing like those in all their scavenging and looting. And walkies were unreliable and unwieldly during stealth ops. With the three team members hidden locally, Elliot would have to rely on them knowing their jobs and doing their jobs. When things were safe enough, they could resort to walkie communications again.

One of the small monitors across the table had been powered on for the last hour. Elliot switched the others on, too. Nothing interesting on any of them except grayscale images of their various locations. But they'd come into play soon.

The SERPs had a klick-and-a-half hike ahead of them, in low light. If they stuck to the road and came in fast, it might take them as little as ten minutes. If they took it slow, well, that depended on *how* slow. Though they'd surely scouted this area at some time in the past, there was only one road leading past the petrol station; the SERPs had to come that way. He didn't think they'd break off into the forest and approach the house from cover. Too much potential noise. Too much unknown terrain. A road was simpler, and these were cops, not soldiers. They were urbanized. Sneaking through dark bushland in mere moonlight wouldn't excite any of them.

He slung his short-barreled MCX across his chest and tightened the strap so the rifle wouldn't hang too loose.

It took seven minutes before movement appeared on one of his screens, the one he'd powered up the longest, the one whose camera was perched in a tree down along the highway behind a hiker's gate into the forest. And it was not the movement of the wild dogs he'd seen earlier. This was people. Eight human shapes in dark clothing, helmets and ballistic vests. A line of SERPs spaced two metres apart. None turned toward the camera, toward the gate and the path into the bush. By now, their leader would have spotted the fuel pumps and the SUV parked at them. When most of the line had filed past, they paused, the final two still in frame and taking a knee to wait. Elliot imagined the leader with an IR hunting monocular to one eye, scanning the fuel stop for heat signatures, listening carefully for telltale sounds. Checking for tripwires across the road, even.

"No tripwires here," he whispered to the people on the monitor. "None anywhere. Us dumb Downsers haven't protected our base. Too slack. Too cocky. Not up to *your* level of competence and carefulness." That was what he *wanted* them to think, to believe.

Please.

The SERPs on his screen remained crouched in place. If one hadn't turned their head toward the person behind them, Elliot might have thought the image had frozen. Whoever that leader was, they weren't suicidal.

Was it the woman Erikson? he wondered. Was it Da Silva?

"C'mon, you assholes, *move*," he hissed.

Sturgis would have a clear view of the targets. He would have been watching them come up the highway for the past couple of minutes, probably...

The property with the house and fuel stop ran north-south, with the home's back fence to the north, and the gas pumps to the south. Sturgis was positioned 400 metres south-west of the gas pumps—across the highway and deep in cropland where the farmers had placed a small equipment shed. By now he'd already be on top of it, lying prone with his long gun, with a clear line of sight up the hill to the west side of the house. If the SERP contingent had numbered only two, he might have attempted a couple of headshots already. But if a group this large scattered...

No, it was best to stick to the plan.

Rit had positioned himself in the storm drain along the dirt road running northwards up the east side of the property, with bracken branches affording camouflage. His position was level with the northern edge of the house. Angie had a similar position in the drainage ditch at the bottom of the hill, across the highway from the petrol station and facing up the dirt road. Uncomfortable and cold it might be, but they'd laid their ditches with drop-sheets—and they were bundled up in multiple sweaters for the time being.

All were placed to improve the chances of containment if anything went ass-up inside the house. And all had plenty of bush and farmland to retreat into if necessary.

The SERPs were moving again, the end of the line passing out of camera shot. Elliot turned his attention to the next screen, the one he'd hidden on the west side of the petrol station and facing the road, sandwiched between an old vending machine and the wall. It took a minute before the line of targets appeared again, moving more cautiously. The trailing four went down on a knee in the middle of the roadway again while the leader headed for the shop entrance, vanishing from sight. The second in the stack went with them, while the third and fourth came toward Elliot's camera.

Don't notice it, he thought at them. *Don't notice it.* They didn't. Soon, they too were out of camera shot—and about to discover the ladder where Rit had left it around back of the petrol station. It leaned there, leading to the roof. Chances were good that the SERPs had planned to leave a sniper on overwatch somewhere; it was better that Elliot controlled where that somewhere was. The ladder provided the bait, the way up to the perfect overwatch position. It took thirty seconds or more, but finally a helmeted head appeared on Elliot's third monitor screen, peeking over the lip of the station roof. Once the SERP had ascertained there was no one up there, he climbed all the way up, signaled to someone below them and dropped into a crouch with his weapon covering the house up the hill. The idiot didn't bother checking the aircon unit directly behind him, where the camera was hidden—along with another nasty surprise.

The leader must have signaled to the four out on the road because they rose and surged forward as if one creature, headed directly to the house along the west side of the fuel stop. Less than a minute later, seven SERPs appeared on Elliot's fourth cam set up to watch the west entry to the house. Exactly the route and ingress he'd predicted experienced cops would choose—rather than the potentially creaky porch on the opposite side of the home, the back entry had a single, cement step up to the door into the laundry room.

Elliot had also placed a camera over on the porch, but

it was unlikely he'd need it. The remaining cameras were placed internally. One in the living-dining room facing back into the hallway—this would catch most of the activity once they'd entered. One between the towels in the linen closet facing across the doorway of Bedroom 2 into Bedroom 1. One in the heating vent midway along the hall ceiling. Several doors within the house had been left fully open to make the triggering of traps easier and more effective—the sliding door between living room and hallway; the door into the kitchen; the sliding door on the hallway linen cupboard; and the door to Bedroom 2 which faced back along the hallway.

Relying on shock and speed, the SERPs burst into the building. The leader smashed open the door and plunged through first, crossing the laundry in three strides before hooking right into the living-dining room. Close on the leader's heels, the second cop darted across the hallway and into the kitchen, while the next three swept left into the hallway. The final SERP stayed in the laundry at the door—on-camera, Elliot could see the back of their vest poking out and over the step. Two of the three cops in the hallway made straight for the bedrooms at the end while the third checked toilet and bathroom.

"Showtime," Elliot whispered as a cop reached the open doorway into Bedroom 2 ...

The device Elliot had placed there was a variation on the old Viet Cong bamboo-and-spike spring traps. Yesterday, he'd removed a leaf spring from the rear suspension on a derelict truck, then drilled holes in it, fitted spikes through the holes and lugged it up into the crawlspace above the bedroom ceiling. After carving a hole in the plasterboard, he'd mounted the leaf spring to a ceiling joist so that it hung vertically across the narrow doorway. Using a hand winch—also securely mounted in the ceiling—he'd cranked the spring back and up until it was shaped like a U with the spikes facing outwards. The trip-wire was formed from the finest fishing line he could find, running down from the ceiling, along the inside of the doorframe, then across it. Tripping that line would knock the winch's ratchet out of position and release the tension on the spring.

The SERP at Bedroom 2 tripped the wire as they made to storm the room—and died instantly, Elliot guessed, as the leaf spring smashed into the man with enough force to punch the spikes through the vest's armor plate like it was paper. Elliot could see the after-math on several cameras—the man drooped from the leaf spring like an abandoned puppet. He wasn't moving. The cops who'd checked Bedroom 1, bathroom and kitchen appeared in the hallway; though their jaws were hidden beneath face gaiters, Elliot imagined them gawping at the carnage. The one at the back door shouted an enquiry that carried clearly to Elliot's posi-tion. The one in the lounge started back toward the hall. Elliot started flicking switches on the spare drone controllers and extra walkie on his trestle, triggering the other devices Angie had placed in the main bedroom, linen closet, living room, kitchen and laundry room—igniting the various mixtures of brake fluid, pool chlo-rine, gasoline, powdered detergent, bug spray, sparklers, and Vaseline.

What happened next was lost in static as multiple

small explosions and fireballs ripped through the small cottage, destroying the internal cameras. The booms and cracks came to Elliot on the air a second later. He poked his head quickly out of the tent to see an orange glow already showing through and above the trees. He ducked back inside, tapped the monitor screen that showed the sniper on the petrol station roof and said, "Bye bye."

The man had half-risen in shock. Elliot lost sight of what happened to him next as the IED in the aircon housing behind him went off. Before Elliot could fully give in to a surge of relief and celebration, he realized the guy on the roof wasn't the only one he'd lost sight of. There was also the asshole at the home's back door. Had he been inside when the devices went up? Had he made it out? The rear camera on the house still operated—but Elliot couldn't see him on it.

Swearing, he toggled his main walkie and told the others, "Hold position. I'm coming in."

He flicked the rifle's selector from safe to single-fire and headed out and down the hiking trail. He'd walked this trail many times in the past two days, in light and in dark; he was familiar with it, treading surely, safe as he hurried. With the breeze coming toward him, he smelled the acrid stink of the burning house—and thought he caught a strangled scream. The home's boundary fence was almost in sight when the remaining SERP appeared ahead, backlit by the glow from the flaming house, moving in a stumbling jog, one hand wrapped around his rifle grip, the other in front of him at face level as if blind. And perhaps he was. He'd yanked his goggles down over his face to his throat, dragging the gaiter with them. But with the only light behind him, Elliot couldn't see his face, couldn't tell if he were wounded or just dazzled. The man's rifle was pointing at the earth, useless.

Elliot's right boot found a depression in the drying mud. He anchored himself there, raised his own weapon. The SERP's torso and neck were protected by armor. At ten metres, it wouldn't matter, even though the rounds wouldn't penetrate. Elliot fired several shots, center-mass, knocking the man back on his ass—and kept on firing, moving in on him as the guy screamed and flailed. By the time he stood over him, the SERP was still. Elliot put another round through his face to be sure. And then he moved on.

THEY WERE DEAD, EVERY ONE OF THEM. THOSE WHO'D BEEN in the house had died there. The one who'd taken overwatch lay crumpled on the concrete behind the gas station, the exposed parts of his body riddled with shrapnel, his neck broken from the fall.

After gathering spare magazines from him and from the man Elliot had killed on the path, his fireteam regrouped, checked the SUV at the fuel pumps had been left operational by the SERPs, then took it toward the spot where the cops had left *their* cars.

Halfway there, all their walkies burped quietly. Angie was fastest to answer. "Go for Angie."

Spider's voice was subdued, serious. "Heard the noise. All good there?"

Elliot gestured for her to pass it over. He sent back, "No casualties. Headed your way."

"We're at Checkpoint Rat Run."

At the east-boundary stormwater drain, Elliot thought. *Under the walls of Jericho.* He rested the walkie against his cheek. "One more time, Spider. Just so there's no mistakes."

"Bourbon and I go through first. He cuts left, I cut right. If there's no contact, Wolfsister comes through. We head north along the fence, take out the sentries at Checkpoint Portal—"

The eastern gate, Elliot decoded.

"—open it, then move three klicks to the closest worker billet and set 'em free."

Angie took the walkie. "Free them, don't arm them. Get them back to Checkpoint Portal and make sure they can get out."

"I know, I know," Spider said.

"Good luck," she told him, tone softening. At a look from Elliot, she passed it back.

He told Spider, "Make sure any workers know the way out to Waystation." Their code for the town of Oatlands.

"Yep. But what if they don't want to go there? What if they don't trust us?"

"Once they're outside those walls, they can do whatever they want—go to Waystation, go to Hobart, hold hands and sing kumbaya for all I care."

"Gotcha. I mean, copy."

"What's next after that?"

"Once we clear that billet, we head to the next one."

By that time, Elliot thought, *we should be at Pankhurst, halfway to the Facility.* "Good. Good to go?"

Rustling against the mic indicated movement; Spider's voice dropped in volume. "Ready to be heroes. Our songs will be sung—"

"Out," Elliot said—cutting off the sudden resurgence of Spider's Vike bullshit—and handed back the walkie.

WITH THE CAR STOWED OUT OF SIGHT OF THE WALLS, THEY jogged in diamond formation through a wedge of forest before gathering to crouch at the forest's edge. The body still hung at the gate, but the gates stood wide open. It didn't necessarily mean that Spider's group—now observing radio silence—had opened them before heading for the first worker billet.

"Open gates might still be monitored," Angie murmured, her thoughts running parallel to his.

Sturgis added, "Might be a trap."

"Eight dead SERPs mean there's three left," Elliot said. "Da Silva will definitely be one of them." There'd only been two bodies he could check back at the safe house. Neither had been Da Silva—and although the rest were still cooking inside the fire, he was sure the big muscle-bound bastard wouldn't have risked his own life on that mission. "By now, the others have missed a check-in. He knows they're dead." When the dead ones had missed whatever all-clear signal had been prearranged, red flags would be squirting adrenaline into the blood-streams of the remaining three.

"Might be right inside there, ready and waiting for a counter-ambush," said Angie. "They might have taken down the Vikes."

"They're more likely still in their bunker where it's safe," said Sturgis, "figuring out what to do next."

"Or running," suggested Rit. When they glanced at him, he added, "I can dream, can't I?"

Angie caught Elliot's gaze and inclined her head toward the easy way into Jericho. "If someone *is* watching that choke point, we should take the storm drain, like the Vikes did. Dirtier and harder. But safer."

Elliot felt a brief fluttering in his gut as her eyes broke contact. He watched her scan the tops of the wall, chewing her lip in thought, one thumb tapping the stock of the assault rifle she'd taken from one of the SERPs. Her tactical decision was absolutely on point.

God, I think I love this woman.

Before she—or the others—could notice him staring, he said, "Agreed" and led the way through the trees in the direction of the drain opening.

07:50

ONCE THEY'D MADE it safely through the drain, they formed up behind an abandoned water tank. From there, they plunged into the native forest between the walls and Jericho's closest farm, spreading apart in diamond formation with Elliot taking point. Elliot, Rit and Angie carried small packs strapped tight to their backs. These contained the ingredients for a Timothy McVeigh mini-bomb spread between them, ingredients separated for safety. Angie walked "drag", stationing herself forty metres behind Elliot and watching the team's six. Rit drifted out left. Elliot glanced at Sturgis out to the right. The sniper had a SERP Smith & Wesson .40 cal in his hip holster; he'd kept his SR98 and carried it over the crooks of both elbows.

Elliot hadn't felt this well-armed for a long, long time. It felt good. Extremely good.

A half hour of pushing through thick forest led to an

hour's trudging south-west through farmland. They were partway across the wheat fields directly east of Pankhurst before they heard vehicle noise: the squeal of a truck's air brakes somewhere north and east of their position. The team dropped instantly into crouches, heads lower than the top of the grass. Elliot caught the faint grating of a bad gear change. And then ... engine noise fading to nothing. Wherever that vehicle was, it wasn't coming nearer. He let out a crow call; as the others rose with him, he signaled to continue.

Elliot cut across an access track through the wheat fields. A farmhouse appeared ahead. He knew a road near it would lead them into Pankhurst, a road he wanted to follow into town. Approaching the house through the stalks of grain, with the new day's light coming in over their shoulders, he recalled a morsel of Driscoll's intel: this farmhouse was a militia homestead. That intel was confirmed by the high wire fence now visible around the yard. He was approaching from the side and front of the house. Rit and Sturgis drew level with Elliot at the boundary wall where the wheat stopped. A long driveway arrowed away to their right, aimed straight at the town road. He crow-called for Angie to come in close, nodding toward the compound when she arrived.

"Let's skip it," she said.

They had an unhindered view straight through the gates, because those gates stood ajar. Elliot put field glasses to his face, grunted, lowered them. "House front door is wide open."

"Do militia leave their gates and doors open during the day?"

"Would you?" Elliot asked.

"Smart arse." She took a breath, blew it out hard. "You want to check it."

"It'll take time, but it's not wise to leave armed hostiles at our back."

"Roger roger."

"I'll take Rit." He lay down his pack before slinging the rifle over his back.

Angie got her pack off too. "Not much in these, but they get bloody heavy."

"You should try the packs in basic training." He patted her thigh, then pulled his handgun and connected a suppressor as he moved toward Rit.

THE FRONT DOOR WAS WIDE OPEN. THE LONG CRUST OF bread lying on the stoop provided a landing pad for small black flies. Beside the step up onto the porch, Elliot rested his forearms on the railing with the pistol toward the door, listening for sounds of habitation. Nothing. Movement at his periphery told him Rit was about to tread on the step. Elliot hissed and made a cutting gesture then pointed at the underside of the stair.

Rit made an *Oh yeah* face and stooped to check, then indicated it was clear. But he still stepped over it as he hopped onto the porch. The boards creaked a little. Rit went one side of the door and Elliot the other. While Elliot kept cover, Rit inspected the jamb then pulled his knife and used the tip to lift a wrinkled carpet runner from the tiled floor, checking for trip wires or pressure plates. Elliot gave him a nod of approval.

You're learning, buddy.

Beyond the door lay a short hallway. A door led off each side halfway along it. Didn't appear to be anything hinky along the walls, so Elliot moved inside, pressing left to make way for Rit. From back of the house came a long, wet breath, someone snorting air through snot.

Deader! screamed his instincts. Rit winced at the sound.

Mindful of traps, Elliot checked the door on the left, as Rit took the one opposite it. His was a small living room, messy, but devoid of people. Rit's was a bedroom, he saw; Rit emerged and gave a thumbs up.

They froze. There it was again, that sniffling. Something scuffed against bare floorboards in back. The sound of clothing maybe. Or loose flesh. Then a low click as a plastic object was put down.

Not deaders.

The hall ended in a T, with an open bathroom facing back down it. Elliot trod lightly to the bathroom first as Rit went right at the T into another bedroom. They met outside the bathroom and exchanged shrugs. Only one more door to open. Elliot pushed it with his suppressor, Rit staying behind him. He saw—

A kitchen, square, clean. A square table in the middle, four chairs. A woman sat the other side of the table near the open back door, nursing a teacup. Bread crusts lay on three plates sidelined on a counter. Beneath the table: two kids, girls probably. One might've been three or four years old, the other closer to ten. The smaller stared at them with frank eyes and sniffed a string of snot back into one nostril. The older girl continued brushing the younger's hair without acknowledging the strangers who'd entered her home with guns drawn.

The woman's voice was dull and thick when she asked, "Gonna kill me?"

Elliot signaled Rit to clear the back yard. After he'd gone, Elliot told her, "Not necessarily."

"That's good." She raised the tea cup and drained it, licked her lips as she pushed it center-table.

Elliot stared at her. She stared back. There was nothing at all in her affect. No emotion. No care factor. Was she high? Or stunned? A disability maybe, intellectual, psychological.

"Where's the others?" he asked.

Her shoulders lifted in a listless shrug. "Gone. Left me."

He pointed under the table with his chin. "Left them too, huh? They yours?"

"One is." Another shrug. Her gaze turned inwards a moment, as if she couldn't remember which one. "Doesn't matter. I love 'em both."

Shit.

One hand went into her cardigan pocket. Elliot's aim shifted toward her midsection. She pulled out a Snickers, tore the wrapper. Where had she gotten that?

Rit came back, gave a headshake, then crouched to squint unhappily at the girls.

"How many lived here?" Elliot asked the woman.

"Huh?" Her mouth was full of nuts and candy.

"How many adults lived here?"

She chewed, swallowed. "Three. Plus me."

"Who left?"

"No one's left. Just me."

"I mean, who *went*?"

"Oh. James and Andy and Amy."

"Took guns?"

"Mm-hm."

"Where's your gun?"

"Never had one. James wouldn't let me."

"Where'd they go?"

She puffed out her cheeks. "Beats me."

"Bloody hell," Rit complained.

"Listen to me," Elliot said. "You are my enemy. I have a weapon. You need to cooperate."

Her jaw stopped working, and for the first time her predicament appeared to register with her. Or maybe she started worrying about the kids.

Elliot continued, "Where did they go and why did they go there?"

"They... They heard that the cops should have..." She frowned a moment, thinking. "Some cops went to get the people who'd been raiding us. And they should have reported in. But they didn't. And Andy and James got worried. So, they shoved stuff in bags, and grabbed the other two kids and then ... they just pissed off. Left us with nothin'." The hand without the Snickers brushed some bread crumbs from the table. The other hand vanished beneath the table and came up empty, the candy passed on to the kids.

"This could be good for us," Elliot told Rit, "if they're *all* abandoning ship like this. Means it's been working."

"Maybe. But what about...?" His gesture encompassed the two girls. By default, it meant the woman too.

Elliot checked her again—she'd closed her eyes, her tongue chasing peanut fragments around her teeth. He allowed himself a small headshake. When it came to black hats and white hats, sometimes it was easy to tell the difference. Other times, not so much.

"We'll come back for them," he said. "Once the workers are free and they find these three, they might be angry enough to... you know."

Though he left the thought unfinished, Rit gave another wince. "Taking them home will be messy."

"Wanna leave them here?"

"Not at all," Rit said. "I'm just saying."

"Whole damn thing's messy."

"I could take them. Now, I mean."

"Shit."

He scratched at his jaw a while, then crouched like Rit had been, catching the older girl's eye.

"Sweetheart, is this lady your mom?"

"Hers," the girl replied in a raspy voice.

"Your parents left you here?"

The girl shook her head. "They died. Amy was looking after me when she got together with Andy."

Holy Christ, there's a backstory here. And I don't wanna hear it.

"Sweetheart," Elliot said again, "what's your name?"

"Emma."

"What's the lady's?"

"Brittany."

"Emma, has Brittany been mean to you? Does she

make you do things you don't want to?" He didn't even know what he was asking.

Oh, yes you do.

Emma's face tilted toward the woman's legs then back again. "She's nice. No one else is. Are you gonna hurt her?"

Elliot shook his head. "Nope."

"You said mean things."

"I did. And I'm sorry. Listen, this other man, his name is Rit. He never says mean things. He has kids. The place we live has a lot of kids. Food. Games. This place here is dangerous now. How about...?" He raised his head above the table a second. Rit nodded in encouragement. "How about you and Brittany and this little one go with Rit to a safer, funner place?"

Funner? You dipshit.

The girl nodded, tugged at the little one's shirt and began climbing from under the table.

Elliot rose and Rit rose with him, stepping back to make room for the kids.

"You sure about this?" Elliot asked him.

Rit screwed up his face. "Maybe I should hide them somewhere close and come back to help you. Sorry, I wasn't thinking."

Elliot raised a hand. "You *were* thinking. You were thinking good. If we're not here to protect people who can't protect themselves, then what the hell are we doing?"

"But what if she's—" He pointed to the woman; she was now watching Emma straighten the little girl's clothes and wipe her nose with a dishrag. Elliot thought

Rit would make a koo-koo gesture, spin his finger round his ear or something. Instead, he said, "—faking?"

The woman didn't so much as blink at this.

Elliot shook his head again. "Your call."

Rit studied the kids and the woman a few seconds, then asked Elliot, "Are *you* sure?"

"Yep."

"You'll be okay without me?"

Elliot allowed himself a brief smile. "Got pretty far without you for a long time."

Rit snorted. Then he came around the table and gave Elliot a hug he wasn't expecting. As Rit pulled away, he didn't meet Elliot's eye. He took off his pack and pulled out the part of the McVeigh bomb he'd been carrying, crap sealed in plastic ziplock bags and wrapped in plastic. He placed it on the table. "Tell the others I said sorry."

"No need."

He moved to the back door. "Then, tell 'em I said stay safe."

"Shall do."

"Ladies, we're going this way," Rit said at the door. "Couple of hours' walk, then we'll jump in a car and go see some really nice people." His eyes rose to meet Elliot's as the children trudged outside silently and the woman rose to follow them, mumbling to herself. "Also tell the others to break a leg."

"Copy that."

"See ya round, chief."

"Yeah. You will."

And they were gone.

"*Shit*," Elliot hissed. He picked up the bomb package and went out the front and back to Angie and Sturgis.

"Where the fuck is Rit?" Angie asked, her eyes on the parcel he carried.

As he handed the package to Sturgis and reclaimed his pack, Elliot explained what had happened in bullet point form. The pair accepted it with grim silence then hopped the fence to join him on the farm driveway.

Elliot took a moment to take in his surrounds again, noticing how tight he was wound, how tight was the knot in his gut. Jericho was a bad bad region. And he was headed now for the worst spot in it: Pankhurst.

The home of the Night Court and trial-by-combat the SERPs watched for fun.

Pankhurst.

Where Jimmy had been bitten and turned.

Goddamned Pankhurst.

It was like going back to Al-Kasrah.

WHERE THE NARROW ROAD CROSSED A SHALLOW CREEK, THE trio veered off and along the banks. Ten minutes' further walking brought them to Pankhurst's back fences. Like many small Aussie towns, it had a highway for a spine, and the population didn't spread far from that. Elliot knew from maps that some commercial properties and yards were set on the far side of the highway back behind civic buildings like the school and hospital. This side was all living space, a couple of wide avenues with cottages lining them. Elliot figured Pankhurst's pre-Collapse population might have numbered a hundred. With a district school, it might even have been higher. As his team scanned the back yards of the outlying cottages, he decided there was low probability that anyone lived in these homes these days. No razor wire; no chain link fencing; no guard dogs. Driscoll had told him the town's only wire-and-dogs defenses were around two stores on the main street where two militiamen lived. Right now, he heard no dogs, just wind in the branches, insects, birdsong, a frog in the creek.

"It's goddamn quiet," he murmured to Angie. There hadn't yet been any indication of the Vikes' activity, either —no shooting.

"Hopefully a good sign," she replied.

Exactly what I was thinking.

Sturgis went first, climbing the fence of the nearest home, disappearing from view as he broke into the house, then—Elliot hoped—went out the front door to scout as far as the street. A shadow passed over their position, clouds rolling in to obscure the early sun. Three minutes ticked by on Elliot's watch before Sturgis's shock of red hair appeared and his hand signaled *all clear*.

Elliot and Angie entered the back yard of the next property over. She gave a low hiss as they crossed the yard, indicating something to their left with a jerk of her chin. Up on top of a child's plastic slide, a black cat watched them. It rose, arched its back and mewled softly, wanting attention, saying hello.

Angie tossed a clod of earth at it, discouraging it from following them.

"Real nice," he told her.

"Never liked cats," she replied.

He tried the back door while she covered him. Unlocked. He led her through a dusty and ransacked home, clearing each room, each closet. A series of someone's personal treasures left brief imprints on his short-term memory as he passed through. All were abandoned now, forgotten, trash not treasure. A leather-bound Dickens novel on a sideboard, its cloth bookmark showing the reader had been two-thirds of the way through it. A porcelain doll in Victorian clothing, reclining on a toy swing. A half-finished tapestry. A polished teak liquor cabinet, open, empty.

"Let's not bother with the rest of the street," he told Angie and she nodded agreement. There was no one back here.

Outside, Sturgis had crouched by a car at the curbside. Elliot went first across the road, providing cover when the others came across. Leapfrogging positions, the three moved through the next property and over its fence into someone's graveyard for farm machinery. No more cats. No dogs. Not even rats. A crow, however, gave them some side-eye from the top of a rusting tractor before taking to the sky.

Across the next street. Through a bed-n-breakfast yard. They reached the high wooden fence marking the boundary of the district school. Climbed it. Dropped into the playground. Took cover at various equipment and fittings.

Since the school occupied one side of a low hill, parts of Pankhurst's modest downtown were visible from Elliot's new position. He'd seen this downtown for himself during his last visit. It consisted of nothing more than a scattering of modest homes, six shops across the road from the district hospital, the hospital's parking lot beside the school here, another building Driscoll had told them was combination town hall and library and meeting rooms—and then a park down where the creek crossed under the highway.

Pankhurst appeared deathly still. Birdlife only. The crow cawed from somewhere nearby.

The three teammates exchanged uncertain glances before leapfrogging each other's positions again, scurrying from cover to cover through the school grounds, their rifles slung, handguns-with-suppressors in hand. They reached the main school building without contact, and hugged the shadows along it. Sturgis gripped Elliot's shoulder, indicating it was time to find a way up to the roof. His other hand extended past Elliot's nose, pointing toward...

Elliot grunted in surprise: he couldn't believe he'd missed it. A steel breezeway ran at right angles off the far end of the building. And a maintenance ladder leaned against it.

Someone already up there?

Driscoll's intel had been rock-solid so far. According to him, sentries weren't posted at Pankhurst. Just those two militiamen living in a former shop to provide a little local monitoring. There certainly hadn't been sentries posted last time Elliot was here.

Maybe we've got them so shit-scared they've changed their protocols.

Down by the building's other corner, Angie's shoulders and free hand were raised in a *WTF* gesture.

Elliot gripped Sturgis's sleeve, yanked him close, murmured into his ear. "I'll go up. You—"

Sturgis pulled away, murmuring back, "No. My job."

Elliot helped him wrestle the SR98 and pack from his back, placing them against the wall while Sturgis jogged to the ladder. Using one hand to climb, his .40 cal ready, he scaled it quickly enough. Angie shifted away from the building to a tall eucalypt, a position better suited to watching the roofline. Sturgis eased himself onto the breezeway and crept to the edge of the main building. From the metal walkway he stood on, it was only five more feet up onto the main roof. He disappeared from Elliot's view. Silence followed, stretching for almost a minute before there came a muffled enquiry and the low *chump-chump* of two rounds fired through a suppressor. More silence. Then the rasp of clothing on brick before a figure appeared again on the breezeway roof. Sturgis. He crouched at the edge, performing the hand signals that said *one hostile, now dead*.

Elliot signaled Angie to watch the windows. Scooping up the SR98, he ran it over to the breezeway and passed it up. In exchange, Sturgis passed down a battered hunting rifle that looked older than he did.

Elliot gave him a thumbs up and left him to climb back into position. After hiding the rifle in a cluster of agapanthus bushes, he joined Angie and murmured, "We're back on plan."

From there, they moved across the school's side fence and into the overgrown lawn and gardens between it and the hospital, keeping pace with each other, staying twenty feet apart. At the low brick wall marking the hospital parking lot's boundary, Angie covered Elliot while he vaulted over.

A van had been parked nearby. He ran to it, crouched at the front bumper, peered around. Nothing to see but a couple more cars that looked clean and cared-for. The van hadn't been used in a long time from the looks of it, windows coated in thick grime, the tarmac beneath it gritty with rain-carried dirt and leaves. The tire nearest him was completely flat.

Elliot glanced back at the school—Sturgis was out of sight as he should be. He braced himself to head for the next-closest car, then froze and hunkered down at a rattle of distant gunfire. Six shots from an automatic rifle. Maybe three klicks away. Maybe five. Three more shots, with four from a different weapon overlapping them. A pause. Another two shots. Five klicks away, Elliot decided. Impossible to tell if they'd been fired from Spider's weapon or a SERP's. There were three ex-cops left. There—

He tensed when footsteps sounded lightly at his back. Only Angie. She slid in beside him. "That didn't sound good."

"Might've been good, we don't know."

They listened a little longer, Elliot beginning to feel naked and exposed out here in the lot. No more shots were fired. And the noise hadn't provoked movement from any of the buildings around them. He itched to get out his walkie and check in with Spider, but it wasn't the time or place for that. "We keep moving," he repeated, jerking his head toward the hospital building.

"Militia houses, I get, but we should skip this place."

"Driscoll said this is where they keep that 'Rooster' guy."

"A guy you've never seen. A guy you heard about—"

"Who was in the same damn situation I was in."

"Elliot, I get how he'd feel like a kindred spirit—"

"Never said that."

"—but just coz he survived several Night Courts the way you did, doesn't mean he's a good guy. Might be the opposite. Might be a psychopath as bad as Da Silva and Kyle."

"He's a survivor. He was just like me and Jimmy, forced to do something..." Elliot's mind stuttered, couldn't find a word to complete the sentence. A word other than *evil*. Because it was an evil act that *he* had been forced into doing out there on that killing floor behind the hospital building, cutting down innocent people so he could survive.

Shut the hell up, he ordered himself.

"Pankhurst is deserted," Angie was saying.

"There was a guy up on that roof."

"The Facility is the priority now."

"Not for Rooster, it isn't. If Spider frees workers and they come this way, they won't take kindly to Rooster after the things he was forced to do. Also, it won't hurt us to have an extra ally."

"This is all conjecture. Let's just—"

"Could we have this discussion maybe somewhere not in the open with our asses exposed?"

She sighed. "He's in the hospital basement?"

"So Driscoll said."

"Hospital basement, then. But let's make it quick."

"Definitely quick," he said as he headed for the cover of the next car. Because after they checked on Rooster, he needed closure on Jimmy.

8

09:55

THEY TRIED A SIDE DOOR, the same one Elliot had been led through in the aftermath of the Night Court. It wasn't locked. Elliot led the way into a hallway cool and dusky. Weak morning light reached them only grudgingly from east-facing ward windows. Side rooms contained nothing of interest, and no people. It wasn't until they were a third of the way up the main corridor that Elliot saw the chain.

It hung across the passageway fifteen metres from his position, drooping from inside the ceiling—where someone had removed an overhead panel—and disappearing inside a ward room to their right. He dropped into a crouch, pointed to it and received a trademark *WTF?* look from Angie. Could they be lucky enough that Rooster had been moved up here?

Or was this some new horror?

He crept toward it, light on the balls of his feet, letting Angie check the other rooms in his wake. A wet cough from the room with the chain made his heart rate spike, made him crouch again. The chain shifted, rattling. Another phlegmy cough. A gasp for air.

Goddammit.

Had they moved a deader up here? Maybe to guard stashes of medication.

As he started forward again, the chain rattled, moved, drooping lower as whoever was attached to it moved toward the corridor. Elliot's .40 cal was up and ready.

The woman who emerged from the ward didn't look healthy. But she wasn't dead.

Short and slight—so slight that Elliot briefly flashed back to Birdy dying in the bush as they escaped the Dead Line—this woman wore a nurse's uniform that hadn't seen the inside of a washing machine in weeks and no shoes. She also wore a single handcuff attached to the end of the chain. She was the same shape and size as Birdy, but *this* woman's ancestors hailed from a different part of the world. As she whirled in shock toward Elliot, the name tag on her uniform came into focus: *Indira*.

Her face drooped in resignation. Her expression said, *This is the moment someone finally kills me.*

Elliot put a finger to his lips, tilted the handgun away from her, formed a question with his face, and pointed at the room she'd come from. He raised one finger, then two, then three.

The shock on her face melted—first into confusion and then into comprehension. Without concern for volume, she said, "There's one person in there. And he can't hurt you."

Cringing at the level of her voice, Elliot murmured, "Quietly."

Her head shake was long and slow. "No need. No one here but us. And as you can see——" She gave the handcuff and chain a little jiggle. "——I'm not exactly guarded by anyone. I'm guessing you're the ones who've been causing all the trouble?" she added, her accent softened by a pleasant Indian lilt. "And I'm guessing you're the American who broke out of here a month ago?"

"I——"

A burst of wet, hacking coughs came from the room. Elliot tensed.

Indira made a tired face. "Come see. It's not a biter, if that's what you think. It's a militia bastard who's no danger to anyone."

Elliot looked back to Angie, who murmured, "I'll keep watch" as she approached the nurse's station that Indira had been headed for.

When Elliot drew level with the door, Indira gave him space. He checked inside, registering a bearded man in the bed, hooked up to a drip, with a piss-bag hanging down beside him. No weapons were in sight; his hands were clasped on his chest. He appeared to be asleep, or unconscious.

Elliot gestured with the .40 cal. "You first." Indira shrugged and went in ahead of him. He glanced up into the gap in the ceiling where more cuffs secured the other end of the chain to exposed water pipes. The chain was just long enough to allow her to move between this room and the corridor work station, but not to climb up on it. Nothing else lay within reach to climb on and reach that pipe and the other cuff. Presumably, whoever had stuck the nurse here expected her to sit and sleep on the floor. There were water jugs and a toilet bucket tucked inside the door; Elliot smelled the piss now. No food though, not that he could see.

Indira lifted the man's sheets as Elliot circled the bed. No weapons visible. The man coughed and moaned, but didn't open his eyes. There were bandages around his torso. Indira pointed to them.

"Your handiwork, I'm guessing."

"Was he on sentry duty at the southwest perimeter?" Elliot asked. "Shot?"

She nodded.

"He'll survive?"

"Who knows?"

"Who operated on him?"

She took a long breath and let it out slowly and tiredly. "Doctors out in the bunker. You know about the bunker?"

"Windowless building with one floor above ground? Out that way?" He pointed. She gave another nod. "But you have *doctors*? Surgeons?"

"Two of them. And a dentist. At least, I hope we still do."

"Why *hope*?"

"Things haven't been exactly stable since you people started making trouble."

"You're angry at *us*?" Angie asked from out in the corridor. "You're chained up by SERPs and you're angry at *us*?"

Indira passed a hand across her face. "I'm angry at the

whole bloody world, my dear. The world and God and the universe and anything else responsible for this mess. You think you bunch of vigilantes are making it better? Well, maybe you are. And maybe you aren't."

"How about I get you out of that cuff and let you leave?" said Elliot. "That convince you we've made things better for you?" Stubbornly, she did not reply. But she accepted the offer with a mild tilt of her chin and softening of her expression. He said, "Follow me."

He went around back of the nurse's station and found a dusty old container of plastic ID bracelets, took out his knife and split one lengthways until he could peel off a three-millimeter-wide strip. He held it up for her to see.

"Makeshift slim jim. And not the eatin' kind, either."

When she frowned in confusion at the American junk food reference, he shrugged it off and mimed holding out her wrists. He inserted the plastic strip into the hole between the locking arm's serrated teeth and the cuff's frame. Gently, he tightened the cuff one notch while pushing the shim in with it. With the teeth now disconnected from the locking mechanism, the cuff opened easily.

"Damn," she said. "Wish I'd known about that earlier."

"Oh, yeah," he replied as he worked the other cuff. "People think handcuffs and cable ties are unbeatable. As you can see, they ain't. You are now free to go."

Indira rubbed her wrists. "Thank you. But I can't leave."

"Why not?" Angie asked.

The nurse glanced at the chain where it met the pipe above. "This wasn't the only thing keeping me here."

"They've got your kids?"

"My boyfriend."

"Bastards."

"Are you safe around the 'workers'?" Elliot asked her.

Indira's left eyebrow rose. "I'd call them slaves. But yes, I'll be safe. I've treated many of them. I've delivered three babies. I've—"

Angie raised a hand to quash the storytelling and Elliot returned to the ward room. Behind him, she said, "Head toward the east gate. Cross country. Keep off the roads, and be careful."

"Why?" Indira asked. "Why the east gate?"

"Our people have cleared that area. They're freeing slaves and directing them out and toward Oatlands. Find somewhere safe that way until we tell you the fight is over."

"*Or* I can go wherever I want."

"As long as it's not to warn the SERPs, sure. Wherever."

While they talked, Elliot stood over the injured militia man, watching the rise and fall of his chest, hearing the rattle of his breath. *I should probably end him*, he thought. Cut his throat.

Out in the corridor, the nurse said, "Fat chance I'll warn those bastards. Just promise me you'll *try* to protect my boyfriend."

"He's in the Facility?" he asked her over his shoulder. "The bunker?"

She came in and joined him at the bed, her presence

unwelcome given what Elliot was considering doing. "Yes. As are about twenty others."

"Shit."

"If you're heading there, there'll be casualties and they'll need me. I'll stay here. To treat them when you're done."

"All right," he said. "You stay here. But you find a window where you can watch for who's approaching. And if it's SERPs, you get the hell out, lady. You stay low and you head for the east gate. You hear?"

She folded her arms, face blank. "And him?" She nodded to the man in the bed, but her eyes were on Elliot's knife.

So was Elliot's right hand. He hadn't realized he'd gotten so close to drawing the blade.

He grunted. "Can he fight?"

"Even if he could *walk*, he's got a lot of drugs in him."

Angie had come to the doorway. "Nice of your lords and masters to take such good care of him."

"The two who brought him in were talking about needing as many hands as they could keep. But I think the main reason they brought him here was for morale. They didn't want the others reminded of how shaky things were getting."

Elliot took his hand off his pommel and leaned it on his rifle. "Up to you whether or not he lives through the day. Or has an overdose of pain meds."

Indira looked down at her hands. "I'd been considering that anyway."

"Might be kinder than workers getting their hands on him," Angie added.

"Why are you doing all this?"

"Kyle's mob killed our people is why."

Indira accepted that with a nod. "You're going to the bunker now?"

Angie scowled impatiently at Elliot. "Soon."

"Good luck, then. You know where to find me afterwards."

"Eat." Elliot fished a ziplock bag of trail mix from a pocket and put it in her hand. "One more thing. A month ago, you had a guy in here named Rooster?"

Her face clouded. "Him? He's one of yours?"

"No. Is he still alive?"

"Yes. What do you want with *him*?"

"I feel like I should have found him last time I was here, let him go."

"He's not a nice person."

"Who is, darls?" asked Angie.

"He's been forced to kill other people to survive," Elliot said. "That's all I know about him. He's not alone in that."

Indira wrinkled her brow. "I have a feeling he *murdered* more than a few before he came here. You can make your own mind up. Just keep him away from me. The militia made him a special cell down in the basement."

"Ange, you wanna keep an eye—"

"—on the front doors?" she finished. "Indira can do that for us. I'm sticking with you, so let's go find your little friend."

"He ain't my friend," Elliot said, then thought, *Don't*

really know what he is. But the workers will kill him if I don't let him out.

————

IN ONE CORNER OF THE LOW-CEILINGED BASEMENT STOOD A square chemical storage cage made of steel bars and chain link. The SERPs had turned it into a cell and furnished it with a hospital bed, a flashlight and batteries, a cardboard box with paperbacks and tins of food, a toilet bucket and a folding chair. Two clear water bottles stood empty against the inside of the double-padlocked door. Stretched out on the cot was a short, stocky man with long greasy locks pulled back into a pony tail, and a beard that reached his chest. He was dressed in grimy leather pants, a t-shirt that might once have been white and—eccentrically—a knitted vest. The man was awake and reading a paperback with help of the flashlight. He put both down as he caught sight of Elliot approaching. He sat up.

Elliot recognized him.

The man was missing the tip of his nose. And all of his ears.

Maggot Rider, Elliot thought and allowed himself a grim chuckle. "No way."

With a groan of effort, the former biker leader eased off his cot and came to the wire. He pushed his face against it, the scarred stump of a nose placed center of one of the gaps, and angled his flashlight beam into Elliot's chest. His chuckle was husky as he jiggled the wire. "Well, fuckin', well. If it isn't the American. What is it with you, me, and fences, eh?"

"You ... know each other?" Drawing level with Elliot, Angie wore a look of mild disgust. Perhaps it was caused by the man's deformity, although he couldn't imagine Angie judging anyone that way. More likely, it was his general filthiness—or the stink coming off his toilet bucket. She said, "This day just got a little freakier."

"It's a freaky world, love," the Maggot Rider said. To Elliot, he added, "Good to see ya again, mate." Then his flashlight dipped to Elliot's .40 cal. "I hope."

"Here to release you," Elliot told him. The man let his flashlight drop to his side, the beam bouncing off the concrete floor. Elliot could now see the tattoos reaching up the Maggot Rider's neck toward his missing ears. The injuries had scarred over, but when Elliot had last seen them, they'd been fresh, still bleeding. "*You're* Rooster?"

"Actually, no." The biker backed up a few steps. "They needed a name when they caught me. That's the one I gave 'em."

"You gave them a fake name?" Elliot said. "In the aftermath of the apocalypse?"

The man gave him a long, lazy shrug. "Force o' habit. They're cops."

Elliot shook off his surprise and confusion, pulled out a leatherman and got busy cutting a doorway into the wire. "So, not 'Rooster' then. We call you...?"

The man was bending down, pulling at something under the bed. It turned out to be a leather jacket. He dumped the flashlight and put the jacket on. Tapping one of the patches on it, he said, "Well, I'm the last o' the

Maggot Riders, so people these days *call* me Rider. People I like, that is."

He likes me, Elliot thought wryly. *Nice to know.*

"You were part of another group?" he asked, still cutting. "Before Jericho captured you?"

"I was. But I don't know you well enough yet, American Bloke. Not to tell ya about *them*. Her either. No offence, love."

"None taken," Angie replied quickly. She'd angled herself back toward the stairwell. "Is one of you gonna tell me *how* you know each other?"

"I will," said the man. "American Bloke's busy."

"His name's Elliot," she said.

A pause while Rider looked him up and a down with a skeptical expression. "*Elliot?*"

"Better than Rooster," Elliot answered.

"Not by much. And what's your name, love?"

"Well, it's not *Love*. Angie will be fine."

"So, Angie. Ya mate Elliot here..." He broke off, watching as Elliot pulled back on the panel of wire to create a way through. "Ya know, I had you pegged as a Tom or Ben or Hank."

As the man ducked through the hole, Elliot asked him, "How do you know Elliot's my first name?"

"Hah! Fair point."

"Hey!" Angie clicked her fingers a few times. "Less sidetracks, more answering the damn question."

Outside the cage now, Rider straightened and rolled his shoulders. His haphazard teeth flashed within the tangle of his beard. "Long story short, love, Elliot saved me arse a few years back after some Death Druid pricks done this to me." He indicated his nose and ears.

"Wait," Angie said. To Elliot: "This was when you found Claire and Jimmy."

"Yup."

"You never mentioned this guy."

"This guy," Rider muttered. Evidently, he liked that about as much as Angie liked *Love*.

"Never came up," Elliot said.

"I should be offended. But I'm not." Rider clasped Elliot's right hand, his grip iron-hard. "That's two I owe ya, mate. And I hate owin' anyone anythin'." He released the hand, slapped Elliot's shoulder and stepped back to consider his gear. "Cop stuff. Cop guns. Please tell me you ain't joined 'em."

"Would he be here if he had?" Angie muttered.

"You and I are well and truly on the same side— again," Elliot replied. He could not believe who he was looking at. A man he'd known for less than fifteen minutes three years back, who'd helped him clear that Druid compound. "And the SERPs and I are not exactly friends."

"I'm jokin', brother. These last couple o' weeks, the nurse kept tellin' me there's someone makin' an arse-load o' trouble for Jericho. Never thought it'd be you." He scratched at his beard which was gritty with the remains of past meals. "You realize you're in the middle o' their territory here."

"If all goes to plan it won't be their territory by midday. You're free now. Guess you have the choice of running or staying to help."

"You fuckin' jokin'?" He winked at Angie. "If you're killin' these pricks, I'm stayin'. Need a gun, but."

Elliot raised a hand. "If you help, this time you do it my way. *Completely* my way." Now he'd said it, he thought he shouldn't have given that option: this guy's "help" last time had been erratic and reckless, despite the fact it had worked. "Maybe you should stay and keep the nurse safe."

"She's upstairs?"

"Yup."

"Who's she lookin' after? Militia?"

"Yup. Unconscious and halfway to death."

"Good fer him. I'm not stayin' with her. If you're slaughterin' the pigs, mate, then I'm helpin' ya. But sure I'll do it your way. I do owe ya. So, no worries."

"One hundred percent what I say?"

The Rider saluted. "Aye aye, Cap'n. Least I can do. I'd still like a gun, but."

Elliot chewed it over a moment before realizing he shouldn't waste any more moments on chewing things over. "All right. We have someone on a roof outside who needs to know we're still alive." He caught Angie's eye. "We'll let him know we are, then we've got one last thing to do before we break into the Facility."

Rider's laugh was more like a cough. "The bunker? Hooley-fuckin'-dooley. This'll be good. What's the other thing ya gotta do?"

"You've been a guest at the Night Court?"

Rider's swagger vanished into a scowl, as scowl so fierce that Elliot actually took a wary step back. "Too many times."

"Well, I'm gonna put the jurors out of their misery."

THE DEADERS USED IN JERICHO'S TRIAL-BY-COMBAT WERE held in an underground pump room, just as Sturgis had reported a few days earlier after scouting this area. Access was via a couple of steel cover plates set in a concrete framework out in the grounds behind the hospital. When Elliot reached them, he glared toward the makeshift arena the SERPs had called the "killing floor". The wooden walls around it hid the grid he'd fought on top of. That grid faced the set of bleachers the assholes had set up for their gladiatorial bullshit. With ice in his gut, he forced himself to look away. Sturgis and Elliot had taken positions on his flanks, keeping look out. Before he realized it, Rider had lifted one of the cover plates to reveal a narrow steel staircase—and had both feet inside.

"Wait," Elliot told him. "Stay here and stay low."

"I wouldn't mind endin' a few of those things down there."

"One of those things was my friend. This is for me to do."

Rider sniffed and looked away, then moved off.

Elliot descended with a balance of speed and caution, finding himself at a solid wire gate across the bottom of the staircase. It had been bolted but not locked. He slid back the bolt and stepped into a cold, concrete chamber, wedge-shaped with the stairs at the narrower end. Pipes ran along the wall to his left. The air pulsed with the noise of a pump motor and the pipes gurgled every few seconds, creating a thick cloud of sound around Elliot that had him glancing reflexively over his shoulder to ensure no one was creeping up on him. The ceiling had been set low, mere inches above his scalp; a large part of it was grated, open to the air above. Morning light streamed through to form a bright chessboard on the dirty floor, a floor cambered toward gutters that were obviously intended to drain off rainwater.

And blood, he thought, *from the Night Court.*

At the far end of the chamber: another barrier, a set of double-gates formed from galvanized steel wire that opened both ways once someone raised the lock bar securing them. Anything past those gates was rendered invisible by shadow, any noise it made hidden beneath the hum and churn of the working pump—a pump whose purpose Elliot didn't even know. Stormwater? Clear water? Sewage?

Who cares? He shook himself.

He tugged his bandana up from his throat and over his mouth and nose, focus on that double gate. What the hell had the SERPs done each time they had a Night Court? How'd they get the "jury" out? How'd they get them back inside? No doubt, both jobs had been given to militiamen.

Something brushed against the inside of the gates as he approached. No mewling, but they were in there. He could smell them. Their leaking pus. The pseudo-shit soiling their pants. He squinted to see inside, but couldn't. He tried to remember how many hands had been reaching through the grate above him while he'd tried to keep Jimmy safe above it—tried to remember this without getting sucked down into another flashback.

There were ten of them, he thought. *Twelve, maybe.*

The magazine in his pistol was fresh. Fifteen rounds. Enough for twelve headshots and then some. He used his left hand to switch on the rifle's flashlight and angle the beam into the room beyond the gates—and although he knew what he'd see, he couldn't help scooting back a little. Those faces. Those goddamn, pus-leaking, black-toothed, should-be-dead-and-buried faces. He'd hoped never *ever* to see one again. And there were ten of them. Right there at the wire, pressing into it now and making the lock bar clink, drawn like demonic moths to his light.

He growled at himself and stepped closer, lining up his .40 cal's suppressor with gaps in the wire, putting two rounds through two heads. The female zombies collapsed where they stood. The remaining pressed toward him, jaws snapping. He dropped five more.

And then saw Jimmy. Down in the back by the pump housing.

The kid had his back to Elliot and the remaining pusbags, his head against a pipe rising from the pump. Maybe he was warming himself. Or cooling himself. Who the hell knew what the undead felt or thought? It was definitely the kid, though, his posture as slouched in death as it had been in life. He wore the same shitty long-sleeve tee as the night he'd died, one of those sleeves torn by deaders clutching at it through the grating, the shoulder ripped by SERP rough-handling before that. Bare scalp and bone showed through patches where his long hair had fallen out—or been chewed out by rats maybe. And just as he'd been in life, Jimmy stood separate from the rest of his group, withdrawn, alone.

Another deader fell over the bodies of its fallen compatriots, recapturing Elliot's attention. Filthy, peeling fingers hooked the hard metal wire and shook it as well, testing it, wanting passage through it, wanting *him*.

He shot them all. One by one. Center-forehead. Until only Jimmy remained. Still slouched against the pipe.

The circle of flashlight bobbed about; the .40 cal shook in his hand, and Elliot stepped right in and steadied it through the gate. A glance over one shoulder, making sure Rider hadn't come down the stairs, then Elliot let the words come out, said what he had to say—

"I'm sorry, kid. Sorry this world fucked you up. Sorry I let you go on that mission. Sorry I let these bastards catch you. Make sure you find some kinda happy afterlife, okay?"

—and squeezed the trigger.

Jimmy fell. Left side down. Landed first on the wrist and knee that had dipped below the Night Court's grated floor and gotten him bit. Crumpled. Settled.

At peace. Finally, at peace.

"I hope," Elliot whispered. And turned back to the stairs.

———

THE TWO CARS IN THE HOSPITAL LOT WERE UNLOCKED AND their keys lay on their dashboards. Angie kept watch while Elliot and Rider checked the vehicles thoroughly for IEDs.

A gunshot from close by made them all press flat on the earth. Moments later, Sturgis came running out of the school grounds, long gun held in front of him. "All good," he told them when he reached the cars. "I just got down the ladder when this militia guy comes around the corner of the building. Wearing a ballistic vest." He indicated the rifle. "From ten metres away, he may as well have been wearing a t-shirt."

"Nice," Rider said with a low cackle.

"This is Rooster?" Sturgis asked Elliot.

"This is Rider. We just thought his name was Rooster."

"Fun fact," Sturgis replied, and got the rifle braced on a car boot to cover the street.

"What's the point of wearing vests?" Angie asked. "You said that leaf spring trap would cut right through one. It made no difference against his gun."

"Told you before," Elliot said and put his head back under the car to check it. "Tactical vests are bullet *resistant*, not bullet *proof*. They're designed primarily for handgun rounds or rounds with far less velocity. His 7.62 bullet would penetrate a quarter inch of steel with relative ease at a hundred yards."

"Mansplaining again?"

"You asked. I answered."

He and Rider found nothing of concern and the vehicles started without issue. Elliot made Angie and Sturgis take one of them while he and Rider piled into the other.

They took the same road out of town that Elliot had taken when he'd escaped Jericho the first time. Back then, it had been night: with his head full of horror, he hadn't noticed the unsurfaced side road with the chain across it. With Driscoll's map in mind, he sure noticed it this time.

"Pull up here," he told Rider and pointed to a cutaway on the verge. Rider braked harder than necessary as he swung into it.

Angie stopped their car on the road. On foot, they entered the bushland. While the other three took up secure positions, Elliot spent twenty minutes scouting to ensure there had been no sentries posted near that gate and there were none ahead of them. From there, his team spread into a diamond formation and started their five-kilometre hike toward the Facility.

9

11:33

THE LAST TIME Elliot approached the Facility, he and Woodsy and Jimmy had cut a hole in the back fence before entering the big windowless box via the underground garage. The garage had been wide open, a trap, and there was no way Elliot was putting all his eggs in one basket this time. Not when *eggs* meant *people.*

While he and Angie waited out front of the property —sheltering on the far side of the track from the small parking lot—Sturgis and Rider circled around back. Their orders were to take a position overlooking the down-ramp into the garage.

Angie slapped a bush fly from her arm, cursing softly. All the bugs seemed to be going for her today. The single most maddening thing about Australia was its propensity for bugs, many of them bigger than they had a right to be. Like the fly currently attempting to land on Angie's neck again. Elliot lashed out, grabbed the sucker from the air, crushed and dropped it.

"Thank you, Mr. Miyagi," she murmured.

"Welcome."

He refocused on Sturgis's shirt as it wove in and out of trees along the Facility's left-side perimeter. Rider had gone around to the right, armed with Angie's Glock with its double-drum magazine. Turning it over in his hands before he'd left, the former Maggot Rider had said, "Pretty sure this was one of ours." Angie had replied, "Pretty sure it was a Death Druid's." Which she wasn't. But the biker had accepted this with a shrug anyway.

Elliot began emptying the three packs with Angie's help. Carefully, they placed the contents on a patch of bare, dry earth. Because of Driscoll, he now knew what he couldn't have known that first time: there were no cameras or other sensors out here in the woods. It had been the ones on the building corners that had picked up his original team's approach. He also knew the reach and scope of each of those cameras. Sturgis and Rider would remain unseen as they covered the rear exfil route for any remaining SERPs.

In terms of getting explosives to that front door—a single-paneled steel personnel door with a keypad beside it—Elliot couldn't avoid the front cameras. But that didn't mean he had to put himself at risk of hostiles bursting through the door while he carried the charge over there. As Angie carefully mixed the ingredients for the small fertilizer bomb, Elliot blew dirt from the propellers of the small drone that would ferry the IED to the building. Next, he took out two parts from a garage door opener:

the handheld remote activator and the receiver normally fitted onto the door motor. The receiver would be used as the detonator, the remote to send the activation signal to that.

The walkie in his thigh pocket suddenly crackled, scaring the shit out of him since he was readying to make an explosion—

Almost had an explosion in my shorts.

After a couple of calming breaths, he got the radio out and thumbed the transmit. Softly he said, "Talk to me."

A moment, then Sturgis replied in equally quiet tones, "Movement back here. Someone's loading up a Land Rover."

Angie lay down the containers she'd been holding and flashed Elliot a hopeful look. Like maybe they wouldn't have to finish assembling the IED.

"Militia?" Elliot asked Sturgis.

"Hold." A few moments pause, long enough for Elliot to wonder if the guy had been discovered. Then he was back. "Yeah, looks like one militia, one civ, maybe someone from inside the Facility. Can't see them properly."

"Garage door up?"

"Up all the way, yes. Completely open."

Elliot lay the drone alongside Angie's materials with a grim half-smile. Thumbing the button, he asked, "You in position?"

Meaning was Sturgis in cover outside the fence corner closest to the garage door.

"Yes."

"We'll see you in three. Out."

"No boom-boom?" Angie asked.

"*Maybe* no boom-boom." He brushed off his knees as he rose, swinging the rifle off his back. And led the way, following Sturgis's footsteps—sometimes literally where the navy man had been none too careful breaking foliage or stepping in soft earth. He saw Sturgis before Sturgis saw him—the man was down on his belly at the fence and using a patch of dry grass as a screen, rifle beside him and handgun ready. Elliot gestured for Angie to loop around and retrieve Rider, then he crawled the last few metres to Sturgis's position.

The Facility's rear grounds were as he remembered them, thick with overgrown lawn, the derelict white van unmoved and rusting where he'd last seen it. But a mid-2000s Land Rover stood at the top of the ramp outside the roller door, its tailgate and four doors open. Elliot could see cardboard cartons stacked inside, along with a couple of big-ass water cooler bottles, both full. Someone moved on the far side: Elliot caught the flash of clothing then a carton shifting within the car.

"Militiaman," Sturgis murmured. "The civ went down the ramp just after I called you. Hasn't been back."

"Slave-worker, you think? Or collaborator?"

"Hard to say. Didn't have a weapon that I could see. Mind you, I couldn't see much." Sturgis tensed, gesturing with his chin. Elliot had seen it too: the militiaman making a brief appearance around the back of the vehicle before dropping out of sight down the ramp.

"Has to be another vehicle or two down there," Elliot said.

Sturgis grunted.

A stick cracked off to their left. Elliot rolled onto one hip and signaled Angie and Rider closer. Angie's belly-crawl was so controlled he couldn't hear her above the forest's ambient bird and insect noise until she was right on his boots. Rider wasn't as good—and he was red-faced and sweating when he joined her.

Elliot said, "Sturgis, I want you out front covering that front door." Sturgis made no comment, simply rose into a crouch, gathered his weapons and duck-walked back into the scrub. To Angie, Elliot added, "You're providing cover now. Can you move a little further that way—" He pointed toward the road "—to see the garage entry better?"

"You and him are going in?" Her eyes flicked to Rider and back. Elliot nodded. A brief scowl was the only sign that she'd prefer to be the one going inside with him. But she moved off without comment, maintaining that careful crawl with her rifle carried across the crooks of her elbows.

Rider's eyes dipped toward Elliot's pockets. "Got them wire cutters?"

"There's a hole in the fence over there." He jerked his head at a position halfway down the long boundary. *At least, I hope there is.* He'd cut it a month ago; maybe the SERPs had patched it. "It'll make less noise and shake the fence less than cutting a new one."

Rider accepted this with a grimace, perhaps not looking forward to a long crawl. Elliot let him off the hook by rising into a crouch and leading the way in fast darts from tree to tree, checking the Facility yard between each change in position. He was relieved to find the hole remained; perhaps the SERPs had thought it the least of their concerns, and with camera coverage on the corners, it probably had been. He had to hope Da Silva was too short-staffed to have anyone watching those feeds.

It was a gamble—but he might secure the underground entrance if he made it to the Land Rover, then rolled it back and under the door to prevent the roller from closing. With the garage entry/exit covered, and Sturgis covering the front, they'd have themselves a siege at the very least.

And likely get a bunch of civilian hostages killed while Da Silva and I trade ultimatums. He pushed through the gap in the fence and shoved aside that concern. *As if we won't get collaterals anyway if we storm the place.* Wasn't much choice except be as fast and professional as possible.

Waiting for Rider to make it through, he let the rifle hang from its sling and pulled the .40 cal. He was still running the suppressor on it and he'd replaced the magazine since popping the Night Court deaders.

There was no sign of movement at the roller door. Elliot used hand signals, telling Rider to head for the decaying white van and then around it for the far side of the Land Rover. As Rider lumbered away—doing what he was told, thank God—Elliot sprinted directly across the open ground, flattening against the wall at the middle of the building the same time the biker reached the van.

A scuff of soles on cement announced the militia-man's return. A moment later, he reappeared from the garage, muttering beneath his breath and lugging a water cooler bottle in each hand. Elliot raised his pistol, tracking the oblivious hostile as he swung a bottle up and into the Rover's cargo space. He repeated the maneuver with the other bottle while Elliot ventured closer, making his shot easier with each step. The guy straightened and threw an arm across his face to mop the sweat from it. Elliot was maybe twelve or thirteen metres away now, still unnoticed. But when the man lowered the arm, he did see Rider clomping out from behind the van. The militia-man's jaw dropped—then *he* dropped as Elliot put two rounds into his side. He came closer and added another in the man's head, completing the old Mozambique Drill he'd been taught two decades before.

When Rider arrived at the hood of the Rover, he leaned there a moment to flash Elliot an *all's-well-that-ends-well* thumbs up and grin. Elliot replied with an impatient hand signal: *stay there and stay down*. Elliot moved along the wall until he could peek into the bay— and looked straight into the eyes of the female SERP named Erikson down near the base of the ramp—and then into the eyes of the man walking beside her with a sealed carton in his arms, the man Elliot knew as Woodsy!

Time slowed for a moment as Elliot took in several details at once. Woodsy's unkempt hair and beard, the shock in his eyes and in Erikson's, the woman's fully stocked ballistic vest bristling with flashbangs and spare magazines.

Erikson moved fast, yanking Woodsy awkwardly in front of her before Elliot could sight on her. Unbalanced, she stumbled back, lost her footing on the ramp's incline, dumped her ass on the flat expanse of concrete at the bottom and pulled Woodsy down and across her body.

Elliot could see her peeping around the older man's shoulder while her hand fumbled with her .40 cal holster.

"Easy!" Elliot called, keeping most of himself sheltered behind the wall, his own .40 cal ready, a clear shot not there to take. She'd start shooting at *him* soon if he couldn't talk her round. "Easy! Doesn't have to end in more bloodshed!"

"Bull*shit!*" she threw back at him, wriggling to find a less awkward position and failing. Though Woodsy's expression was stiff, he flailed like an oversized child, moving as she moved, with both arms trying to reach around to the left and behind him, presumably for balance.

"I know that guy from somewhere," Rider said from the far side of the entryway. The Glock hung by his side, resting against his thigh.

Locking eyes with Erikson again, Elliot told Rider, "No, you don't." As a former criminal, Rider probably *did* know Tasmania's one-time Assistant Police Commissioner. If he remembered this, he might even kill Woodsy for old time's sake.

Erikson fired and Elliot forgot about Rider, flinching as the bullet chipped the concrete above him. He withdrew into cover, his left cheek pressed against the wall.

What now, smart guy?

Rider was also forced to withdraw as the next shot came within inches of punching his clock. From across the wide entry, he waggled his eyebrows at Elliot and grinned his gap-toothed grin.

If Elliot didn't act fast, Erikson might scoot further

back into the garage and out of sight. Given her current position on the floor, it was ridiculous she had the upper hand, but she sure did. Neither he nor Rider could sight on her without risking a bullet to the brain. And they couldn't fire around the corner indiscriminately because of Woodsy.

Goddamn you, Woodsy. Always—

A double-flash, a tight stutter of super-bright light. A god almighty *crack!* that Elliot felt as much as heard.

He backpedaled reflexively, reeling.

What in—?

Rider recovered before Elliot did, already at the doorway squeezing off shots. Elliot yelled "Stop!"— surprised he could hear himself since he was sure that had been a flashbang going off down there. Or maybe even two...

He peered down the ramp to find Erikson curled up on the floor beneath a fast-dissipating smoke cloud, her weapon discarded and blood pooling beneath her. Woodsy was sprawled forwards and near her. Neither one of them was moving.

"Holy shit!" Rider whooped—actually whooped. "Holy *shit!*"

"Help me!" Elliot barked as he bolted down the ramp. There were no other vehicles in the garage, nowhere for hostiles to hide. He took a knee beside Woodsy, breathing in flashbang smoke and coughing. Before he could put a round through Erikson's head, he saw that Rider's wild firing had already done that. He kept his weapon trained on the door into this level's main access corridor until the biker came up beside him. The door was wide open. "Go there, make sure no one comes through."

When Rider was in position, Elliot felt for Woodsy's pulse. There wasn't one. A grenade pin was looped around the dead man's right index finger, an identical pin around the other index finger.

"You crazy sonofabitch." Elliot stood and used a boot to half turn Woodsy over, saw the mess the stun grenades had made of his insides and lowered him again. "You crazy, heroic sonofabitch."

The SERPs used M84 stun grenades, classified as "less" lethal rather than non-lethal. By activating two of Erikson's at that range, Woodsy had effectively detonated a small suicide vest. And he must have know it, *must* have. Erikson had stood as little chance as he had, vest or no vest. Her clothing smoked a little from flash burns; there was blast and shrapnel damage to her forearms and throat. She'd been dying before Rider finished her.

Elliot got out his walkie, thumbed the transmit. "Angie. Need you down here now!"

"What was—?"

"Now," he said and put the device away. "Anything?" he asked Rider.

The biker shook his head.

When Angie started down the entry ramp, he stopped her with a raised hand. "Stay outside the door. Cover our six from the Land Rover."

"Who's down?" she asked.

"Erikson." He swallowed. "And Woodsy."

"Ah, fuck."

"Watch our six. We're going inside."

"Head on a swivel," she told him.

"You, too, please."

Over on one side of the garage bay, the goods lift stood open. Elliot shoved a heavy box into the doorway to ensure no one could call it down to a lower level and get behind him. He entered the access corridor hugging the left wall while Rider hugged the right. While Rider stayed by the stairwell and interior passenger elevator, Elliot stalked the upper level which proved to be an unimaginative grid of short corridors and large rooms, mainly offices. Three had been converted into billets. All rooms were empty, though there were signs of recent use. A store room held nothing but a spilled box of AAA batteries and some candy wrappers. A security room had its camera screens powered on; one showed Angie keeping an eye on her surrounds from the shelter of the all-wheel-drive. Finding two swipe cards, Elliot tried one at the front door, relieved when it popped open and outwards.

He pulled out the walkie. "Sturgis."

"What the hell's happening?"

"Front door's open. Come on over." He waited there until Sturgis came running across the front lot, the SR98 in one hand, the .40 cal in the other. As Sturgis came inside, Elliot let the door swing closed and lock automatically. "Follow me." He led the way deeper inside, saying, "Angie's outside the garage. One SERP down, one militia. Also ... Woodsy."

"What!"

"Pressed up against Erikson and pulled the pins on two of her flashbangs."

"Holy..."

Rider nodded a greeting when they came around the corner.

"Stay here," Elliot told Sturgis. "Rider and I'll take the stairs. Anyone uses the elevator without us notifying you, kill 'em."

"Of course." Rider had opened the stairwell door and had his back turned as he peered inside, so Sturgis jerked his chin at him with a question in his eyes.

Elliot put his mouth close to Sturgis's ear. "Keep your weird-ass maybe-allies closer."

Sturgis nodded unhappily.

The real reason for taking the biker with him, Elliot had to admit, was the possibility of further firefights. He would much rather lose Rider than Sturgis if it came to it. As he approached the biker, he heard a muffled shout from within the stairwell. Rider stiffened, then made room for him.

"Woman down there. Askin' for you."

Elliot frowned. "Woman?"

"What I said."

Rider retreated as Elliot braced the door open with one elbow.

"Identify yourself," he called.

A moment later, a tremulous voice from below replied, "My name's Glenda Lavery."

Who?

"Is that Elliot?"

"How do you know me?"

"You met me the last time you were here. Sort of. Remember? In the lunchroom. While ... While Kyle..."

There came a pause. Perhaps she was picking her words carefully, or fighting the rising emotion that had laced her voice.

Elliot completed her sentence. "While Kyle interrogated and tortured us."

"For real?" Rider muttered. "Thought that shit only happened to me."

Another pause, then: "Yes."

A memory surfaced of a slender, pockmarked woman taking notes for Kyle until he sent her fleeing the room. Elliot had a vague idea that Kyle had said Glenda was a member of the Tasmanian government. The reminiscence was disturbed by Sturgis tapping his shoulder and asking quietly, "Friend or foe?"

"She's not a foe. Unless Da Silva's wired her with explosives."

"Happy days," muttered Rider.

"Or another SERP is holding her as a meat shield," Sturgis added, then withdrew a metre, grumbling. "I really wish you hadn't said *explosives*."

Elliot raised his voice again. "Glenda. We'd like to come down there. Before we do, do you or anyone else have any surprises for us?"

"No! No surprises here. But be careful. Erikson is up top somewhere."

"You hear a big commotion a few minutes back, Glenda?"

"No."

Sealed that deep within a concrete bunker, it was probably true.

He told her, "No more Erikson."

"Oh. Okay."

"But we appreciate the heads up. The two we're concerned about are Da Silva and whoever's left."

"Miller," she filled in. Elliot couldn't have chosen a more deserving asshole to visit some final vengeance on: Miller was a thug with a personality as flat as his nose. She said, "Gone. They're both gone. An hour ago, a bit more."

"Gone? Gone where?"

"Didn't say. Erikson was meant to meet them somewhere."

That certainly gelled with what he'd seen outside.

And Erikson's dead so we can't ask her where they were meeting, dammit.

He asked, "You absolutely sure there's no SERPs or beard-boys down there with you? I really do hate surprises. And if they're down there, they're gonna get found out anyways. May as well get the negotiations started now before more people get hurt."

"There's no one here 'cept us," came a younger voice, a girl's voice.

Glenda shooshed, then called, "Sorry about that. That's my daughter. I assure you, sir, there's no one here but a bunch of scared and tired and *unarmed* non-combatants. Men, women, children, teenagers. Some of us are medical and engineering subject matter experts. We can help you. We only ask for a chance to ... to live free."

Before Elliot could form a response to that, Rider leaned past him. "Lady, you don't hurt us, we don't hurt you. That's a fuckin' promise, love."

"Oh," said Glenda, sounding uncertain. "Good. Okay."

Elliot made a slashing gesture to shut Rider up. He waved the man back from the door; he stank like a deader. One last time, he asked Glenda, "Definitely no SERPs with guns to your head? No booby traps on the stairwell?" and listened for tell-tales in the woman's response: extra nervousness, trying too hard to sound calm...

None of that entered Glenda's tone as she patiently replied, "All safe, Elliot. I assure you there's no traps. They left us alive in case they could come back and get us again. But they were more intent on getting out quickly than worrying about you coming in after them."

Quickly? Elliot thought. Had Erikson and her militia sidekick drawn the short straws to stay back and load up two more cars? Or had that been her decision, her greed?

"Um, Elliot?" Glenda called up into the silence.

"Yeah?"

"Terry was up there too. Is he... Is he...?"

Terry? Oh, Woodsy. The former cop's real name was Terence Woods. "He's... He's dead, Glenda. He intervened with Erikson and stopped her hurting anyone else."

There was no reply to this news, but Elliot was sure he caught a muffled sob from below him. He glanced at Rider, an idea forming. "I have a man up here who's enjoyed custody at the hands of your former dictators. He could use a checkup."

"Uh?" said Rider.

Elliot made the slashing motion again, then continued, "You said you had medicos?"

"Doctors, yes," said Glenda.

"More than one?"

"Two."

"Send them up the stairs. Just them for now. The rest of you we'll leave in place for the moment until we know things are safe."

There was a commotion at the bottom of the stairwell, voices, movement. Glenda called up, "Two coming up the stairs. With medical kits."

Elliot motioned to his men, but both had already dropped into crouches. Elliot pushed the door all the way open and trained his .40 cal on the furthest riser he could see below him.

Listening to the heavy tread of people climbing, he felt disappointment where he should have felt relief. Sensing the turning of the tide, Da Silva and Miller had fled and this had prevented a final shootout with its accompanying collateral damage—maybe even prevented casualties among Elliot's team. But, damn, he'd really wanted to end those bastards.

He thought of Jimmy being dragged away from the Night Court with the zombie virus surging through his bloodstream. He thought of the half-starved slaves forced to battle to the death on a grid above hungry deaders. Of dead Jericho workers hanged at the gates as a warning. Of sick people slaughtered in The Downs's Infirmary.

The stairwell began to spin and he had to shut that shit down fast.

Breathe, dumbass. Breathe.

His first sight of the people on the stairs was a pair of

red-and-black medical bags held with two hands above the people's heads.

"Don't shoot," a woman said.

The bags lowered to chest level as the carriers' heads and bodies came up into view. Two shocks of greying brown hair. Glasses. Pale faces flushed with the exertion of climbing. Narrow shoulders under thin long-sleeve shirts, skinny arms struggling with the weight of their bags.

The two women stopped on the landing, gazes swinging between the two guns pointed their way from the corridor. The woman who'd spoken first raised her chin as bravely as she could and said, "You're Elliot?"

"Fall back," Elliot told his men.

Rider blinked at him, but complied, moving to join Sturgis along the corridor. Elliot stepped closer to the women, letting the door close behind him. Neither appeared nervous about the contents of their bags, but he wasn't taking chances. Just like he wasn't taking chances that any explosion would reach Sturgis and Rooster.

He gestured with his weapon. "Bags on the floor, open all the compartments."

The pair exchanged a look, but followed the instruction. Elliot tensed as each zip was pulled, relaxing only when it was plain the bags contained nothing nefarious. He gestured for them to zip them as much as they needed to, then called to Rider. When the burly man poked his head in the door, Elliot told him to accompany the doctors out to the garage where they could look him over. He scowled but complied.

"And send Angie *inside*," Elliot added.

The doctors seemed glad to move on as they hurried into the corridor.

"*Woodsy*," Elliot heard Rider say from around the first corner. "Now I know who he was. Christ, this day gets weirder and weirder."

When Sturgis joined him on the landing, Elliot risked a glance down the middle gap in the stairwell between flights and railings. Two levels down, an oval face was raised toward him framed by more greying brown hair.

"Hey there, Glenda."

"Good morning, Elliot. I ... I'm pleased to see you survived your encounter with our former ... dictators."

"And I'm pleased our incursion didn't cost you and yours your lives."

Glenda accepted that with a grim nod. "Are you coming down to us?"

Elliot pulled back and turned to Sturgis. "Thoughts?"

"I'll go first," Sturgis said. "Someone has to if we want to check for antivirals *et cetera*."

Elliot chewed the inside of his cheek a moment. "I think we wait a little longer. No hurry if Da Silva's really gone."

"You think he is? They are? There's two of them, right?"

"Two of them, check. Really gone? Yeah, I think they are. Cowards."

"Smart cowards. They couldn't know how many of us there are. And they lost most of their main force this morning, in one hit."

"Smart or dumb, they're still cowards. And they're a goddamned loose end. Loose ends can kill you."

So can distractions, said Radler's ghost in his ear. *The here-and-now, Sparkles: be in it. Be circumspect.*

He called over the edge, "Glenda, you feel like a walk up the stairs?"

"Sure. Did you say ... Woodsy ...?"

"Come on up. If you're up to it, you can see for yourself. Just you, though. Not so safe for your daughter or anyone else yet."

"Okay." Her face vanished as she moved to the nearest riser.

Angie appeared while Glenda was still a flight away.

"They're really gone?" she asked.

"Seems so."

"Well, that's an anticlimax."

"Rider playing nice with those doctors?"

"Seems to be. They seem nice too. God, I wonder what they've been through."

GLENDA CAME UP ONTO THE LANDING AND LEANED A HAND on the rail, short of breath. She nodded a hello to the three Downsers standing there. "Thank you. Thank you so much. Not sure exactly what you've been doing. But it's been enough. We ... We've already been discussing this, us survivors. We'd like to negotiate the next steps forward. Maybe some kind of treaty with your group. You have a group? A settlement?"

Elliot said, "Yeah, but, we might hold off on treaties and such right away. Not that we don't trust you, but we don't *know* you. You might be okay. Until one of the workers we've freed turns out to be a bigger narcissistic psychopath than Kyle was."

"Or Da Silva comes back once we're gone," Sturgis added.

"We'll make sure neither of those events occur," said Glenda. But the promise was knee-jerk. It was the latent politician in her, saying whatever she could to keep the audience onside.

"You can't guarantee that," Angie said, but her tone was gentle, kind.

Elliot continued, "I've seen this in the Middle East. I've seen it in the USA. And now I've seen it here. When there's more to gain from cheating and killing and stealing than there is from treating people right, there'll always be some sonofabitch who goes that way. And no shortage of assholes who'll follow him. Primary reason we're here is to protect *our* group. No offence. We're mopping up, then we're gone."

"Elliot," Angie started before Elliot cut her off.

"We can talk 'treaties' down the track."

Angie bit her lip, clearly irritated, but keeping her thoughts to herself.

Elliot had a job to do—and while he'd never been one for 'victim blaming', Glenda had been a member of a government that kept signing off on the procedures that led Kyle and Da Silva to bring her here and ultimately to take over. He suspected there'd been nothing like Secret Service or even private security protecting government members as a countermeasure against the SERPs' monopoly on brute force.

He went on, "In exchange for what we've done for you

today, we want some of these antivirals you have. That was the original reason Woodsy and Jimmy and I came here in the first place."

Her face flashed anxiety before she covered it with an apologetic expression. "If there's none in Erikson's car, then we're both out of luck. They were the first things Da Silva and Miller carted upstairs."

"Oh, man," Sturgis muttered.

"You might find them in insulated containers if you check her car..."

"You don't mind if we check downstairs too?" Angie asked her, tone remaining gentle. "Like Elliot said, we don't know you."

Tentatively, Glenda reached out and touched Angie's arm. "You've liberated us from a bunch of maniac bullies. Our house is your house."

Angie took Glenda's hand and held it a moment.

Elliot pointed to the notepad poking from one of the woman's cardigan pockets. "Maybe you can start making a list of what you have left for Angie while she and Sturgis hold here."

"Where you going?" Angie and Sturgis asked him together.

"I'll check that Rover outside for 'insulated containers'. And see if Rider's hanging around to help us here." He gave Angie's shoulder a gentle squeeze as he turned away, then slapped Sturgis's arm as he passed him.

"Shout if you need something," Sturgis told him. He sounded hopeful Elliot *would* need him—perhaps he was sick of inactivity. Perhaps he didn't feel he'd executed enough payback today.

Yeah, that's the problem with vengeance, Elliot thought as he turned a corner back toward the garage. *It's never enough.*

Reckoning was not recompense. It could never bring back the people who'd been lost.

Radler. Eames. McGovern.

Birdy.

Jimmy.

Kim and Dylan and Little Abby ...

Goddammit all to hell. Even winning ain't enough.

As he came up from the garage and into the open, Elliot sucked in air like he'd just surfaced from deep water. He removed the suppressor from his .40 cal, then holstered it and leaned on the Land Rover. Rider went back into the Facility to find a body bag. The two doctors had come up the ramp behind him and started pacing the grounds, faces toward the late morning sky, enjoying the first moments of their freedom. In the end, there'd been no collateral damage as he'd thought there might. None except for...

Brave thing to do, Woodsy, he thought.

He couldn't get it out of his mind. He should be thinking about where the final SERPs had gone, should be planning another mission, but his mind kept sliding back to the subject of Woodsy's sacrifice. Had it been sheer selfless heroism? Was it anger at the SERPs, a chance at his own form of vengeance? Elliot would be left wondering about that for the rest of his life.

He shook his head and stretched and breathed the fresh air and watched a parrot spear across the sky above him. Today had been a very long day. And there was more to do yet.

Hearing the crunch of shoes on the concrete driveway, Elliot whirled toward the corner of the building where two men appeared. He whipped out his .40 cal, then relaxed a notch as the men faltered and stumbled to a stop. In response, Elliot angled the weapon aside. The two had to be workers. Had to be. Emaciated, the skin tight over their cheekbones, their pullovers stretched and stained, their denims torn and filthy. They sure weren't militia. Their long hair hadn't seen a shampoo bottle in years. Small-caliber hunting rifles dangled loosely in their right hands, .22s by the look of them. Even these pea-shooters seemed too heavy for the men, their barrels drooping toward the ground.

Where the hell'd they get rifles? He'd given Spider clear orders not to arm anyone. He sighed in frustration. Spider wouldn't have disobeyed the order; but his idiot friends may well have.

Or—to be fair—these two might've found their weapons among gear left behind by fleeing militia.

He lifted his chin in challenge. "What are you doing here?"

"Here to help," one returned. He had a long and wispy beard. One eyelid drooped, appearing to be a permanent disfigurement.

The other man said nothing. Elliot peered hard at him: a younger face beneath the grime, a guy Lewis's age perhaps, all dark eyes beneath a dirty brow.

Wispy Beard added, "The lady with the Viking tatts told us you'd be here somewhere."

I knew it! Goddamn toker morons.

"Did she?" Elliot stepped up beside the Rover and ran his left hand over one of the windows, testing their interest in it, their intentions. They didn't so much as glance at the car or its contents. "Thanks, guys, but we don't need help. Best thing to do is get the rest of your people free of the other billets. You can gather them in—"

"You're American," the dark-eyed teenager interrupted. His voice was stronger than his companion's, stronger and deeper. He flipped the .22 up and across his chest to catch the forestock in his left hand—weirdly, he looked a little like a Buckingham Palace guardsman at parade rest.

Elliot nudged his own weapon's business-end closer to the men again. Pea-shooter or not, .22 rifles had killed people plenty of times. And these ones were less than thirty feet away. "Yeah?"

"You're *the* American," Dark Eyes continued.

"The one and only American in Tasmania, by all accounts."

Abruptly, the teenager's face curled into a sneer. "You remember what you did at the Night Court?"

Elliot tensed. He remembered the Night Court, all right. The flashback hit him hard—*whipping his belt at the guy they'd sent in to fight him, the two female workers losing their footing on the grating and falling, their limbs disappearing through the gaps, their faces contorting with pain and terror, and one of them pulling free from the grasping deaders beneath the floor, her arms running red and the flesh hanging ragged above her wrists like torn sleeves*—so he got a grip on it fast, pushed it away hard.

But not fast enough. The men were already moving.

And Elliot was a second late in reacting ...

Time broke into fragments, into bullet points of action and sensory detail.

The muzzles came around to point at him.

He fired his own weapon.

Wiry Beard took a round in the chest.

The .40 cal swept on toward Dark Eyes.

The .22's muzzle flashed.

Elliot heard a sharp, electric crack.

Felt it too: snapping his head back and right.

And felt the world dissolve into madness.

Gurgling cries.

Shouting.

Whose?

White hot agony. It tore at someone's head, tore their head from their body. Ripped at someone's skull. Someone's jaw.

Mine!

What...?

Choking. Choking.

what what what what what what what: a machine-pistol question, hammering at the world.

His body lay far below him and it arced, lungs straining to draw air through a wet mess that should not be there. Should not. Be there.

The shouting. Panicked. Angry. Angie?

The world was night. The world was a white, searing night. Blaring with words shouted, words screamed.

"On his side! His side!"

"Give him this!"

"Hold him, dammit! *Hold*—!"

A pinprick of sweet bright pain dropped somewhere in the ocean of agony.

Needle?

Seeping warmth. Treacle. A lover's comfort. The torment, the horror, rolling away and out from him. The white collapsing into grey. Dark grey, curdling.

"Get him!"

The darkness clouding.

The darkness everything.

The darkness—

Nothing.

PART TWO

HURTING

I stand a wreck on Error's shore,
A specter not within the door,
A houseless shadow evermore,
An exile lingering here.

Adah Isaacs Menken

10

November 6

HE IS on a street in Hobart and Hobart is gray and noisy and chaotic. He is on the street with a compact handgun welded snugly to each of his palms. The fuselage of a crashed Cessna lies between him and a horde of screaming, snarling dead people. And Hobart is on fire. And the plane is upside down, lying on its roof and wings. And its propeller spins. But how can the propeller do that? Because the plane's lying on its roof on a city street and the propeller is turning *through* the asphalt, but not chopping it up like it should. And the dead people on the other side of the plane, they want him, want to eat him, and there are thousands of them and they *could* come around the sides of the Cessna, except they don't, and that's fine with him, and all these dead people are kind of *not*-dead because some kind of science-fiction microbe is keeping them animated and making them violent and making them attack other people, people like him. And there aren't many people like him left, at least he can't see any. These two stubby handguns in his hands are warm, they feel *great*, and he's able to fire those handguns across the flipped airplane, so he does, he fires them over and over and over and he never needs to reload just like in a movie and it's awesome coz it saves time. But there's a problem: his bullets are hitting the dead people, he shoots hundreds of them, right in the head, right in the middle of their goddamn heads, but the suckers don't go down, they don't fall down, they don't die, they keep snapping and growling and screaming. And then there's one of them on his side of the plane. One of them right here with him, tall as he is, and she has sandy blonde hair. She's a *she* coz she's a woman—or she was once—and she leans in like she'll kiss him but she doesn't kiss him coz she's not looking for romance. She opens her mouth real wide and closes her jaws on *his* jaw right along the jawline, right along the righthand side of his face.

And slow as you like, slow as she can, she sinks those teeth in *deep* and she eases her head back—slow as you like—and his skin comes off in her mouth and his jaw bone comes off his face, just that half of it, just that side of his face, and he can see it clearly half-hanging out of her mouth as she grins around it and his blood drips off her chin. She's torn off his jaw. And he's asking himself, *Is it weird it doesn't hurt?*

And then.

It hurts.

"HOLD HIS ARMS! NO, *HOLD* THEM DOWN!"

"He won't let me."

"Just come round here. *Lean* on him here."

"Christ, Elliot. It's *okay*, babe. Let them get the needle in."

The voices came to him through a sickening, wavering blur of light and movement. He'd been dreaming about Hobart—and he wanted to go back. It was better than this agony, this madness.

The first voice shouting above him was female, old, authoritative, confident. A stranger's voice. An *anybody* voice. The second was male, and the third belonged to another woman—and Elliot knew these two voices, but he also didn't. And his eyes wouldn't focus. And his mind wouldn't focus. And he couldn't feel his body except for the searing pain in his head, in his face like a living thing, crawling, biting, gnawing, freezing...

"Please, Elliot."

"That's it. You've got him. Now. Elliot we're just—"

Something something: the words dissolved into buzzing. The pain dissolved too. Melted away. And the white, blurry world went with it.

11

December 25

CLAIRE'S VOICE was bright as a shell burst.

"Merry Christmas, Elliot!"

The impact of her happy, hurried steps traveled from the Infirmary front door, though the floor and up the frame of Elliot's bed to hammer tiny nails into the base of his skull.

He kept his eyes firmly closed.

Didn't look at her. Didn't want to. Didn't need to. Being summer now in the southern hemisphere, the morning was warm already, so Claire would be wearing a t-shirt, a Christmas t-shirt. He knew this without having to look. She'd have something Christmassy on her head too, an elf hat or Santa hat—some such shit. Yesterday, it'd been a headband with felt reindeer horns on it.

Not horns, he scolded himself. *Not called that.*

What was the word?

Did it start with an *A*?

Fuck it. Who cares?

Claire would not be carrying breakfast, since his morning fruit smoothie was already sitting on the bedside nightstand. He couldn't remember who'd brought that and it didn't matter. The only thing Claire would be carrying was that irritating cheerfulness of hers. She'd be wanting to give that cheerfulness to him. Pass it on to him. Like a virus.

"Big day today, E."

She'd been calling him that for a few weeks, since around the time he'd started getting a grip on what had happened to him. The letter-name felt worse than stupid. It was a mark of her pity for him, a nickname you'd give a sick child.

She was still talking. "I need you to finish your breakfast. Then we can start getting you ready, okay?"

He did open his eyes then, turning them away from her and toward the bed stand, to the glass of mashed-up fruit and cow's milk he didn't want. He wanted what the other Infirmary patient had. Nance was in here after burning her arm fighting a grassfire last ... whenever it was. Nance had a real breakfast. Elliot wanted that: the huge, thick slice of fresh bread cut into a jagged Christmas tree and smeared with butter and jam; the lamb chop and mushrooms.

The damn liquid diet they had him on was insult-to-injury.

Injury, he thought. *That's kinda funny.* But he didn't laugh, couldn't.

Whoever had brought the breakfast had also brought his communication board, leaving it on his lap.

He lifted it for Claire to see, though he still didn't look at her.

"Oh, yay!" she effused. "Talking's good, E! What's up? Wishing me a happy holiday? Want a book to read?"

As she prattled, his trigger finger got busy tapping at letters. He'd been using the thing a lot the last few ... was it weeks? ... and no longer needed to check the positions of the letters and punctuation marks. That freed him to finally give Claire his full focus.

She did indeed have on a green *Seasons Greetings* tee along with those goddamn ... antlers!

As his message became clear, her cheerfulness melted into a scowl. She gave him a good long dose of stink-eye, then said, "No, Elliot. *You* fuck off."

He grunted in satisfaction, dropping the board.

Her brightness flared up again. "You're not spoiling my Christmas, dude. And you're not spoiling a positive day for you."

"Reckon he'll give it a good try," Nance chuckled from the other end of the room. "Merry Christmas, Claire, love."

"Merry Christmas, Nance. How you feeling?"

"If I was any better, I'd be dangerous. And no matter what he says—or writes or whatever—you're doing a bang-up job, dear."

Their conversation came through to him as if from a slightly different direction to where they actually were. There was a dull spot in his hearing on his right side, as if someone had stuck a Tupperware bowl over that ear. The result of the pressure wave from the bullet passing through his cheek and out below his jaw. He'd been lucky his mouth was open at the time. Someone had told him that. Angie, maybe. He'd been lucky the bullet missed main blood vessels. But it had done plenty of damage even without nicking an artery. With his missing teeth, unreliable hearing, the memory issues, the decreased mobility of his right arm and shoulder, Elliot didn't feel lucky. *Broke dick* was the term they'd used in the Army for a guy like he was now, unlikely to ever be one hundred percent again.

His bandages were off at least. And though he'd done it fifty times before, he put a hand to his jaw again, expecting it to meet a cartoon-style swelling from his face. The hand met no swelling. Tenderness certainly. The rough patch where a bullet had pierced his cheek. The same in the soft skin beneath his jaw.

Claire had shaved him yesterday. Like he was a child. If kids needed shaving. She perched now on the far end of the bed, taking care not to jostle him. He dropped the hand in mild embarrassment, but she didn't seem to notice.

"Do you remember what's happening today, E?"

Of course I do, he thought. *I'm not a moron.* But there were gaps in his memory. A lot of them. And he had the distinct feeling people had been telling him things over and over.

Remaining snarky, he spelled out *Xmas pudding?* in reply to her question.

She made a face at that. "Sadly, no, but you got the day right. I seriously want to know if you remember what else is happening today."

Reluctantly he spelled out *Visit from doctors.*

Claire clapped her hands in delight. The sharp sound sent an arrow through his brain pan. "Yay! Awesome. Your memory is so much better the past fortnight." She clasped her hands in her lap. "Jericho radioed us this morning to confirm. Gayle is the surgeon who worked on you." She paused and he gave a cautious nod to show that he remembered that detail. "She's coming. Also Ranesh, the dental specialist. And James the physio."

Why dentist? he spelled, and hoped that wasn't a detail he'd already been told. Claire's unfazed reaction indicated it wasn't.

She said, "Assessing you for dental implants." She pointed to the side of his face he now thought of as disfigured. He thought of it that way because it *was* disfigured. "Month or two, you'll be able to eat toast."

Whoopee goddamn doo, he thought but didn't write it down.

He spelled out, *False teeth. Like an old man.*

She gave him a mock pout. "Never told you, but my upper teeth are a denture. And I'm not an old man."

Shit. Way to go, wise ass, he thought.

She went on, unperturbed. "James will guide you through some more recovery exercises. See if you can get that arm and shoulder working better."

Now that was something he was looking forward to. Along with the face damage, the bullet's passage had messed up the right side of his neck and the shoulder, causing constant hot stabbing sensations, and impeding his ability to raise the arm very high.

"And yes, they'll be staying for Christmas lunch."

He tapped out, *Wasn't asking that.*

"Grumpy pants." She stood and pointed at the smoothie. "Drink. Alyssa is bringing another one in an hour. You need to get your strength up and get some more meat on your bones. Doctors will be here around eleven."

With his left hand, he grabbed the smoothie and took a small sip. Then another. It wasn't that bad, he supposed. And at least he was alive to drink it.

But, he thought with a glance at the lamb chop Nance was currently cutting up, *this shouldn't have happened in the first place*. He didn't remember the shooting, but he'd let his guard down. He was sure of it. To his dismay, he realized that he'd once again forgotten the details that Angie had told him. He grimaced, frustrated at losing so much information, and the tiny muscle movements of the grimace caused fresh pain to flare and flow across his cheek and into the bone of his jaw, down his neck, up into his skull.

Goddamn it. It's gotta get better than this.

———————

AT A LITTLE AFTER TEN, ANGIE ARRIVED.

"Morning, babe," she said, her smile as bright as Claire's had been. Was she genuinely happy to see him? Was she putting it on? He'd taken a good long look at the right side of his face in the mirror while washing up; no way was she in love with that thing.

Sitting now in the armchair beside the bed, he grabbed a pen and pad from the bedside stand. He shielded it from her as he wrote the message. He was about to show it to her when he realized she was still smiling, her eyes liquid. Probably, she expected a warm greeting in return. He scrawled something at the top of the page above the main message, so as not to disappoint her.

She took the pad, sat on the bed with her knees close to his. Unnecessarily, she read the message aloud. "'Morning. Your hair looks nice today'." She paused to give him a little side-eye. "My hair looks like it always does: badly cut and stuck in a ponytail."

He shrugged. It had been worth a try. He leaned forward to tap the pad with his pen.

She read his main question. "'Where is Spider?' Yeah, he hasn't been in to see you because he went back to the Vikes." She dropped the pad onto his lap.

He wrote *When?*

"The same day as this happened to you. He never came back with us. He's been out of contact since and we think he feels responsible for the pricks who shot you finding out where you were. And arming them to 'protect themselves'." She used air quotes around the last two words, then sniffed and studied her fingers as she lowered them.

He did that? Elliot wrote.

"He didn't. His two mates did." Quietly, she added, "Arseholes are lucky I didn't shoot them too."

Too?

"My, we are talkative today. This is a good sign. You asking questions. Communicating." But there was a distinct concern in her eyes which he read as *I already told you this and you don't remember.*

He tapped the spot where he'd written, *Too?*

She glanced at Nance—who was snoring softly in her own armchair—then leaned closer. "*Too* means I got the guy who got you. And Spider's two mates were lucky I had to keep you alive or I'd have been after them too."

Snatches of information about what had happened to him began surfacing in his head. Some of it came to him in Claire's voice, others with Angie's face attached to the memory. Some of it was just impressions. He still didn't remember getting shot. They'd told him he never would. He remembered walking outside the garage and watching a parrot skate across the morning sky. After that, he had a series of fragments, images of recovering here in the Infirmary, or people treating him or talking about him. He did remember Claire explaining his wounds to him. But the *how* of it eluded him.

He wrote, *Tell me again. What happened to me?*

Her left hand reached for his. Although it irritated him, he let her take it.

She said, "I heard shots just as Rider came in to find a body bag. He and I sprinted outside. The two doctors were on the ground, cowering and whimpering. You were on the ground, bleeding." She sucked in a deep breath and there was a slight shudder in it when it came out. She closed her eyes. "There's a Jericho worker down and dying because you shot him, but his buddy is staring at you with his rifle pointed at your chest. He's, like, *glaring* at you. But there's this smugness in his expression." Another deep breath and her eyes opened but they were focused somewhere not-here. "I knew he'd done it to you. I absolutely knew it. He noticed us, but didn't have a chance. He tried, though. He lifted the gun, but I hit him twice. Rider got him a third time. He fell down, still alive. Turned his head at you and said 'That's for Kelly'. Then I shot him again. And I checked on you. The doctors crawled over. And..." She winced, her left hand closing tighter around his. "God, so much blood. I turned you on your side so you didn't choke on it. You were in bad shape. The bunker doctors got you down to an operating theater on one of the underground levels. They worked on you for two hours, and when you were stable enough to move, I forced one of them to come home with us. The same one who's coming today. Lucky, she forgives me; I wasn't exactly nice about it. And she's a good person. Sturgis and Rider grabbed a car each still loaded up with SERP supplies, and we came back here. And I tell ya, when we were leaving, I was ready to kill anyone in Jericho who even looked at us funny. But we didn't see a single one of their ex-slaves. Doctor Gayle stayed here for a week, instructing us in a deep clean after the flu infection we'd had, and she told us we didn't need to threaten her to help us: she was grateful we'd saved her, and she was happy to look after you and the rest of us. But, eventually, she wanted to go back to her husband and kids. Adult kids, it turns out. Her husband is the dental surgeon coming soon. Her son's the physio."

She released his hand; he was glad for it, picking up the pen and scribbling doodles on his pad.

She continued, "Bloody government had their nest feathered in that place, that's for sure. They had some pretty decent specialists in a bunch of fields ready to lock down in there, though the SERPs apparently couldn't evacuate them all out of Hobart when the original zombie shit hit the fan. Gayle's family were chosen because of their specialties. Anyway, a week after she left here, she brought others back to work on you some more, around the same time as all the other Downsers were coming back home and resettling. You remember they'd left here in case the SERPs wanted payback for Kyle? Yeah? That's good. So, Gayle and her crew brought one of the slave-workers, an old bloke who apologized for what his grandson did to you and asked if we could form a pact with them."

He remembered something about that. He wrote, *Claire told me about the pact. Shouldn't have rushed it.*

Angie pursed her lips while she read this. "So far, so good, babe. We're helping them rebuild and they've been helping us here. For example, after Ranesh looks at your teeth, he's staying two days to give everyone else a check-up. Pretty lucky to have dental care in this day and age."

Ranesh? he thought. *Oh. The dentist. Focus, idiot.*

He shrugged.

She scowled at his scowl. "What?"

Don't want it, he wrote.

"You don't want what? Jericho helping us? Or Jericho helping you?"

He scratched at the stubble on the left side of his face and avoided her gaze.

"Elliot, what is it? Are you suspicious of them? Or don't you like people helping you? Things have changed since—" She caught his eye then gestured to his face. "—this."

His gut clenched and his face flushed. He was angry

with her, angry maybe at her use of the word *this*, maybe at the way she wouldn't stop trying to bright-side him. Maybe both. He scribbled the next message, suspecting he was being a dick but unable to stop himself. He held it up for her: *They already put a bullet through my mouth. Don't want their hands in there.*

She read it, face tightening. Forcing tolerance into her tone, she leaned back on the bed. Her knees no longer touched his. "Don't be like that. The doctors didn't shoot you. They've been helping you, and they've done a good job. New teeth is a good thing. The temporary dental plate you'll get first is good. Don't you want to chew a steak again some time?"

He couldn't believe she'd said it, offering false hope like that. It was cruel. The way his jaw was, dentures or no dentures, he couldn't imagine eating anything but breakfast smoothies for the rest of his life. He wrote, *don't want to discuss it!* and tossed the pad to land beside her.

"You don't..." Grip slipping on her patience, she rose to her feet, glowering at him. "You wanna shut us out? That your goal here? Shutting us all out, including me, *especially* me? Because you're doing a bloody good job of it."

He raised both hands, palms up, asking when he'd shut her out. That wasn't his wish at all. He just... He just wanted...

With a glance toward Nance, still snoozing, still snoring, Angie lowered her voice but grit her teeth and backed away from him another step. "Oh, you've been shutting me out, Elliot. Every time I come in here, I'm glad to see you. But you give me nothing back. Nothing but attitude and cold shoulders."

His head pounded. His wounded cheek and neck twitched and stung. He snatched up the pad and wrote some more, then held it up to her. *No idea what I'm going through.*

"I'm trying to understand. I'm trying to be here for you."

She broke off because he was scribbling again, writing in caps now.

YOU'RE NOT THE ONE IN PAIN, he showed her.

"Oh, I'm not? I'm not hurting too? God, Elliot."

Nance had woken, staring at them both in silence now, the goddamn busybody.

Elliot scrawled another response.

Angie's eyes widened as she read it, then shifted to his. They stayed wide, brimming with shock, with disbelief. Her expression brought him a pang of shame. He really was an asshole, he thought, and he wasn't sure he could help it.

She took a step back, hands on hips. "If that's how you feel—how you really feel—then fuck you, Elliot." She moved toward the door on shaky legs. "Fuck you and your pity party and your whole 'I'm a loner' bullshit. I'm done."

A second later, she was gone, the door banging in her wake.

Nance rubbed one eye and mumbled, "Sounds like someone's just made things worse." She snuggled in her chair. Moments later, she was snoring again.

Elliot looked down at the final note he'd written. And wished he hadn't. *What the hell is wrong with me?*

The note read, *I DON'T NEED YOUR HELP. I NEED SOME FUCKING PEACE!*

AN HOUR AND A HALF LATER, TWO SURGEONS AND A physiotherapist looked him over, asking questions and making reassurances about his long-term prognosis. When they lapsed into doctor-speak between themselves, Elliot lapsed into introspection. He was an idiot for two reasons.

First, it had truly been a dickish thing to "say" to Angie, and he didn't know why he'd done it. Angie was the best thing that ever happened to him. Ever. And she was only trying to help.

Second, it felt like he'd been channeling Uncle John. His step-father's number one maxim was playing in his head again: in the end you're all you have.

Still got your hooks in me, you ol' bastard, John, he thought as the dental surgeon began to gently assess him for a denture. *Not even Angie could purge you.*

He wanted to ask these specialists what exactly his positive prognosis was. He had to admit, they didn't seem like enemies, just like Angie had said. Uncle John's shitty proverbs weren't the only thing with their hooks in him: his real enemy was his mental state, his struggles with memory, and the black gloom that had settled over him and which he couldn't find the strength to fight.

The female doctor—Gayle?—was talking to him. He

had to blink his way to focusing on her and ask her to repeat what she'd said.

She smiled patiently. "I said, we have a Christmas present for you."

She placed it in his hands. A small box, a cube, wrapped. He used his thumbs to tear off the tissue paper and opened the hinged box. A wristwatch, its body and band coated in black rubber. Digital.

"A smart watch," she said. "Remember these? It performs a whole bunch of functions, including measuring your heart rate, reading the air temperature around you, counting steps."

He thanked her with a careful nod and a thumbs up, then submitted himself to her husband's ministrations again, turning the watch over and over in his hands. More than four years since the world had broken, but this thing was still ticking. Or whatever digital devices did instead of ticking.

Eventually, Gayle's husband—*Ranesh! Thank Christ, I can remember something!*—said, "I'll have a plate for you in two weeks, Elliot. We'll start the process for implants in a couple of months. Next thing on today's list is your shoulder. James will keep assisting you with that." He patted the young, polo-shirted physiotherapist on the shoulder.

Forcing himself to channel a little Claire and Angie, Elliot wrote on his pad, *Appreciate the help, folks.*

"Least we can do," Gayle told him. "We're eternally grateful for what you and your team did for us."

So you should be, he felt like writing, but didn't. That, too, would be dickish.

As James helped him get off the bed, the young man

was saying, "The bullet damage to your neck muscles has affected the mobility of this shoulder, and there's a lot of inflammation still in there. We'll take it slow today, Elliot, but we'll see if we can improve it a little."

He babbled on. Elliot let him do what he needed to, following his instructions when asked to try this and hold that. And all the time, he wondered if the arm would ever carry a rifle again.

If he would ever be himself again.

12

January 25th

ELLIOT's new wristwatch said the time was 13:11.

He thumbed a button and the display showed the outdoor temperature. *28.0 Celsius, 82.6 Fahrenheit.* A pretty near perfect temperature to be lounging around at a beach—even though this was a rocky beach with water too cold to swim in. That was okay; he'd never been one for swimming, and he'd learned while showering that getting water in his bad ear truly sucked.

Elliot had brought along two towels as a pad to sit on. His back now pressed against what *had* been a sun-warmed boulder when he'd first wandered down here after another unsatisfying lunchtime smoothie. The rocky shore lay a few hundred metres across the coastal highway from The Downs's entrance. Up the hill behind him and to the left, over by the old lighthouse, the wreck of a cattle truck still stretched there. The truck that had brought Elliot—and Angie, Lewis, Heng, Dylan—to

Settlers Downs in the first place...and in vastly different circumstances to those of today.

A few clouds scudded past across the ocean to the east of The Downs. A breeze was flowing up the coast from the south, carrying a hint of Antarctic chill even this deep into summer. A big pacific gull hovered offshore, braked perfectly against the wind and interested in something moving beneath the gentle waves. Minutes earlier, Elliot had swung around at a shushing sound in the grass to find an echidna traveling past—a rare sight outside of forest habitats and an indication the critter felt safe out here. When he'd first come out this morning, two pelicans had flown in from the north, their huge wingspans and heavy bodies making them look like seaplanes coming into land. They'd stayed in the area and were now paddling around interested maybe in whatever the gull was interested in. A half hour earlier, a crowd of silver gulls had dropped by to check if the human was eating anything and if he'd share it. He wasn't and he didn't. And with disapproving squawks they'd moved on to the north.

Elliot soaked in the quietude of waves, the healing embrace of the sun, the caress of the breeze. And he thought, *Life really is shit.*

The wristwatch said 13:12 now.

He hurt. Constantly. Pain pulsed outward from the side of his face in waves. A patch across his head and neck seemed to swell, contract, swell, contract—in time with his heartbeat, as if that whole area were a new heart attached there and beating, beating, beating. He still couldn't lift his right arm higher than the shoulder, but like an idiot he tried again now, and when it didn't work he dropped the hand into his lap with a snort of disgust.

This is what you get. For jinxing yourself. You used to make comments about getting away unscathed while your friends got shot up or blown up. Now look at ya. Shoulda kept your dumb mouth shut.

And his mouth was the main problem. The aching jaw where he'd lost teeth. The tight and itching flesh around the cheek wound—it felt like a bug was in there, crawling, digging. The headaches, the goddamned headaches like the bitch he had going right now. There was also the dull spot in his hearing that threw off his balance and made him glance around all the time in case he'd missed something—and then the goddamned glancing around would spike his neck pain and upset his balance all over again.

He growled wordlessly in frustration at it all.

Even with this reduced hearing acuity, he heard someone approaching him now, long before Lewis appeared at his side.

"Hey," the young man said and dropped into an easy squat. He rested a small shoulder bag on the ground between his knees.

"Hey," Elliot replied.

The word came out hoarse. Talking was difficult. Forming words worked his jaw and his throat in ways they didn't like.

The next minute passed in silence as the two men regarded the sky, the surf, the big gull and pelicans.

"Good talk, as always," Lewis said finally with a light laugh. He reached into his bag and slid out a bottle, passed it over. It contained a caramel-colored liquid, one-quarter-full. "Brought you some pain relief."

Elliot read the label. "Smooth Honey Bourbon Liqueur."

Lewis dropped onto his butt, moving the pack onto his thighs. "Found it up in the hills in October and kept it as a Christmas gift for you."

Elliot unscrewed the lid and sniffed inside. "Not bad," he said. "Christmas was a while back." And what a shitty day that had been, the last day Angie had spoken to him.

"Now that your drugs have been scaled back, I thought it might be time to give it to you."

"They do say honey's good for you," Elliot replied.

"Yes, they do."

Elliot raised it, sipped it. Smooth fire purred across his tongue and down his throat. The sun had warmed his outsides; this stuff began warming his insides. He sighed in pleasure, then tilted the bottle toward Lewis.

Lewis declined with a smile. "Still not much of a drinker."

Elliot sipped again and savored it before screwing the lid back on. "Thanks, Cochise."

"*De nada.* So. How is it?" Lewis's hand waggled toward Elliot's face and neck.

Elliot thought about the little shocks he felt at intermittent intervals, shocks almost electric in their own way. The impotence and frustration of trying to train himself to use his SIG MCX left-handed and fire handguns from the hip with his right hand. How could he explain all of that? And why would he invite further conversation about it? He simply replied, "Fine."

Lewis chuckled. "Right. The tough guy answer."

Elliot gave him some side eye, avoiding turning his head. "You asked. I answered."

"Yeah, but it's *me*, mate. I mean, you used to talk at me when I didn't want you to. Now I actually want you to."

It was Elliot's turn to let out a reluctant chuckle. "Yeah, that's a turnaround, all right."

Another long silence, then Lewis said, "Well, I know you're having a hard time. So, if you need to talk, or like, you need some natural pain relief or something, come find me, yeah?"

"Sure."

"Did you hear we had a message from the Maggot Rider?"

Elliot turned the top half of his body toward him. "Rider was here?"

Lewis shook his head. "Went to Jericho last week. Ranesh told us when he was doing dental checkups yesterday."

And Ranesh didn't tell me. That's weird.

Or maybe Ranesh had. And Elliot had forgotten. God, he hoped that wasn't the case; his memory had been so much better these past couple of weeks.

"What was Rider's message?" he asked.

"Just a hello. And giving instructions for how to contact him if we need him."

"And what are they?"

"There's a town called Evandale, up near Launceston Airport. He said to leave notes in the fire station letterbox."

"That's it? He doesn't have a radio or something set up there?"

"Dunno. That's all the instruction said. Just chuck messages in the letterbox."

"A dead drop? Christ, the guy's more security-conscious than I am."

"That," Lewis said, plucking a dandelion stalk and slipping it into his shoulder bag, "is impossible."

No address to find the guy. Elliot admired that. He seemed to remember Rider mentioning he'd been part of a community of his own before the SERPs captured him. What kind of community would a messed-up biker like him fit into? And how had Jericho reacted to him turning up again when he'd been the SERPs' unwilling executioner at the Night Courts?

"Did Rider give 'em anything else? No other ... news?" Goddamned Ranesh, not telling him this. Elliot would have pumped him for more information directly. And he definitely would have remembered this if Ranesh *had* told him.

Lewis plucked another dandelion, put it away. "Mmm ... Something about him hammering them with questions about the last couple of SERPs. Is it Da Silva and Miller?"

"Yup."

"Yeah. He just was trying to find information to help him track them down. I think. Something like that." Lewis shrugged like this was the least important thing in the world, and picked more dandelions.

"Dammit," Elliot said. "I need to go to Jericho."

Lewis actually startled at that. "Um. Why?"

"To find Rider."

"Really? *Seriously?* You wanna chase the SERPs around Tazzie? The way you are now?"

"Jesus. Could you ... I dunno ... make me sound less like a basket case?"

"You need to keep getting better."

"I need something to *do*. Something important."

"Getting better is important."

"Sitting round on my ass is..." He clenched his frustration into his fists and finished the sentence with a growl.

Lewis leaned in. "Getting better," he said, "is important."

Elliot started to get up. "I—"

"And Rider already *left* Jericho. Who knows where the hell he is now?"

Elliot settled back down, instantly deflated. "He didn't tell them."

"He didn't tell them where he was going, no."

"Shit." Lewis was right. And Elliot could go leave a "message" at that town up near the airport—or wait there for Rider—but he might be waiting for months for the asshole to turn up if Rider was out hunting through the south of the island or something, or in Hobart. Elliot would just be trading locations to sit on his ass achieving nothing. "*Shit*."

"It's okay, mate," Lewis told him, touching his arm briefly. "Stay here with us. Try to be part of us again. Just get better. There's other things in life to do besides shooting people. Especially now. Things are getting way better, you know."

Other things in life? Of course there were. But there wouldn't be for Elliot until the threats to The Downs were dealt with. Da Silva and Miller still out there. Hell, *Waxer* was still out there, the last surviving Death Druid who'd led Elliot to Alyssa's location three years ago ... then escaped from his temporary prison by the time Elliot had returned for him.

Goddamn loose ends.

When finally, he looked around to see what Lewis was doing, the young man was gone. Nowhere to be seen. So was the pacific gull. Elliot checked his watch again.

13:59.

He'd blanked out for a half hour or more. That wasn't good.

Christ, he told himself. *None of this is good.*

13

February 18

"Wait!" Elliot snapped.

Wilma, his dog, froze at his side with her hackles up, unhappy at being stopped right when she'd been about to leap upon the threat. A leap that would have caused her serious injury. Elliot's own hair was up on the nape of his neck, his gut doing flips.

Four yards past them stood a humongous feral cat— orange with brown patches—arching its back from a fallen tree trunk, hissing demonically. The thing was easily the size of a beagle.

Feral little fucker. Worse than deaders.

Probably, the cat had a litter somewhere nearby. Then again, given her species and her size, a cat like this probably needed no excuse to go toe to toe with intruders. No doubt she enjoyed a good fight. Ferals were bad for wildlife, bad for people who stumbled across them. The MCX was already in his hands—he still couldn't sling anything from either shoulder—so that made it quick and easy to take aim.

Elliot was poised to kill her and make it quick. But he didn't. Wilma grumbled at his hesitation. A second later, the cat chose the better part of valor and fled into the scrub. The dog lurched forward, trying to round the roots-end of the dead tree. Elliot had to snap at her again, forcing her to stay. The yelling made his headache spike. Wilma obeyed, but stared at him like he was crazy.

"I probably am," he muttered, his voice thick. It seemed to come to his right ear via the inside of his head rather than the mouth, traveling up through his slow-healing jaw and directly into his skull.

The dog's head turned to where the cat had gone. She grumbled again.

"Waste of bullets," he told her.

She sat down in the dry grass, looking dejected.

There were other reasons not to kill the cat, besides spending a bullet. If he'd shot her, the dog would have leaped onto the twitching remains to rip and shake them apart—and the frenzy would remind Elliot of old-time deaders feeding. The shot might also alert the wrong kind of people out here in the bush.

Also, he believed the cat was a mom.

So, he took Wilma away from the area, skirting the tree line until they found another fallen tree where Elliot could rest from his afternoon wanderings. Sweat sheeted his face, soaked his polo shirt, his socks, his hair. Damn hair—it was longer than he'd grown it since he was a kid, almost at his collar. But no one other than those Jericho docs was gonna be touching his head with sharp objects

—or, worse, vibrating trimmers. He stroked the mess of beard that had spread down his throat. Not touching that, either. Not for a while yet.

Laying the rifle along the tree trunk, he pushed his sunglasses up onto his forehead and consulted the step counter in his watch. Nine kilometres. He'd covered nine klicks since passing through The Downs's front gate at midday. And he had more in him. The first hour had been the toughest, but the activity seemed to have burned away much of the dizziness, the nausea. He hurt, of course; that never went away, it just traveled. From his right ear to his jaw to his throat to the whole of his trapezius then back again. And if he slept the wrong way, or snapped his head round too quick, or bumped the shoulder on that side, all those pain-spots would join to remind him that he couldn't do that stuff, normal stuff, without consequences.

Nine kilometres. The distance satisfied him. Some of that had been wandering the expanded fence line around Settlers Downs; the rest had been spent testing his limits. And doing the scouting that others should be doing but weren't anymore. Did the damn fools think that pushing their fences out wider and rebuilding the guard dog runs along them was enough? How many crises did it take for them live in vigilance?

Elliot carried no pack, since carrying the damn thing would be problematic. All he had was the rifle, a .40 cal, spare mags for both, a knife, and two canteens clipped to his belt. One canteen held water—that was half-full now. The other held a "soup" Lewis had made him because he still couldn't chew: vegetables stewed and blended into a sloppy pulp, with egg added. And sea salt, thank God. He wasn't hungry, but the bad taste his injuries had left him —that sour, turned-milk taste—was in his mouth again, so he needed something to cleanse it. He took some soup in small sips. The dog glanced at him, then away, knowing he wouldn't share this. Finished drinking, he reclipped the soup canteen, then used the water to rinse the holes where teeth had once been. He'd left his dental plate in his tent in a glass of water; unless he was eating, the thing was more hassle than it was worth.

He made a low whistle, using his tongue against the roof of his mouth. Wilma's ears perked up and she came to his thighs, tongue lolling, a ball of energy. He dipped a hand into a side pocket, brought out some of the dried cat food pellets he kept there, fed them too her. When she was done, he pointed further along the tree line and she trotted ahead. A couple more hours hiking seemed a great way to spend the afternoon.

Just no more wild cats, Universe.

ONE HOUR LATER, ELLIOT WAS CROSSING THE OPEN FIELD behind The Downs toward the property's back fence line, intending to check it one last time for rust and indications anyone had tried cutting it. All day, the wind had been blowing from seawards, across The Downs, over these fields, and toward the bushy hills behind them. Suddenly, it shifted around to the north, gusting. Wilma froze in place, head snapping to the left as she literally caught wind of something. Following the line of her snout, Elliot saw what she'd scented. Above the waist-high grass: the top of a head, facing away from him and toward the curve of escarpment north-west, its long fine hair billowing in the breeze.

His first reaction was alarm.

Drybones!

His second was relief as recognition kicked in.

Claire.

What was she doing, kneeling out here in the grass? He scowled as the answer came to him. She was communing with nature, that's what. He made the dog sit and stay, then pushed through the grass toward her.

Five metres out, she spoke without turning. "We live in a beautiful spot, eh, Elliot?"

He held onto his answer until he arrived at her side. She shifted from her kneeling position to fold her legs as close to lotus position as she could. Her back was straight, eyes closed, hands resting in her lap. The wrist she'd broken in the BearCat ambush was out of its cast now; he'd seen her using that hand lately without wincing, so hopefully it had healed fine. A water bottle stood beside her, a clear plastic bag of dried apples by that.

He replied, "It's a dangerous spot."

She opened her eyes to squint at him, then indicated the hills. "It's a beautiful one. Remember that old song? I see trees of green? This is a wonderful world, Elliot."

"I remember those lyrics used sarcastically in a movie."

"I think the word is *ironic*."

"And I give not one shit about semantics. Do you even

have a weapon with you?" He couldn't see one—not on her, not on the ground.

She took a long easy breath. "I'm traveling light."

"I'll stay with you then. Till you're done doing whatever you're doing."

"Meditating."

"Right."

"Don't say 'right' like that. I'm making the most of the season—the literal and metaphorical season." She gestured to the azure sky and the high hills that rose like a barrier north and west. "Great weather. Great view." Another long, slow breath, in, out. "I came out to enjoy this and I came without a weapon because we live in peace now. To bring a weapon would upset the peace I carry within me."

"Seriously?"

"What now?"

"You're sitting in the middle of a goddamned field. I saw you from twenty metres away. My dog smelled you just fine. With the wind hissing in the grass, someone could sneak up on you, if they wanted to."

"Elliot. I want a *life*. A life without worrying about bogeymen coming to get me. I feel like that life has come back to me. I really do enjoy feeling peaceful. Don't piss on that."

"It's not just people, Claire. Okay, so maybe most of the bad guys are gone. For the moment. But you're out here in nature without a care in the world."

"Ah, so you are listening."

"Nature's plenty nasty even without drybones, SERPs or scav-rats."

"Nature," she said, turning her face to the sun, "is magical."

"There are snakes out here. Feral cats, feral dogs."

"And bees and flowers and birds and wallabies and dragonflies. I saw a big, fat echidna this morning. Very cute."

He went to shake his head in frustration, but the movement had him clutching the side of his head.

"Oh, sweetheart. Come on, sit down a sec. I've got some Jericho painkillers with me if you need one."

She unbuttoned a shirt pocket to reveal a small first aid kit inside it. Perhaps she wasn't so trusting in Mother Nature after all.

"Fine," he said. "I'm fine."

He forced the hand to drop from his head and latch onto his belt, turned around in a three-sixty. The maneuver served the triple purpose of monitoring their surrounds, checking Wilma was still following orders, and also to prove he could do it without losing balance.

Claire reached out and patted his boot. "Listen. Turn off your hypervigilance for five minutes. Sit with me, breathe this air and take in this view. Clear your mind." She lifted her healing wrist. "Meditation works really well for managing pain."

The side of his head was pulsing as if some living thing were trying to get out. The left side of his peripheral vision had a stinking great white blotch in it. He probably *should* rest a while.

"Come," he called the dog. Her ears flattened in friendly fashion as she approached and caught sight of a human she knew well.

Claire said, "Can I pat her?"

"For a moment," he replied.

Once she'd scratched Wilma's neck and given her a rub on the chest, making baby noises all the while, Elliot said, "Okay."

The dog looked to him.

"On guard."

With nose to ground, Wilma vanished into the grass, headed north.

Elliot stomped some grass flat, then eased himself onto the pad he'd made, laying the rifle beside him. He drank deeply from his own water. He and Claire sat in what she probably thought of as companionable silence for a time, and then, with his injuries hammering fresh nails into his sanity, he gave up resisting and said, "I'll take one of those meds."

She fished out a pill and handed it over. He swallowed it with water.

"You're sweating a lot, but you look good today," she told him.

"I'm fine. Like I said."

"Getting fitter."

'Fitter', not 'fit', he thought. He said, "Almost ready to go tie up some loose ends."

"The two SERPs?"

"And Waxer."

"Waxer? There's a name I haven't heard mentioned in a very long time."

"Still out there somewhere."

She pursed her lips. "Maybe. Maybe he's now a part of a lovely, forgiving group of people in Devonport or somewhere. Maybe he's found Jesus and he's walking the land as an itinerant preacher. Or maybe he's dead. Why don't you forget about him? Him and the SERPs."

"Can't do that."

"Why not?"

"It's dangerous, Claire. How many different ways can I say it. We can't have threats like that roaming around out here unaddressed."

"Sure we can. The world has always been full of threats and dangers. But we can choose to live without anxiety even so."

"You can, maybe."

"You could too. If you focused on what you have here and enjoyed it, you might stop fretting about things that might not ever happen."

"Yeah, well..." He plucked grass and tossed it into the breeze the way Lewis had tossed a dandelion a few weeks back.

"Yeah, well?"

"I probably screwed up the chance at enjoying things here."

"You mean Angie?"

"Her. And other people I've been a dick to recently."

"Like me?" She grinned at him a second then turned her face to the sun again with eyes closed. "And I still like you. How about that?"

"Sure, but ..." He didn't know how to finish that. *Angie's not as nice as you? Angie's a lot more hard-ass than you?* Saying something like that wouldn't really fly, would it? He hawked then spat to the side. And held his breath in horror as the wind snatched the loogie and whipped it

Claire's way. He let the breath go when the snot flew a good couple of feet in front of her.

"You haven't screwed anything up, Elliot." She turned her face to him again. "If that's what you're afraid of."

"I'm not afraid of it. I'm just realizing and accepting it, is all."

"Well, don't accept it. Angie's still there. You're still here. You've built bridges before."

He let out a sigh. "Not over a mess like that one." Why had he written what he'd written that day, freezing her out? Why hadn't he called her back in and apologized? Why had he left it so long, until it was too late to say anything?

"The big secret of life," Claire said, "is that life is messy. Everyone who's still alive in this world has been traumatized. Brutalized. I can't imagine what you've been through with your injuries. You can't imagine what I experienced in that Druid camp. But we both know it hurt like hell and still does. Psychologically. Physically."

He stared sideways at her as a thought hit him. "You still got ... physical pain? After the Druids?"

"Yes, I do, mate. Yes, I do." She didn't elaborate. He didn't press her. Over the years, he'd wondered what she'd been through. But the idea of her suffering some ongoing physical damage...

"Those bastards."

She made a dismissive motion. "Dead ones. Dead and in the past."

"But—"

"I'm living now, my friend. Or trying to. And maybe

eighty percent of the time, it's working. I really like that eighty percent. It's working for me."

Another silence stretched between them as birds chased insects above and through the grass, as the dog returned to check on her master before pursuing another scent trail, as puffy clouds slipped across the sun, as the breeze made the long grass sigh.

"I'm trying to conjure some wise words to take away your pain and improve your quality of life," Claire said finally. "Here's the best I can come up with. You know how you've spent the past three-and-a-half years trying to get the rest of us to be more like you? Well, you succeeded. We have conquered. We're safer. It worked. And we know it worked, because now we live in peace. Like we keep telling you. So maybe, just maybe, it's time for you to become more like the rest of us. Think about that." She patted his boot again and when he looked at her, her eyes had closed. Her hand returned to her lap and she wriggled herself back into a meditative posture. "And now, my beloved friend, either meditate here in quiet with me ... or piss off."

14

March 19th

ELLIOT WOKE with a stiff neck and stiff jaw. And that sour, turned milk taste in his mouth again. It took fifteen minutes of stretching and massage to ease the joints enough to consider facing the day. The turned milk taste was chased away by a sip from his honey liqueur. He left the tent with a mind open to the idea that the day ahead might just be okay.

For maybe the first time ever, he came early to a Community Centre meeting, arriving ahead of the crowd. A half-dozen people folded the breakfast tables against the back wall and positioned rows of chairs to face the kitchen. Elliot offered to help. They told him *no, sit and relax, we've got this*. Hating it, he complied. His head didn't hurt, not at all, and it hadn't yesterday. The neck wound where the muscles had scarred and tightened did hurt. He still couldn't lift that arm higher than the shoulder, but although it was weak, he could have helped these people drag chairs around a room.

Instead, he took a chair from the back row and nestled it into a back corner, in beside the folded tables. There was a window sill there, low enough for him to lean his right arm on it and take that weight off his shoulder and neck.

Soon after, other Downsers began filing in. Angie was one of the last; she gave no sign of noticing him down at the back as she picked out a front-row seat. The militia wife that Rit had escorted home from Jericho sat in the row behind Angie, alongside Huy and Chariya; their children and her children sat on the floor to the side beneath a window with their heads over coloring books. Unlike many past meetings, children were welcome at this one, and though they made a little noise as the meeting started, Elliot thought they were pretty well-behaved. For them, a gathering like this must be boring as batshit; he'd certainly felt that way about most of them.

Claire, Heng and Sturgis—the new Council—leaned against the kitchen servery counter, facing the room. After Sturgis outlined the agenda ahead, Claire led everyone in a minute's silent honoring of those they had lost in the crisis of the previous year.

Elliot spent that minute reciting the names of the thirteen who'd died during his first ill-fated visit to Jericho and the subsequent SERP incursion into Settlers Downs.

Kim. Dylan. Abby. Ben. Tony. Faye. Macca. Piers. Raj. Garry. Ilse. Jen.

Jimmy.

Gently, Claire cleared her throat and intoned, "Rest in peace, beloved ones. We'll remember you until the day we eventually join you."

An awkward chorus rolled around the room, composed of *amen*s, *yeah*s, *mmm*s, and one *too right*. Noses sniffed, chairs squeaked and scraped, and Claire beamed a loving smile at the group.

"We belong to Settlers Downs."

"A place where peaceful people settle down," the small crowd responded.

"A lighthouse of hope," she continued.

"In a dark world," they responded.

"May we increase the light and decrease the darkness." She cleared her throat again, changing gears. "Well, Settlers Downs, this is our second meeting back here since Elliot's team resolved things for us. But it's Elliot's first."

More chair-scraping as people twisted toward him. He heard variations on "Thanks, Elliot", "Glad you're better" and "How ya feeling, mate?" He weathered the attention with his left hand held up in acknowledgment and his gaze on the floorboards. When it passed, he locked eyes with Claire. He couldn't tell if Angie had turned to look for him; all he could see of her was a blonde ponytail.

Claire spoke over six rows of heads to tell him, "You're continuing to look well today, my friend."

He thought that was a kind-hearted lie, but didn't say it.

Moving on, she told the room, "We're now four months into our pact with Jericho, and it looks like Nine

Mile River has finally joined it, too." Over a ripple of excitement, she added, "Yesterday's parlay with them went extremely well. With the Vikes on board, this region is looking safe and secure."

Elliot had been told about that, and about the fact that the Vikes would soon be handing back the sole-surviving BearCat as a gesture of good faith.

Finally, he thought.

"That's great news, Claire," Nance said. "About bloody time Tazzie got back to normal."

"Furthermore," Claire went on, "the Daves went south yesterday and managed a second conversation with a small group of people sheltering in Freycinet."

"Scav-rats," someone muttered, mid-room.

Claire's face tightened in disapproval. Before she could say anything, Dave Two spoke up near the mutterer.

"Nah, mate, we shouldn't call 'em that anymore."

From the back row, Dave One added, "They're just people. Just stuffed-up people. They're alright when you get talking to them."

Chariya asked, "Do they want to join us?"

"Nope," said Dave Two. "Not yet anyway. They don't trust us yet."

"And fair enough, too," said Sturgis. "Can't say I blame them. For the moment, we'll keep in touch. Dave One and I will be meeting with them in five days' time, and Jericho are sending a doctor and nurse as well. Maybe these folks want to keep their own autonomy, which is fine. But we'll help as we can."

Jericho are sending a doctor, Elliot thought. *And, no doubt, an armed escort.*

The idea of an armed escort was a smart one from Jericho's perspective, but it worried him that many SERP and militia weapons were now in the hands of people he didn't know.

What the hell you talking about? he chided himself. *You were born in a country where there were more civilian firearms than civilians.*

That was maybe true, but it hadn't been like this. Tasmania was fast becoming a new Wild West.

Angie raised a hand and Claire acknowledged it. "So, we're talking about a new reality, right?"

Yeah. A Wild West.

"We are."

"Outside Jericho, back in October," Angie continued, "we saw a fresh dead body."

We saw, Elliot noted she'd said. *Not 'Elliot and I saw'.*

Well, that's what you get for writing such dumb shit to her, Radler's ghost muttered.

And don't I know it.

"He'd survived almost four years out there," Angie continued. "Possibly alone. There must be lots of other survivors like him who've hunkered down all this time. And there's plenty of good places to do it."

Sturgis nodded. "Jericho are sending scouts to the Huon Valley soon."

Angie said, "Now the deaders are basically gone— and the SERPs and bikers too—maybe more of those survivors will be open to joining groups like ours. Is that where the Council's thinking of taking things?"

"Yes," Heng said, stirring himself for the first time. "We know small groups are up in the mountains."

"That's exactly what I was thinking," Angie replied. "Nance's old crew is probably still up there. Might be time to try harder to make contact. Like the Daves did in Freycinet. And we should get onto it before we can't find usable petrol anymore and we're all riding horses."

"Excuse me, but what if the people you find are arse-holes?" The voice came from mid-room. Di, a woman whose husband Raj had been murdered by SERPs in September. She half-stood to add, "Two SERPs are still out there, we don't know where. And as we know from them and the Death Druids, bad people seem to be best at surviving." She sat again.

Hoorah, Elliot thought. *A voice of reason, finally.*

"We survived," Claire said. "And we're not bad people."

"Not so sure about that," said Nance. "Heng did take the last fritter at breakfast."

Polite laughter followed, clearing the air. Claire allowed it to die out naturally before saying, "Angie, you look like you have more to say."

Angie stood and faced the room, though she didn't look directly at Elliot. "I keep thinking about that poor dead bloke and how well he did for four years, only to meet the wrong people at the end. A Jericho militia sniper got him, in case I didn't mention that earlier. There's probably a thousand other people out there like him. Good people like us. Or slightly annoying people like Heng," she said with a grin over her shoulder.

Heng flipped her a half-hearted bird. From the second row, Chariya scolded him for it.

Angie continued, "It's not just about giving people a chance. There's safety in numbers."

"Also," Sturgis said, "more people makes industry easier, and it allows for healthier genetic diversity." Two months back, there would have been a combination of awkward coughs at the topic of procreation, accompanied by some whispered witticisms and giggles amongst the community's jokers. Today, those gathered accepted Sturgis's comment with sober nods.

With a nod of her own, Angie went on. "I've been thinking of going back up to the mountains, but searching further than we did before. Up between St Marys and Launceston."

Now came nervous coughs and whispered comments. Remembering the way Birdy had described Launceston in the weeks following the outbreak, Elliot found himself leaning forward.

That's insane.

Lewis gave voice to Elliot's thoughts, and to those of many assembled. "Elliot and I met someone coming from Launceston once, and she said it was a war zone. Infected everywhere. Lawlessness amongst the survivors." He glanced at his sister two seats over, probably hoping the word *lawlessness* wasn't strong enough to give her flashback.

Sorry, Cochise. Everything probably gives her flashbacks.

Dave Two shifted in his seat, facing Lewis. "Neil and I came from Lonnie, didn't we, Neil? We know how bad it was back then. But so was every other big population center. By the time we got out, we weren't seeing many survivors at all. Like we said, the deaders are gone and the bikers are gone, so it's probably not that bad now."

"Dunno, Dave," Lewis persisted. "There might still be groups there we don't want to run into. Sorry, Angie, I reckon the cities like Lonnie and Hobart and Devonport should be off limits still."

Preach it, Lewis.

Voices rose to argue multiple viewpoints on this topic. Eventually the racket was quelled by Heng putting his fingers in his mouth and whistling shrilly.

In the lull, Angie said, "Appreciate what you're saying, Lewis, Dave, but I wasn't actually going into Lonnie. There's enough small hamlets around those hills to keep us busy scouting for months."

"You want to go for *months*?" Rit asked.

She shook her head. "Two weeks to start with. Tops. Just a look-see, leave some messages behind, go back in a month and see if anyone's left a reply."

"Not a bad idea," Sturgis said.

"Glad you think so, I've actually been planning it." Sturgis accepted this with a nod while Claire gave a good-natured eyeroll, smiling as if to say *Of course you have.* "If there's no reason for me to hang around, I'd actually like to leave mid-afternoon today. But it's a two-person job. I need someone riding shotgun."

Elliot rose to his feet. "I'll come," he said, forcing volume into his rusty voice, directing the comment to Claire.

Heads turned. Angie's included. He kept her in his peripheral vision while he focused on Claire.

"Elliot," Angie started.

"You're still recovering, mate," said Claire.

"Exactly," said Angie.

"I'm recovered enough to—"

"Not enough for this," Claire interrupted.

"The hell you say. I've been out scouting for weeks without problems."

Dead and awkward silence descended, while people faced forward or avoided his gaze—including Angie, whose gaze—he saw when he finally glanced at her—had lifted to the roof as if in prayer. What the hell was he thinking, he asked himself now. Did he really want to be in a car with her for days when the past three months had been so awkward?

Hell yes, I do, he thought. *If it means keeping her safe. If it gives me a chance to fix things.*

"Elliot, you're not ready, dude," Lewis was saying as he also rose to his feet.

"I'm fine to sit in the car with a rifle and cover someone."

"I can shoot rifle from car," said Heng. "I go support her."

Angie gave the old man a *good idea* look that incensed Elliot, set his head to pounding. Heng *was* an old man, for Christ's sake!

"You think you're fitter than me?" he snapped.

Lewis sat down in the lull that followed. Angie turned her stare toward a window.

Elliot counted eleven seconds of silence before Heng spoke up. "Angie want to make people relax around her. Elliot, you a little bit … scary." Murmurs of complaint rolled around the room, forcing Heng to elaborate. "Not scary-looking! Not scary-*looking*! Just scary. You a scary man." He searched the room for support. "True, yeah?"

Dave One mumbled, "That's a bit rough, mate."

But no one really denied it.

Mindful of children present, Elliot bit down on the cusses roiling in his mind, tamping down his anger. As much as he could, at least. "What are you all saying? You think the crisis out there is over? You think there's nothing for old soldier Elliot to do anymore except sittin' on the sidelines lickin' his wounds?"

Well, isn't that the way of the veteran, though? Risk your life in defense of your people, then go vegetate on the margins once they no longer need you to fight?

"That's not what anyone's saying," Claire said.

"The hell it's not."

"Elliot," said Angie, and her voice had that *don't-mess-with-me* tone in it he'd always respected, always loved— until now. "You're not coming. You made it pretty clear you didn't need my help. Well, I *don't* need *yours*."

He swayed a little with the shock of it, then stomped down the side aisle leading to the door. He had to catch himself against a wall once before he made it there, and that just fueled his anger.

He didn't slam the door behind him. But it was only because of the children.

ELLIOT COLLECTED WILMA FROM HER DOG RUN. THEN HE went to the barn, gathered fishing gear, and left The

Downs, storming across the highway. His mind was filled with white noise—the same noise hissing and whining in his ear like a living thing. He passed the lighthouse and came to a stop on the rocks beyond it where they jutted into the ocean. He still hated fish, but they were clean protein and when he cooked them right, he could eat them without chewing. Also, this gave him some-goddamn-thing to do.

He stood there on the rocks, stewing on his thoughts, cursing the Universe, while Wilma zigzagged around the area, rudderless without orders from him.

After catching only a couple of fish, his temper was cooling along with the day. Enough was enough. Packing up the gear, he showed the inside of the bucket to Wilma. "One for you, one for me."

She wagged her tail in enthusiastic support of that idea.

He was past the lighthouse and the truck carcass, most of the way up the slope, when he heard motor noise up on the road. The top half of a Land Rover appeared above the crest. From the driver's window, a blonde head turned his way. Blue eyes held his.

Then the car was past.

And it was just Elliot alone on the hill with his dog.

15

April 4

ONE MOMENT ELLIOT was in Jericho, lifting aluminum sheeting to search beneath it for SERPs. The next he was sitting up in a sleeping bag, listening to a voice outside his tent. He blew out a breath, hoping the dream hangover would go with it, reaching for reality.

"Did you hear me?" asked the voice. "We're pretty worried."

Krystal. It was Krystal. He was back in his tent in Settlers Downs—and it was Lewis's girlfriend talking to him from outside. Was something wrong with Lewis? He tried to ask as much but his mouth gummed up and the words came out as garbled nonsense.

"Can I come in?" she asked.

He made another noise—an affirmative—then peeled the sleeping bag off his legs. He swung them over the side of the camp cot, glad he'd worn track pants to bed. The flap unzipped and the young woman duckwalked inside.

The tent was large enough for a kind of mud-room at the front where Krystal could crouch without encroaching on the inner sleeping compartment. It was daytime, he saw. Early. The light over the teenager's shoulder was grey. Misty rain slicked her jacket and pattered the tent walls.

Elliot raised his wristwatch and blinked until he could make out the time. 08:44.

Yeah, I should be up anyway.

He said, "Someone's worried about something? What have I done now?" He opened his mouth wide to stretch the tension from his jaw.

"What? No, it's not you." She shuffled closer. Her face, he saw now, was drawn with concern. "It's Angie and Heng. They're three days late getting back."

What? Shit!

Since the injury, he'd been losing interest in things like the date. And their mission had been someone else's concern, not his. But when he checked his watch again, it confirmed what she'd said.

Krystal asked, "Can you meet with the Council at the Office in five minutes?"

"I'll be there in three." He was already reaching for his jacket and boots.

KRYSTAL FOLLOWED HIM INTO THE FREESTANDING SITE office near the property's original homestead. It was in this small square room that Woodsy had first suggested searching for antivirals at Jericho seven months ago. On that occasion, the three-person Council had been cut to two by Faye's illness and quarantine. On this occasion, it was again cut to two by Heng's MIA status—Claire and Sturgis. They sat at either end of the table. Dave One, Lewis and Rit had squeezed along the side facing the entrance. Elliot and Krystal entered the silent room and took up spots either side of the door, standing.

Those seated all nursed mugs with steam curling out of them. A thermos stood on one of the side counters beside three spare mugs. Sturgis gestured toward the thermos, but Elliot waved away the offer and spoke before anyone else could.

"You lost radio contact with them?" He winced as he said it. It must have been the way he'd slept: his neck kept "zapping" him, shooting random bolts of lightning across the back of his skull and down into his shoulder.

"We did," Rit replied. He leaned over a map spread across the table center-room. "Last contact was six days ago."

"That's nice," Elliot replied. "Six days. And you're doing something about it *now*. You're telling me *now*."

Sturgis bristled, straightening in his chair. "Well, if you were part of the community again instead of wallowing in self-pity, you'd have been part of the conversation already."

Elliot blinked back at him. It wasn't like Sturgis to give him shit like this. "What, I live so far away at the back of the property that Krystal's the only one fit enough to make the journey? Or is she the only one who can be bothered talking to me?"

"You're not the only one who suffers around here—" Sturgis had started rising, but Rit grabbed his jacket sleeve and yanked him back into his seat. He landed with an *oof!*

"We're all worried," Claire said. "So, can we have a productive discussion without voices being raised and insults thrown?"

"Sure," Sturgis mumbled.

"Fine with me," said Elliot. "Angie radioed six days ago. Anyone actually been out to look for her—them?"

Lewis elbow-nudged Dave One and Rit either side of him. "Us three took a drive up around St Marys and Rossarden. Rossarden's the last place they radioed from. They'd left some wall-scrawl messages for locals, but we found no other sign of them. We looked for a while, Elliot. We only got back this morning."

The three men did look pretty road-weary, he noticed. And there was more than a little body odor pervading the room.

"Where's Rossarden?"

Both Lewis and Rit pointed to it on the map and Elliot leaned in close. The area west and north of St Marys was peppered with place names, and most of them weren't actual towns. The island state of Tasmania had been sparsely populated before the Collapse, and that sparsity was more pronounced through the interweaving chains of low mountains covering most of its triangular north-eastern third.

Elliot said, "They could have left one of those access roads to hike into the vales."

Sturgis nodded, his flashy temper apparently under control again. "Or even into the forested areas over some of these hills. In their last radio message, Heng said they'd tried that at least once."

"Good way to get lost," Dave One said. When they stared hard at him, he added, "I don't mean it's their fault if they did. I'm just saying it'd be *easy* to get lost up there. It's happened a million times around Tazzie."

"And we don't have rescue helicopters this time, if that has happened to them," Claire said, raising her face towards Elliot. "Thoughts?"

"I got a few," he said, surprised that he actually did. "Dave, I want that BearCat fueled in the next thirty minutes with spare gas in the back. Krystal, can you find Wilma and bring her to the garage? Claire, whatever first aid and medical gear you think should be in the BearCat, put it there. Cochise—" He felt his own hard glare soften a little as it passed to Lewis. "—get food for me, the dog and Heng and Angie."

"And for *us*," Sturgis said, looking at him hard.

"BearCat's mine. Mission's mine." With that, he turned and stamped out of the Office before anyone could object.

No one chased him, but as he marched away, he heard Rit complain, "He didn't ask me to do anything."

———

BACK IN HIS TENT, HE CHANGED INTO TACTICAL PANTS, sweater, wool cap and a sleeveless parka vest. The vest had two button-down pockets on the outside and two deep pockets inside.

Opening a sports carryall, he packed changes of

underwear and socks—jocks and socks, as Aussies loved calling them—then added the holstered .40 cal, two spare mags plus a toothbrush, floss and paste. He zipped up the sports bag, lay the MCX between the handles and grabbed them with his left hand.

His ballistic vest stood upright on a shelf unit Dave Two had built for him; after a moment's hesitation, he left the vest there. It was too heavy and uncomfortable to wear with the way his neck and shoulder were—and if he did things smart, he wouldn't need it.

When he reached the garage, Krystal had the Bear-Cat's passenger door open and was patting Wilma who sat on the passenger seat. The rain continued to drizzle; beneath the cover of the garage roof, three men and a woman waited in a line. Sturgis. Rit. Lewis. Claire. They held small packs. And weapons. All wore ballistic vests, and they blocked Elliot's path to the armored car.

"No, no, no," Elliot said, dumping his carryall and glaring at them. Angie had once said something like, *I can live with a lot of things on my conscience, but not with getting good people killed.* She'd also said she'd never forgive him if *he* got other people killed while trying to save her life—and made him promise never to do that.

"We're coming with ya, boss," Rit was saying. He pointed at Sturgis. "Him and me and you: we're your fireteam, remember? And Claire and Lewis, they love you. And all of us love the people we're going to find."

Emotion rose in Elliot's chest. Raw and unwelcome, it kept on rising until it reached his throat and he had to swallow to keep from choking up.

"Out of my way," he grated.

Lewis said, "Elliot, you need us."

It was easy to dismiss the other people standing here, to be a dick to them. He didn't know why. But he couldn't be that way with Lewis.

Eyes on the ground, he replied, "Maybe. Okay. I've needed you all to help me get well. And I've been a royal asshole about that, sure. And ... maybe you were right about my lone wolf, pity party bullshit. You and—" He looked at Claire and Sturgis. "—you. And ... and Angie. Sure, I'll accept that. But this isn't that. I just ... can't take any of you with me."

Sturgis said, "We're coming."

"If what happened to Angie and Heng is because of hostiles, I don't want any of you out there with me."

"We're coming!"

"You're *not!*" Elliot locked eyes with each of them in turn. "Sturgis, you got a wife and kid. Rit, you got a wife and kids—and a widowed sister-in-law and *her* kids. They need you guys. Claire, you're the mother of the whole community—they can't lose you. And you, Lewis. You got Krystal there. You got your sis. You got a whole camp full of children who look up to you as the best big brother they could ever have." He raised an index finger and swept it across them. "I'm not taking any of you away from the people who need you. If I've proved anything the last few months, it's that you get along fine now without my input. So, this is my mission. This is my ..." He faltered then found his words again. "This is my problem. That's my friend out there, and it's my ... the best woman I ever met. She once made me promise *not* to put other people's lives at risk to save hers. And she'd sure as shit hold me to it. So, I'm keeping that promise."

Stubbornly, Sturgis held his gaze, jaw working. But the others had already relented, their shoulders drooping.

"Well, jeez, if you're gonna be an ass-hat about it..." said Lewis. He dipped into his pack and laid a plastic bag on the concrete. "You can take this. Extra bandages and a bottle of homemade apple juice. Angie likes apple juice."

Carefully, Elliot nodded his thanks.

Rit blew out a breath and mimicked Lewis, placing three plastic baggies next to the young man's package. "Trail mix and dried fish. I know how much you *love* fish."

Elliot accepted the joke—and the gift—with a grunt.

Sturgis growled before he took something from his pack. The small bottle held about a half-pint of amber liquor and clinked as it touched the concrete. "Brandy. In case it gets cold out there." He pulled a spare MCX mag from a vest pocket and balanced it on the bottle. "And a pack of arse-kickers as backup."

The three men stood back and looked to Claire. She made a face as she reached inside her pack. "I don't really have anything like that." She pulled out an opaque fast-food tub and stood it beside the pile. "Mixture of stewed apples and apricots. Lots of energy. Easy to chew. Best I can do, sorry."

"Pretty damn good, Claire," he told her.

She looked away as tears brimmed.

The group stood locked in an awkward tableau for a moment until Lewis broke it by coming over and offering Elliot his fist. Elliot bumped it, left-handed.

Lewis grinned. "Watch your back, ass-hat."

"You watch yours or I'll be *kicking* your ass."

"Nah, you're too old and slow for that. Hey, Krystal, let's get the gate for him." He started off without waiting for her and Elliot thought it was because the young guy's eyes had started shining like Claire's and he didn't want anyone to see.

"Sure." Krystal gave Wilma's chest a final rub and skipped over to Elliot. She leaned up and kissed his good cheek. "Good luck, sir."

He crooked a smile a little at that, remembering how Angie had often called him that to annoy him. Before he could think of a retort, the girl was gone, jogging out into the drizzle after Lewis.

Sturgis was next to say his goodbye: a firm left-handed handshake and an encouragement to radio in every twelve hours.

"How about 0700 and 1900 hours?"

"Perfect," Sturgis said and, shouldering his pack, he marched away.

Rit gave Elliot a gentle tap in the gut and a hand-shake. "Be bloody careful out there, boss, yeah? And when you see Heng, tell him he missed Chariya's birthday yesterday and she's pissed at him."

Elliot flinched at that. He'd missed it too. "I didn't realize—"

Rit laughed. "Her birthday's really next month. But Heng won't remember that anymore than you did." A wink and Rit was headed out as well.

Claire hugged him, being mindful of his tender neck

and shoulder. Into his left ear, she said, "I second what he said. Be bloody careful."

"That's the plan, Mom."

She snorted, still holding him. Then, after a long unsteady breath, she whispered, "We're the same age. You're my brother, not my son." A final squeeze and she too was out in the rain. She'd left her weapon—a shotgun—on the ground beside the pile of gifts. Elliot left it there as he ferried the other things into the back of the Bear-Cat: he would have enough trouble handling a rifle left-handed. And Claire might need it.

He slammed the back doors of the truck and went around to close the passenger door that Krystal had left ajar. And paused.

Lewis's sister Alyssa had come in under the edge of the garage, her duffel coat pearled with raindrops. As the others vanished into or behind other buildings, and as Lewis and Krystal reached the gate, Alyssa ventured closer. Her hands were deep in her pockets. Was she going to give him a gift, too?

After a moment's hesitation, she dashed across the last few metres and threw her arms around his middle.

He returned the hug.

As she broke away, and hurried away, he heard her say, "I'll pray for you."

That hug and those words were the best gift she could have given.

PART THREE

HUNTING

"If all you have is a hammer, everything looks like a nail."

Abraham Maslow

"In enemy territory,
everything *is* a fuckin' nail!"

Elliot's FTX instructor, US Army Ranger School

16

April 4
Year 5, Post-Collapse

THE RAIN STUCK AROUND, forcing Elliot to travel slower than he wanted as he steered the BearCat up into the hills. There'd been heavy winds the day before, so the vehicle's cow-catcher had to push through plentiful debris. The asphalt was slick with runoff and mangy after years of neglect, forcing him to skirt car wrecks and larger fallen branches rather than bully them aside. He took a good many bends and corners at walking pace. In their smaller vehicles, the previous two Downs expeditions would have had to do the same, even without this rain.

It was a full two hours after leaving Settlers Downs that he pulled over beside a large graveyard one kilometre southeast of the St Marys township. It was as safe a rest stop as any. Out here, the terrain was mostly rugged bushland: there were no houses this far out of the town, and no farms across the steep hills. The only potential hostiles he could imagine lying in wait on a day like this inside a graveyard were—

"Drybones, maybe," he said to Wilma.

He reached into one of Rit's baggies and produced some dried fish to feed her, then refolded the map against the steering wheel to consider options. So *many* damned options. The main highway—such as it was—ran west to a town called Fingal. There, he'd have the choice to either continue further west and into the string of towns leading eventually out of the mountains, *or* to branch north-west. This would lead deeper into the hills to Rossarden where Angie had last reported from.

A third alternative would be taking a ridge road north out the back of St Marys: it would snake for dozens of kilometres through what the map called "heritage" forest before eventually plunging into a valley hosting a modest open cut mine. West of the mine—where the ridge road ended—sat a settlement of some sort, accommodation and amenities perhaps for mine workers.

Other narrow roads branched north from St Marys. They all led to apparent dead ends in the middle of nowhere. He didn't remember considering trips up those the last time he'd studied this region. Of course, back then, traveling even the short distances to places like St Marys or old Jock's town had seemed dangerous enough without venturing further. Others led to small, self-contained hamlets such as Cornwall which was a mere seven kilometers north-northwest of St Marys. It was like many of the townships smattered throughout the north-east mountains: a tight and tiny grid of streets—and sitting at the end of a single access road, meaning one way in, one way out. Given Australia's legendary propensity for bushfires, Elliot found that kind of town planning reckless. He recalled Downsers investigating Cornwall years back, finding nothing but bodies and a couple of pusbags in need of putting down. Another team had checked it out again last October while Elliot's fireteam harassed Jericho; finding no signs of recent activity, they'd marked it as a potential alternative to Settlers Downs if things went bad with the SERPs.

Wilma gave a short whine and Elliot checked the windows, the mirrors, but saw nothing through the drizzle. And Wilma wasn't looking out there anyway; she was staring at him. Maybe wanting more of the fish he'd sealed away. Maybe wondering why they were sitting here doing nothing.

He gave her chest a rub. "Not doing nothing. Planning next steps. We'll get outdoors soon enough."

She relaxed, curling up on the seat, and Elliot returned attention to his map. St Marys and Cornwall would be the first places he'd search, despite the fact that Lewis's crew had just come back from here. Might be clues they'd missed.

And after that? If there's nothing there?

Well, after that there was west, there was north, or...

He unfolded the right edge of the map as his finger traced a thread of single-lane highway that snaked northeast to meet the coast twenty-five klicks north of Settlers Downs. Angie hadn't mentioned going that way, and it was the Nine Mile River faction's area to explore. That alternative was a long way down the list of possibilities for him, but tonight he would radio home and have someone check in with Nine Mile.

Radio home, he thought. *Home.*

Home was a place where you belonged. Where you felt able to be fully yourself. Elliot was sitting in an armored truck with a rifle in the rack, a sidearm on his belt, a map under his palms and a mission burning clear and fierce in his head.

This is home.

A burst of buttery light surprised him, snapping his attention outside the cab. The rain had let up, he realized, the clouds parting between the cemetery and the sun. The graveyard was fenced in wrought iron pickets, and a tiny shape darted in to land on one of the spikes. Against the shallow browns and greys of the graveyard behind it and the Aussie bush around it, the blue of the male wren's plumage was all the more startling, magical. A moment later, it launched again. He ducked his head to watch it, but it was gone. Gone where? he wondered. The bird had the run of an island the size of West Virginia.

As did Angie.

The thought brought a new tightness to his chest.

She could be goddamn anywhere.

As he'd driven up the mountain, he'd noted the property gates screened by walls of high weeds that marked the entrances to the farm holdings hidden behind tracts of pine or eucalypt forest. There would be dozens or hundreds such homesteads in this region, no matter what direction he concentrated on. He and Wilma could spend weeks carrying out house-to-houses in Cornwall, St

Marys and Fingal; Angie could be lying injured—or captured!—in one of these homesteads. Or in some out-of-the-way hay shed, or a birdwatcher's hide high on a mountain peak, or at the bottom of a ferny gully, or...

It was overwhelming. The enormity of it. What if she'd been snatched by someone and driven to the far side of the island? What if the Death Druids weren't all gone? What if—

What if Da Silva had tracked her, lain in wait, taken her?

The anxiety had been building steadily since Krystal woke him. It now exploded through his torso, rushing through him like poison, whining in his ears, constricting his throat, drying his mouth, twisting his bowel, dimming his vision, pounding at his head.

I'll never find her I'll never find her I'll never find her I'll never

The truck cab dissolved around him as reality fragged into a dozen pieces.

He was in an arid place with sandy soil and tiny rocks and a wide black crater with his team in pieces. He was there and wanting his team back, wanting to undo it, unable to make that happen.

He was in a dusty village hovel with a baby hugging the leg of its mother who streamed blood from a bullet hole in her sternum.

He was in his classroom with the air turning black and the oxygen growing thin as the teacher explained that Tommy Harrison had had an accident at the train tracks and Elliot could think of nothing except that it was his fault and wanted nothing but to run outside and turn the world backwards, the way he'd seen Superman do in that movie to turn back time, but he couldn't he couldn't.

He was back in his childhood bedroom with his wooden chair hooked tight under the doorknob and Uncle John slamming against the other side of that door, howling for his blood and Elliot yanking and dragging at the shitty window catch that wouldn't give, needing to get out, and so damn close to doing it but knowing that the heaving of the door and the telltale scrape of the chair leg meant he wasn't going to make it, that he would never *ever* make it—

"*ENOUGH!*"

The word rang in his left ear and in his mind, loud enough to drown out all the other crap, the tinnitus, the flashbacks. He'd screamed it loud enough to strip his throat raw and twang on the tender muscles in jaw and neck. And the pain cleared his head. He was here. He was now.

Inhale for five seconds, hold it for five, release it for five. Rinse, lather, repeat.

And his vision cleared and he could focus on the steering wheel clutched in his hands, on the half-folded map that had slipped between thigh and door. On Wilma sitting upright with her head cocked in concern.

"I'm okay, girl," he whispered. "I'm okay."

I'm not. But I have to be.

He leaned back, pressed his head into the rest. To Wilma, he said, "God, I thought that shit was a thing of the past." Flashbacks. Angie had helped him chase them away. The thought of her name gave the anxiety a little fuel, made it flare a little, but he went through the breathing exercise again, and told the anxiety to go fuck itself, and that seemed to work. At least, it slithered back into its box where, he now knew, it would simmer, awaiting another chance.

"Never really go away, ya dirty bastard do you?" Just like the memories. Just like the ghosts of Uncle John and Radler.

He took a hand from the wheel to pat Wilma's neck and back. The action settled him further—and reminded him that he was sitting in an idling truck, wasting fuel.

"Okay," he told the dog and took the shifter out of park and pushed into gear. He fished with the other hand for the map. "We drive through the town ahead, then we check Cornwall. Then we go west and scout around from inside the truck. Big picture first. If that doesn't get us anywhere, we work our way backwards, house to house, building by building." He folded and tossed the map into the footwell below her. "That okay with you?"

She faced forward as he eased the BearCat off the shoulder and onto the road, her head and eyes tracking anything that looked like movement.

"I'll take that as a yes," he said.

———

IT TOOK THE MORNING AND AFTERNOON TO WIND HIS WAY through the towns he'd chosen first, driving down every street. Next came a couple of 9-hole golf courses where he and the dog left the car to clear the various buildings. He found nothing there but evidence of years-old looting, and of cats, rats, mice, possums. The looting told him only that people had been in these places *sometime*, not that they were near here now. He saw zero signs of recent habitation. And zero signs of Angie or Heng—apart from one of their messages in Fingal, spray-painted across an inside wall of the town hall:

MARCH, YEAR 5 AFTER THE COLLAPSE: WE'RE PEACEFUL PEOPLE FROM THE COAST. THINGS ARE BETTER NOW. COMMUNITIES JOINING TOGETHER AND REBUILDING OUR STATE. IF YOU WANT TO PARLEY, LEAVE A MESSAGE HERE. WE DON'T WANT YOU TO JOIN US. WE JUST WANT TO CONNECT.

Elliot had used a permanent marker to add:

THIS IS ELLIOT. ME OR SOMEONE ELSE WILL BE BACK HERE IN A FEW DAYS. WAIT FOR US. OR COME ON HOME. PLEASE.

At the Fingal golf course, the dog spooked a possum in the clubhouse. On impulse, Elliot spent a bullet on it for fresh meat. As rain returned, darkening a sky in which the sun had already sunk behind the hills, he stood on the café's outdoor area, glad its roof was still intact, skinning and gutting the critter. The heart and liver he tossed to Wilma and found a clean plastic bag to seal the rest of the carcass for later cooking. There'd been a trio of drybones in the parking lot: on leaving, he ran over their heads.

From Fingal, he took the branch road to the right and to the west, the BearCat's headlights picking out debris and the occasional wallaby. Once, he saw a waddling echidna that must have been insane if it thought that ants would be out in this weather. The townships of Manganga and Rossarden held a smattering of large, private properties and a half-dozen commercial buildings spread along small clusters of streets. It took very little time to cruise them; by 1800 hours, Elliot had pulled over on Rossarden's Baker Street to consider next moves. This town was the last place he'd chosen to visit today. The map told him that a location north of here—Story's Creek—held an abandoned mine site and a couple of small farm holdings. Also waterfalls that had been a tourist spot before the Collapse, so there might be a ranger's cabin or café there.

"May as well head there," he told Wilma. "Gotta stop somewhere tonight, and it's not far if the road's not blocked."

Clouds gathered overhead. The wind picked up. Hailstones hammered his windows. By the time he made it to the sign that said *TURN HERE FOR STORY'S CREEK HISTORIC WATERFALLS*, visibility was so bad he was moving at a crawl. When his headlights picked out a sign advertising a hobby farm and bed and breakfast, he turned through the open gates and up the weed-covered driveway. There were no lights on in the main house or the two nearby cabins. Not wanting to bog or lose the BearCat, he reversed it under the farmhouse's side carport before powering it down.

Maybe he and the dog could sleep in back. Claire had stacked five rolled-up swags in there. But since there was no connecting hatch between the cab and the rear compartment, he would have to exit via the rear doors in the morning and this would expose him to anyone who might have seen the vehicle during the night and lay watching it. Though only the hardiest of hostiles would choose to lie in wait during a freezing cold night, anything was possible. The house would be safer: more windows to use to check their surroundings in the morning. Easier to get out of and escape into the forest if need be.

"Let's just hope the house is wind and hail proof," he told the dog.

He spent a minute listening to the roar of the hail on the carport roof: noise like that could combine with his bad ear to mask all sorts of hazards. And the storm would drench him if he scouted around now. But it would also make observing him tough for hostiles prowling out here. So he pulled a thin anorak from under the passenger seat and climbed out. Without moonlight or starshine, Elliot was forced to fit a flashlight under the pistol. He made Wilma stay under the carport while he kept the anorak pulled over his head with his left hand and held the .40 cal beneath it, reconnoitring the outside of the house. Safer for him and not the dog—since dogs weren't always on the lookout for tripwires. The possum carcass stayed with her; he could trust her with it. He stepped from weed patch to weed patch to silence his footfalls after inspecting each for traps first. Fifteen minutes later, he returned to the carport, collected the dog and made her carry the bag with the possum in her mouth. The back door had been wide open and there was no porch around there to creak underfoot, so they went in that way, entering a laundry room first and then a kitchen that opened onto a dining room and living area.

Place was a mess. He couldn't imagine anyone living here in the past couple of years. There'd certainly been no defenses outside. Still, only a real dumbass wouldn't check inside too. After sweeping the torchlight around the room and seeing no trip wires or makeshift pressure plates, he signaled Wilma to head down the dark hallway that ran off to the bedrooms. She vanished silently into the maw of the archway there, leaving Elliot to curse the surf-hiss in his injured ear as he tried to listen for her. He folded a mat and wedged it beneath the back door to fix it closed as best he could since the wood around the latch was swollen and rotten.

Thirty seconds later, Wilma was back. But she'd paused in the archway, her way of saying *something here you should see*. Treading between curls of leaves, trash and animal shit, he followed her to a closed bedroom door. He had one SERP flashbang, but he didn't want to use it. Wilma didn't seem particularly antsy, nothing to indicate she'd caught some scent or sound beyond the door that concerned her. He had trained her to be thorough, and that's what she was doing.

Still...

With the pistol to the crack, he eased open the door. No one was inside. It was dusty, but appeared to have stayed sealed from human and animal incursions. Even so, he patted Wilma's neck in recognition of her caution. After checking the rest of the house, and barricading the other two outside doors, he drew the curtains, then dragged a relatively clean mattress and duvet in front of the fireplace. There was a wood pile there, enough wood to warm the room and cook their dinner before he extinguished it. The cloud cover outside would make chimney smoke tough to pick out, and the drapes were heavy enough to hide the fire's glow. If any people had cleaned this place out in the past, they'd left plenty of crap behind: herbs and spices, canned soup and beans, baking powder and such. More importantly, they'd left a whole box of steel wool. He tore off a chunk then located a loose 9-volt battery in a kitchen drawer. Baking powder, steel wool and batteries were way more useful in Elliot's opinion than canned food and oregano. For one thing, steel wool made a great component for weapon suppressors. For another, it was useful in lighting fires.

A quick test of the battery's terminals against his tongue told him it had charge. He pulled the steel wool into shreds and mixed the fibers in the base of the fireplace with some dried leaf litter and pages from a paperback for kindling. Touching the terminals to the steel wool created a flame which quickly caught in the kindling. He added a couple of logs to create a modest blaze.

"Food and sleep," he told Wilma. "That's our agenda."

And although Elliot expected his thoughts and situation would keep him awake throughout the night, they did not.

17

April 6

A YEAR AGO, or maybe two, a scrub fire had swept down from the hill behind Mosely, taking out fourteen of the hamlet's houses plus its lone corner store. Mostly, this village south of Fingal was a blackened ruin: a few more years of hard weather and resurgent nature would see it vanish as it crumbled to dust and the bushland moved in to reclaim it. But one patch of houses had survived unscathed, two single-story bungalows facing each other across Mosely's only side street.

Elliot swung a leg over the first property's knee-high brick fence, squatting while Wilma leaped over to join him. The house might have survived, but it didn't appear anyone was using it. The open front door creaked and shifted in the morning's light wind, indicating airflow: an open back door or a broken window somewhere. The dog knew the drill by now. She trotted ahead, slipping past and around the door without touching it. Elliot moved onto the stoop and waited for her with one foot holding the door open and his rifle aimed along the central hallway. Breeze from within the house ruffled his stubble and carried the familiar abandoned house odors of rot and animal waste. Along the hall, Wilma disappeared, reappeared, disappeared, clearing the rooms. Less than a minute after entering, she came and sat on a clean patch of carpet with her ears calmly back, indicating there was nothing of concern or interest inside. He motioned *come on out* and she did, following at his heel as he moved on.

The second house took a couple minutes to clear, since every interior door was closed. A family of mice inhabited it—Elliot got to stomp a few on his way in and the dog quietly took another one down on the way out. The mice shared the home with roaches, so maybe there'd been people here not so long ago, leaving enough scraps to attract and feed the vermin. Or maybe the fire had driven them here. Any human squatters had done nothing to maintain the vermin house's once-pretty garden. From the porch, he could make out a bench seat beneath the gum tree that grew in the center of the lawn. But the hip-high grass remained wet from days of rain and dissuaded him from resting there. Elliot lowered his ass onto the edge of the porch instead, gaze still ranging up and down the street, the scorched bushland beyond.

Although it was early, and the air and ground were damp, the sun was out now, making him squint, giving him a headache. After seeking permission, Wilma came and sat against him with her head on his shoulder. He took out his canteen, took a pull, then poured some into his palm for her to lap at. From a belt pouch, he fed her a half-dozen pellets of old cat food and fed himself some blackberries he'd picked at dawn, emptying the little plastic container he'd kept them in and putting it back in his vest pocket. He raised his chin to the sky, stretching muscles and joints while the dog stayed vigilant for both of them.

"Goddammit," he muttered.

His third day now of searching town to town and house to house; his neck and shoulder were stiff, and anxiety had fast given way to despondency. *All this work and nothing to show for it.* It was time to stop this fine-tooth comb shit. Two things were obvious: first, it was taking too long; second, he would have to widen the search grid. Leaving the other Downsers at home might have kept his promise to Angie, but it severely limited the ability to search quickly and thoroughly. In his defense, he'd imagined interference from the surviving SERPs, or Death Druids unaccounted for in the biker war, or a hive of scav-rats, or some new posse of outlaws. Yesterday, any of these eventualities seemed highly likely to him. But there'd been no sign of anyone, least of all threats like that. Now, he thought, if she and Heng were injured or captured, all his slow and methodical skulking was creating a delay that might be fatal.

"I'm wasting time." The dog responded with a brief grunt that seemed to acknowledge this fact.

He consulted his watch: 09:19. Ten hours until he was due to check in with The Downs again. When he did, he'd be eating humble pie. He'd be asking them to come back up here with a sizeable group and finish combing the region. The one good thing about the three days' scouting was an assurance they'd be entering a relatively secure environment. The first place they should go would be that mine north of St Marys and the old accommodation site behind it. From there, they could systematically check the individual farms and other mine sites off the main roads.

The same two possibilities kept niggling at him: one, Angie and Heng were dead or taken; two, they'd changed their plans without telling home base and ventured outside the agreed region. It was maybe the latter he should start acting on. Closing his eyes for a moment, he conjured up the map in his head, unfolding it to picture the area west of here.

Bournstowe, he thought.

Thirty klicks past Fingal, the mountains peeled away and to the sides of a widening plain. Bournstowe was a small town placed near the confluence of two rivers. For no reason beyond caution, no Downsers had explored that far, ever. Even Angie had been pushing agreed boundaries by going as far as Fingal. He had a moment of perspective, looking at this country through the eyes of someone pre-Collapse. Thirty klicks here. Fifteen klicks there. The distances they'd been traveling slowly and cautiously were *nothing* to someone driving around these lands pre-Collapse, sightseeing or delivering a new fridge to someone up in the hills.

"Thirty klicks from Fingal, forty klicks from here," he told Wilma.

In the old days that'd take well under an hour, even with all these winding, narrow highways.

Now, with crap all over the roads, and with careless wallabies darting in front of the vehicle, it'd take him a few hours. And that was if a tree hadn't fallen across the road along the way.

And if it has?

If it looked as if it had been there a while, he'd know she didn't go that way. He'd have certainty.

Unless she was taken by someone and forced to walk there.

"FUBAR," he said. Wilma glanced at him hard this time. Something in his tone. He scratched the back of her neck. "Just talking to myself, girl. Just making myself crazy."

The best antidote to crazy was action. He had to stop mulling and do something. When he eased himself to his feet, Wilma came off the porch and raced to the sidewalk ahead of him, eager for the next house.

"Sorry, girl," he told her. "No more clearing here."

He pointed back along the street to the truck. Taking his meaning, she bounded off ahead of him.

I'll radio the Downs on the way to Bournstowe. If someone's listening, they can come up here and finish covering this area while I start looking further out.

"And if there's a tree across the road, I'll get out and goddamn walk."

THERE WASN'T A TREE ON THE ROAD.

There were two.

The first had fallen eight klicks beyond Fingal. A huge and soaring pine, it had originally stood a long way upslope to Elliot's right, landing so that its trunk lay within the woods. Only its crown encroached upon the road. With a drop-off on one side of the highway and heavy forestation on the other, Elliot thought this proved fortuitous. He stopped the BearCat fifty metres short and sat there for a good three minutes, squinting through the windscreen and then through his field glasses. Unable to detect any sign of a trap or ambush, he pushed ahead, steering around the thicker ends of the branches along the cliff-edge, plowing through and over the ones he couldn't avoid. The truck handled it fine and there were no traps...

But when he reached the second tree five klicks past the first, he was equally vigilant. *We are concentrating circumspectly,* Radler's ghost whispered in the back of his mind. Elliot agreed with him. The new tree was a eucalypt and this one thankfully had crashed down along the siding. Its branches choked the narrow highway, but not its trunk. He checked the road for signs of bullet casings, checked the mud around and across the tarmac for scrapes and boot marks, checked what he could see of the trunk for indications of axe or chainsaw.

Nada.

A small earth slide, it seemed, had freed the roots, caused it to topple and roll. The foliage was still green, and the wounds in the earth where it had come from looked fresh enough that this may have happened during the last week's rains, even yesterday. Recently enough that if Angie had passed this way a week back, the road would've been clear.

"She could be in Bournstowe," he told Wilma. "*They* could be."

He moved the shifter out of park and eased forward, muscling through and over the outer edges of the tree, grateful for a eucalypt younger and smaller than the pine had been.

From here, the road zigzagged as it followed contour lines around hillsides, but it began widening out. And the only things barring the way were the occasional fallen branch, a single rusting car hulk, and a trio of wallabies sunning themselves. The marsupials startled to life, two leaping off what Elliot thought of as a cliff along the left side of the highway. It was a source of constant amazement to him that these things could traverse terrain like that at top speed without killing themselves. The other bounded along the center line for a good twenty seconds before it too vanished over the cliff. Wilma pressed her nose to the glass as they rolled past the place where the last animal had disappeared.

"Some other time we'll bag one of those for dinner."

The A4 highway had already been angling steeply downwards as it neared the lowlands. Soon after the wallabies, it arrived in the valley proper, leveling and straightening out. And it was here that Elliot braked the truck hard in the center of the tarmac, leaning closer to the windshield with his heart pounding and his throat tightening.

Four klicks in the distance, the bush gave way to the valley plains and revealed a grey-brown smudge of human construction nestled in the apex where two rivers converged. There was something odd about the way

Bournstowe looked from here, something that pinged at the back of his mind; he couldn't make out with the naked eye.

But it wasn't the town that he focused his binoculars on. The thing that really caught his attention was the vehicle wreck five hundred metres down the road. The glasses only confirmed two things that he'd already noticed without them: the Land Rover had slewed sideways off the road to smash passenger-side into a telephone pole then bounce off and into the grass; and it was the same make and model Angie had been driving when she'd left The Downs.

No no no no no no!

He had already shifted his foot from brake to accelerator before he tossed the glasses aside. Fifty metres out, he pulled over and cut the engine. He snatched the MCX from its rack and was halfway between BearCat and car wreck before he realized he should sweep his surroundings first. When he halted, Wilma crashed into the back of his knees and peered up at him with mouth open and tongue drooping. Elliot made a circular gesture and hissed, "Scout!"

Her head snapped left and she bounded into the high grass along the verge. Elliot turned three-sixty, seeing nothing but open land and the birds wheeling and darting above it. He lowered the rifle and jogged toward the car. The carcass of a large kangaroo lay stiff and bloody in the gravel ten metres past the wreck. The car's front end angled back toward the road and the roo, the damage to it clear evidence the animal had caused the crash. Elliot had been told a hundred times by Downsers that a ute or SUV might survive a collision with a wallaby, but not a kangaroo. Might as well hit a cow.

His boots were off the gravel and in the dirt now, and while he didn't want to keep staring at that driver's side window, he had to and he did. The windows had become soiled with dirt adhering to the rain-spotted glass, but through it he could make out a shape that wasn't one of the seats. Also, he saw a smudge of brown the width of a finger that streaked across the glass low down.

No no no no no!

His hand was a half a metre from the door clasp when his boot came down on something small and hard and round, bringing him to a stumbling halt. Brass glinted up at him, reflecting the sun. A 9mm casing. He picked it up, stooping, turned his head to see another nearby and— over by the front tire—the weapon that had fired it. A Glock. Angie's Glock. Turned ass-up with its double-drum magazines facing the sky.

He tossed the brass and lurched to the door, wrenched it open. The stench hit him like a fist to the gut, but he was accustomed to such things. It was the sight of Heng's bloating body that threatened to drag up the blackberries he'd eaten earlier. Dark fluid leaked from the old man's nose and mouth, glistening in the sunlight filtering through the dirty windshield. The chassis had caved in beside him, and must have shattered his shoulder and ribs just as the impact of his head against the door frame must have crumpled his skull. One of Heng's eyes protruded like something from a Halloween costume.

Elliot took it all in within seconds before he dropped

away from the car and landed on his ass in the wet grass, the rifle falling beside him. He struck the meat of his thigh with his fist, once twice three times, keeping himself anchored, and beating out a rhythm for his grief.

No. No, Heng. Buddy. No. No.

But even while the shock hollowed out his innards and danced cold fingers up his spine, Elliot felt another emotion sneaking its traitorous way in.

Hope.

It made him feel dirty.

A good man was crumpled there, dead. His *buddy* was dead.

But Angie: she got out! Angie got away!

He felt around in the knee-high weeds, found another 9mm casing.

She got out. But she was shooting at someone.

That realization crushed his hope into a tight ball and threatened to toss it away. She'd hit a roo and crashed the car. The noise had attracted the attention of a local faction. They'd come for her. She'd gotten out and started shooting at them. But she'd dropped her Glock by the car. It was here and she wasn't. Very wrong.

Leaving his rifle where it lay, he crawled across to the front wheel, picked up the Glock. Its sides were slick with moisture. He racked the slide, but no round ejected and nothing was visible within the chamber. He detached the double C-Mags and a few loose rounds tumbled out of the top. A bad spring, then. Angie had rarely fired the thing in the years she'd had it. It was a biker-modified weapon and they'd screwed it up. The drums had held almost a hundred rounds. He searched around a little and only found a couple more. So, she'd fired as few as four before the thing jammed up on her.

But why leave it? He'd shown her how to check a weapon, how to remedy things like this.

She dumped it and ran.

Or someone took her.

"They *took* her."

This had been his greatest fear, that terror eating away at him for two days now. She and Heng had had an accident in a new faction's territory. She was hurt. She hadn't been able to fight them off. They'd taken her.

She could be right down there in that town, alive. She could be murdered and lying dead in the grass beyond that rock over there. She could be taken a hundred miles away to some sick bastard's harem—

"*Gone,*" Elliot whispered and it was like his spirit left him. He crumpled on his side, curled in the fetal position with his face in the weeds as a hole seemed to open beneath him, gravity dragging him down down into its depths, into the universe's heartless maw.

Gradually, he became aware of shifting patches of sun. They crept towards and over him, then past. A rough, thick canine tongue had started licking the exposed skin of his face and hands.

"Wilma."

The dog whined, nudged him. He got off his side and onto his ass, knees hugged to his chest. That seemed to satisfy the animal for now and she raced off to scout again.

What now? What now?

Angie was gone.

And Heng was dead. Dead. This tough old bastard who'd survived the Khmer Rouge in his youth. This man who had survived poverty and carved out a new life in a new country with a new language. This man who'd avoided the sickness that had befallen The Downs last year, who'd fought the undead, who'd fought with Elliot against slaver-bikers and prevailed. Killed by a random car crash. And if Elliot could find the strength to get up out of this grass and think of what to do next for Angie, he'd have to leave the poor old coot to bloat and rot in the wreck.

"Sorry, buddy. I'm so, so sorry."

He'd attended more than a few ceremonies for fallen vets. A fragment of an Army prayer surfaced and though Heng was probably some kind of Buddhist, Elliot hoped it meant something, hoped it would help him on his way to somewhere so much better than this. Claire would do the ceremony better, when finally someone came to take Heng home. But at least this was something.

"Keep in your mercy this man who died in the cause of freedom...and give him peace." His breath hitched in the middle of saying it. Like he had asthma.

Man up, said Uncle John's ghost.

You do the man thing your way, asshole, and I'll do it mine, he told him back.

No one was gonna stop him grieving a friend. And there was nothing the hell wrong with being lost and empty without ... without the woman you loved ...

"Nothing's changed," he told himself. "Nothing's changed." *Mission's the same. Still a search-and-rescue. At least I know I've come in the right direction now.* "Get up, asshole." And he did. He made himself stand there, anchored, although the world seemed to sway around him.

There was some kind of commercial property down the road a ways, close enough to see the shape of the building and a sign out front that marked it as a big store, far enough away he couldn't make out what kind. The next step was going there.

He'd start there.

He found an empty standard magazine for the Glock in her pack and reloaded it with ten rounds from the C-Mag, then slipped it into one of his vest's large inside pockets. The vest sagged with the weight of it. Then he shook his head, ignoring a mild twang in his neck. The bag and the Glock just lying here was a weird thing: if someone *had* taken her, then they would have taken these too. Unless they'd been watching too many old movies and feared an explosion from the Land Rover. Or maybe she *had* run and drawn her attackers away from the scene, and from Heng. Of course, she might have been shooting at wild dogs. Getting out and getting away meant she might be relatively uninjured; leaving her gear behind suggested a head injury, a concussion.

So, she's alive and mobile. Next step is that store.

No, he warned himself. Next step was moving the BearCat out of sight. Scoping out Bournstowe on foot would be slow-going, of course, but he'd be a helluva lot stealthier and more agile than he would be in an armored truck. There'd been a picnic area a klick back. Elliot took the truck back up there, driving slower than he wanted, keeping the noise down. He parked it behind a screen of

wattle trees. From his pack, he transferred some important shit to two field pouches and fixed these to his belt.
He stuffed a little more into his vest and trouser pockets.
The 9-volt battery, the steel wool, survival cord, a bag of
Lewis's trail mix, another bag with dried rabbit, a walkie,
and two of his three spare rifle mags—the other spare
being already in his tactical pants' right thigh pocket. A
magic marker for leaving messages, his multi-tool and a
spare mag for the .40 cal. He had his holstered sidearm, a
first aid pouch, a pouch for his flashlight, and fresh
canteen. The hunting knife sheath was already strapped
to his left calf, above his boot. In case he came upon some
new kind of stink like he had in the car wreck, he tied a
bandana around his throat.

He climbed out and locked the rear of the truck.
Wilma sat out on the asphalt with her back to him,
watching both ways along the highway. At his approach,
she glanced over her shoulder before resuming her
duties, keeping focus.

"Good dog. Good role model." He scratched her neck.
"Ready to roll?" She looked up at him, stood, tail
wagging. "Then let's go shopping."

THE SIGN READ **TALBOT'S HARDWARE AND TRADE
SUPPLIES**.

Or it *had* before years of bird shit and scorching sun
had blotted and bleached the writing. Still, there was
enough there for Elliot to piece it together.

He crouched by one of two tire piles framing the

parking lot entry while Wilma scouted the perimeter. The store's front glass automatic doors were closed, but he could see a side door ajar. Wilma sniffed at it when she reached it, looked back at him. He motioned her to continue around the outside and she obeyed. There were rainwater tanks and tractors in the fallow ground on that side of the building. A truck sat in the lot with a car smashed into the back of it. Another, cleaner car had been parked beside them. No bodies that he could see. No skeletons. When the dog appeared at the far end of the building, she had her ears up and she'd focused on the front doors as if to say *lemme in, lemme in.*

He gave a crow call to get her attention, then made the hand signal that meant *sit.* She did, reluctantly. She could guard outside while he went in quiet and slow. He crossed the gravel lot as fast as he could with his unreliable sense of balance, made it to the side door without contact, entered Talbot's Hardware at the storage/receiving area along the back of the building. This was an open area with shelves for lumber around two sides, a wrapped pallet of boxes in the middle, and a cold forklift rusting by the locked rear roller doors.

Also, two people.

Both were dead. Each had a bullet wound in the chest, and another in the head. Four small-caliber casings lay near them by the opaque plastic swing doors leading to the customer area. But there was an open office in the far corner back here, and Elliot could see the legs of another body inside.

Please, don't be her.

He headed over, his nose wrinkling against a waft of something like bad cheese or old vomit.

The dead woman in the office wasn't Angie. She was mid-forties with short hair. She wore a parka and jeans. Elliot adjusted his bandana. The stink was worse in here, the cause immediately apparent. Her jacket was unzipped, revealing that the front of her work shirt was matted with puke. There were spots of it on the floor nearby and again by a narrow bookshelf holding files and folders. A sawn-off rifle had tumbled to the ground just beyond her head, a .22 from the looks of it—the same caliber they said had been used on his face. His jaw itched at the memory. Judging by the burn mark around the bullet hole beneath her chin, and by the bloody mess in her hair, the lady had used it on herself.

What the hell was this? She took out two men in the timber store then puked and shot herself?

During the days of the outbreak, infected people often puked on their way to becoming zombies: people like Claire believed it was the body attempting to evict the virus, or whatever the infection was. Bandana still raised, he leaned toward the woman. No bite or blood on her exposed skin, no blood on her clothes other than that caused by the gunshot wound. He went out into the store and checked the two guys from a distance. Signs of vomit; no signs of bites. And they looked like regular dead folk, dead as long as Heng, little longer maybe, but not people who'd been zombified for any length of time before the final bullet.

"Poison, maybe?" he muttered.

A suicide pact? Then why'd she shoot 'em twice when once would do it?

There'd been a large hiker's pack set upon the office desk. And there was a viable weapon on the floor there. But all of it was potentially compromised. If these three had been sick in any way, Elliot didn't want it.

He checked the front of the store, then he and Wilma hiked down the road toward Bournstowe.

Once he was closer, what had seemed weird about it earlier became apparent. The town was surrounded by a trench. A massive trench.

He took Wilma up into the bush where they skirted the town for the next two hours. When he returned to his starting point, he sat down, drank from his canteen and poured a little in his palm for Wilma. "They did a damn fine job of defenses here," he told her.

There were no walls for attackers to climb or set afire, no chain link fences to cut through. These smart bastards had used excavators to carve a fifty-foot-deep dry-moat for their border. Then they'd carpeted the trench floor with jagged metal scrap, broken window panes and tangles of barbed wire. From what he'd been able to see, the trench was broken only where the narrow highway entered the town grid here on the east side where excavators had left the earth undisturbed for a fifty-metre strip, forming a kind of land bridge. At the far side, this "bridge" was barred by a head-high ridge made from pressed dirt.

This ridge—this barrier—arced around between the two ends of the trench. It was split in one place only, by a gate made from corrugated iron and—his field glasses revealed—mounted low on an assemblage of car axles and tires so it could be pulled aside. On the far side of the breastworks, two double-story houses provided perfect sniper posts. Within the trench, he'd seen the occasional ladder and pulley system, perhaps access for people to get down and clear the moat of rotting deaders where needed.

Now that'd be a shitty job, he thought. He leaned against a pine tree, considering the whole enterprise through his field glasses again, jealous.

"That's what The Downs should've done." Wilma responded with a low whine of enquiry. "Hell, it's what *Jericho* should've done."

If the people here were friendly, Claire and the others might convince them to loan out their machinery and personnel to repeat this back home. In trade for food and some of the Jericho antivirals. Then again, people with defenses *this* good might not be all that friendly.

If there are still people here, he reminded himself. While scouting earlier, he'd traveled uphill a while to see down into the town. From up high, he'd made out a modest downtown area with some sizeable stores, maybe sixty or seventy homes. Sports grounds had been converted into crop fields, as had the open land north of the town, though it was difficult to see details. There were plenty of tall trees to obscure details. Two tall windmills rose above the trees in the north-eastern corner of the town. Midtown, he saw laundry flapping on a line. But no people were visible, no one was moving around. And the only sounds in the little valley were the sounds of nature. Maybe Angie *had* been shooting at feral dogs.

But what about the people in the hardware store, then?

Christ, he hated questions. No, he hated *unknowns*.

Eliot sighed and pulled out some small pieces of dried rabbit and shared it with the dog. Neither of them chewed it, Elliot because chewing was hard, and Wilma because she was a dog. After that, he pulled out a plastic baggie filled with some little black and butt-shaped berries he'd found in a gully two days earlier. Lewis called them pepperberries.

A flash of memory hit him hard and stark as he opened the bag. *Oh hell, no way. These were growing on that hill outside Lewis's home the day I—*

He tried to cut off the thought, but it pressed through anyway.

—I didn't stop those bikers taking him.

He growled at the surge of years-old guilt. So long ago. So damned long ago. And he'd been so damned ignorant. He'd sat on that hill above the Oussefs' home, his belly aching with hunger, and these goddamned pepperberries had been growing right there next to him, begging to be eaten.

He scooped out a half-handful. Sniffed them. Popped them. Chewed carefully and slowly. Swallowed. Good to their name, they followed the initial fruity flavor with a good dose of spicy aftertaste.

"Not for you." Wilma folded her ears back in disappointment. "We'll get you something more later. Promise."

Elliot put away the berries. His jaw ached, probably from the chewing. He slowly eased it open and shut, open and shut, using his index fingers to massage the tiny muscles at the hinge. And he thought about egress into that town. And about the lack of human activity.

Maybe they're incredibly disciplined. Maybe they all moved out. Maybe they're dead.

A viral illness had hit Settlers Downs last year; it wasn't a stretch to think something similar might hit this faction hard. Not enough to kill them all, but enough to send many fleeing for a cleaner location.

And if they're really dead or gone, then I'm no closer to finding Angie.

A cloud passed across the sun. The temperature dropped and Elliot checked his watch. 13:15. Four-and-a-half hours until sunset. He stroked Wilma's back and shivered as a fresh southerly wind slipped in through the armholes of his vest. A wide sheet of clouds was headed in from the west; if they hung around it would mean another night without moonlight or starlight. Wilma licked his cheek and the scar on his jaw. He chuckled and gently pushed her head away, then got to his feet. "Come on, let's move."

As they walked, he told her, "We'll head to the hardware store. I'll set you up in there for the moment—away from those bodies." If he had to spend the night inside Bournstowe, it would keep her safe from any feral packs in the area. And if he didn't come back at all, the others would come along and find her after he missed his radio check-in. Wilma gave a low whine as if she'd understood what he'd told her. The dog was so damn smart that maybe she did. "Yeah, I'm sorry about leaving ya. But I wanna check that town alone. Alone and fast. Might be some climbing to do and you ain't that good at climbing. And if there's a firefight ..."

He reached down and fluffed her back hairs. To save time, he was leaving the BearCat where it was.

Shit. I should be wrapping Heng up in a tarp or something. Not real fair if Rit comes along and finds him like that.

But he really did want to move fast. Needed to.

"Speaking of which..." he said to Wilma and broke into a jog, ignoring a burst of fresh pain, squashing that down.

By the time he'd locked her in the store with food and water, it was past 14:00 hours. To save time, he tried starting an electric forklift parked around back. It started first time, purring softly. As long as he avoided manipulating the forks, the thing would stay pretty quiet. He'd found a white towel inside the store's lunchroom, so he tied that to the vehicle's frame like a white flag and trundled out onto the highway and down toward Bournstowe.

18

ELLIOT THOUGHT of the double-story buildings beyond the moat-trench as OPs: Observation Posts. Place a sniper and spotter in the upper floors and you could watch the eastern approach to town day and night from shelter and relative comfort. These buildings were a concern, which was why he'd put the white flag on the forklift. But nobody fired at him as he approached, then parked the forklift on the bridge. He climbed out and lifted both arms to his sides and away from his weapons: still nothing. No shouts of challenge and, thank God, no shooting.

He hadn't seriously expected either, not with the strong deserted vibe that was coming off this place. In keeping with the vibe, the gate had been pushed slightly aside to create a two-foot gap Elliot could slip through.

The first thing he inspected was one of the OPs. Empty—although a chair and table against a top floor window suggested they had used snipers in the past. Ahead of him, the Esk Highway became Bournstowe's High Street. But he wasn't yet ready to try that, so he moved along the inside of the moat then onto a back street. Immediately, he came across bodies in the road. Two people and a dog, a Doberman. From a distance, they looked to be dead a week or ten days.

He skirted them.

Zigzagging along the street, Elliot gave the houses cursory inspections, calling Angie's name softly each time he entered one. When he reached the first intersection, he froze. A young bull stood in the middle of the cross street to his right, down toward the main strip. Facing him. Staring at him. It was maybe a hundred meters away, a little less. The nearest house was thirty. He could make it if he had to, if he sprinted. He took a slow step in that direction. The bull just eyeballed him. Elliot took another step. The bull snorted once. Elliot tensed. Then the animal wheeled and fled in the other direction, hooves clattering along the asphalt as it veered left and out of sight. The echoes from its passage eventually faded.

"Okay," he said and took a deep breath to slow his heart rate. "You just *keep* your distance, fella, and we'll get along fine."

Crossing the intersection, he ducked onto the sidewalk. And found another body in the first yard he entered. This time, Elliot went in for a closer look. It was a woman, maybe a week dead. Crows and other scavengers had been at her: the exposed bone along one forearm had the frayed look that came from animals gnawing or pulling at it. In life, she'd been wearing a blue summer dress and yellow knit cardigan. Damage across her torso was consistent with multiple puncture or bullet wounds. And someone had definitely shot her in the face.

Deaders? he wondered again. His fingers tightened reflexively around the rifle's grip before he growled in self-disgust. Deaders were always his first thought in cases like this. And it was the kind of old thinking that Angie and others had been trying to snap him out of the past few months.

The deaders are dead and gone, he told himself. The fresh ones were, anyway. He'd put an end to the last of those in the pump room at Jericho.

So, intruders, then. Or locals murdered by intruders.

Perhaps he'd be better off performing a big-picture sweep of the town first, drilling down later. He continued to the end of the street where it ended in a T-intersection, hugging property lines since there were no more parked cars along here. Two more bodies lay in the middle of the next street and in similar condition to the woman he'd inspected. Six more lay in yards he passed, and another three where the new street crossed the main highway. He didn't stop to check cause of death with any of them. What was the point in that? He had to make certain this place was uninhabited. After that, he could walk around shouting her name until after dark if need be.

This new intersection placed him at the western edge of town. The downtown precinct was two blocks back down the highway, the main street. Best to check that next. He kept hugging the boundaries of properties along the north side of the road, detouring through a few at random. The few houses this end of town had their curtains drawn, their doors shut tight. Closer to the shopping strip, a gas station's doors were wedged open by another corpse. Elliot didn't investigate. More bodies were scattered along the main road between the shopping district's stores. Elliot counted nine.

A small department store mid-strip presented a potential place any survivors—or intruders—might have holed up. Or be keeping things of value—including captive blonde women. Its front windows were intact, its front entrance closed. Elliot circled back and around to the service lane behind it. No bodies back here. The department store's loading dock had a long, high roller door, partly raised to reveal a couple of feet of dark space beyond. He approached it from the side and peeked inside, squinting through the low light. A tidy stock and parcel area. He listened. Nothing. He got his ass up onto the edge of the dock and, rifle slung on his back, squirmed his way underneath the roller door. A stray hangnail of metal tore at his shirt at the shoulder. Thinking of tetanus, he swore quietly and felt his skin beneath the tear. Nothing. No scratch.

Thank Christ for that.

Inside the loading dock now, he folded himself up into a crouch, scanning the dim space. The place stunk better than most old-world places these days. Someone had maintained it since the Collapse: a couple of neat piles of boxes still on pallets; shelving units along the side walls; an open door leading to a white-walled hallway; a sorting table with two opened boxes of men's underwear on it; a desk with a pile of papers held in place by bottled water. Some dirt and leaves had blown beneath the door, but the floor was relatively clean. No corpses that he could see—although a long breath through his nose convinced him something or someone had died in the building here in the past few years. A rat maybe—it smelled kinda stale, so he dismissed it.

Hunkered there by the roller door, he slung the rifle on his back, took out the .40 cal. A little dizzy from his exertions, he nevertheless felt more stable than he'd been in months, fitter. He strained to listen through the ever-present white noise in his right ear. He stayed that way a good while, only standing when he'd marked off five minutes on his watch. A moment for his blood pressure to adjust to the new posture, a moment for the headspin to fade, then he moved to the desk. The papers were tally sheets, tracking stock. Clothing, mainly. Some medicines. The dates were recent, running from three years to two weeks back.

Yeah, something real bad and real sudden happened here all right. Another alternative occurred to him. *Some kinda civil war?*

If so, there might yet be survivors here.

He put the water bottle back on the papers and with an eye and ear on the open doorway into that hall, he went to the stock shelves and moved down one aisle, checking labels on boxes. They had a plethora of very good shit here. And they'd stored it methodically. Up at the top of one fixture where it met the wall, he could see handwriting:

PERFUMES: CHYPRÉ AND CHANEL.

Chypré. Apparently, it had been a damn expensive

perfume in the Old World. And it was one of Angie's favorites; she'd hoarded a whole carton of the stuff herself, and used it liberally when they weren't out killing SERPs.

Elliot suddenly wanted that scent again. Craved it. Needed it. More than anything. Laying the .40 cal on a lower shelf, he reached up with his left arm. It was just out of reach.

"Screw it," he said and removed a box of brassieres from the shelf beside his pistol so he could climb. He got both feet on the shelf, his right arm trembling as it grabbed the fixture frame to anchor him. He got his left hand on the side of the perfume box, leaned back to see better.

And knew instantly he'd done a dumb thing.

The collapse of the shelving unit was immediate and unstoppable. And the only thing Elliot could do was drop to the floor and curl into a ball as it all came down around him, as the fixture crashed over into the next and shelves and cartons fell and banged around him. The carton of perfumes must have slipped into the mess above him because when the mayhem was over, it was dripping down onto his pants, soaking them.

"You ... big ... idiot."

Two shelves had landed edge-first against his ribs. They were heavier than he expected, pinning him in an awkward position to the concrete floor. He was damned lucky they hadn't cracked a rib, but he'd have some bruises after this, all right. He was pinned there, but he felt like he'd be able to move out from under this mess. Once he got his breath back. Once his head stopped ringing from whatever had hit him when it fell off its shelf.

Yeah, great idea, he thought disgustedly. *You just take a minute, Elliot. You just lie here and do nothing. Under the crushing weight of this goddamned shelving unit. With all this goddamned perfume making you smell like a whore at Christmas. Get moving, soldier.*

He unfurled himself, shifting position, ready to worm his way loose. And heard something.

For the first time since reaching Bournstowe, Elliot heard the sound of human movement. Footsteps. The scrape of shoe on cement.

Twisting his head up and around until his forehead pressed into the cool metal of a shelf, he caught sight of two boots, work boots. Cleanish and newish, they shuffled to the point where one of his own feet was sticking out from under the fixture. One heel dragging, the feet passed his. Then stopped.

Goddammit.

His handgun. Where was it?

He felt about, trying not to disturb boxes and pieces of metal and glass, tying not to draw attention to himself —draw *any more* attention to himself. Still strapped to his back, the rifle was trapped behind him. Useless. The boots looked like men's, maybe because they were big. They shuffled forward one more step each, froze again. One foot was turned a little inward. The other dragged, as he'd already noticed. When the owner took another step, that boot caught on something and the man almost pitched forward, catching his balance just in time. Whoever it was moaned softly.

And hearing that moan, Elliot thought, *Ah, shit.*

The moan. The shuffling feet. Junkie? Town drunk? Insane scav-rat?

Deader?

No. It couldn't be a pusbag. The boots were too new, the trousers too clean. And it was walking. It couldn't be. Could it?

A wet, snuffling intake of breath dealt a blow to Elliot's certainty. The undead in Jericho's Night Court had been fresh enough. Fresh enough to walk, to snatch at him and at Jimmy. To bite.

Ah, shit.

It was swaying right there, a metre away from the sole of Elliot's right boot, listening, sniffing the air, smelling his sweat and maybe the dried rabbit on his breath. Hunting him.

He turned his head as far as he could, scanning for the pistol, fingers searching for it in the other direction. It was lost. He wasn't going to find it without making enough noise that the deader would hear and crawl in after him and find the bare flesh where the accident with the shelf had shifted his trouser leg up above his boot. And it would latch its damn teeth into him—

He gave up on the gun and found his hunting knife along his left calf, drew it out and held it by his thigh while the other hand and his left knee braced against the shelf, ready to push up and give him wriggle room. If it came for him, he might just spin himself around enough to get the blade closer to the deader than his bare shin currently was. Maybe. The mess on top of him was heavy and unstable. The blood roared in his ears, adding to the latent white noise. He needed to hear! He slowed his breathing. Just like he did whenever the panic attacks came upon him. He drew on the pain for focus, for clarity, craning his neck as best he could and straining his eyes to keep the dead man's boots in sight. They moved again: one step, two, four, six. Moving away. Moving on.

Thank Christ.

The boots paused again.

Then the deader vanished from sight. Twenty seconds later, it knocked something metallic onto the floor. Even with his compromised hearing, Elliot could figure that had been at fifteen metres away. At least.

What in God's name just happened? he wondered, knowing it should have sniffed him out. The newly infected undead had a damn keen sense of smell when it came to prey. And this one had been well and truly close enough to smell him ...

Elliot put his free hand to his nose and took a whiff of spilled Chypré. He huffed a laugh. "First time it's been a good idea to wear this much perfume."

HE CAUGHT THE DEAD GUY HALFWAY ALONG THE WHITE staff corridor to the main shop area, felling him with a blade to the brain stem. As he was cleaning the knife, he confirmed that the guy wasn't long turned and had bite wounds to his left hand and wrist.

Fresh pusbags. Just what the world needs.

But how?

Elliot went to the plastic strips marking the entry to

the shop area and parted them with his rifle barrel. The store beyond was modest: ten by thirty metres, so choked with racking and shelving that Elliot didn't feel safe venturing further.

"Angie," he stage-whispered. Then repeated it louder. Someone wheezed to his left. He leaned through the plastic strips to see better. Another deader had crawled from behind the register counter, arms pulling her along while her ichor-soaked legs dragging uselessly behind. One glance told him it wasn't Angie.

Through the dirty front windows, he saw two buildings across the street that it made sense to investigate next: a family doctor's offices where a wounded Angie might seek supplies, and the two-story pub beside it where a town might also stockpile such things and set up further medical services.

The pusbag's milky eyes searched for him. Her lips peeled back, teeth gnashing. He decided not to spend a bullet on her and withdrew to the back of the building, closing the door to the hallway to keep her inside. He left the way he'd come in.

Five deaders waited in the alley. Clustered together, all were children, sniffing the air. Where the hell had they come from? They were definitely undead, easy to discern even from twenty metres away. Their milky eyes, their shuffling, jerky movements. Upon seeing him, however, they broke into a shambling run—*not* something Elliot had seen deaders do before.

"Holy—!"

He sighted the MCX best he could left-handed and squeezed off three bursts, nine rounds—a wasteful amount to drop five bogeys. Then he jogged out of the far end of the laneway and around into the main street, stopping to catch his breath out front of the Chinese restaurant beside the department store. There was another deader, another child, crouched dormant in the sunken entrance to the restaurant. Elliot's arrival roused her from dormancy, set her to blinking, then smacking her gums, then snarling.

Elliot cried out in surprise and fired two bursts, shattering the glass door behind her and bringing her down on the sidewalk only a meter from his feet. That was three close calls in five minutes; this was getting ridiculous. Things hadn't been this pusbag-crazy since—

There was movement within the restaurant. A lot of movement. Chairs scraped. Bodies bumped things. Something mewled.

Elliot backed onto the street.

And the first of the undead within the building tumbled out through the shattered front door. More appeared past it, squeezed together, pushing out the remaining glass in the door, tripping over the first one still down on the ground.

Elliot checked down the street both ways as he kept backing off: figures had emerged from the gas station, and from a side street, drawn in by the gunfire, no doubt. A *lot* of figures, their movements jerky.

Jesus.

He sighted on a cluster of four, switched to single fire and dropped three of them.

The scrape-squeal of wood on metal drew his attention to the top floor of the pub at his back. An older man had his head out a window and waggled a finger in rebuke. "Don't point your gun at me! Just come round back and get inside."

Elliot lowered his aim an inch.

"I would've shot you already, if I wanted to," the man said, though Elliot could see no weapon. The man pointed toward the restaurant. "Better if you don't shoot them either. Only draw more in."

Dammit, he's right, Elliot thought, glancing up the street at the scattered clusters of pusbags trying to locate him by scent and by sound. The restaurant door continued oozing undead. They toppled over the sill, fell over each other, sprawling and crawling on the sidewalk. Seven of them. Eight. Ten. Elliot hurried along the narrow pedestrian path between the pub and the medical center, watching the roofs either side of the path for murderous, treacherous assholes. He emerged into an asphalt parking lot round back. Four deaders were there, one prone and unmoving, the others sniffing the air.

"Here," someone hissed at him. A rear door was ajar and a woman had her face to the gap. She stepped back to let him in. He yanked the door closed behind him. The woman was his age, tall, her red hair tied back, her wool-lined hoody unzipped over a Woody Woodpecker t-shirt. A t-shirt was tied tight around her cargo pants over her left knee like a bandage. She limped along the pub's side hallway to give him space.

Another lady in her early thirties sat back where the corridor reached the main bar, sat there in a wheelchair, holding a bow with an arrow nocked but not aimed at him. *Not yet*, said her expression.

Red Hair wrinkled her nose, looking him up and down. He'd forgotten the perfume stink all over him. *Better than zombie stink*, he felt like telling her. The woman's gaze shifted to his right, to a stairwell. The man from the window had come to the landing and was looking down at him. A lean, sour-faced man in late middle age. In one hand, he held a sawn-off .22 like Elliot had seen in the hardware store, but it dangled toward the carpeted stairs.

"David Caufield," he said. "Mayor of Bournstowe. Not trying to be rude, but would you mind showing us your wrists, your neck? That's great. Turn around please."

"You gonna shoot me in the back?"

"I told you before—"

"Yeah, yeah. Turning. There, satisfied? No bites. Just —" He dipped his gaze toward his pants. "—perfume all over me."

"I noticed," the older man said. "Would you also mind handing your machine gun to Rita?" His gesture indicated that Red Hair was Rita. When Elliot didn't immediately comply, Caufield added, "You can keep the pistol. We just want to even things out a little. That okay? I mean, we're giving you shelter."

Elliot glanced out the wooden door's small window at the trio of pusbags coming their way. "Giving me shelter? Or trapping me in here with you?"

"We're not the ones who woke 'em all up," said the archer.

Elliot ignored her. "And it's a rifle, not a machine gun."

Caufield waved the correction away. "Simple situation

here. We're strangers in a stressful situation and all of us are armed. We need to build trust, and lower the stress levels, and avoid accidents. You keep your pistol, but let Rita carry your rifle for the time being. Take the clip out if you want."

"Magazine," Elliot corrected him. "Question first. You know a woman named Angie?"

Caufield nodded as if expecting this. "Blonde hair, late twenties. Slightly injured in a car crash. She's safe. Relatively speaking."

Elliot's heart actually did a little skip at the news. Rita reached for the rifle, but he turned a shoulder, keeping his body between it and her. "How 'relatively'? How 'slightly' was she injured?"

"Mild concussion. Strained wrist. A few cuts. She's okay. But the young lady's not here in this building. She's in the yards with Pham and Tom."

"Yards?"

"How about we talk upstairs? Best you give our dear departed less to look at through the window. We'll talk. We'll feed you. We'll explain. And maybe you can help us."

Elliot couldn't smell cooking. Only unwashed bodies. "You have a *lot* of deaders in this town."

"Deaders?"

"Undead people."

"We call 'em nesters," Rita said.

"*You* call them that," Caufield interjected.

She ignored him and added, "So, yes, we definitely have a problem."

"Why're you all still here then?"

"Why not leave, you mean?" said Rita with a little heat in her voice. She glanced back at the lady using a wheelchair. "Because we have people upstairs who can't run around and climb and duck for cover. And the jury's out on whether it was worth sending people to the gates —or even to find a working car."

"You *did* send people through the gate, though, right? Two men, one woman?"

Caulfield frowned. "Three days ago. When Angie arrived *five* days ago, she told Pham and Tom about your settlement. Our trio were headed your way to ask for your help."

"Shit," Elliot said, relaxing a notch.

"You met them?"

"I *found* them. In that hardware up the highway."

"Turned?" Rita asked.

"Turn*ing*, I think," he replied, "before the woman shot them, herself included. They were covered in puke. That a common symptom now?"

Please don't tell me it's a new way of transmission.

"When they're first bitten," said the woman with the bow. "We think it's the body trying to get the virus out. And that makes 'em extra hungry when they ... you know."

"Damn," Elliot muttered. Two of the undead in the lot had tracked him to the door, butting against its window. He ejected the MCX's magazine and pocketed it, ejected the chambered round, pocketed that too. He swung the rifle behind him. "It's empty. I keep it. Talk to me about Angie."

"Follow me," said Caufield and went upstairs.

The archer and Rita remained on the ground floor as Elliot followed the older man. From the top of the stairs, they emerged into a function room. Some furniture had been cleared to one side. Tables, chairs. Plastic water jugs and cardboard boxes of supplies lined another wall. Beneath some of the tables, three beds had been made out of blankets and tablecloths. The far end of the room had an interior wall with three doors, one for a kitchenette, two for restrooms. The front wall had windows with street views, one of which was still open. The strangled mewls and groans and gasps of the undead came through it from below.

Caufield had gone to stand with four other people near the stacked chairs and tables: a man and woman in advanced old age. A young woman Angie's age. A toddler perched on the knees of the old man.

A shotgun had been left on a double stack of tables and out of the kid's reach. The boy rubbed his snot-crusted nose, regarding Elliot with open suspicion. The adults wore pretty much the same expression, minus the snot.

"You're guaranteeing me that Angie is safe?"

"Safe but surrounded. By our departed," Caufield clarified.

Well, who else would surround her? Elliot thought, forcing himself not to grind his teeth.

"Your name is...?" Caufield asked.

"Elliot."

"Well, I guess it's a pleasure to meet you, Elliot."

"This is all of you?"

"All of us left," said Caufield.

"You had an outbreak here? Or the undead arrived from someplace else?"

"Outbreak."

"*How*?"

"Fella came back from a resource run bit," said the young woman.

It took Elliot a second to get his head around her syntax. "He got bitten?"

"Yeah."

"Where? I mean, where was he?"

Caufield pointed vaguely south. "No idea exactly where. But I'm sure you know *old* ones are still out there. Decayed zombies. Our Craig must have stumbled into some long grass or sat down in the wrong place or something."

"And one infected guy destroyed your town. Infected all those people on the street out there."

"He got into the restaurant," said Rita, exiting the stairwell behind him. "The one you shot the door of. He got in there at breakfast time. No one knew he was infected. And he started biting and puking. Probably infected a dozen people before he left and chased down more."

Caufield added, "None of us expected it. No one was on guard. None of us had many bullets left, even when we did get to our guns." He shrugged. "You know how these things go."

"I know how they *used* to go," Elliot told him, and found a spare chair.

"And this is a little different," Rita said. "The younger the nesters are, the quicker they move."

"I found that out for myself."

"And once they infect you, you turn quicker than you would in the early days."

"Jesus, what a mess."

"Mess is worse now you let the restaurant ones outside. Took a whole bloody day to trap them in there."

"My bad," said Elliot, though he didn't feel particularly guilty. "The three in the hardware went to alert my people—and musta got bitten on their way out the gate. You send anyone else anywhere? Jericho, for example?"

The lady Elliot had realized must be the toddler's mom said, "Jericho's in the middle of nowhere, isn't it? Isn't that just farmland?"

"What's there?" Rita asked.

Before he could answer, Caufield said, "A few went east. Well, they were *meant* to. We think they became the zombies who attacked Angie after she crashed her car. Some other folks went west for help, and they had no radios, so we've heard nothing from them."

"*Where* in the west?" he asked.

"More northwest," Rita clarified. "Devonport way." She bent over a box of apples and fished two out, then limped over and handed him one.

Caufield said, "They went for guns and ammo from a guy we met once."

The old woman at the back stirred for the first time. "I told you all I didn't trust that man."

"You didn't even meet him," Rita muttered as she returned to the wall by the box of apples and slid down it, stretching her injured leg in front of her and wincing.

"It was worth trying him, Aunty," Caufield told the old woman, trying to sooth her.

It didn't work. "He probably killed them all," she said.

The toddler's mother shooshed her, eyes on the kid.

"What 'guy'?" Elliot asked Caufield, suspecting he might know exactly who it was.

"Ugly man," the old woman muttered before settling back and folding her arms.

Rita said, "He was scruffy and scarred and he said he had weapons to trade."

Elliot put his left hand to his ears and nose. "Scarred as in, missing these?"

"You've met him, too?"

"Couple times."

"Is that right? Well, it was me and Pham who met him on a resource run a couple of years back. We parleyed and that's as far as it went. Haven't contacted him since. Really didn't trust him."

"And yet you've sent people to find him."

"Desperate times," she said.

"His name's Rider. And let me guess: he left you instructions for a dead drop, to leave messages for him. In a town called ... In a town starting with E?"

She nodded.

"He's an okay guy, Rider. By today's standards. He wouldn't hurt your people if they didn't try and hurt him first. But he might be kinda busy right now."

Out hunting SERPs.

"Your folk might still be sitting out there a long time waiting for him."

"Or they might be on their way back with guns and bullets," Rita said.

"Or cutting their losses and setting up a new life in a new place."

"Not the way our people act," scolded Caufield. "We're a community built on mutuality, on being there for one another, on love in *action*."

As if confirming the sentiment, the toddler chose this moment to twist around and wrap his arms around the old man's neck, burying his face in his shirt.

Geez, kid. Way to make a Hallmark moment.

A thought hit him then, distracting him. Those dead-heads Angie had shot at were outside the moat, and the gate had been cracked open when he'd come in. Meaning this outbreak might not be contained so easily. And if Sturgis and others came looking for him in the morning, and he was still in here without any way to warn them, they'd be walking unprepared into a pusbag party.

With a sigh, he said, "I'll do what I can to get you out. But my priority is Angie."

"No reason why you can't get her out and us at the same time," said Caufield.

"You can really get us through all those departed?" the old lady said.

"With some planning, some luck and the weapons I have with me, I don't reckon avoiding a few 'departed' is gonna be all that tough."

Ironic laughter swept the room. Even the old lady joined in.

"What," Elliot asked suspiciously, "is so funny?"

19

Rita chuckled again. "A *few* departed?"

"A few, yeah," Elliot said. "There's maybe twenty out along the street. A handful in the parking lot out back. Wait. You said they were *surrounding* Angie's position?"

"At our peak, said Rita, "Bournstowe had eleven hundred and eighty-two people. Men, women, children."

Elliot gaped at her. There were six other people in this room and another downstairs. "Are you telling me...? *This* is all that's left? Out of twelve hundred people?"

"Plus the six headed for that weapons guy at Evandale. Plus Pham and Tom."

"The rest *turned*?"

"Or died," Caufield said with real sadness.

Elliot turned back to the window, watched the milling, living dead below him. "How many do you estimate are out there? Total?"

"Best guess," said Rita, "six hundred. Maybe seven."

"Holy shit," he whispered. He got it now. Rita was injured. No one else in the pub—except maybe Caufield

—was fit to dodge deaders and get a vehicle to the door to collect them. The only potentially fit people were trapped somewhere—with Angie—not by a few zombies, but by hundreds. He turned back.

"Where are they? Where's Angie? Exactly?"

Caufield drew him over to a wide town map tacked to a wall. The ragged square of the moat-trench had been sketched in thick pencil and someone had marked other internal boundaries and important locations with a thinner pencil. The square containing the town was tipped on its side, so the corners lined up almost exactly with the cardinal compass points. A large swathe of the northern corner was devoted now to "crops, cattle, chickens". Elliot hadn't heard or seen any animals. Apart from the bull.

"We know Pham and Tom are in the coolstore yards, in Building A." Caufield pressed a finger to a location toward the side of the crops area. "When your Angie stumbled into Bournstowe, she turned right for some reason and wandered through the crops. Lot of departed around there."

"Maybe she saw the windmills and wanted some height," Elliot replied. "To scope her surrounds."

"Whatever her reason, she was lucky Tom saw her outside the coolstore fences and fought to get her inside. She was pretty wonky on her feet. Pham was a student doctor before the world crashed. He treated her. Says she'll be fine."

"Pham and Tom are gay," announced the old lady suddenly. Elliot turned her way. She added, "And Pham's Asian."

Caufield grunted irritably. Rita eyerolled, not bothering to hide it. Elliot went one better, speaking his mind.

"And why is their sexual orientation and ethnicity relevant?"

The woman's pale skin turned red across her cheeks and throat. "Oh ... I'm just saying..."

"Well, don't." He turned his back on her, telling Caufield, "What *is* relevant is: are Pham and Tom healthy, and are they armed?"

"Healthy enough, but out of bullets," Caufield replied, hiding a tired smile behind the hand that scratched his long beard. He seemed happy that Elliot had put one of his people in their place. Perhaps he was sick of doing it. Perhaps it was good politics to let someone else do the rebuking. "They have short-blade knives. Plus a couple of shovels."

"How are they getting in touch?"

Rita pointed to a walkie on one of the tables. "Their battery's toast though. They told us it was dying the last time we talked and we haven't heard from 'em since."

"Bad batteries. Maybe your crew out trading for weapons had bad batteries too."

Caufield ignored this, focused on the map. "The irritating thing is: there are car chargers in the yards—for electric cars. But not chargers for smaller batteries. Bit of an oversight on our part, I'm afraid."

"These guys went there for a car?"

"They did. We're basically out of petrol here. We mostly use electrics and hybrids, which we keep at the yards where the windmills can charge them. We had a bloody good thing going here, you know, before idiot Craig brought the virus back in."

And it proves I'm right to keep on at Claire about security, much as she wants to enjoy the peace. This coulda happened to us.

"They went for the cars," Caufield continued, apparently committed to telling the entire *Ballad of Tom and Pham.* "One of them knocked over some scrap metal. Because the yard gates had been left open, departed had gotten in and—" He gave Rita a small glance. "—*nested* under some of the cars, some of the tarps, in the base of the windmill. Pham got the gate. Tom managed to put down the departed inside. But by the time the gates were bolted, a crowd was gathering. Tom thinks they'd been nesting out in the crops and got drawn in by the ruckus."

"Why the hell are hundreds of deaders congregated over that way?" He arrived at the conclusion himself a moment later as he took a fresh look at the map. "Ah. Your livestock."

"Yes," said Caufield. "They pretty much ate them all."

"Well," said Rita, "they ate *parts* of them, anyway. But they did *kill* them all."

"Not all," Elliot said. "You have a young bull running around town."

Caufield said, "That'll be Max. Glad he's made it this far. He's a smart one. Shame the poor fella can't make it out the gate."

Elliot turned to face the room. "Speaking of the gate, I have a truck outside. A BearCat, if that means anything to you." Shrugs all round. "Anyway, that east gate seems like it'd be heavy to open."

"Two-person job," Caufield confirmed.

"If someone can help me get it fully open, I can bring the truck in and around to your parking lot. Someone else distracts your departed out on High Street. Everyone else piles into the back. Then the distractor legs it down the alley to join us. But I pick up Angie and your other two guys first."

"You're putting me in the back of a truck," the old lady said unhappily. "Hope you won't drive too fast, young man."

"It'll be like a limousine ride, Miss Daisy."

Rita snorted. Caufield frowned at him.

"Daisy? My name's Glynnis."

"My mistake," Elliot replied. "So. Who's coming with?"

"I will," said Caufield

But Rita was rising. "Nope. These guys need someone here who can shoot."

The archer was obviously following some of this conversation from downstairs. Her voice called up the staircase, "I can shoot, dammit."

"Two people who can shoot," Rita called back. To Caufield, she said, "I can make it, David. If I keep the wrap tight around my knee, I'll be fine."

"I don't like it," he said.

"There's nothing *to* like," she returned. "I'm going."

He raised both hands, relenting.

"We have three bikes down in the front bar," Rita said to Elliot.

"Motorcycles?"

"Bicycles, sorry."

"Shit. Okay, then. You sure your knee is up to riding?"

"Just said it was. Better question is, can *you* shoot while riding?"

"Well enough," he answered.

She waved an arm toward the stairs. "You take first pick of the bikes."

"Just tell me they're not the kind with baskets."

20

ELLIOT CHOSE the .40 cal with the suppressor to take down the deaders at the back door. Then he headed into the front bar with Rita and started reloading his rifle. A sudden wind gust swept spray across the windows there.

"Goddammit. Of course it starts raining now."

"No, that's good," Rita replied, climbing onto a barstool. "Rain makes it hard for nesters to smell us. Hard rain blocks their vision."

"Well, duh," he replied testily. "The old ones were the same. Also makes us cold and wet, and makes metal surfaces like the gate slippery." And the cold of the past couple nights had set the muscles in his neck and shoulder and jaw twitching at times, not something he wanted happening when he was firing a weapon.

Scowling at his attitude, she added, "But these new ones are different. They don't like rain any more than you do. We think there's something about the sensation of cold they hate." She pointed to a fresh hiss of rain against the front of the building. "If this sets in, they might all try to nest again."

"Seriously?"

"They've done it before."

He checked his watch, then moved to the window. There were twenty or so of the bastards out there. But some of them were flicking hands and waving arms at the downpour. Not something he'd seen the undead do before. "Okay. We'll give it twenty minutes."

She toyed with her ponytail a few moments, then crossed her arms. Maybe her stare was so hard because she didn't know him, didn't trust him. And maybe it was hard because he'd said "duh" to her.

He returned his attention to the undead outside and the weather. "It's good intel, what you said. You're right: they're smacking and waving at the rain like it's alive. That's new behavior."

"These ones do a lot of things we never saw before."

"It's a variant. Of the virus."

"Duh."

"Touché." A couple of pusbags had shifted under cover along the department store windows. The zombie child returned to the restaurant doorway and curled up again. "Twenty minutes more of this and they might even forget they were out here looking for lunch."

After half of those twenty minutes had passed, Rita stirred. "Any chance I get one of your guns?"

He hesitated, then pulled Angie's Glock and walked it over to her. "Ten rounds only. No safety. Is it offensive for me to order you not to point it at me?"

"I have used guns before." She looked it over. "Have you chambered a round?"

"The pleasure is yours."

She jacked the slide back and let it slip forward. Then she took a shoulder bag off the counter and slung it across the front of her body. The Glock went inside it.

More minutes passed. Because the archer had long since vanished into one of the pub's back rooms, and because they were alone now, Elliot asked Rita, "Why haven't you left yet?"

"Me, personally?"

"Yeah."

"You're looking for a reason apart from me being a decent person?"

"I'm a curious bastard, is all."

She tapped the wrapping on her knee. "Maybe it's this."

"You're coming with me, so it can't trouble you too much."

"Then I'm still in Bournstowe because I'm a decent person."

"Fair enough."

She was squinting one eye at him. "You see everyone new as a threat, don't you?"

"Don't you?"

A purse of the lips. A shrug. She changed the topic. "How long you been out there? Outside town, I mean, looking for Angie?"

"Hours."

She hummed and looked away.

"What?"

"Couple of days back," she said, "I risked some scouting at the edge of town. I thought I saw someone moving in the bush across the river."

His turn to squint at her. "What exactly did you see?"

Another shrug. "Movement. There and gone again. Probably nothing."

"Probably some of your damn nesters."

"Why would they wander in the bush when there's a decent road out there? Why would they leave the food sources in town?"

He stretched and sighed. "Add that to the list of mysteries, sweetheart. How'd they get out? Where'd they come from? How'd they erupt all over the world at virtually the same time?" He checked then tapped his watch. "That's twenty. Let's ride."

THE MOMENT HE WAS OUT THE PARKING LOT DOOR, A DRIP of water off the roof hit him square in the eye, making him wink. The weather, however, had abated.

Without speaking, they rode their bikes onto the service laneway behind the pub and toward the east gate, making another left onto a cross street before a right again onto High Street. That whole stretch of the journey had required speeding past a number of undead who emerged from behind fences to snatch at them. All had been adults. Although they gave chase, Elliot and Rita easily and quickly outdistanced and lost them.

No nesters lingered around the east gate and they opened it without incident before riding as fast as they could manage up the sloping highway toward Talbot's Hardware, then past it. When a fresh shower passed across them, Elliot hoped it would discourage deaders from investigating the open exit point from town. Several hundred of them within Bournstowe's walls was a big problem; hundreds of them spilling out into the countryside might be a bigger one longterm...

His thighs were burning by the time he brought Rita into the picnic area with the BearCat.

"Nice rig," she said when she saw it. "That should do the trick."

"Can't see them biting their way inside," he agreed, and led her around to the rear compartment. In the cubbies at the very back were two drones as well as two tennis ball bombs. He handed the IEDs to her with a brief description of what they were. While she went to put these in the cab, he checked the charge in the drone batteries and inserted them, fired up the controllers and handed her both as well. "In case we need distractions," he explained when Rita came back.

"Good idea," she said, turning one over in her hands.

He dragged a big set of bolt cutters halfway out of another cubby hole. "Will I need these? To get into the yards?"

"No. All the gates are latched, not padlocked."

He shoved the cutters back in with relief. One less thing to carry.

He came outside, forcing her to step back, closed the door again then slapped it. "Think you could you drive this?" She gave him a withering look. Another Angie-like response, to go with all the other Angie-like responses she'd given him over the past hour.

"You're asking because I'm a woman?"

"I'm asking because it's a military vehicle."

"I drove lorries for my parents' nursery business. I spent a year driving road trains through the Northern Territory. If this thing has pedals and gears, I don't think I'll have any trouble."

He gave her some side eye. "We'll see." He'd only got this damn truck back. Now he was trusting it to a complete stranger. "Once we clear the pusbags away from the yards—"

"Wish you wouldn't use words like that."

"—you'll drop me nearby, then drive round back of the pub."

"Drop you? Seriously?"

"You want your people outa Bournstowe, right? Once you evacuate the pub, you'll come for Angie and me."

"And my two friends in there."

"Right."

"Which means you're trusting me? Or you consider my two friends an insurance policy."

"I'm trusting you. So, your friends better be where you say they are. Angie too."

"Why would we bullshit you about any of this?"

"Why do people do anything? Why did someone decide to break the world with this virus? Why are assholes assholes?"

"You finished?"

The question—and the jut of her chin—reminded him so strongly of Angie this time, it actually pinged him right in the chest. And got him moving. He went around front and put one drone on the floor, passenger side. The other, he placed on a nearby picnic table.

"You drive," he said. "I fly these."

He climbed in and slammed the door.

When she'd started the motor, he added, "And we pick up my dog from the hardware store on the way back."

———————

THEY PAUSED AT THE EARTH BRIDGE INTO BOURNSTOWE. Elliot had been flying the first drone directly above them while Rita drove. He now sent it zipping across the moat, then a thatch of thick bushland, a wide field of corn with the ears rotting on their stalks. Finally, he slowed it above the yards. One of the town's windmills was indeed within the fences here. Also, ten large sheds. *Outside* the fences...

"Holy Christ, that's a lotta pusbags."

The showers had passed. Fifty or more nesters had remained out in the open, hunkered down against the cold, concentrated around the north and west boundaries of the yards.

Elliot hadn't seen so many undead in one place since ... When? Where? If there really were hundreds more sheltering in Bournstowe's bushland and crops, he hadn't faced this many since the days of the Dead Line. He shook off the thought before it made him think too hard about Birdy.

He showed Rita the drone controller's video screen. "Rain hasn't dissuaded those ones."

"They remember there's food inside the fence."

"*Remember*? You think their brains have that kind of functionality?"

"We have a doctor—well, we *had* a doctor, before she went to contact that Rider guy. Anyway, she thought these new infected are better at retaining muscle mass and some higher brain function."

"That's all we need: smart deaders." He set the drone skipping northwest, getting a better lay of the land.

"Also, there's probably a vicious cycle going on. Only takes a few nesters to keep the noise up near the fence and others keep returning to check out what's going on."

"*Vicious* is the word for it."

Past some fenced-in corrals and paddocks, between them and a stretch of the moat-trench, the camera eye located a young horse sheltering behind a tractor. Elliot dropped the drone lower, unconcerned about the noise: if it drew zombies away from the yards, all the better. The horse seemed to be keeping an eye on a pusbag group who'd curled up underneath an open-sided shed. While they "nested" in relative comfort, this poor bastard was out in the weather, just trying to stay alive. And if that horse was having a bad day, things were about to get a whole lot worse for it.

"This goddamn world," Elliot muttered.

The drone zipped out and over the trench, then circled around toward the horse, staying low. The animal bolted, just as Elliot intended. He used the drone to herd it back along a path toward the yards.

"What are you doing?" Rita asked, leaning over to see the screen. "That's Socks!"

"Sorry about this, Socks. You or us, pal." Once the horse passed the shed where the nesters slept, Elliot sent the drone straight up in the air and into a hover above it. "Bombs away," he told Rita, and released the tennis ball IED.

The boom sent the nesters crawling out from underneath and in all directions. Bringing the drone down low, he flew it back to the yards to hook the interest of the nesters there, then sent it back toward the fleeing horse. Before long, plenty of the undead had caught sight or smell of the animal. They pursued it with a collection of children out in front and sprinting. Socks wheeled and reared and tried to find a way out of trouble. He ran straight into a stretch of wire fencing and had to change direction again, panicking.

Rita slapped Elliot's arm. "You bastard."

"Let's go," he replied. She put it in gear, muttering. He added, "You can build Socks a statue when this is over."

"You're an arsehole."

"Sounds about right."

He sent the drone whizzing across the heads of the nesters who'd stayed near the yards and in the direction of the pub, hoping the stragglers would follow the noise. Buzzing the small crowd on High Street, he crashed the drone into the asphalt out front of the petrol station.

"That noise'll distract the ones out front of the pub," he said.

"Hope you're right." Through the gate now, Rita turned off the highway and onto a rutted dirt track that led toward the yards.

Elliot dumped the drone controller in the footwell by

the other drone. Then he took his rifle from the rack. Referencing his memory of Caufield's map, he knew they were a couple hundred meters from the yards. He could see the windmill through gaps between gum trees.

"Let me out here."

She pulled up with a mild squeak of the brakes. "You sure?"

"Totally," he insisted. He cracked the door. "When you return, come in slow. Unless they hear you and try to intercept. If they do, you get to us as fast as you can. Have someone ready to open the back door, probably Caufield. Your archer friend can sit up here with you and maybe use the mayor's rifle."

Rita gave him a *good luck* nod and then he was outside. As she reversed along the track, he slung the MCX over his back and pulled the pistol, staying close to the interlocking banksia trees that lined the western side of the track. A deader detached itself from among them but it was slow because the branches had snagged in its clothing. It snarled in frustration. A headshot later, its troubles were over.

Ahead of Elliot, the grass grew long on the east side of the track and two abandoned mountain bikes poked out of it. Two bodies lay sprawled near them and—because he figured the bikes belonged to Tom and Pham—he went over to them. But the corpses looked and smelled like deaders—and neither one of them had been Asian. Elliot's attention whipped to his left and ahead where something briefly shook the banksia branches. He steadied the .40 cal with his left hand, wondering how many nesters would emerge this time.

A moment later, the pistol flew from his hands, gone, as if yanked away by a string. His hand stung. It took him a second or two to compute what had happened. Instinctively, he swung right. A man wearing a Ghillie suit emerged from the grass near the bikes, training an MCX rifle on Elliot. The rifle had a makeshift suppressor fitted to it, explaining why Elliot hadn't heard the shot with his bad ear.

Then from his left where the branches had been shaking came the voice of another man. A man climbing out of cover. "You're a hard man to find," he said.

Elliot had to squint a second to recognize him. The former cop still wore his cop clothes, but had his face gaiter scrunched down around his neck. He wore no armor. But he did have a rifle.

Elliot's heart seemed to gum up within him. He hissed, "Da Silva."

The man in the camouflage suit—the man who'd shot his pistol out of his hand—ventured closer. He growled, "And I'm Miller, in case ya forgotten. *He* reckons you're hard to find. But I don't reckon you'll be hard to kill."

21

DA SILVA PLUCKED Elliot's fallen handgun from the path, then circled him, popping out the magazine from the .40 cal and pocketing it. He tossed the damaged weapon aside. Miller kept his distance and kept his angles, denying Elliot the chance to reach for the rifle on his back or the knife on his leg.

"You look like shit, Elliot," Da Silva said when his inspection was complete.

Back atcha, Elliot thought. Da Silva had dropped a ton of weight since he'd seen him last. His beard was heavy, and his hair had twigs in it.

"What happened to your face?" said Miller.

Mind churning, Elliot did not reply. The tinnitus in his right ear was peaking, probably coz his blood pressure was. He wanted to tear out that ear, tear it off and jam it—

"That your drone drawing the zeds away from the windmill compound?" Da Silva asked him. "Seemed to work pretty well." He glanced up the road; Elliot realized he could see one corner of the chain link fence from here. There were maybe a dozen deadheads left in sight near it, and all of them faced away from him, noses in the air and ears cocked. North of them, the commotion from the ones who'd chased the horse grew in volume.

What could he do, what the *hell* could he do? Neither one of these pricks was going to make a mistake, drop their guard, give him an opening.

Da Silva sniffed and wiped his nose on the sleeve of the black sweater he wore beneath his tactical vest. "Hah! I can see those wheels turning in your head there, mate. But there's no way outa this one."

"Waited too long for this," Miller confirmed.

"We been waiting it out in a farmhouse west of here, listening to these Bournstowe dickheads radioing each other about their troubles. Pretty lame entertainment, but you know: entertainment's been hard to find since you ruined Jericho, you sonofabitch. It got better the other day, though." He lifted a finger to one ear, miming listening. "A newcomer's voice came on the radio. A woman stuck in the windmill yards. A voice that sounded a *lot* like the bitch who radioed Jericho and said, 'Scheduled transmission to Miller. Richardson made it here safe and you should bring all the meds and ammo when *you* come.'"

Miller swore softly. "Caused a lot of trouble, that bitch. Made a lot of trouble for *me*."

"I never doubted you," Da Silva told his buddy. To Elliot, he said, "But her little stunt made plenty of others doubt him. Luckily, karma's as big a bitch as she is. And she and you are gonna find out how bad karma can be."

Miller's turn to sniff. "When the bitch said on the radio here she got injured in that car crash, I said to Jason, 'What if Elliot comes lookin' for her?'"

Commencing another circuit around Elliot, Da Silva continued, "And *I* said, 'Or what if he got hurt too, but he's hiding out in the bush somewhere nearby?' And how about that? Here you are. In the flesh. All—"

"Ah, Jason?" Miller said, gesturing to his right.

A pod of three undead had detached from the others up by the compound. They ambled onto the path, heading closer.

Da Silva rolled his shoulders, cracked his neck. "I'll take care of 'em. Cuff this prick while I see if the bitch is still in the compound. We'll try'n start one of those cars in there, chuck these two in the boot."

If Elliot could attract a couple hundred pusbags to the compound gate, no one would be driving a car through them. That might upset Da Silva's planning enough to force a mistake, an opening for Elliot.

Yeah, that's good. Welcome back, brain.

"Hey," he said before Da Silva could march away. He said it loud, speaking over the whining hiss in his right ear, speaking loud enough to maybe make some early trouble and keep the SERPs away from Angie. "You're the man, huh? Big man on campus? You wanna prove that? Lose your weapons, and take me on, *mano e mano*." Remembering something Rider had said when they'd first met, he added, "Let's dance."

He knew he was in trouble if Da Silva said yes. His chances were poor, his fitness nowhere near where it used to be. But it was something. And if it—

He blinked in surprise. There'd been a moment, just the finest fraction of a second where a look passed over Jason Da Silva's face. Not hunger. Not amusement. But anxiety. Fear. Fear of *Elliot*. In that moment, he saw the man for the coward he was. Compensating for it by a lifetime of bulking up. Spending his adult life hiding behind a badge, a weapon and body armor. This was Kyle's successor, the heir to the SERP and Jericho throne. A total coward who'd lost his position, who no longer had body armor—and who wouldn't in a million years come out from behind his weapons.

Da Silva recovered his swagger fast and simply laughed off the suggestion. Then he jogged toward the trio of approaching deadheads, pulling a narrow-bladed bush knife.

Miller made Elliot place *his* knife and his rifle on the ground, made him kneel, then secured his hands behind him with a double-looped cable tie. He slipped his rifle strap from his shoulders before slinging Elliot's rifle over his back. The knife, he ignored. He used his boot to prod Elliot to his feet.

Da Silva was already out of sight by the time Elliot was being pushed along the path. The three nearest zombies lay face up, each oozing gore from an eye. Three more lay near the compound gate, which Da Silva had closed behind him. Through the fence, Elliot saw several cars and a scooter inside an open garage shed.

They get us in the trunk of one of those and we're dead meat, he thought.

He drew in a lungful of air and shouted Angie's name. As loud as he could. It hurt to shout. Even more than the rabbit punch he then received to the back of his head. By the time he'd regained his balance, Miller had his rifle's suppressor pressed between Elliot's shoulder blades. The infected who'd been pacing haphazard patterns thirty or forty metres away had turned toward the sound, now sighting human targets even with the rain beginning to thicken. From the corner of one eye, Elliot noticed more emerge from the bushland that stretched between here and the back of Bournstowe's shopping strip.

Elliot turned, expecting Miller to be reaching for the gate. But he wasn't. The ex-cop had his back to it, and he had a twist to his lips that was probably meant to be a smile. Elliot had a good idea what the guy was thinking.

Shit.

22

"WE GOT TIME," Miller said. His rifle indicated the closest four undead individuals. "You wanted to dance. Away ya go."

It was a sidetrack. A distraction. Elliot wanted to beat on SERPs, not Bournstowe's walking corpses. He wanted to get inside that compound after Da Silva.

"Git," Miller told him. "Go git 'em."

With no choice but obedience, Elliot moved closer on an intercept, then shifted his angles to meet the nearest zombies one at a time. But if he succeeded against these first four, there were plenty more coming up behind them. Others had appeared on the path from the highway, also; they must have been nesting out in the bush behind Da Silva's hiding place. Miller had his back to them—so maybe Elliot's endgame here was distracting Miller long enough to get him nailed from behind.

He tried a little fancy footwork, boxer style, surprised when his legs obeyed him, surprised he didn't topple onto his ass. The first deader to reach him took a front kick to the knee. The second took a side kick in the same place. That put both on the ground, but didn't stop them dragging themselves at him.

He skipped around them toward the third in line—and missed his next kick, almost falling. The nester was female and she was skinny, but the grip she got on the side of his vest was firm. Elliot was forced to whip his body sideways, breaking her grip and sending her stumbling past. Christ, if his hands weren't pinned behind him by cable ties, he could have punched her in the ear, he could have gotten one of his spare rifle mags out and used that to break her skull. All he could do was continue the pivot he'd started, use his bodyweight to keep her moving past him, then stamp on her achilles.

When she fell on her face, arms spread, he stomped hard on the soft area below the back of her skull. Then he hopped back a few steps to get his breath and his bearings.

Through the roar of blood in his right ear, he could hear Miller laughing. The SERP called, "Hey, Irish Dancer, this is as good as the Night Court. Better." He chose that moment to check behind him—and dashed Elliot's hopes. His rifle spat a few rounds, dropping the first of the zombies back on the path.

Watching this, Elliot made a misstep and also fell, landing on his side. The next deadhead in line made a dive for him. Elliot barely avoided it, managing to roll out of the way and leave his attacker to hit the mud where he'd been. The reaction was desperate, uncontrolled. His neck screamed where it joined the shoulder.

The zombie turned his way, jaws gnashing, one hand clawing. Elliot channeled energy from his agony and got up. When the deader's next swipe went wide, he slammed a boot into its face, then crushed its temple with his heel. It wasn't *dead* dead—it still twitched—but it didn't rise again.

Four down. Many, *many* more incoming. He needed a new endgame. He needed—

He froze in place when the unmistakable sound of a gunshot came from within the yards. It was muffled, but clear. A handgun fired from within a building. The only person in there with a handgun was Da Silva.

Elliot looked to Miller.

"Don't worry about that," the SERP warned him with rifle raised. "Just focus on yer river dancin'."

Elliot hesitated, his whole body aching, his whole body wanting in to that compound. "I will *kill* you, Miller. And it'll goddamn hurt when I do."

Miller laughed. "Ya haven't killed me yet." He took one hand off his rifle to shake the gate. "And I'm closer to safety than you are."

Another noise, then: from the air above them, the high-pitched whir of something fast, something inbound. Miller jerked his head up and around toward it. A drone struck him full in the face, rebounding to land upside down in the mud. There was no sign of the BearCat; presumably Rita or someone else on that truck had grabbed the spare drone he'd left behind and flown it over for a look-see. And seen an opportunity. And saved his life.

Miller crumpled against the chain link gate, hands

against his face, blood sliming his fingers, his rifle falling into the mud beside the drone. Elliot was already running before the man's knees touched the earth. Reaching him, Elliot kicked him over onto his back. One of Miller's hands reached out for his fallen rifle. Elliot dropped his right knee onto the cop's exposed throat, putting his full weight into it. Immediately he bounced up, and braced his shoulder against the fence. He kicked Miller in the temple and stomped hard on his face, again and again and again, until he realized that Miller had stopped squirming.

"Told you it'd hurt," he said.

Plenty of chain link wires had been tied off nearby, producing short and narrow metal spikes. A few of these poked from the fence. He turned his back to one of them and got the wire-end jammed into the gap between one of the loops around his wrists and the plastic locking mechanism. Three firm jerks downwards and the lock snapped off. Set free, his hands flew out to the sides while one of the plastic loops sailed away into the mud. The other was still fixed to his wrist like a hospital bracelet, but that was fine with him.

Elliot squinted along the path from the highway through the screen of rain and approaching undead: no sign of the BearCat. Lifting the edge of the fallen drone with his toe, he gave the camera a *thank you* look. The picture would be upside down on the controller screen, and he had no idea if its crappy microphone was working, but he said, "Wait for us outside the gate for thirty minutes. Don't let any strangers in the truck." Then he let the drone drop, snatched up Miller's MCX and—

wielding it lefthanded—sprayed fire into the closest infected. When the magazine was spent, he ejected it and fitted a spare from his pockets. He chambered a round before transferring Miller's .40 cal to his own holster.

Then Elliot went through the gate and into the yards.

23

THERE WERE ten buildings in the coolstore yards, including the windmill in the north-east corner and the open garage in front of him.

Ten buildings in two rows.

Ten buildings, but no sign of Da Silva. Or of Angie.

That might mean Angie was successfully avoiding her hunter. It might mean Da Silva was being careful and thorough. Best-case scenario, she'd gotten the drop on the prick and put a shovel through his head.

When was the last time you experienced a best-case scenario? Radler's ghost asked him.

Right eye squinting in rhythm with the spikes of pain in his neck and shoulder, Elliot headed first to the garage where there were lots of vehicles to hide in or under. It proved to be a simple shed, no offices at the back, no toilet or kitchen.

And no sign of Da Silva. So he ventured well inside and out of the rain, stage-whispering Angie's name.

Deeper inside, someone shuffled their feet. He caught a glimpse of an Army Surplus camo jacket as the person scuttled between cars, seeking better cover.

"You Pham or Tom?" Elliot asked them.

A man rose slowly from behind a black Toyota hybrid, his hands up. A young, white man with a receding hairline. "Tom."

"Drop your hands, Tom. Seen an armed stranger sneaking around here? Apart from me?"

Tom just blinked at him, mouth opening and closing.

Something occurred to Elliot. "The gunshot: your partner?"

Tears welled in Tom's eyes. Instantly.

"Shit," said Elliot. "Focus on me, man. It's bad, but it'll get badder if you don't help me. Where is the guy who shot him?"

Tom pointed a shaky hand. "The... The shed behind the one next to us. He *was* there," he added hurriedly and swiped at his eyes.

Elliot heard his unspoken thought: *before I got away.*

Elliot edged sideways, watching the front of the building. "And where's Angie?"

Tom pointed again. "Windmill."

"Okay. Tom. You're—*Tom!* Listen to me. You're gonna stay in here."

"No," Tom hissed and shuffled forward. "Don't leave me alone."

"You're safe in here. Stay here. Might take a few hours, but Rita or I *will* be back to get you. In a big-ass armored truck, okay? You're safe here. Get down, or get in one of the cars, and keep your head down."

Tom wiped at his eyes again. "Who is that man?"

"Someone I'm about to kill," Elliot replied.

When he left the shed, he did it with his head on the best swivel he could manage, vectoring toward the windmill. The rain pounded on the metal roofs and walls around him. He slipped along the grassy path between two sheds. Open ground lay at the end of it—beyond that, back fence. The windmill would be to his right when he came out of the grassy alley.

Shouting erupted from that direction, voices rising above the drumming of the rain. A woman. A man. Elliot hurried to the end of the alley and peered around the corner with rifle up.

Caufield's people had erected a simple tin shed around the windmill's base with rubber-coated cables snaking out of it and overhead toward the other buildings. This small shed had a single door on this side. It was open. Angie came out through it, swearing over her shoulder.

Her appearance was a shock. She looked even more ragged than Elliot had expected. Her face and hands were filthy, the dirt streaking in the downpour. Her hair was untied and draped limply across her shoulders, water plastering strands of it to her ears and cheeks and forehead.

A hand appeared from the gloom in the shed to latch onto her shoulder. Da Silva appeared at her back. He wasn't taller than her, but he was wider. Both shoulders were exposed, as was the arm with the .40 cal, the arm not holding her.

Neither of them had seen him yet. Elliot tried to sight

on the SERP, but the far end of his rifle wobbled, wouldn't stop wobbling. He lowered the weapon a moment, took a couple of breaths. In that time, Da Silva pushed Angie ahead of him, heading for Elliot's position. He raised the rifle again. And again, the damn thing shook in his hands.

Angie froze. Da Silva's weapon came up as the SERP finally caught sight of him. From a distance of thirty metres, he fired.

The bullet pinged off the side of Elliot's building before Elliot had even withdrawn out of sight.

Well, this is a problem, whispered Radler's ghost.

"You're telling me," Elliot muttered back, and let the rifle hang from its sling. He pulled the .40 cal with his left hand. It was lighter. Hopefully, he could hold it more firmly. He dropped down low and risked another peek around the corner.

Da Silva and Angie were gone.

She called out for him then, telling him to leave her and help the "other people". And she meant it. He knew that. But all she'd done was give him a direction, tell him which way to go to follow her.

He ran back the way he'd come, along the makeshift alleyway away from the windmill, then peeked to the left at the corner. He counted ten seconds, fifteen, thirty. Then Da Silva and Angie emerged from behind the far end of the next building down, headed for the garage. The ex-cop checked Elliot's way, but didn't appear to see him. And he was behind Angie, turned side-on. He was open. For the next few seconds, as they crossed the gap between buildings, he was open. Pre-injury, Elliot might have taken the shot. At this range and with a rifle, it would have to be a good one, but he could've done it. It might not kill Da Silva outright, but it would hurt him enough to make him stumble, make him drop his weapon, give Angie the opportunity to finish the job. But Elliot's damn arms kept trembling. He wasn't the man he used to be and there was no way he could risk trying that shot.

He fired instead into the open air ahead of them. It had the desired effect, herding Da Silva back the way he'd come, away from the garage. Angie resisted then, tried for an elbow strike to her captor's cheek—and received a hard slap to hers that sent her to her knees. Before Elliot could think about using the opportunity, Da Silva dragged her to her feet again and on toward the cover. Elliot tracked their retreat with the handgun up, swearing. They were gone in seconds, headed no doubt for the fence at the back of the yards.

There would have to be another gate there somewhere. A pedestrian gate. There was no reason for the Bournstowe folks *not* to install one back there, for convenience. Da Silva had obviously realized that Miller was gone. He could either shoot it out with Elliot or look for such a gate and flee through the cornfields.

He would also expect Elliot to return back up the narrow alleyway. So Elliot hurried the other way, toward the wider space where they'd just been, unable now to sprint, but pushing himself as hard as he could. His one advantage, he thought—and it wasn't *much* of an advantage—was that the SERP didn't know how badly the injury to his face had affected the other muscles and tendons, had made him drop a whole lotta fitness.

He's running coz he thinks I'm the same guy who escaped from his custody, who took Jericho from him.

It might make the bastard rush, make a mistake. Mistakes might give Angie a chance.

Or get her killed.

When he finally reached the corner where they'd disappeared, he came around it and instantly saw the pedestrian gate to the cornfields. Forty metres away from him, with another ten-metre gap between it and the closest corn. It stood wide open and he hustled toward it. Because there was no sign of Angie or Da Silva.

There *were* nesters, however. A bunch of them heading into the cornfield. Two standing on the edge of it and hesitating as if they couldn't remember why they'd emerged from it. And a cluster seeping *into* the yards through the newly opened gate. The leader of this cluster saw Elliot as he closed the distance between them. The *thing* had been a teenager when it was truly alive; young enough in unlife to start running toward him ...

Elliot experienced a moment of detachment.

This was like the moment in a movie. The moment where everything went to shit at once. Where the hero had to fight a battle on multiple fronts. A moment where that hero would always say something snappy, some clever one-liner. But the only thing that came into Elliot's mind was ...

"I ain't no hero."

Firing from the hip, he nailed the teenage deader and the first two deaders who'd followed it inside. But it took a lot of bullets to do it. He switched out the handgun for the rifle to kill the rest of the cluster.

And after that, Elliot passed through another gate.

24

Bournstowe's nesters were everywhere, phantoms in the forest of cornstalks, haunting Elliot's peripheral vision.

Stumbling into his path, half-blinded by the rain.

Wasting more of his bullets.

Distracting him from finding Angie.

Some of the damn things whirled on the spot; they reminded him of that stupid cursor-circle computers once put onscreen when having trouble with processing. Others thrashed about in the certainty of nearby prey, bending and breaking corn stalks.

When Elliot was so far into the field that he couldn't see where he'd come from, the nesters thinned out. Shielded by the driving rain from the ones he could see, he could focus better on his pursuit. Only, he wasn't sure for a moment if he was even heading in the right direction. If Da Silva and Angie had left any sign of their passage, the weather and the churning left by dozens of deadheads was obscuring it. When Elliot caught sight of a narrow workers' path between this field and a neighboring one, he veered out on to it.

He pushed himself. Though his lack of conditioning was starting to tell. Though his spiking pulse rate poured electric shocks into his neck and face. Though he'd started getting white patches in the corners of his vision. Though his legs kept trying to disobey his brain.

He felt sure he was falling behind, playing tortoise to Da Silva's hare. Even if he could keep out of the pusbags' bite-range, he could be screwing around out here for hours without tracking down Da Silva. Except that the SERP wasn't stupid: he *had* to be headed for the earth bridge through the moat. And that gave Elliot a direction.

A moment later, this direction was confirmed as the right one when Angie shouted something caustic at Da Silva, swearing up a blue streak.

I'm coming. I'm coming, babe.

Out of nowhere: an almighty commotion to his left. A brown smudge hurtled through the cornstalks. A horse burst out of the crops ahead of him—*Socks!*—then plunged immediately into the next field. There were fence posts all over the place here; lucky for the horse, the wire had been removed some time in the past. In the lull that followed, Elliot paused and braced himself, knowing what was coming. And sure enough, a dozen child-zombies boiled out from the crops in chase of Socks. Only one of them emerged close enough to Elliot to notice. He had his knife out by the time it changed direction. When it was close enough, he sidestepped and tripped it before plunging the blade into its brainstem. The others were out of sight already, but audible as they howled for horse blood. That sound cooled Elliot's own blood: he'd never heard that before, deaders baying like pack predators, deaders calling to each other on the hunt. *New virus variant. New species.*

Gunshots erupted from somewhere in the middle distance. Ahead, the path cut to Elliot's right in the direction of the highway. He forced himself into a staggering jog toward the turn. Easier than pushing through crops. Better visibility.

At the corner, he leaned a hand against a bare fence-post to catch his breath and take his bearings. The new path ran for two hundred meters ahead, laying a border between the corn and another long field blanketed in chest-high bird netting. The netting had come away in some areas, exposing torn vegetation and uprooted planter stakes. The same stakes—for tomato plants maybe—poked through the netting in other places. Close to Elliot's corner, zombie bodies writhed in it, all tangled up.

Halfway down the path stood Angie and her captor.

Boxed in by the undead.

Through the swaying bodies, Elliot could see that Da Silva was using her as a shield with an arm hooked around her midriff while he fired his handgun at their attackers. The ex-cop turned Angie around and around in a tight circle as he made headshot after headshot. He was making progress. But there were more deadheads than he had bullets—and to reload or swing the rifle from his back, he'd have to release Angie. If he didn't push her into the pusbags as bait.

The bare fence posts lined the pathway here too.

Elliot took a knee behind one and made it a bench-rest for his rifle. He blinked water from his eyes and sighted along the weapon. It no longer wavered—although he could feel the fatigue threatening to take over his arms and ruin his aim. He'd only get a couple shots off at most before Da Silva reacted to him. And he had Angie and nesters between him and his target. Given the noise Da Silva was making and the fact that Miller's rifle had its suppressor, Elliot felt safe squeezing off a round. A sighter. It took out a pusbag to Da Silva's left as the SERP swung around toward Elliot again. Da Silva didn't notice. Angie did. Her eyes found his—before another zombie stepped in front of her.

Elliot knew by the sudden lull in the firing and the spike in Da Silva's swearing that his magazine was dry. He tightened his grip on the rifle, blinked away water, let out a half-breath and wished to hell that deadhead would get out of his line of sight. Then Da Silva and Angie stumbled to Elliot's left—and Elliot was bracing for his opportunity—and it came when the SERP released Angie momentarily to go for a reload—and Angie whirled on the spot to take another swing at him—and Da Silva dodged it, so that she missed and fell on her ass in a big puddle.

And Elliot took his shot.

Da Silva jerked and swung around one-eighty degrees to stumble into the embrace of a nester. But he brushed it off before it could latch on tight and he threw himself into the cornfield.

With Angie down and scrambling around, Elliot fired three more times, opening up a path for her. And then she was coming to him, swaying and skidding as she ran, almost losing her footing at one point. Elliot stood and let the rifle swing down by his left thigh. He took four steps forwards, reaching for her.

A preteen zombie exploded out of the corn, slammed into him, pinning his right arm and riding him down into the mud so that he landed sideways on top of his rifle. The deader's jaws latched on his shoulder. Elliot wrestled to get his left arm free from under him, waiting for the bite pain to kick in, expecting to see his own skin coming loose in the kid's teeth. When finally he'd rolled enough to free his left arm, it still had hold of Miller's rifle. Elliot brought it up and over, cracking the top of the frame into the zombie's head. Then, as its jaws unlatched from his shoulder and it reared for another bite, Elliot remembered the serrated rail-system fitted beneath the barrel for mounting handguards, lights, grips...

Swiping backhanded, he got the underside of the barrel in the path of the deader's oncoming bite, jammed it in hard as the kid bit down, and ran the rail against its face, feeling and seeing the skin tear back from the mouth, some teeth popping free until the deadhead's skin gathered taut enough to catch it—then Elliot heaved against it, turning the head, forcing it away and up, got his other hand to the rifle barrel and flung the pusbag around and off him. He was struggling to get up on his knees so he could hit it again when a boot came out of nowhere, knocking the deader onto its face, then coming down fast to crush the back of its neck. Angie hopped away from it, checking around them. Elliot slapped at his shoulder, feeling for the bite wound, finding nothing but a small split across the fabric of his vest where the zombie had torn at it. Next thing, Angie was helping him to his feet. Then she was pressed against him and Elliot was kissing her hair and her ear and her cheek, and he was dragging her around and behind him so he could see back down the path. Two adult deaders remained in sight, coming for them. The other four that had been there had gone into the corn after Da Silva.

"I think I hit him in the shoulder," he said. "Left shoulder. Not sure."

The .40 cal slid from Elliot's holster as if by itself, then Angie fired past him to drop the oncoming nesters. "I like this better than my Glock."

"That was Miller's. Yours, now."

"Miller's dead?"

"Yep."

"Excellent. Got a way out of here?"

"We get outside the gate and Rita picks up in the BearCat." Did Angie know who Rita was? he wondered.

"You wanna do that now?" she asked. "Or you wanna get Da Silva?"

"I wanna finish the job."

"Me too."

More noise from the side, splashing, heavy panting. Wilma, coming in fast. Elliot stooped over her, ran his hands over her. No bites. "Good dog. You're okay. You run away from the truck?"

Angie pulled him upright and turned him toward her and it was her turn to look *him* over. "You okay to move?"

"Too right," he said in a bad Aussie accent. He needed

to keep going a little longer, just a little, just enough to put another bullet in Da Silva.

"On me, then," she replied in a bad American accent.

She led the way along the path to the point where the SERP had fought off the pusbags. Blood had splashed across the puddles and mud and weeds. Not the blood of deaders: this was lighter, richer. Human blood. The blood of the living. And there was a lot of it.

Elliot blew out a breath. "Didn't think I hit him that good."

"Let's follow it before the rain washes it away."

"Or the nesters start licking it up."

"Thanks for that image," she said as she entered the corn.

Elliot wanted to lead. Angie had a handgun; he had a rifle. Also, he loved her: she should be safely behind him, with him taking the higher risk. But she was too damn fast. She was on the trail, and he was stumbling along in her wake, feeling half-zombie himself. In fact, he thought, if he hadn't felt this shitty ten minutes ago, he might have believed the teenage deadhead actually infected him.

It still could have. He shuddered.

He watched their six and watched their flanks while she watched the ground. Soon she stopped, letting him catch her up. Ahead, a deader actually *was* lapping at blood on the ground. Elliot dispatched it with his suppressed weapon.

They'd only moved on another thirty metres when she let him catch her again. A body rested ahead of them, face down in a long puddle between cornstalks. Black clothing. A short-barreled rifle strapped to its back. Blood misted the water around it. Face down in water, the man should be dead. But Elliot had seen stranger things...

This time, he did get in front of Angie. He put a knee on Da Silva's back—wondering if he'd have the strength to get back up. No reaction from the prone man. Elliot felt for a pulse. None. His fingers came away warm and slick with blood. Wilma gave the man a sniff, then turned her head away. It was an effort to get to his feet. He cleaned his hand against the wet leaves of a cornstalk, afraid to bend over a nearby puddle in case he fell into it.

"I did hit him in the shoulder," he said. "Must've nicked an artery."

"Huh." Angie came over and prodded the dead man with the toe of her boot, then put a bullet through his brain anyway. She shrugged. "Now, there's an anticlimax for you."

"Well," he replied, "I'd rather this than—"

Noise exploded from south of their position. A brown blur thundered past, flattening corn, kicking up spray. Socks the horse. Hot on his trail came a cloud of undead children and teenagers, slashing their arms at the water spray as they came, some tripping on crushed cornstalks but immediately finding their feet again.

Elliot exchanged a tense glance with Angie: if that animal had veered five metres to its left...

"Um," she said, "we're leaving town now?"

Elliot waited a few moments for the tail end of the horse-chasers to pass, then lurched in the direction of the gate. "You're goddamned right we are."

PART FOUR

HOME

Monday's child is fair of face,
Tuesday's child is full of grace,
Wednesday's child is full of woe,
Thursday's child has far to go,
Friday's child is loving and giving,
Saturday's child works hard for a living,
But the child who is born to survive Doomsday
Is blessed and cursed in every way.

Children's Rhyme, first documented in 66 PC (Post-Collapse)

25

New Easter Weekend
Year 6, Post-Collapse

ELLIOT STOOD by a Community Centre window, squinting through warm autumn sunshine at the shenanigans outside. Directly below him, Nance and Alyssa had set up a trestle table and laid it out with different kinds of paint. Nance led a bunch of older children in decorating the shells of hard-boiled eggs while Alyssa painted the faces of the younger children, transforming them into animals or comic book heroes. One of those kids, Elliot saw, was the toddler from Bournstowe who giggled each time the brush tickled his cheek. Alyssa's responding laughter brought a half-smile to Elliot's face.

Beyond the painting table, other Downsers had set up plastic picnic tables. Indira the nurse sat by one—she'd moved into camp permanently to take care of The Downs and nearby Nine Mile River. Bournstowe's Rita and Caufield sat with her, Rita dealing cards while Dave One sent lingering looks her way from an adjoining table. As Elliot watched, a twenty-something couple from Nine Mile joined the card game; they'd ridden horses down the coast in time for the celebration, another gesture of the growing trust and unity between settlements.

Elliot's dog Wilma came bounding up to the old woman from Bournstowe. The woman pried the stick from Wilma's jaws and tossed it a couple of tables over, cooing and clapping her hands in encouragement as the dog raced off in pursuit.

Past the picnic tables and across the small creek, a flat area had been commandeered for the day's sporting events. Plenty of noise rolled from there toward the Centre as Chariya and Huy officiated over a three-legged race, organizing the competitors and clarifying rules. Spider seemed to be the competitor giving them the most grief, holding up proceedings by arguing over something with his partner, Dave Two.

Typical goddamn Spider, thought Elliot. His grin broadened enough to stretch his scarred cheek while his focus shifted to Spider's wife and son; they were the audience Spider was really playing to, and they looked on proudly. *As well you should*, he thought. *That man's done good by us, and by you.*

At the painting table below his window, the Bournstowe toddler squealed in delight as Alyssa held up a mirror and the child saw the tiger he'd become. He ran off in search of his mother to share his joy.

Within the Centre, the clanging and clatter of work spilled out through the kitchen door and servery: Neil and Rit, Di and Sturgis, prepping Easter lunch. The aromas of frying meat and roasting vegetables wafted Elliot's way.

Elliot sighed. Eighteen months earlier, Settler's Downs had been forced to fight for its life. Twelve months back, it had been Elliot and Angie fighting for theirs. Smelling that food and looking out this window, Elliot found it hard to imagine that any of that period's horrors had actually happened.

There was one person missing from this scenario, however. At least in Elliot's mind. *Rider*. There'd been no contact from the former biker since the day they'd freed him in Jericho. Despite the fact that twice, Downsers had gone across to Evandale and left him a message in his dead drop. Was he still out looking for SERPs?

Mentally, Elliot kicked himself. There was more than *one* person missing today. Those who'd died at the hands of the SERPs, for starters. Also, Heng...

After escaping Bournstowe—and before returning to cull its deaders—Angie had picked and laid flowers by the car where Heng died, while Elliot and Rita bundled the old man's body into a blanket for the journey home. She'd stopped talking about it months ago, but he knew she still felt guilty—though no one believed the accident was her fault.

Raising his eyes to a passing cloud, Elliot thought, *I hate to say it, Heng, you cranky ol' bastard, but I miss you. Be at peace, buddy, wherever you went to next. You sure earned a rest. You—*

Behind him, Angie screamed. Elliot whirled unsteadily to face her where she was squatting by one of the tables and panting hard.

Kneeling on a folded towel in front of her, Claire reassured her, "Almost there, Mama, almost there."

"Better be!" Angie snarled, then squealed again.

Lewis and Krystal hovered behind Claire, holding another towel and a basin of water, awaiting further orders. Claire flashed Elliot a wry smile. Hell, she didn't need to be psychic to see how goddamned nervous he was: he'd been pacing the room for almost three hours.

"My leg's cramping," Angie gasped through clenched teeth as the latest contraction eased up. She half-fell, half-lowered herself onto her ass and then her back, one hand still gripping the table top above her.

Claire repositioned her folded towel to kneel between Angie's feet, and rolled Angie's long black t-shirt back to check on the proceedings. As she found the cramping muscle in Angie's leg and started massaging it, she said, "You're doing good. It's going well."

"Is the *baby* doing well?" Angie replied.

"Baby's doing fine and baby's going to *be* fine. Comes from good stock." Another smile Elliot's way.

"*Dammit!*" Angie rasped, squeezing her eyes closed, forcing out tears that mingled with the sweat on her cheeks.

Watching, grimacing, Krystal draped the spare towel over one shoulder, then rubbed at her own slightly swollen belly. Noticing it, Lewis put down the water basin and wrapped his arms around her, placing his hands over hers.

Elliot now turned his back completely to the window and the commotion outside, to the shouting, the laughing, to the barking of his dogs. Everything that mattered now was in this room.

Just, please, God. Been enough suffering these past few years. Get her through this safe. Get our kid through this safe.

Angie shouted, "Get a goddamn *zombie* in here to *kill* me and get it *over* with!"

Enough of this keeping my distance shit. Elliot moved across and knelt behind her, resting her head against his thighs while Claire fussed and encouraged.

Angie reached for him. He slapped his palm to hers. He took a risk and brushed her hair from her forehead. She didn't flinch or pull away.

He told her, "Biggest mission of our lives, babe. I'm proud of you."

"You should be."

"You're gonna be okay," he said. "The three of us are gonna be okay."

But she wasn't hearing it, groaning through gritted teeth again and Claire was telling her to push, push, and her fingers were a vice around his.

Then Claire said, "Okay, stop pushing. Rest. Breathe. I see the top of someone's head." She grinned and told Lewis beside her, "That's the head crowning."

He grinned too and glanced over his shoulder at Krystal; the young woman didn't look so enthused.

Claire was leaning forward again, busy with her hands.

"Everything okay?" Elliot asked while he stroked sweat from Angie's brow. "What's happening?"

"Everything," Claire said, "is perfect. That's it, Angie, keep on breathing. One last push now, yeah? Ready?"

"No, but okay," Angie moaned and raised her head from Elliot's knees. She gave a final grunt and cry, fell back against him a moment before raising herself to look.

Elliot's own breath caught in his throat.

Claire held a slippery, wriggling, purple-skinned baby. Beaming at it, she checked it over and cleared its throat. She was talking. Lewis was talking. Angie was talking. Elliot heard none of it.

A child. Our child.

"Did you hear me, Elliot?" Claire said.

"What?"

"I said, it's a boy."

She laid the baby between Angie's breasts. The curly snake of the umbilical cord trailed out behind it. *Him.*

"Hello, bubby," Angie said. "Hello, bubby."

Elliot reached across her shoulder and cupped a palm around the sticky, wispy-haired scalp. "You did it." He wasn't sure if he was talking to his son or to Angie. Maybe it was both.

"He's perfect," Angie told him.

"He is. *You* are."

Decades before, Uncle John had told him over and over, *In the end you're all you have.* He'd said all sorts of things about women too—none of which Elliot was ever gonna bring to mind again, because every day since he'd met her, Angie had proved John wrong.

Claire and Lewis were giving them space, discussing subjects like the afterbirth and how long to wait before cutting the cord.

Angie tilted her chin again and met his eye. "One thing we have to get straight," she told him.

"What's that?"

"The name Elliot. First or last?"

The others looked his way, curious.

Lewis rocked back on his heels and nodded. "If this kid's getting a hyphenated last name, well, we know Angie's."

Oh, Christ.

Under the circumstances, he could hardly claim it was too painful to admit his full name. After a couple of deep breaths, he managed to say it. The whole thing. Without stuttering.

"Alvin Elliot Clutterbuck."

Lewis, Claire and Krystal averted their gazes, finding other things to look at.

"Clutter..." Angie started. Then: "We'll just go with my name."

He nodded. "Copy that."

Shit just got real, Sparkles, said Radler's ghost.

Sure did, he told him back. *And I'm all for it.*

There was more fuss for a while, the passing of the placenta, more checks for the baby, Claire helping Angie to get the little one positioned for nursing, Lewis shooing the nosey cooks back into the kitchen and moving tables as a privacy screen. Elliot watched it all with a pleasant hum in his chest. For most of four decades, his life had revolved around him. The last three years and more, it had begun orbiting around this community—and increasingly this woman on the floor, now nursing his son.

A child. I have a child.

No. Not just a *child—the* child.

And Elliot would spend the rest of his life doing everything he could to make the boy's life good.

Claire and Lewis had come around to him, he realized. He looked up at them. Claire was holding the umbilical cord. Lewis offered him a pair of shears.

"Ready?" the young man asked him.

"Ready," he said, and he cut the cord.

ACKNOWLEDGMENTS

MY PROFOUND THANKS TO …

Joy Killar (aka Sarah)—who connected me with a whole bunch of wonderful human beings in the zompoc community. *Vale*, Sarah. Be at peace.

James Jackson, Rich Restrucci, and William Todd Rose—who supported and advised me across this series. Go check out their books.

Authors D Robert Digman and B.B. Burdock, and good mates Liz and Dave—for helping me hammer a lacklustre story into a sharp and shiny one.

Janine the series Proofreader.

Noel Osualdini, *this* book's second and much esteemed Proofreader (and, let's be honest, editor).

And *you*—for journeying with me, across post-apocalyptic Tasmania and (I hope!) beyond …

AFTERWORD

I started writing *Reckoning* early in 2019. I finished the final draft (except for my proofreaders' edits) late in 2021.

"Why'd it take so long?"

I'm so glad you asked.

Couple of reasons ...

The first was my lack of planning for the series. I'm a far better writer when I've planned a book or series, when I know where it's all going. (Well, I'm a less grumpy one, anyway. And far more productive). When I wrote the original *Doomsday's Child* novel, it was only ever intended as a one-and-only, a standalone story. I'd always wanted to put my own spin on a zombie apocalypse. When I released it, I was ready to move on to other projects. (Yes, folks, that cliffhanger ending was always meant to be there). However. The moment I released it, friends and career experts told me I needed to turn it into a series. And I listened to them. I'm *glad* I did, don't get me wrong. I love Elliot as a protagonist. I've loved setting a saga in Tasmania, my favourite place on Earth. But the mission to write two more novels and two novelettes became an uphill battle ... simply because I hadn't planned on it. With *Reckoning*, I had many false starts and rewrites as I worked to make it all fit together and *go somewhere*.

The second reason the project stalled was COVID-19 (as well as certain events and trends in America and home here in Australia). During 2020 and early 2021, the world suddenly felt quite *pre*-apocalypse. The idea of sitting down and writing a dark, *post*-apocalyptic tale lost its appeal. I like reading (and writing) this genre precisely because it's *not* reality. I found it tough to work in a dystopian fictional world when I was living in a real one.

Eventually, however, the planets aligned. I kicked my own authorial backside and nailed it to the chair so my authorial hands could pound away at my keyboard. I thrashed out the sticking points with good friends.

We got there.

And you came with me. I've had so much positive feedback from readers who've journeyed with Elliot since 2017. I've included something at the end of this book that I used to only give my newsletter subscribers. I'd like you to have your own copy of Elliot's prequel novelette. I set *Half Past Doomsday* two weeks before Elliot met Lewis, and based it on a throwaway thought he'd had somewhere in Book 1 about being stuck early in the Collapse with a bunch of dumbasses in a resort, watching things go pear-shaped.

Bon Appetit ...

HALF PAST DOOMSDAY

PETE ALDIN

1: Golfing the Apocalypse

THE DEAD WOMAN *came to rest at an intersection where the rural road split in two. She stood at the stop line and swayed there with no way of deciding which way to turn. Her skin had begun blistering from exposure to the summer skies. A part of her brain was aware of the sun's heat, that it was both nourishing and dangerous. And that was as far as it went—no thought of sheltering from it, no thought of benefiting from it. No thought at all.*

A minute after she arrived there—or perhaps an hour later, or perhaps two—clouds covered the sun and rain pelted her. She opened her mouth to the sky for a time, let the water collect, swallowed. She fell awkwardly to her knees and lapped more from the puddle collecting in a pothole.

Taking in the water gave her a kind of emotionless satisfaction. She needed water. She needed sun. She needed nitrates and sugars. She no longer had words for these things and didn't truly think about them, but she yearned for them all.

When she was done drinking, she stayed on hands and knees, swaying gently as the rainstorm passed and the sun came out to suck at the moisture in her moldering clothing, her hair, the road. Steam rose from the asphalt like wraiths. She noticed none of that. She stared ahead, at the fork in the road.

For the moment, there was nowhere to go, nothing to do. But wait.

"THESE PEOPLE ARE GONNA DIE."

After four days of coming up to this vantage point on the clubhouse roof—four days of watching over his fellow refugees—Elliot was convinced of it.

Every single one of them was another tragedy waiting to happen.

The three men and one woman out there playing golf.

The small groups wandering the resort's paths and gardens, chatting amiably.

The young couple sunbathing on the practice green, horsing around with the hose.

The elderly couple socking a ball around the tennis court behind his position ...

"They're all gonna goddamn die."

The "time share" resort buildings graced the north-facing slope of a low Tasmanian hill, looking out over a small valley of horse agistments which lay beyond the resort's own 9-hole golf course. The buildings were simple and modern, brick and glass, their eaves and doorways painted in earthy colors that Elliot thought more suited to Australia's deserts than this lush and temperate southern island.

The designers had arranged the resort around the main structure: a restaurant and clubhouse. A man-made shelf had been cut into the hill behind that to carry tennis courts, a hot tub and pool, now carpeted in leaves and grit since no one had cleaned them in a couple of weeks. Twenty-four studio apartments—incongruously called "Cabins"—flanked the clubhouse, twelve fanning out to the east and twelve to the west.

Maintenance buildings peppered the grounds past the edges of the easternmost and westernmost cabins where they'd be out of sight of every guest's window, and a parking lot took up another excavated shelf of rock above the pool and tennis court, with thick bushland capping the hill above it. The parking lot was full. Each building had an uninterrupted view of the valley. This included the clubhouse roof which made it the best sentry position on site.

One of the golfers shouted "Fore!" and the others' laughter floated up to him on the breeze.

The thing that pissed him off most was that he was the only one on watch. The only one vigilant and aware.

Thirty-something dumbass people doing dumbass things while one prepared-and-alert dumbass PMC watches over all our dumb asses.

Behind him, the elderly couple paused between sets and tipped back water bottles, plucking at their sweaty McEnroe whites and congratulating each other on form. They'd introduced themselves to him as Mr and Mrs

Chisholm—proud retirees from a life of wealth-gathering. They'd been busy spending that wealth on a nation-wide tour of golfing retreats before the cannibal pandemic had put a halt to that. *For the moment*, he'd heard them chuckle to someone.

He caught himself grinding his teeth together and forced himself to desist. But it was so goddamn insane. The Chisholms acted like it would pass. Everyone here acted like it would pass. Like a stock market crash. Or swine flu. Elliot had seen what he'd seen in Hobart. He'd heard what he'd heard over the sat phone and secure internet links in the first few days when they'd still operated.

This wasn't going to pass.

Civilization was over, uniformly collapsing around the globe. The long-awaited apocalypse was here.

And Elliot was surrounded by the sounds of idiocy.

A golfing iron connected with a ball and men cheered.

The young man on the putting green guffawed as he angled the hose-water in an arc and his girlfriend caught it gracefully in her upturned mouth.

An engine in the parking lot started up, revved three times and was shut off again.

The resort manager and her chef wistfully discussed gourmet recipes over the squeaky wheels of the trolley carrying a large propane bottle toward the kitchen's back entrance.

Mr Chisholm shouted encouragement to his wife, followed by the *thock* of a served tennis ball.

The muffled braying of an argument rose from the

restaurant below; maybe someone's sleeping bag had encroached on someone else's. Or perhaps they were squabbling over food allocations, attempting to bully resort staff into letting them raid the stores without thought to later consequence. No one had yet been brave enough to organize and go scouting-scavenging nearby hamlets. They were telling each other their fantasies, masturbating each other's hopes: *the authorities will come for us, the government will help us, it's only a matter of time.*

And meantime, they kept eating through their stores.

Not Elliot though. Elliot had his suspicions about packaged food. He'd kept a little in his backpack. But so far, the nearby apple and cherry orchards had been keeping him alive, along with meat he'd caught for himself.

Jesus, he thought, remembering one reaction his new habit of living-off-the-land. The bespectacled beanpole of a man had lumbered around a cabin corner, his tiny daughter in tow, maybe getting in his three minutes of daily exercise and forcing her to do the same. His eyes had been on the grass but they'd looked up at Elliot—at the exact moment Elliot twisted a captured magpie's neck. Beanpole Dad had swung his daughter up into his arms, given Elliot his best *how dare you* glare and turned heel. The girl hadn't seen the bird's death—but should have.

Sitting on the roof, he muttered to himself, "Kids should be learning this shit."

Hell, he thought, *the grown-ups should be too!*

He wiped sweat from his brow, smacked his gums. He'd had two Coke bottles filled with water up here in the sun for the full two days he'd been here, long enough for UV to kill any bugs in them. He reached for one. It would be warm, but it would be safe. He screwed off the cap. It paused halfway to his mouth as he saw *her* coming his way along the path that snaked around the gardens between the fairways and the clubhouse.

Oh, great.

Brin. Athletic and sun-bronzed, her Gucci halter top showing off skin at cleavage and belly button, grey leggings hugging the lines of her hips and thighs, expensive bracelets and wristwatch. Fake blonde hair with a dark stripe of regrowth showing along the part.

Brin. Holding court with that regal tilt to her chin, her faithful entourage in tow: the short brunette with self-esteem issues, hanging with the head cheerleader to be cool, plus three guys, an assortment of body types, ages and haircuts.

The saddest thing was that these boys and the girl were not teenagers; not a one of them was under twenty-five and the oldest guy was easily in his mid-forties. Brin herself had to be thirty, but the body language that evidently served her well in high school hadn't changed in the fifteen years since.

Brin, he thought. *Queen of No Country, Duchess of the Deader Plague.*

Every one of her group had a half-empty champagne flute in hand, the men's containing beer, the two women's red wine. The booze was in use despite resort manager Carolyn's prohibition from using the bar; no doubt they were using their own stash more to flaunt the rules than to actually get hammered.

He tore his eyes away from them and got the water bottle to his lips—where it froze again. Something caught his eye out on one of the greens. A flash of light. He raised the glasses, found the cause and swore several times. He must have done it pretty loud because when he lowered the glasses, Brin's sycophants were all smirking up at him.

"Something wrong, Mr American?" the Queen herself cooed. A couple of snorts amongst her group, a titter, a muttered insult he didn't catch—vocal offerings made in tribute to her.

Elliot ignored them. On what he thought to be the fourth hole, the four players appeared from behind a line of stunted trees, towing golf bags on wheels. And on the fairway beyond them, the one running parallel, an equal number of deaders were fast-staggering closer. One of the undead wore a large belt buckle which kept flashing sunlight Elliot's way. He raised the glasses one more time to be sure and yeah, the apocalyptic golfers had neither seen nor heard the approaching danger, lost in loud and demonstrative conversation.

Leaving his backpack and bottle behind, Elliot turned his body over the edge of the roof, found the ladder with his boots and descended as fast as he dared.

"What's the big hurry?" the brunette understudy cooed as he dashed past. Pleasingly, the males' mocking expressions had begun wilting as he'd gotten nearer.

Elliot didn't reply, caroming down the gentle grass slope between the pressed gravel path and the first tee. The group of golfers were maybe five hundred yards away. Now that he was almost on their level, they'd disappeared behind another screen of trees between fairways, and into a gully. At least the screaming hadn't started.

Maybe he'd get there in time.

Maybe I won't.

As the turf levelled out and he reached the low fence along the course's side, he cursed the universe. He'd had a three-day reprieve from this. Just three short days.

The undead were always going to reach this not-so-remote location sooner or later. There'd been maybe a quarter million people in Hobart, probably twice as many again scattered throughout the rest of this large island state. More than all the bullets he could ever find, especially in a nation with sphincter-tight gun laws. There simply weren't enough survivors or weapons to cull the infected.

A shout from the fourth fairway. Another. A series now.

Christ!

He reached the lip of the gully they were in and paused to suck breath and take stock. The golfers were a hundred yards away. And they were fighting for their lives. Luckily—and it *was* luck, dumb luck—the quartet were armed. Each had an iron in hand; three were swinging away at the approaching undead, two of the men and the woman.

But the fourth balding accountant type had taken to his heels, his club waving above his head as he legged it toward Elliot's position.

Coward. He'd left buddies behind, left a woman too.

Elliot had a piton hammer he'd looted from a camping store, his two knives, and his empty SIG-Sauer.

Hadn't been able to find more decent weapons, or more 9mm ammo. His team had abandoned him, fleeing their Hobart shelter only to be swept up by the tides of infected, their weapons lost with them. The four dead cops he'd come across getting out of Hobart had been weaponless, their holsters empty—even the one that was still moving, the one that had come closer than any other deader to getting its teeth into him.

Elliot pulled hammer and tanto knife and set off again. When he drew close to the approaching coward, he shifted direction enough to shoulder-bump him, knocking him off his feet. Without waiting to explain, to abuse or to answer the man's whiney questions, Elliot kept on toward the embattled trio, his SIG bobbing uselessly in its side holster.

To their credit, the golfers had already stopped one of the deaders permanently, evening out the numbers again, but they were making a meal of those remaining.

Meal. Elliot almost found it funny under the circumstances.

He darted in with a downward swing of the hammer, denting a living corpse's skull. One of its knees buckled, but it righted itself and came at him without concern for its oozing head wound. Elliot swatted its sun-blistered hands away with the hammer, dancing back, looking for his moment. The pusbag had lost an eye in the past; there was some scoring on the brow above it and Elliot wondered if someone shot it but missed the brain—and wondered where in Christ they'd gotten the weapon.

The other eye was as good a target as any: when he next dodged its grasp, the deader unbalanced and Elliot thrust his tanto blade up and into the socket, releasing the handle as the deader fell. He could retrieve the knife later. He stooped to the grass, wiping lukewarm gore from his hand and checking the situation around him.

Two of the golfers were tag-teaming the undead guy with the big belt buckle. But their swings weren't hitting it well enough, bouncing off shoulder muscles and thighs.

"Gotta hit bone!" he yelled at them, but they weren't listening.

The third golfer had her club braced against the final pusbag's chest, keeping it beyond arm's reach. Elliot came up behind it and swung the hammer twice to remove it from the game. The golfer sagged and forced her gaze away from the exposed brain of the deader toward his friends, her eyes wide, face flushed with more than sunburn.

"Hit it in the head," Elliot told the others. "Swing downwards."

One listened and did as he was told. Their opponent shuddered under the blow, then recovered enough to surge forward toward its prey. Instead of attacking, they backpedaled.

Elliot was about to step in when the woman he'd just rescued jumped in and began hacking away with his iron. Soon the deader with the fancy buckle was a true corpse —very little of its head remained.

"Thanks mate," puffed one of her friends.

"Appreciate it," huffed the other and looked toward Elliot. "You too."

The hacker tossed her messed-up club and wiped her trembling hands on the grass. "You're the best."

"I have to hand it to you folks," Elliot started to say and surveyed the area, even though there was no way more hostiles had crept up across the open ground.

"Yeah?" asked one, an adrenalized smile forming on his stupid flushed face.

"You're probably the dumbest dumbasses I've ever met. And I've met many."

Their shoulders dropped. Faces flushed deeper. Then one man tapped the other on the shoulder, pointing out across the fairways.

More swaying bodies staggered across a hillock a hundred yards off, ten of them, then twelve ...

Elliot stopped counting at fifteen. One stopped to sniff the air. The golfers turned frightened faces toward Elliot.

"Maybe we should warn the others," one said.

Moving over to retrieve his knife, Elliot said, "Ya think?"

2: ANY OF YOU DUMBASSES WANT TO LIVE?

THICK PILLARS of midday light streaming through the restaurant skylights. The clubhouse's back windows that overlooked the valley had their blinds drawn all the way to the floor, leaving the skylights to do most of the work in lighting the place. The three golfers who'd danced with the undead had showered and changed and now huddled in a corner amidst their nest of air mattresses, passing around a scotch bottle they must have brought with them. From his vantage point seated on top of the bar, Elliot couldn't see their former friend's nest of bedding but he knew it to be there behind that upturned table against the far wall where he'd dragged it after banishment from his friendship group. The little wuss was currently slumped in a lobby armchair where Elliot had insisted he do penance, watching the three foyer entrances.

Before the golf course attack, nine people had been camping in the clubhouse restaurant, including Elliot. In the hour since, twenty more had dragged their bedding and belongings from the cabins into the increasingly crowded space, figuring on safety in numbers. Unfortunately for Elliot's sanity, Brin's group was amongst them —though their "bivouac" was out in the pro shop where they'd pushed display racks to the edges to create more room.

The clubhouse had been designed around the central restaurant, with two wings running off the sides and a broad foyer out front. This foyer continued out to the sides along the wings—Elliot liked the options for escape this provided, the lack of choke points. The west wing contained a manager's office, restaurant kitchens, a small function room and set of restrooms; the east wing was changing rooms, the pro shop, and storerooms. There were exterior doors at Reception—locked shut—and at the kitchen, at the ends of each wing and from the storerooms out the east side of the building. The wing doors and Reception doors were all glass; the Reception doors had been locked and Carolyn the resort manager had wisely powered down the wing doors—they had to be manually slid open and closed.

Twenty-nine people including kids sharing the building—Manager Carolyn had run the headcount twice—while the remaining six people had chosen to stay hunkered down in the luxury cabins they'd been renting at the time of outbreak. Elliot assumed this included the elderly Chisholms, although he wouldn't be surprised if they were out playing tennis again. The club-house air curdled with the stink of unwashed and under-washed bodies, of food dropped and mashed into the carpet, of overused restrooms. It was hot, the beginning of summer and they'd cut the aircon to reduce any noise that might attract unwelcome visitors. The resulting stuffiness wasn't helping the smell—and may have been a major reason Brin and her group had claimed the pro shop.

There was food in the kitchens and storerooms, supposedly monitored by Carolyn and her small staff. From what Elliot had seen, they were eating it too quickly —if they should be eating it at all. Before internet and satellite transmissions had turned to white noise, a prevailing theory had been that the infecting agent was widely distributed in drinking water or in processed foods. Collecting, catching and cooking his own food early each morning gave Elliot something to do and removed that risk. There were plenty of rabbits and bird life around. Apple and cherry orchards lay north over the hills and he'd eaten his fill there early that morning, lugging a sack back to his bed in the space behind the small bar. Though water still ran from taps, Elliot preferred filtering it, as he had with his bottles on the roof. He'd had a charcoal rig set up in a tree outside but one of these idiots had taken it down for some unknown and probably ridiculous reason. No one had owned up to it, but he suspected Brin's group.

He was hungry. And he was thirsty. And the small restaurant bar behind him was still half-full of booze and very tempting.

While pockets of people murmured with heads together, comforted the small number of distressed children, or paced nervously, Elliot field-cleaned his SIG-Sauer, the handgun's empty magazine in his pocket for the moment. Maybe one day soon, he'd come across some 9-mil ammo.

"While there's life," he muttered, then glanced down at movement near his feet.

The daughter of the Beanpole stood there, a kid the size of a Sesame Street muppet and no more than three years old. Her father loitered nearby, watching Manager Carolyn carry a chair through the crowd with constant apologies and course corrections. The little girl's very blue eyes stared up at Elliot's work, her lips pursed, hands on the hips of her blue and white check dress. One of her sneakers tapped a rhythm on the floor, giving the butterfly pattern on it the illusion of life. Elliot raised his brows; she caught the movement and raised hers in return. He put his bore brush down and leaned back to snatch an apple from the sack of them he kept. He held it out and she nodded once, very seriously, and took it. Elliot nodded back.

A hand reached over her head and snatched the apple away.

"Great," said Beanpole. "I'll find a knife and split this between us. Thanks."

He strode away through the maze of tables and

sleeping bags. The little girl remained, watching after him.

Elliot shook his head very slowly, refrained from swearing aloud for the kid's sake and gave her another apple. She gave him another nod as she took it and headed in a different direction to her dad. "Good choice, kid," Elliot said and picked up the brush.

Into the space the girl had vacated stepped one of the young sunbathers from the putting green earlier. In contrast to Beanpole, this guy was short, even shorter than the young woman he'd been hanging with, and up close, his skin bore the remnants of old acne. He offered Elliot a hopeful smile as he began to round the bar.

"Nope," said Elliot.

The sunbather faltered. "There's heaps there," he stage-whispered.

"Yep. Because Carolyn and I have been stopping people getting drunk and stupid on it. There's already enough stupid here," he added, his gesture encompassing the room.

"I won't get drunk. I ..." He leaned on the bar, dropped the whisper a few decibels. "I'm a bit scared, mate. I need some liquid courage."

"'Liquid courage'? That's clever. You think of that one yourself?"

The young man brightened, perhaps thinking an American wouldn't know that expression. Then he read Elliot's face. "You've heard that one before?"

"I have," Elliot replied. "Booze is off limits." He pointed to where his sleeping bag and bedroll poked from behind the bar. "My bedroom is off limits. If you're thirsty, there's bottled water over there. If you're scared—" He pointed his brush to where Carolyn was climbing her chair mid-restaurant. "—then it looks like you're about to get a chance to discuss it." He put the brush away, dropped the SIG's barrel back into the slide and locked it in place, then followed it with the recoil spring. The guy was skulking away when he looked up again.

"If I can have your attention," Carolyn called, arms up and making jazz hands. Heads turned her way. Hubbub trailed off. "I thought it might be good to talk through some practical issues. Toilet roster. Rationing food, as well as the gas in the few propane tanks we have left. Sentries."

At least someone's making sense, Elliot thought. Carolyn was good people, doing her best despite being wholly unprepared for an apocalyptic shitstorm.

There was a laugh from the restaurant doors: a thirty-something yuppie with sand-colored hair had poked his head in, one of Brin's male devotees. "Sentries! You a General now, Carolyn?"

Elliot shook his head in disgust, got the slide back on the frame, taking care with the ejector. He held the slide back with one finger, pushed the slide lock back in and made a wager with himself that there'd be some kind of argument within the next sixty seconds.

"Yes, sentries," Carolyn said, puffing up her chest. "Or a watch. Whatever you wish to call it, Elliot has been the only one doing it and we were darned lucky he was."

There was murmuring of assent from the golfers. Brin's face joined her friend's at the door.

"I think sentries are a waste of time," she said. "They don't actually do anything besides standing around. What we need is some brave men to get rid of those ugly zombies then build some fences to keep others out."

"Fences!" Carolyn exclaimed.

Elliot got the depleted magazine out of his pocket and slid it home. Out of habit, he put the safety on.

Here it comes, he thought.

She took a step inside the room, encouraged by his attention. "Also, someone needs to go into town and see what's happening there."

"Town?" asked a woman's voice in back.

"Yeah, maybe things are improving and we're just not hearing about it."

"Ridiculous," the woman responded.

Carolyn said, "No one's leaving here!"

The background buzz rose again as side conversations broke out, people already taking sides.

Way less than sixty seconds.

"If we can find some authorities, we might be able to get help." Brin's voice didn't rise in volume, but as she spoke, side conversations dropped off anyway. Many of the women scowled at her. But more than one man wore an open expression, their focus way below Brin's eyes as they listened. "We can find out how long this is going to go on before we can all go home."

There was some response to that: side conversations, some scoffing. A burly man, Carolyn's chef, called Brin a dickhead.

One of the male golfers said, "She's right. I don't wanna stay here forever."

Desperate to get attention and control back, Manager Carolyn drew herself up, sucking in air to project her voice, but Elliot barked two words that drew the attention his way and cut the noise off in an instant.

"*Christ Almighty*! You people have been behaving like this will pass you by. Out playing golf, for the love of God. Taking morning walks around the property and talking crap at the top of your voices." He shot a look toward the door where more of Brin's group had appeared behind her, including the brunette acolyte. If they were embarrassed by his comment, it didn't show on their cocky faces. "Tennis matches," he added.

"But that's exactly what we should be able to do," Brin said. "What's the point of being stuck here if we can't enjoy ourselves? I mean, what's the point of *living*? We should kill those uglies, get more food and help from the town up the highway and then we can relax a bit. We can live like civilized people instead of bloody refugees."

"But you are refugees!" Elliot snapped.

"You might be, Mr American. We're in our own country."

He shook his head. "Don't you get that this is the end of civilization? Someone didn't press the goddamn pause button, they pressed delete. This is the end of countries." He pointed to a man at the back leaning against the windows. "You. I've seen you charging your tablet and checking the internet every hour on the hour. You think it's coming back online? The power grid around here will fail soon. The piped gas already stopped. Power failed in Hobart a week before I got here. It's failed most other places in the world, I'm sure of it. There is no internet anymore, and there probably never will be. There are no police or authorities and there probably never will be. Not unless enough of us uninfected survive long enough to rebuild a civilization."

There was stunned lull, one that actually gave Elliot hope. They were all of them facing a new dark age but it hadn't occurred to them that it might be permanent, that the problem might not just go away. But they were listening; they might yet get it.

"Keyword: *survive*," he said, realizing a few people were staring at the SIG he'd forgotten was in his hand. He holstered it.

"We're not *all* that stupid," objected a blonde-haired woman over near the compulsive internet-checker. She wore a canary yellow tee, hugging two grade-school age kids to it. Her voice was quiet but firm, a teacher's voice. On first meeting, he'd suspected she'd rescued the children from her school—but then someone else had handed back her baby. The kids had to be hers, the older two consistently pale, wide-eyed, mute. "I came from Hobart," she continued. "I saw what you saw. I get it. I've been really careful, because I'm *not* stupid, I'm a survivor."

"Us too." Two middle-aged women in long loose skirts and hippy blouses said it in unison. Their bead-necklaces rattled as they side-hugged each other. One added, "We were at Richmond, but we saw the same horrific things as all the cities. We've been trying to talk sense into different people since we got here, about finding a better place than this where we can grow food and figure this out, where the infected won't find us."

First I've heard of that, Elliot thought, but at least they were on the right wavelength.

Brin clapped her hands together, beaming. "See, that's wonderful! And this could be that place with a bit of work. If the real men went out to get building materials, we could make a fence to keep the infected away."

There was a ripple of offence at the phrase "real men". Someone else commented that building fences would make the kind of noise that attracted dead people.

"You see any building materials around here, honey?" demanded the yellow-shirted mom.

And the conflict erupted suddenly and irrationally, surging around and filling every corner of the room like a simulation of a viral spread. Carolyn tried valiantly and vainly from her chair to shut it down. A kid's wailing was quickly muffled as Yellow Shirt pressed the child into her body. Brin, Elliot noticed, was mid-room now, close to Carolyn's chair and actually beaming at the ruckus. Brin's group had shifted inside the room, all of them leaning or squatting against the wall.

With a couple dozen deaders roaming the grounds, Elliot wasn't about to let this go on forever. He rounded the bar, took an empty Captain Morgan's bottle from the bin and smashed it in the stainless-steel sink. It worked. The room was staring at him and the arguments had stopped.

"Jesus! Get a goddamned grip. There's good ideas *and* bad here. But seriously, the best way of continuing to live is by working together to build a safe and sustainable base somewhere. Just like the ladies with the beads said."

The two women brightened.

Who says I have no people skills? he asked himself.

He kept talking before anyone else could interrupt. "When I went outside an hour back, I counted eighteen deaders roaming the grounds. So far, they haven't caught on to our hidey hole, but you keep making noise and they will."

The crowd was subdued now, watching him. Some glanced at children with horror, while more looked at those same little kids with anger and resentment, perhaps seeing them a liability. The kid that had been wailing was now whimpering. A few men like the internet-checker kept running their eyes over Brin, shifting position to get a better view of that halter top. Elliot tried to ignore all of it. If he didn't move these people toward some kind of rational and moral consensus, there wasn't anyone else here who would.

"Good God," he said, "I do believe some of you listened to that. Let's return to the idea of keywords. The keywords in what I just said are: *working*, *together*, and *safe*. Carolyn up there was making some sensible noises about rationing, but you all might want to take it further and consider eating unprocessed food."

"What? Why?" one of the staffers asked.

"It may be that the agent that infects people is in your processed food."

A man in Brin's group snorted at that. "None of us is sick from the food." A few hums of agreement.

"Not yet," he said and that shut them up. "Maybe you

just didn't eat the right tin of beans. In any case, those boxes of food in the storerooms won't last forever. And before you say we'll go get some more—or go get fencing materials—think about how far you want to travel through hostile infected people and how you're going to carry crap back here and how long that crap is going to last anyway."

"Are you suggesting farming?" said one of the hippy ladies, with a knowing look at her friend or partner.

"I am. And I'm thinking you were right when you said there has to be a better place than this. This has been okay until now because of its remoteness but..." He gestured toward the grounds beyond the covered windows. "So we need to plan a way out of here *and* find more defensible location."

"This place is fine," Brin murmured.

"Until there's a hundred undead out there. Or a thousand. These windows aren't gonna keep those kinds of numbers from coming in here and feasting on you."

Some gasps of horror. The mom in the yellow tee covered her whimpering child's ears with her palms and glared daggers at Elliot.

Nice going, he told himself. *Make the kids even* more *scared*.

Well, what of it? Maybe the kids didn't need to hear this, but their parents sure did. If they lived long enough, they could comfort and counsel them later.

He said, "We're going to have to wait until the infected outside wander away or else we risk some lives leading them away. First option takes patience and like Carolyn said, rationing. Second option is still an option but it's highly dangerous. A show of hands for first option."

Hands began rising as side-conversations started up in hushed tones and that was when Queen Brin had obviously had enough. She coughed for attention and adjusted the straps of her slip-blouse with one hand while waving the other, light glittering from the jewels on bracelets. Not for the first time, Elliot wondered if she'd looted her clothing, her jewelry. She seemed to have a large supply of *God-I'm-sexy* outfits. Or had she been a kept woman? She was certainly goddamned used to being listened to ...

As the room quieted again, she turned a slow circle, then said, "Mr Elliot—"

"Stop calling me that," he muttered.

"—another keyword you used before was *sustainable*. You mean sustainable like the way you've been catching poor little magpies and crows, and cooking them for yourself?"

"What's that got to do with anything?"

"I'm just not sure you have everyone's best interests in mind. You certainly weren't sharing any of that meat with us."

"He brought back fruit for the kids," Carolyn said from the chair. She checked her wristwatch pointedly, as if trying to tell Brin she was wasting time. Which she was.

"And killed and ate some magpies and crows," Brin replied, folding her arms. She nodded at her brunette acolyte. "She saw him eat a cute little duck. He'll want to eat the horses down the valley next."

"Not the horses," the internet-checker hissed in horror.

"Not exactly endangered species," Elliot said. "Not like us."

"Mm-hm. What about the little fires you made out in the gardens to cook on? What if the zombie people smelled that? What if they saw the smoke? What if *you* drew them here?"

There were more gasps. The attention turned on him was no longer as cooperative and considerate as it had been.

"I think you're only interested in saving yourself," she added.

He said, "You stupid bitch. You think a few cooked birds drew the deaders from miles away?"

The insult had drawn murmurs of outrage. She lifted a confident arrogant chin either in challenge or because she was breathing in that outrage as fuel for her fire. She asked him, "You can prove it didn't?"

He was trying to think of a way to shut her up that wouldn't further alienate the parents in the room when a different voice spoke up in his defense.

"You can't prove a negative like that, and you can't argue a point from *lack* of data." The man's voice was so educated it sounded more British than Aussie. Having heard this man editorializing several times, Elliot had already call-signed him the Professor. "The trouble is we don't know anything about these monsters."

"Not monsters, people!" snapped the mother in the yellow tee. "Sick *people*."

Carolyn's burly chef stepped forward in agreement,

pushing through others to close the distance on the Professor. His eyes were puffy, bloodshot. There were a variety of kitchen knives circulating among the crowd and Elliot was instantly glad he wasn't carrying one of them. The man said, "Yeah, my wife and my kid got infected. You sayin' they're monsters too? Eh?"

The Professor backed away until he bumped up against an overturned table. Elliot stalked across and put his arm like a toll gate between them. Burly man drew himself up for a moment and Elliot met his eyes—

Give me an excuse, asswad.

—but the man hissed some names Professor's way, drawing further complaints from the parents, and pushed his way to a crack in the blinds at the back. There, he turned his face to the window like a dog awaiting the return of his master, like a grieving husband awaiting the return of his family.

Elliot had his mouth open to continue talking sense into the living when Brin interrupted him yet again—picking up her thread as if nothing had interrupted *her.*

"And who said you could eat our duck? That duck belonged to the resort, not to you." Her entourage hooted agreement.

"I didn't eat any goddamned duck..." he started.

But even Manager Carolyn was nodding at this, faced pinched. "Maybe we should have kept it and eaten its eggs."

"Know a lot about farm animals, do you?" Elliot asked him. "That duck that hangs around here? It's male."

"And it's *gone*." Brin's sandy-haired friend took up the

fight before Elliot could get the discussion back on track, "Why are we listening to this Yank?"

Yank?

"What we should be doing is trying to reach the authorities," the man continued, "trying to hook up with other groups of survivors, and building fences like Brin says. *And* eating the food we have to keep our strength up."

"Once those infected have moved on, then we—" Elliot started but was interrupted again.

"Notice he's the only one here with a gun," the man said, stabbing a finger at Elliot's hip. He asked the room, "So perfect, isn't it? Always the Americans with all the powerful weapons while the rest of the world has to hope they won't use 'em to kill us. And guess who's trying to tell us what to do—yet again! The American with the big bad gun."

Elliot took a step toward him before he could stop himself. "Pretty simple math, dickhead. I have a firearm because it's my firearm. Mine. Not my fault if your anal gun laws prevent the rest of you from having your own."

People started up again, so many of them saying so many things so suddenly, Elliot's mind couldn't track it all. He heard the Professor say, "Those anal gun laws prevented—"

"I'm not here for a gun ownership debate," Elliot told him. "I'm trying to keep you all alive."

"Well, who died and made you king?" Brin shouted, hands on hips, chest thrust out to the obvious approval of men like the internet-checker.

Elliot had had enough. He shouted back, "Any of you

dumbasses want to live? Like, actually *want* to?" This drew more indignation from people. Swearing a blue streak, he shouldered his way to the restaurant doors and stormed through the foyer. The coward was turned around in his chair, more interested in the arguments raging behind Elliot than in the entrances he was meant to watch. Elliot took hold of his head and cranked it toward the Reception doors, eliciting a whine of pain. Then Elliot headed outside through the east wing.

The path outside was empty. Parrots squawked from the line of gum trees up behind the parking lot, as if mimicking the people arguing within the clubhouse. Someone had left a dining chair on the pathway; there was a paperback still under it, pages fluttering in the breeze. Elliot picked up the chair and launched it out onto nearby lawn as far as he could. He kicked the paperback after it. He should leave this place, he should leave these fools to their deserved ends. He put his fists to his temples and rubbed at them, tried to slow his breathing. If only it was that easy. If only they all deserved to be left to their own misery and deaths. But there were sensible people in there; there were people who'd be led astray by group think and by Queen Bitch's group. And there were children.

He stomped up to the tennis courts, higher ground, surveyed the grounds around him but saw no sign of the undead. He couldn't hear them above birds and the wind in the trees. But they were around. He knew they were around. There were cabins blocking his view, copses of trees, gullies, out-buildings. He stared longingly toward the top of the hill, thinking of the orchards on the other

side and of all the places he could hide and build some
kind of life for himself. If only there weren't children
here, he could be the selfish bastard he was born to be,
the selfish bastard his step-father had modeled and
insisted was the measure of a man.

"Goddamn it," he growled. His step-father had beaten
a lot of things out him when he was younger, but he'd
never beaten out Elliot's conscience.

Elliot had often wished he had.

3

3: JEREMY GETS SICK

NIGHT SET ON HER.

The dead woman's nervous system—what was left of it—recognized cold and the threats it posed to her, driving her to her feet, inducing her to burn calories, compelling her to move. Without choosing, she chose, taking the right-hand fork in the road.

Burning calories meant the further destruction of her own body, the host organism. That too was a threat. And so she lifted her nose to the wind to find food and turned her hearing to sifting through the night sounds to help her find something living.

In the end, she found roadkill, the aroma luring her from a quarter mile away.

Once more on hands and knees, she dined.

· · ·

Elliot spent an hour trailing small groups of undead, counting, getting a sense of whether they were wandering around the property or its peripheries, or they were standing around dormant like he'd seen them do from time to time over the past few weeks.

Most of them, he noted with a sinking feeling, weren't interested in leaving the property. Perhaps they knew there was live food locked in these buildings somewhere. Perhaps they all liked golf in their former lives...

As confident as he was to safely cull a few—he could take down the rearmost individuals from behind then run like hell from the rest—he refrained for the time being. It was firstly an unnecessary risk, and secondly would create the problem of stationary dead bodies that might spread disease. Ambulatory, there was still the hope the pusbags might move on outa town, taking their stinking carcasses with them. Surely they would grow bored soon, smell the sheep over the hills, chase a flock of birds.

When his anger at Brin and the Moron Convention in the clubhouse had abated some, he came back in. Three women met him at the east wing entrance: Carolyn, the woman golfer and one of the hippy ladies.

"Jeremy's sick," the golfer announced.

"Who the—?" he started, preoccupied by the name until his mind registered the adjective. That sinking feeling started up again. "Sick?"

"Really, really sick," Carolyn confirmed.

The golfer added, "Jeremy's the guy who ran away."

The lobby armchair was vacant as if to prove it.

Elliot rubbed at his stubbly beard. "You checked for bites?"

Murmurs of confirmation while the golfer added, "But he wasn't anywhere near those infected people we fought."

"Maybe he had the disease before he got here?" the hippy lady proposed, nodding in agreement with her own hypothesis.

"Where'd you put him?" Elliot asked, ignoring her.

"Cabin 11."

"Was he eating anything just before—?"

He didn't get to complete the question. A fresh ruckus started up inside the restaurant. Heart in mouth and hammer in hand, Elliot bolted for the doors well ahead of the others, expecting to find someone else had turned and started biting.

Instead, he found three men facing off center room. One—the chef Elliot thought of as Burly Guy—brandished a long kitchen knife. The two opposing him were the rest of the golfing group, waving their golf clubs ineptly and snarling abuse. Their prey kept one hand on the chair he was using as a shield. Nearby, Brin had backed into the cluster of her supporters comforting her brunette understudy, who cradled *her* left arm. Blood dripped between the brunette's fingers, staining her long-sleeve t-shirt crimson.

"See what you've done to my *friend*?" Brin shrilled.

Elliot did a double take at Brin when for a moment, just the smallest of moments, the veneer of outrage on her face dropped to reveal something else, smugness, satisfaction, something, before then the pain and outrage were back. And—

You're shittin' me.

—her friend's hurt glances kept flicking up toward Brin, rather than the resort chef.

You are goddamn shittin' me.

"Accident," Burly Guy kept saying and glanced behind him to check for surprise attack. But the people drifting behind him showed no interest in tackling him and more in the people on the other side of the room. During one such glance, one of the double team lunged but his club head met Burly's chair coming up and he lost his grip, his swearing increasing in volume and censor-rating as the weapon fell from his hands.

"I said I didn't mean it!" Burly Guy yelled. "I didn't even notice her."

Brin shouted, "It still bloody hurt her whether you meant it or not! Doesn't it, darls?"

Her friend did not reply, her pale face tightened in pain now.

Brin's sandy-haired male added that Burly Guy should watch where he was going.

As the man who'd lost his club scrambled for it and his partner braced for a new attack, and as blades flashed among other frightened people in the crowd, Elliot decided that this time he would use his automatic, since no one knew it wasn't loaded. He cocked it, causing heads to turn at the sound.

He snapped, "Enough!" The three would-be skirmishers froze and gaped at the muzzle while it shifted between them. "You three will put your weapons on the

floor and kneel with your hands behind your heads."
When they didn't move he added, "I don't like waiting."

It almost worked. Almost. There was a moment
where the three fighters' weapons dipped toward the
floor.

And then one of Brin's sandy-haired fella raised his
voice. "Keep outa this, Yank!"

"You keep out of it," snapped the young sunbather-
dude from behind Burly. "She started this!"

"How'd *she* start this?" yelled the lackey.

"She bumped the other chick into his way. I saw it."

"Bullshit," Brin snapped.

Sandy-hair added, "You're full of it."

"Idiots carrying knives," the internet-checker said, and
the small girl's father added, "The big oaf did it."

"Been telling you all for hours you shouldn't be
carrying knives around," Brin chimed in, using just the
right catch in her voice to regain the attention—and
sympathies—of many.

Elliot noticed it then, surprised he hadn't before.

The room had started separating already. People
with knives were all in the rear part of the room toward
the windows, behind or to the side of Burly Guy. This
included the two sunbathers, Carolyn's waitress, Yellow
Shirt, the other hippy lady. The rest of the room closer
to and behind Brin's clique had no weapons, or they
carried makeshift ones like chair legs, a rolling pin,
more golf clubs—and there were more men on that
side.

"Hey!" Elliot barked and when eyes turned his way
again, he asked Burly Guy, "You cut her?"

"Accident. I keep saying. I was walking through everyone to go take a crap and she bumped into me."

"No excuse," someone muttered to a chorus of agreements.

"You were carrying the knife uncovered through a crowd of people?" Elliot asked snaring a bunch of other people's eyes. He hated to agree with Brin, but it was dangerous. "Like I see a whole lot of you doing right now. Those knives won't help you close quarters with infected people anyway and you're risking further accidents. Ron, you get everyone's knives."

"What do we use for defense?" asked the sunbather dude. He had edged closer, Elliot noticed, perhaps bent on rescuing an ally. That would be just perfect, if the idiots on that side of the room thought that Elliot belonged on Brin's.

Elliot indicated the golf clubs and blunt force weapons in Brin's group. "Things like that. Things you won't cut yourselves with. Plenty of those to go round. Isn't there? Brin?"

She had stepped away from her friend now, gesturing instructions to her oldest male acolyte as he wrapped a resort polo shirt around the brunette's arm. "I think there's a couple left in the pro shop." She inspected some spots on her jewelry with an upturned lip.

"Plenty of wooden and steel stakes out in the gardens too."

"I'm not ditching my knife," said the woman with the kids. "Not when they are armed."

The Professor on Brin's side of the room bristled. "They!"

And then the shouting was back, toing and froing cross the room.

And this is what it always comes to, Elliot thought, his sliding his SIG into its holster. *Someone always decides there's a Them and there's an Us.*

Amidst the ruckus, Elliot heard one of the kneeling golfers ask him, "Not gonna use ya gun then, mate?"

The three men were staring up at him, an oasis of calm irony in the midst of a storm of yelling and threats that risked attracting the attention of a lot of deaders soon.

Elliot jerked his head at the foyer and told the three skirmishers, "Foyer."

Sheepishly they rose and preceded him out there. They stood apart from each other, eyes moving from Elliot's face to his holster to the noise beyond the doors and back again.

Burly Guy said, "Lotta fuss in there, eh?"

Elliot told the double team, "Whether he actually cut her or not, you were ready to kill this guy over a mistake?"

"Wasn't really thinking," one replied.

"Really tense in there," said the other.

"Bit of cabin fever maybe," added the first. He looked at Burly Guy's chest and mumbled, "Sorry mate."

"Yeah, sorry mate," agreed the second.

"No worries," said Burly. "I shoulda been more careful."

They shook hands, hands that had only moments ago borne weapons against each other. Despite no abating of the conflict in the restaurant, perhaps these three guys were a sign of hope for this crowd.

"Well, if you're restless and itching to hurt someone, how about I teach you how to take down some of the infected? Then maybe you can check on the people still in their cabins?"

"That'd be good."

"Yeah, something to do."

"I'll need a weapon like you said," Burly Guy added. "You meant like sticks or something?"

"Garden stakes will work well enough," Elliot said. "Or these guys' nine-irons. Your best bet is a blow to the head. Or two. Or three." He nodded to the east wing doors. "We'll get their clubs, then go that way and get you armed—"

"One thing first," Burly interrupted.

Elliot faced him. "What's that?"

"I still need to crap."

THE NEWEST PACKS OF UNDEAD ENTERING THE RESORT seemed to be drifting in single units or pairs. Elliot supervised the three men in picking off some of the singles. The plan was to take out a few then drag the bodies into the empty ground near the maintenance shed twenty yards west of Cabin 11 where Carolyn had quarantined Jeremy. They could set fire to them later in the day if necessary, or on the following. At first, Burly Guy had been reticent to harm the infected, but when Elliot explained that these people weren't going to recover, that like it or not they were to all intents and purposes *monsters*, and that while they hung around they were a danger to women and kids, the chef bought into it. The three men's enthusiasm and confidence grew until they had taken down nine between them. While they were busy congratulating each other on "head shots" and "shoulder power", Elliot left them to it, and followed up on Jeremy.

One look from the doorway and Elliot confirmed the man wasn't merely sick, but *Sick*.

Jeremy was writhing on his bed when Elliot came in, oblivious of his visitor's presence for a few moments. When he sensed him, his head shot up, thin hair soaking wet, skin pale. He rubbed at his throat and croaked, "Did you bring medicine?"

Venturing no closer, Elliot pointed to the box of paracetamol on the bedside unit. "Got plenty there. That's all you need." Jeremy also had three two-liter soda bottles that had been filled with water. He'd gone through half of it.

"I'm dying here. I think ... " Jeremy's torso curled over in the grip of a coughing fit for several seconds. "I think I have it. I'll die without medicine."

"You'll be fine," Elliot lied. "Seen it up close a lot and this isn't it. You have a bad flu is all."

The sick man moaned and writhed. His hand rubbed at his throat. "This feels really bad. Are you sure?"

"A food allergy maybe," said Elliot, hoping Jeremy was as dumb as most people round here.

"Allergy?" Jeremy's rubbing at his throat turned to scratching. "Then I probably need antihistamine. Don't I?"

"Fair enough, I'll rustle some up." He checked over his

shoulder for sneaky undead and closed the door at his back.

The sick man propped himself up on his elbows and squinted. "Carolyn and the others thought it was the— you know, zombie virus."

"Dude, it's most likely flu, and I don't want to catch it. And we don't want those kids in there catching it. So we'll keep you here. But in case it is an allergy, what did you eat today?"

"Eat?"

"And drink."

"Oh." Jeremy reached for a towel and wiped so hard at his face and throat, he left pink welts. "Some instant soup, you know the packet soup? And some cereal. Corn flakes."

"UHT milk?"

"That ran out yesterday. I used orange juice."

"Which one?"

Jeremy named one of the two brands on site. "I had UHT yesterday."

That wouldn't count, Elliot figured. Not that long ago. He'd seen this thing before, and he'd had the benefit of his satellite hookup for the first day and a half after the breakout to hear other stories from around the world. This thing, whatever it was, usually moved very quickly —though *quickly* could be relative. Whether the infectious agent was a bite or environmental, the reaction always started within the hour. And sometimes, it ran its course within that hour too. Bites had been observed to prompt a reaction within five minutes and death-resurrection within the hour. With others like Jeremy, transformation took a lot longer, prolonging the suffering. "When did you eat the cereal and the soup?"

"Cereal, about eight this morning. Soup while you were outside. Someone took over at the foyer for me."

"What packet soup, Jeremy? I don't remember seeing that anywhere."

Defiance shone in the man's eyes. "It was mine. I'm allowed to have my own food."

Shit.

It had to be that then. It had to be. The pathogen might be some nano-thing or prion. Perhaps something dormant in people's biology activated by time or by an agent in processed foods. But Elliot had to get rid of that soup. Jeremy told him it was in his suitcase in the restaurant and Elliot told Jeremy that everything would be fine. He closed the door on him while the man was still talking.

It was Elliot's turn to feel like a coward.

IT WAS GROWING LATE IN THE DAY. THE SOUP WAS GONE, along with everything else in Jeremy's backpack and the batches of orange juice and corn flakes he'd eaten. Elliot had tried telling people they might have to live with hunger for a day or so until it was safe for him and others to go hunt down some meat and fruit. A handful of people nodded, including the hippy ladies and the yellow-shirted mom. The Professor thanked him. Others ignored him; Internet-Checker told him to "piss off."

Two groups had well and truly separated now. There was the restaurant group who'd refused to give over their knives and practiced math and English with the children, played cards, or sat in small clusters talking in whispers. And there was the Brin group who had pushed all the pro shop fixtures out into the foyer and dragged their bedding in there. Individuals in both camps eyed him with suspicion or resentment; he kept his bedding where it had been since he'd arrived, right behind the bar. At least that way, when he felt like resting he wouldn't have to look at idiots.

He'd been sitting on the foyer seat Jeremy had once occupied for ten minutes now. The pro shop fixtures blocked his view of the west wing doors and he would occasionally stand and check then sit again. Thankfully, the earlier bickering had only drawn in a handful of pusbags and he and his three "enforcers"—as they were calling themselves—had sent all of those to their eternal rest. The three men had reported seeing larger bunches of others further out toward the peripheries, back on the golf course, up in the parking lot, up the hill in the bushland. Two, they said, had fallen into the pool.

He turned at a noise behind him. Burly Guy took a knee beside him, carrying two cups.

"Hot water," he said. "I boiled it twice."

Elliot didn't take it. "And?"

"I used the rain water from the tank we bleached."

"Washed the cups?"

"Rinsed with boiling water and detergent."

"All right then." Elliot took a cup and sipped. "Glad to see you can be taught."

If the chef was offended by Jake's bluntness, he didn't show it. He actually wasn't that bad a guy, when it came down to it. Though he was probably used to running kitchens and bossing other people around, he'd been prepared to do what Elliot asked, and he was fast developing some common sense. He settled on his haunches and sipped his water. "Bloody hungry, I am," he said. "But I'll survive." For a moment, his eyes grew glassy, no doubt remembering his family and their fate.

Elliot wondered where he'd been when it happened, how it had happened, what had brought him back here to his workplace afterwards. But they weren't the kinds of things he'd ask another man. It was enough that it had happened; Burly Guy was doing what good men did, finding a way to go on.

The chef blinked hard and sipped again. "I'll survive."

"If you can convince some people to get smart like you, then yeah, maybe you will."

"That Brin is a piece of work," he growled. "A real psychopath. She's so much like my first wife—everything was about her. As long as she had control, as long as people did what she wanted, no worries. But cross her? Holy crap, you were in for a war then. The opposite of my second wife. My ... She ..." His voice caught. He plunged his fingers into his hair and scratched the thoughts away, centering back on where he'd started. "Bloody psychopath. First Mini-Brin bumps into me and Brin says I cut her—"

"Yeah, well, 'Mini-Brin' did seem more upset with her Mistress than with you at the time. Like the young dude said he saw, I wouldn't doubt it if Brin did shove her into you."

"Right," said the chef. "Right. And now she's in there

whinging to Carolyn about not being able to eat the food. Even though we've got a sick guy out in the cabins. And she wants access to the alcohol—can you believe that?"

Elliot cranked his neck toward the restaurant door but couldn't see her inside. But, now he concentrated, he could hear her. And she was using words like *ridiculous*, *starvation*. And *brave people*, *trucks* and *town*.

"Maybe we can lock her in a storeroom," he muttered. "Let her taste test all the food for us, see what's safe and what isn't."

"You really think it's food?"

"Maybe. Maybe it's water. Maybe it's in the goddamn air."

Burly Guy shivered. "I've eaten plenty of stuff from tins. And packets of rice and chips and shit." He chewed his lip a moment, then asked, "Am I gonna die too? Am I gonna turn?"

Elliot swallowed some vaguely bleach-scented water and put his cup down. "You're not sweating, you're not scratching at your throat. You're not a deader."

"Thank God for that." The man's laugh was humorless. "Why do you call 'em that? Deaders?"

Elliot shrugged. "Call 'em what you like. I was in the casino hotel for ten days. We were fine for the first six, but we'd brought a little food into the country with us. Then my guys got antsy. Once that food ran out, they went looking and ... well, that was the end of them. I was left catching pigeons and rain water on my balcony after I shot out the glass. Watched a lot of bad shit from that balcony. And saw a few people turning as you put it, people who'd been staying on my floor." He shook his head at the memories. "Bad shit. Before the grids went down, the media and the internet were calling them zombies or more politely Sufferers. Me, I saw the truth straight away. Whatever they were—whoever they'd been —they weren't exactly dead but they were sure deader than me."

"Well," Burly said when they'd both been silent for several minutes, alone inside their thoughts. "Maybe by morning all the deaders will be gone and we can go catch some pigeons and magpies of our own."

"Yeah," said Elliot. "Maybe."

Burly Guy drained his mug, stood and winced and swore as his knees cracked. He said, "It's getting dark outside."

Elliot nodded at the reception windows. "I see that."

"You can sleep if you want and I'll take watch."

Elliot was about to reply in the negative when Brin steamed out of the restaurant, nostrils flared and face flushed. Her glare flashed their way momentarily. She hadn't won her argument then. Carolyn had stood her ground.

Good job, Carolyn.

Sensing their eyes following her, Brin flipped the bird before disappearing into the pro shop. The movement made her bracelets jingle.

"Right back atcha, honey," Burly Guy said and laughed.

Elliot nodded tiredly. Now that she wasn't in the restaurant, there was a small chance he could nap in there. "You're sure you got this?"

The chef straightened and snapped off a clumsy

salute. "Yes sir." He laughed again. "Figured you're a cop. Or maybe a US soldier. Are you?"

Elliot stood and grimaced when his own knees cracked. "Maybe," he said and headed into the restaurant. "Or maybe I'm just a guy who can't stay out of trouble."

4

4: Cabin 11

Someone was tugging at his shoulder.

He opened gummy eyes. He lay on his back beneath a bleached-out sky, with dry air and dust in his nostrils, ringing in his ears. Clods of dirt and brick pattered the hard earth around him. A child was pulling on his shoulder, on his rifle strap—a local girl, thinking him dead and fair game for looting until he had the presence of mind to move his jaw and his sandpaper tongue and force out some noise. He bent his limbs to turn his numb body over, and then that kid was fleeing from him, picking her way between pieces of Radler and Eames, surefooted as a mountain goat and ...

And he was not there but he was here. And it was not bright sky above him but a flashlight beam reflecting off the light fittings. He lay not upon the hard-packed earth, but upon a thin camp mattress behind the bar of a restaurant. And it was a man who crouched above his head—an Australian man tugging at his shoulder and not a Syrian girl.

"What is it?" He rose to his knees, rubbing grit from his eyes. His own voice sounded quieter than the whisper he'd attempted, muted by tinnitus.

"You need to come," the man said. He angled the small flashlight down and into the carpet, dimming it.

Elliot realized it was dark in the restaurant and quiet, apart from a murmured conversation somewhere across the room and a whole lot of snoring.

How long have I been out? His watch was gone, broken in a pusbag skirmish while leaving Hobart.

"Time?" he asked.

"Three thirty-ish," the man said and as Elliot's tinnitus faded, he recognized the voice. It belonged to the sandy-haired friend of Brin's.

"What do you want?"

"Sorry to wake you. Can I talk to you in the foyer? Um, you'll need your gear." The flashlight beam played over the lumps beneath Elliot's fallen blanket, his belt with tanto knife and empty SIG-Sauer and piton hammer.

Sucking lungfuls of air to get his head straight, he tightened his boot laces and buckled on the belt. Then he followed the man out, picking his way through sleeping people like that Syrian girl had picked her way through the pieces of his squad. Some people stirred, anxious eyes peering up at him; others turned a grumpy shoulder in an effort to regain sleep. The yellow-shirted mom was nursing her baby by the back windows, watching the stars through a crack in the curtain.

In the foyer, the man led him to the Reception desk and leaned on it. Jeremy's sentry chair sat empty, but in the illumination from the resort's still functioning path lighting outside, Elliot had seen Brin's forty-something male devotee pressed against the west wing door.

"What's going on?" Elliot mumbled. "What time is it?" He'd already forgotten, disoriented. The ringing was abating, but he still tasted dust and blood and smoke.

"A bit before four," the sandy-haired man said. He spoke louder now, but not so loud that folk in the restaurant would hear it. "We had trouble. My name's Tom by the way. So twenty minutes ago, we were on duty, me and Henry down there. Two of those ... zombie-people came right up to the windows, started sniffing and scratching at them."

Elliot leaned back, took a better look at this Henry. Near the man was a definite smear on the glass. "*You* guys were on watch? You?"

The man dipped his head. "Yeah, I know Brin can be a pain, and we've all been arguing a lot, but we're not bad people. We're trying to keep everyone safe too. Anyway, long story short: Henry and I went out the east door, then we went around and led them away into one of the gardens and—" he grimaced and licked his lips. "We killed them. With golf clubs. Not nice, but had to be done." He leaned back on the bar and stared into space, remembering.

Elliot wrapped one hand into a thumbs-up. "Gee willikers. Thank you for waking me to inform me of your incredible heroism. There'll be a commendation in tomorrow's mail."

Ignoring the sarcasm, Tom said, "That's just the start. While we were coming back, we detoured past Cabin 11, the one with that sick guy in it. And. Guess what?"

Elliot raised an eyebrow.

"Guy's door is open. And the guy is gone."

Elliot raised the other eyebrow. "Gone, or you killed him too?"

"What? No way! He was just gone. We had a quick look but there were more of those infected people nearby. We could hear them, so we hightailed it back here."

"*Hightailed*. Why is it so many of you use old American cartoon language when you're talking to me? So, what, you think he's got himself eaten by the other deaders? Cause if he really is Sick, that won't happen."

"Well, no, but we're worried that he hasn't fully ... you know ... *changed*. And he might be trying to get into one of the occupied cabins for help. Or maybe he'll come back here and get us infected too."

Elliot scratched at the back of his hand and considered it. Jeremy was a problem; that was for sure. He was not the kind of man to suffer alone in noble silence. If Jeremy was trying to get into someone's cabin for help and sympathy, the people who'd chosen to stay out there away from the reeking masses in here might just be stupid enough to let him in.

He pointed a finger in Tom's face. "You're coming, and you'll be damned quiet while you're with me."

"Totally and totally. You want Henry too?"

"Will he follow instructions?"

"He will. Promise. Me too."

"Where's your golf clubs?"

"We ditched those, they were pretty filthy when we'd finished ... you know."

Elliot indicated the pro shop doors. "Get another one."

"Everyone's taken them. But I saw wooden stakes in the garden like you said, holding up bushes. We could grab those."

"Do it. Maybe we'll get lucky and come across some vampires while we're out there chasing the rest of the monsters."

HE'D TAKEN LESS THAN TEN STEPS OUT THAT WEST WING exit when Henry tugged on his sleeve and pointed the other way. "Should we check Jeremy's room again? Just in case he went back? I mean, you're the boss, but..."

Elliot nodded. It made sense instead of traipsing around everywhere else first. He exaggerated a *lead the way* gesture and followed Henry with Tom at his shoulder.

"The garden stakes are that way too," Tom hissed.

This time Elliot made a slashing gesture: *all right, shut up.*

A minute later they had their long, pointed sticks and continued on to Cabin 11. The door was still open and Elliot cursed.

"You didn't shut it?" he asked.

The two men shrugged an apology.

He ground his teeth, got his flashlight out of his pocket. He signaled them to wait here and gripped the light with one hand and the piton hammer with the other. He got to the door, felt something at his back. Tom stood right there, peering over his shoulder with interest. Tom offered a smile and Elliot nudged him with a shoulder forcing him to shuffle to regain his balance before he could fall into the spiny bushes beside the path.

"Wait here," Elliot ground out and Tom nodded an apology.

While exterior lights worked because the local grid still had power, one of the first things Elliot had done upon arrival was to go around and remove cabin light globes—much to the disgust of everyone except Carolyn who understood the precaution and supported him. Some people had replaced them; he knew that because two cabins had their lights on. Jeremy's didn't.

He nudged the door fully open with a toe, played the beam both sides of the single room apartment beyond. No one there. The bathroom door was closed, the wardrobe beside it half open. The wardrobe door was glass, a mirror bouncing his beam back at the other side of the room. The bed sat dead center and he could see down both sides of it. Unless something lurked in the wardrobe or Jeremy was shut in the bathroom, it was time to go.

He felt the carpet retract with Tom's step behind him and repressed a groan, was about to let some expletives fly when something solid pricked him hard between his shoulder blades.

"If you turn, you die," Tom said and stepped away, pulling the sharp object with him before Elliot could spin and disarm him. "Spear gun," Tom explained. "It'll hurt."

"Are you kidding me?" Elliot growled.

"Found it in some dead tourist's car on the way here. Hid it in the bushes outside."

"Are you *fucking* kidding me."

He started to turn but Tom made a discouraging noise and Elliot heard the rasp of the weapon's handle shifting against his palm.

"I'm not. And trust me, I'll gladly kill you if I need to. You're not exactly what us Aussies call a good bloke."

Over his shoulder, Elliot said, "So what now, Einstein?"

More movement behind him, Henry entering the room. Two on one, the two with a loaded weapon. A speargun? Christ, but it made sense on an island where spear diving and abalone fishing were main sports. How could he get close enough to get a hand on that weapon, push it aside? Maybe they'd go to lock him in the bathroom; maybe undead Jeremy would be in there and Elliot could somehow unleash him on Tom and his buddy.

And maybe this is all just a dream.

Goddamnit.

"Gun belt on the floor," Tom added. "Hammer too."

"I thought you folk were morons, but I had no idea you were clinically insane," Elliot said. The hammer turned a full circle within his grip. He could throw it. He might get lucky...

Tom merely repeated what he'd already said.

With visions of caving Tom's head in then Henry's, Elliot crouched and laid down the hammer. He unbuckled his belt and let it drop, then stood, still facing away. In the pause that followed, Elliot wondered would this be it, would the sonofabitch shoot him in the back now he'd disarmed?

"Step over to the bed, knees against it," Tom said.

Evidently not. Might be a mistake you regret, asshole.

Grudgingly, Elliot complied. The sheets were stained with sweat and something else—from the sight and smell, the old Jeremy had probably died here an hour or two ago and the new Jeremy found a way to open that door.

Or Tom and Henry had found him newly resurrected and lured him outside somewhere before ending him.

"You killed Jeremy?" he asked.

"Nah," said Henry. "That was the truth that he was gone when we came looking for him. Maybe he went out to top himself."

"Looking for him? What the hell for?"

"Brin's first idea was that if he'd turned, we could get you in here to ... Why am I telling you this? Just shut up."

The mess on the sheets still glistened in the light of the flashlight they hadn't yet specifically told him to relinquish. He hoped he'd get a chance to use it—that or the short lockblade they didn't know was in his right cargo pocket. No way was he giving up weapons he didn't absolutely have to.

From behind him came the sounds of the two men dividing spoils and the thud of the discarded belt. He angled his head to watch them in the wardrobe mirror. Henry had the tanto, admiring the long blade, and he'd taken the speargun. It looked like a compressed air model, extra deadly. Tom shoved the piton hammer handle into his pants and turned the 9-mil over, weighted it. His flashlight beam played Elliot's way and he smiled at him in the mirror. "Feels good. Looking forward to using this."

"Do me a favor. Stick it in your mouth when you do." For all the good that would do. Better he didn't tell them that the handgun and magazines were all empty: having knowledge they didn't have, even a small piece, might give him an edge. Elliot ran a quick calculation as to whether he could get across the room and break Tom's nose and then Henry's before Henry could point the speargun. He didn't like his odds.

"Not nice, Elliot." Tom pointed the handgun at him. "You have spare clips? Them too please."

"They're called magazines, not clips."

"Don't stall. Hurry up and give 'em to me. And chuck that torch back here too."

Another moment of consideration: if he stalled further, they might come over to frisk him. But it was 50/50 as to whether he'd be able to use that moment to disable them, or with a speargun still on him he'd be helpless while they felt his pockets and found his spare knife.

He reached into his left thigh pocket and slipped out a small back up first aid kit he'd found in the camping store. He tossed it and the flashlight backwards. In the mirror, Tom frowned.

"Only thing in there." He added honestly, "The mags are in my backpack, back at my bed."

"Other pocket," said Henry, gesturing with the speargun.

Elliot hesitated before sliding his fingers inside the

pocket with the Shrade. He brushed it but pulled out a thin booklet instead, held that up. "My passport. Don't think that's of much use to either of us."

"Probably not. Keep it."

Elliot dropped it on the floor.

Henry mumbled something and in the mirror, Elliot saw him gesture to the door. One of them had closed it sometime in the last minute.

"First we tie him up," said Tom.

He pointed the SIG at Elliot again, then at the bathroom door. "In there, mate. Sit your arse down in the bath."

Waiting in the bath were four cable ties. While both men watched from the door, Elliot sat in the tub and bound his ankles together with two. Then at their instructions, he got two more loosely around his wrists and Tom tightened them while Henry covered him. When Tom had finished, they were damn tight, tight enough to cause his hands to go numb if they stayed on too long.

Henry continued to cover him, while Tom took a screwdriver to the door handle and disassembled it. As he was finishing there was movement and a bobbing light out in the main room. A blonde head appeared at the door with the internet-checker behind her.

"Hi, Mr Elliot," Brin said brightly. She had a golfer's jacket over her halter, unzipped. She peeled back the sleeve and pretended to check her watch. "Bright and early, huh?"

"You narcissistic, clueless little bitch."

She ignored this, saying, "Hope you'll be happy here for a few days."

"Days? What in hell are you doing?"

"What we're doing is making this place a well-run place. I don't want to live in squalor with babies shitting their pants in my dining room, and people accidentally cutting each other, and Carolyn locking down the booze, and especially not with crazy cannibals wandering our grounds and keeping us stuck inside. And neither does Tom."

Tom was still busy with the door lock; she bent to peck his forehead, lingering over it so he could stare straight down her halter top. She straightened and reached out to rub Henry's forearm. "And neither does Henry."

Henry favored her with a goofy grin, before focusing back on Elliot.

"Dumbasses," he told them.

"Or Tony." She turned her head, lips pursed to blow a kiss to the internet-checker who'd come into Cabin 11 with her—

—and screamed! She slid from the doorway and behind the wall toward the closet.

A half-second later, "Tony" screamed too.

"What the—" Tom started and stood bolt upright in the doorway.

Another scream from Tony accompanied the thump of bodies on the floor. The beam of Brin's flashlight swung drunkenly around the bedroom as she alternately sobbed curses and snapped meaningless orders at the others. Elliot tried rising, but couldn't get his feet under him in the slick tub. Tom pressed against the jamb as Henry squeezed past him, swearing.

"Shoot him!" Tom hissed. "Shoot him!"

"I can't ...get ..." Henry's voice choked off and the speargun fired with a snapping sound. "*Shit!*"

Tom pulled the door shut behind him—perhaps in reflex, perhaps just not thinking—and yelled, "Out the way!" The hammer of the SIG came down on an empty chamber once, twice ...

There followed a hell of a lot more thumping and scraping and shouting. The closed door had left the bathroom pitch black. Elliot gave up trying to stand and put his bound hands to his side pocket, going for the Shrade lockblade.

Outside the desperation reached a new pitch. Brin's voice was no longer among those gasping and swearing and shouting. "Fuck, he got me," Tom said distinctly, then louder: "He got me, fuck! *Fuck!*" Further commotion: Henry and Tom's voices, the sounds of a struggle.

Without light, working by feel, it took Elliot fully two minutes to get the lockblade from his side pocket; by the time he had, there was silence out there. Another minute passed while he dropped it then split one of his nails getting the blade extended. Cursing the growing numbness in his hands, he worked for many more minutes sawing at his bonds. The knife fell from his fingers twice before his wrists broke free. He paused a moment and listened. There were raised voices outside in the grounds somewhere—he couldn't make out their emotional content, but he could guess at it. *Jesus, Mary ...*

Able to grip the lockblade more easily, the ties around

his ankles were far easier to remove. He climbed from the bath, rubbing blood back into his hands and swearing quietly to himself as they prickled with vicious pins and needles.

And a moment after he finally felt the pain was subsiding was the moment the first woman's scream split the air outside.

5: Fools and Dead People

THE DEAD WOMAN *walked again once her belly was full. Once the sun was up and high enough to warm her, she stumbled to a stop along the country road and gradually she went dormant.*

For a time, there was nothing.

When the sun was directly overhead, she became aware of sensation gradually—and gradually that the sensation meant threat. Black shapes fluttered and clamored at her, above her head and behind it. She registered the strike on her eye distantly, threw a hand up to snatch at the crow but only succeeded in batting it away. The eye and one ear were a ruin, streaks of skin and cartilage, vitreous material and sclera pasted to her cheek and her neck.

The two crows, her attackers, retreated to a fence post to caw at her. Moments later, they took to the air when she rushed them, her hands outstretched and her jaw opened wide.

THE SMALL WINDOW ABOVE THE BATH AND SHOWER LET IN very little ambient light. Over the next few minutes, as Elliot felt his way around the door and the hole where the lock had been, the screaming outside did not abate. In fact, the volume and intensity of noise out there made Elliot's hackles rise—and stay risen. What in hell was going on? Had the infected gotten into the clubhouse?

The door hinges were screwed onto the side of the door's edge where it pressed against the jamb. With it closed, he couldn't get to the screws with his knife. Within the hole *through* the door, Elliot felt out the latch bar and the square aperture where the spindle would slot and turn to retract bar from latch plate. His blade was the wrong size and shape to turn it.

While screams continued to rise in quantity and volume outside, Elliot scrambled around the bathroom, a blind man in unfamiliar territory. There was nothing of use to him. The cabin had been unoccupied before they'd put Jeremy in it. No toiletries. Not even cleaning chemicals.

"Shit!"

He climbed on the rim of the bath, peered out the small window. He'd never fit through it. Not even a kid could. It was a little lighter out there now, predawn washing starlight from the sky but helping to resolve shapes and texture out there in the non-public area of the resort. He could make out a quad bike, a gardener's shed, some rolls of turf. There were moving figures also, drawn by the screams. One walked into the corner of the gardener's tin shed, bounced off it with a hollow thud. Something smashed over towards the clubhouse. A rise in the shouting.

Elliot slapped the window hard, thought the better of repeating it when the closest blurry shape veered toward him. He climbed from the bath, teeth grinding. An idea came to him then. He felt around behind the toilet until his fist closed around the plastic handle of a toilet brush. He brought it up to his chest, grabbed it with both hands and snapped it, ran his fingers around the two broken ends, chose one and discarded the other piece. He got to work on it with his blade until he had something that finally fit the hole in the spindle. It had taken minutes, precious minutes. He turned his makeshift lever slowly, slowly, expecting it to snap before he could get the door open. The spindle moved grudgingly while the plastic strained.

"C'mon, you sonofabitch. C'mon."

A *clack*. His heart skipped a beat, fearing the lever broken. But the sound was the latch releasing. The door pulled in toward him and Elliot ventured out warily. Path lights beyond the open door revealed a body down by the bed—it was male but he couldn't make out who. Most importantly, it wasn't moving—*and* a blocky shape on the floor by it was Elliot's SIG. He retrieved it, squinting more closely at the body. Yes, it was the oldest of Brin's acolytes, Tony. Dumbass Tony who must have left the door ajar behind him, allowing undead Jeremy or something else to get in behind him. Whatever had torn out his throat was no longer there, but had gotten out and away, in pursuit of the two other men. Including Tom who'd yelled about being bitten.

How long had Elliot been locked in that room since the room had grown quiet? Ten minutes? Fifteen? Twenty? Sometimes infection a bite moved super-quick —more often than not in fact. Even ten minutes could be long enough to turn someone. So if Tom got back into the clubhouse infected ...

He picked up his belt from where the others had discarded it, buckled it, holstered his SIG and decided he'd be damned if he wasn't getting his tanto knife back. He pulled the small kitchenette's drawers in search of a longer blade. Only found butter knives, but they were longer than his Shrade so he kept two of them and pocketed the lockblade. Tearing the covers from two pillows, he wound them around his forearms, knotting them. The material wasn't that tough but it wouldn't matter: the undead had human teeth after all, not feline or canine ones.

A car started up over in the parking lot as he came out of Cabin 11. He shielded his eyes from the pavement lighting to retain his night vision, squinting. Tires crunched on gravel as the car pulled out of the main lot toward the access road. Elliot caught a flash of blonde hair at the driver's window.

Brin. Queen of No Country. Of course *she'd* get away.

A man, the oldest of Brin's followers, appeared from between two other cars, three deaders in pursuit. He was limping as fast as he could go, arms out toward the car. "Wait!" he managed before the deaders took him down.

He rounded the cabin away from the clubhouse and toward the gardener's shed. He could seed well enough to make out the three deaders right in front of him. They sniffed and reached for him. He slapped away the arms of the first and plunged a butter knife into its eye socket, releasing it and spinning sideways to avoid the spasming hands and the squirt of blood and vitreous fluid. His foot snagged on a sod but he turned the trip into a side roll and swept a leg under those of the next pusbag. It crumpled and took the next one to the ground with it. Elliot came out of his roll into a fast jog toward the shed, watching the indistinct surface to avoid further falls, the second butter knife held away from him to the side.

The shed doors were fixed with a thin chain and a thick padlock. He pulled off a pillow case, used it to grip the edge of one of the double doors, put a boot against the other and pulled, straining against the chain until the latch it was hooked through came free, throwing him backwards and down into the path of one of the recovered deaders now crawling towards him. He turned himself round and planted the heel of his boot squarely in its face, shattering the nose and then what felt like eye socket on the second kick. The deader huffed and keeled over, squirming, still far too animate for Elliot's liking. The other was back on its feet and moving faster than Elliot had anticipated.

He rose to meet it, held up his left forearm ... and realized he no longer had the pillow case there. He whipped the arm down just as infectious jaws clacked shut where it had been. Still driving forward, the pusbag was on him, forcing Elliot to take a good hold on its ear with his right hand, pulling it around and down. Rolling on top, breathing through his mouth to prevent from gagging at its stench, he freed his knife hand and stabbed the blade into its temple. He missed, the blunt blade butting up against bone. Elliot punched with the blade again, but the skull didn't give and the tore off in his grip, the head swinging up at him, teeth snapping. The one with the shattered nose was getting closer again.

Elliot broke off, pushed himself upright and moved to the shed, wishing those bastards hadn't taken his flashlight. He took two wary steps inside and reached a hand to the walls, knuckles brushing a wooden handle. He got a hold on it and pulled it from what must have been a wall rack, went outside again and held it up to see better. A shovel.

"Perfect."

Seconds later, both deaders were finally dead-for-good.

WITH DAWN A TEASE ALONG THE HORIZON, PEOPLE WERE visible running across the golf course. He counted five, two of them distinguishable as the Professor and a hippy lady, hand in hand. Nothing was pursuing them; Elliot could only hope things stayed that way. For a moment he considered following them, offering them protection. But there were others inside the clubhouse, people in the cabins. He went door to door for a few minutes, pulverizing the heads of any infected unlucky enough to be in his way.

The paths close to the east of the clubhouse were

choked with undead, many *many* more than those he'd been tracking during the afternoon. He stood ten yards back from the pack and wondered where in hell they'd all come from? Had they drifted here from other towns? From Hobart? Were they farm workers?

There were more bodies here. Some of them had been deaders and some had not. The other hippy lady was splayed across a pathway with two deaders eating her innards, her face set in a permanent expression of surprise. Many of the still ambulatory deaders were feasting, others pressing against them, eager to get to the meal table. Those who had until recently been his living co-inhabitants had presumably been out trying to take on this horde with their golf clubs and kitchen knives, and they had not been up to task. That's what he thought for a moment, until he looked at the deaders closest to him and realized the body they were eating couldn't have been someone out attacking them.

The body belonged to a child, three of the undead in the bushes with her. A small girl with butterfly sneakers. If it weren't for those shoes, he wouldn't have known her. In life, she'd been as pretty as a doll, stoic and brave despite the palpable fear in the restaurant. Last time Elliot had seen them, her father had been rubbing his hair and face in panic while she rubbed his shoulders and kissed his cheek and brought him glasses of water. Where was he now, the father who should have protected this girl? He wasn't *here* and his girl was being eaten by mindless infected *things* that had once been people like him, like her—

Rage exploded from deep within Elliot, a living force

seizing control of his limbs and swinging the shovel again and again and again until the three corpses eating the little girl with the butterfly sneakers formed a blanket across her, ichor and brain matter leaking from shattered skulls.

Head pounding, he stepped over them and into the eighteen-inch gap between the short scrubby bushes and the wall, an alley he could use. He took off toward the east wing entrance, shovel held above his head.

One of the doors was wedged open by a body, a piece of human meat swarmed by the undead. Making a split-second decision based on instinct, and still running, he planted his boot firmly on the back of one deader, vaulting through the door and onto the carpeted floor beyond.

His rage evaporated, replaced by the cooling draught of self-recrimination at the risky move—

What the hell was that, soldier?

—and just a touch of elation that it had worked.

No infected wanted to follow him, more interested in their current meal than in him. He was inside where most refugees had sheltered, inside where a dozen more people lay dead and dying and bleeding from puncture wounds to their limbs and torsos

Inside and smelling smoke. It curled up from inside the restaurant, spreading through the air in thin clouds. Someone shouted from within and there was crashing. He started forward. He had to get the living out the far wing doors which appeared to have been ignored by the undead, he had to—

Something exploded in the kitchens, blasting wall

panels into the foyer and sending a ball of propane flame blooming in their wake.

Elliot landed on his back, smelled the overlapping odors of the real here-and-now burning building and the burnt-plastic-and-hair smell of an IED's aftermath. He felt carpet beneath his fingers and he felt dry and dusty soil. He heard screaming, more screaming, the screaming of Tasmanian refugees roasting alive in their sanctuary and of Syrian bystanders peppered with shrapnel. He was here and he was there, and he wasn't sure what was better, but in the interests of living, he chose here and he forced himself back to it, forced himself to choose reality. A rogue part of his mind was glad that he was living while others were not and he hated himself for it and he also thought it a sane response. He was working on autopilot now, scuttling backwards from the flames, crab-walking, his shovel abandoned. The area beyond the turned-over pro shop fixtures was well aflame. Burning figures lurched and writhed, mindless with pain and panic. Elliot got himself to his feet and wondered fleetingly if he would ever find out what in God's name had gone so horribly wrong. As he reached for an extinguisher it occurred to him that at some level this was all on Brin. Her hubris was responsible for it all. Had she drawn in the deaders to put pressure on the others to accept her ideas? Had she let Tom back inside? And maybe Henry, bitten too?

Coughing and blinking away smoke-tears, he pulled the extinguisher's pin and took three steps toward the burning people when another propane explosion tore through the building and set him on his ass. He lost time, seconds only, but he came to himself crawling for the door. He couldn't help them. He could barely help himself, the carpet behind him ablaze like grassfire. Flames gobbled at ceiling panels above him.

As he made the door with the taste of cooler air on his tongue, the screaming cut out behind him, leaving only the sounds of crackling walls and carpets, and the hiss and pop of boiling and bursting fat cells in the bodies of the dead. Sucking in oxygen and holding it, he got to his feet, took hold of a restaurant chair someone had dragged out here and swung it at the window to the side of the blocked doorway. For the first couple strikes he thought the window would hold, that he wouldn't make it, that he'd either asphyxiate or be forced to leap into the wall of undead beyond the door. And then the window gave on the third swing. Jagged pieces dropped around him as he leapt through, unaware of whether or not they'd cut him. Not caring. He was clear. He was clear and he could breathe. Air was life.

Veering hard right to escape the attention of the eaters, Elliot rounded the corner and almost collided with a new body standing in mid-path, instinctively raising his fists. But the blow was not delivered. Brin stood there, mascara running, panda eyes visible in the firelight, jaw slack, hair askew. There was blood on her right hand, the hand that was clutched to her body, the hand flesh from its pinky. There was another wound on the wrist. She was missing a shoe and the bracelets she'd worn above her watch were also gone from her other wrist.

He checked his six—the undead still had too much

food in front of them to concern themselves chasing him —then ventured closer, eyes streaming and squinted from the smoke and gorge rising at the battlefield reek of opened torsos wafting from behind him. Brin's wounds were tears, bites.

The blonde hair he'd seen in the car earlier must have been the yellow-shirted mom's. That was real good. "Brin?" he started and couldn't think what else to say.

She met his gaze, hers blank. In a monotone, she said, "People never do what I ask them to do. Not properly. I was only trying to help." She performed a jerky pivot and marched away from him, lifting her chin and adding, "I put your stuff in my cabin."

Elliot followed her a few yards as she lurched like a windup toy toward the parking lot. A deader appeared near her, a thing that weeks ago had also been a woman, the left side of its face a pattern of dried gore and loose flesh. Brin marched right past it while it sniffed at her and continued on through her wake, disinterested. It went to the locked reception doors and pressed against them, drawn to the glow and perhaps the heat. The glass was so hot, her flesh immediately sizzled.

"Jesus Christ," Elliot breathed.

Another smaller explosion sounded within the clubhouse. No way could he help anyone still in there, even if they were alive.

Brin was out of sight along the path up to the parking lot now. He turned around and went to clear the rest of the cabins, to check for survivors.

6: GOING BUSH

ELLIOT STOOD in the parking lot, upwind from the smoldering carcass of the restaurant. He tightened the straps of his pack against his shoulders, shrugging it into a more comfortable position. Chances were he'd be wearing it a while. He'd recovered some of his gear from the cabin Brin must have rented here, Cabin 20: the backpack, his IFAK, his water filtering kit. He'd found one of his SIG's magazines back of the floor of Cabin 11, but the whereabouts of the other remained a mystery. Henry's ravaged corpse was lying out in one of the communal barbecue areas, Elliot's hammer and tanto nearby. Elliot had used a mattock to end the two pusbags eating him.

The sun was well up now, the sky cloudless. It would be hot. Again. He had filtered a few liters of water and put them at the bottom of the pack out of the reach of the sunlight. Cool water would taste like heaven in a couple of hours. He tested the weight. Nothing he couldn't handle; it was a quarter the size of the one he'd used in basic eighteen years ago.

Eighteen years. Half my goddamn life. Where in hell did that go?

A question easily answered. It had gone where the world had gone, where civilization had gone, where its latest dominant species was fast heading. It had gone into the past, vanishing inside a black hole that nothing —*nothing*—climbed out of.

There was another question, one not so easily answered: where to now?

He could go after that mother and her two kids. Wasn't a good chance he'd find them, but he might. She was a survivor, that much was certain. Did she need someone like him around, swearing and killing for her kids to see, or was she better off on her own? Other people had been fleeing over the fairways. If they all met up ...

What then, dumbass?

Did he think they'd fare better than they had here? The world was as screwed as it ever was. As long as more than one person was in a room or a foxhole or a time share resort, there'd be disagreement and strife, there'd be agendas and power plays, there'd be pain and death, there'd be grief for somebody and usually the ones who least deserved it. Manager Carolyn and Burly Guy whose name Elliot had never bothered to ask, yellow-shirted mom and her kids, the lady golfer with the big kahunas, the second hippy lady who he'd found with throat torn out, undead Jeremy and the dead girl in the garden, and whatever goddamned *idiot* had set off the gas explosion in the restaurant thinking it would save them and kill the deaders—these were exactly the reasons Elliot could only ever trust himself, why he would keep to himself. They had all been doomed and there wasn't one thing he could have done to stop it.

No. That was the cynical bastard in him talking. That was trauma. That was the ghost of his step-father. As much as he hated being around other people, he couldn't give up on them all.

Could he?

He recalled Brin's bitten hand and wrist—and then recalled her in the midst of the crowded restaurant, spruiking her bullshit. He heard her arrogant voice, saw the nuances of body language used to manipulate, heard her group laughing. He saw a tinkle of light from her now lost bracelet, saw her check her expensive watch as if she was late for an important appointment, watched her hitch the straps of her Gucci slip on her shoulders and talk a room full of people out of listening to him as he tried to talk sense into them.

Hell yes, he could give up on the human race.

The people fleeing across the golf course had gone southwest. Any cars fleeing the parking lot had left on a highway running east-west. Elliot turned north toward the hills. He was never going to take responsibility for another dumbass human being for as long as lived.

LIGHT REVIVED HER ONCE MORE, REFLECTING FROM THE

shattered glass of her wristwatch. It had broken one of the times she had fallen.

On the road behind her, she sensed them, smelled them, felt the chemical tug of sister infections in them. She turned. The small herd did not pause to wait for her, but it moved so slowly she caught it easily, shambling from the grass where she had stood for hours. The herd walked toward the setting sun, a source of heat and energy.

And the woman once been named Brin followed them, was led by them. Belonged to them.